FALLEN PETALS OF THE
ORION

Dedication

This book is dedicated to a few people who helped me to become the person I am today. First, in loving memory of my Mother Leeann Rabsatt Francis whose kindness is the one thing that has kept me from being the bad girl I always wanted to be. In loving memory of my father,
Denzil Francis Defreitas, whose desire to succeed as a self employed business owner, is the driving force behind all my entrepreneurial endeavors.

To my ride or die Gilbert "Pugito" Heyliger who has always been my biggest supporter.

To my sister, Monique Francis whose persistence has landed her in a size 14 dress all the way from a size 32 and who (I believe) won't stop, until she reaches a size 2. To my brother Preston Francis, my hope in the world….because I have so much hope for him.
Special dreams go out to my nieces Jenique, Shakhira and my nephew Shackhoy

Prologue

A gentle breeze floated in from the ocean washing away the oppressive summer heat. Wind chimes made from seashells rattled making a tinkling sound both pleasing and distracting. Montego Bay, Jamaica was one of the most beautiful, quiet places in the world, and even more so at night.

William Stone walked quietly along the veranda of the Orion Hotel. The Orion was one of the most popular tourist hotels in the region, catering to both excessively wealthy Europeans and overly brazen Americans. Stone was a middle-aged man, with slightly graying hair. His features were stern and centered; yet his eyes were soft and pleasing. When he reached the edge of the veranda he paused, the sound of voices catching his attention.

Moving through the shadows he followed them. As he rounded a corner, he froze. Sitting at a small table out on the lawn, he saw two men, one he recognized immediately. Darwin Stone was a rich and extremely powerful yardie who dealt in drugs, prostitution and more importantly, death. The other man sitting with him he couldn't make out, but knew well from past dealings that he was Darwin's client. The distance was too great for him to get a good, clear verbal understanding of their conversation. He didn't need to hear though; he already knew what was going down. Darwin was dealing death in the form of white powder. He didn't approve of what he was witnessing and didn't want any part of it, but he also knew he couldn't stop it. Despite what Darwin was, he was still his younger brother.

Turning he was about to leave them to their business when something rustled in the bushes next to the veranda, he quickly crouched down. Straining to see who was there, he moved slowly and quietly to the railing his eyes darting back and forth to determine where the noise had come from. Suddenly, he heard the rustling noise again. Then he saw her.

Evelyn Lawson stood as quietly as possible amongst the bushes, it was extremely uncomfortable and she shifted positions frequently to ease the pain that was now growing in her legs. She was on her way home to her two children, when she stumbled upon the two men talking. When she saw Darwin her heart sank, she finally saw with her own eyes what her intuition had known all along. Her former lover and the father of her children peddled death.

Years ago it had been sheer willpower that enabled her to leave him taking their two children Darrius and Eve. At first he was distraught, forcing her and the children to stay at the mansion. They had become his prisoners, until one day, he abruptly let them go. That was the time she was scared the most, grabbing the children and running. She expected to feel the pain of a searing hot bullet from one of his many guards as she hurried away from his spacious home. Darwin provided everything, everything a woman could want – at least materialistically. He lacked though the one thing he would never be able to give her, a stabile loving home, which she wanted desperately for her children.

He did nothing though and just watched her leave. That was many years ago. He never bothered her, never asked to see his children, yet once a week she found an envelope on her doorstep. Inside was a large mass without any identification as to who sent it. At first she wanted to throw it back at him, accuse him of suddenly forcing his way into their lives after not giving a damn, but times were tough, poverty was high and even the slightest morsel of anything, meant surviving for another day.

She swallowed her pride and used the money to better the children's lives.

Even from the distance she now stood from them, the very sight of Darwin made her heart race. He was a handsome man, short, but extremely muscular. Both his light brown locks and complexion added to his handsome features. However, beneath it all the man was psychotic. Tossing aside his features she couldn't understand what made her fall in love with him and even more, sleep with him. He was like a burning flame and she the moth.

Darwin suddenly stood up. Smiling, he shook the other man's hand then handed over to him a small case. The other man grinned and looked inside. Moments later he pushed over his own case placing it at Darwin's feet. The second man grabbed his briefcase and quickly left, Darwin turned grabbing his own case when he suddenly stopped. Evelyn froze, her breath catching in her throat. She had recognized the second man; it was Magistrate Heyliger. A prestigious lawman whom she had always believed loved his country and his people, obviously this was not the case. She wanted to be anywhere but where she was right now.

From behind her, she watched Darwin's brother William walk down from the porch. She prayed that he hadn't seen her in the shadows. Keeping as still as possible, she continued to watch them.

Darwin grinned when he saw his brother. He loved him, loved him more than life.

"Good to see you my brother," Darwin beamed. "We must talk," William said softly.

Evelyn watched as William grabbed his brother's arm and walked him further away into the shadows. It was her chance to back out of the bushes and get as far away as she could. Heading back into the hotel, she walked as quickly as she could to one of the other entrances. She would take the long way home.

She knew also what she had to do. Both of her children's futures were at stake. Darwin would eventually want to include them into his world - his world of death. She must let the authorities know what she saw, someone she trusted; her friend Winston George, II would help her.

Leaving the hotel she quickly headed down the long winding entrance of the hotel. It would be over an hour before she could get to Winston's house, an hour of walking through the dismal and often dangerous streets of Montego Bay's outlying community. She had done it so many times in the past; she knew which way to go and what to avoid. Tonight though was different, time did matter.

She took a direct path.

The night became very still. The wind coming off the water had died down and the oppressive heat had returned. Evelyn began to perspire soaking her dress. Soon her walk had turned into a run. Fear swept through her, the same kind of fear like she had felt when she walked out of Darwin's mansion. Her mind was playing tricks. Though the night was dark, she could make out shapes and images.

The crescent moon provided just enough light for her to see and just enough light for her mind to imagine things that weren't there. Then a soft noise arose from behind her, she wanted to look over her shoulder but her fear wouldn't allow it. She began to run faster.

Finally, she forced herself to turn and look. Two pairs of headlights shone in the distance and were rapidly closing in on her.

"Dear God!" she muttered aloud, then dashed from the road into the dense underbrush but not before the headlights cast a glow over her.

The vehicles came to a halt. She dashed from palm to palm her breathing becoming labored as she ran even quicker. Stumbling she fell landing hard on an exposed palm root. She let out a small yell as she hit. The pain in her arm caused her eyes to water, fighting to control it she forced herself back onto her feet and continued through the night. Ever so often, she would glance back to see if someone was following. She had no idea where she was heading or what direction she was going. At this point, all she knew was that she had to get home to protect her children, get them away, anywhere out of their father's reach.

She had no idea how long she ran or how far she had gone, but she came back out onto the road. Glancing in both directions she tried to choose the correct way. Suddenly two headlights emerged out of the darkness casting their brightness directly on her. She froze, the twin beams paralyzing her like a scared animal. The vehicle came to a halt, both doors opened and two men emerged. She held her hand up blocking the light trying to see who they were. Then she saw the light brown hats. It was the Montego Bay police.

"What you do in' out here so late at night?" one of the men called out to her.

"You must help me! There are men after me, back on the road," she pointed in the other direction.

"Come with us, we will take you back to the station," the other officer said.

Evelyn let out a sigh of relief. She quickly went around to the passenger side of the car where one of the officers opened the back door for her. Moments later they continued down the road.

"You know it is not good to be out on this stretch of road this late at night," one of the officers said to her.

"I got off work later than I expected, I must get home to my children," she replied.

"Do not worry, we will make sure you are safe," one of the officers grinned in the rearview mirror.

Evelyn felt a chill; it swept through her with such force it almost took her breath away. Glancing out the front windshield, she saw two more vehicles parked alongside the road. The chill she felt suddenly became excessive.

"That's them! They're the ones following me!" she pointed.

The two officers glanced over at each other. The car slowed and finally stopped, the headlights casting upon the dark, sleek and shiny form of a limousine.

"Wait here," one of the officers said to her.

She watched as they got out and walked over to the limousine. The side window lowered and one of them leaned over. She couldn't see who was inside but she already knew, there were very few limousines on the island. Only the extremely wealthy could own such things, Darwin owned this one.

The officers moved away from the limo heading back to their car. Suddenly one of them opened her door.

"Please step out the vehicle," the man asked.

"What are you doing?" she said not moving.

"Come with us," the man said extending his hand.

Fear rushed through her, turning she bolted for the other door. Opening it, she jumped from the vehicle right into the arms of the other police officer.

Kicking and screaming the officer held fast to her. The other one came grabbing her by the legs. They walked her to the limousine. She continued to kick trying frantically to lash out at the men in an attempt to break their hold on her. Out of the corner of her eye she watched the door open, she was then roughly forced into the car the door slamming shut behind her.

Instinct drove her into the corner of the seat. Her eyes darted back and forth finally settling on Darwin. He watched her, calmly showing no emotion. She bolted for the door. A clicking sound instantly sounded, she tried the handle but the door but it wouldn't budge.

"What were you doing watching me earlier?" he said his voice stern.

Evelyn turned looking at the man, and then tried the door handle again. Finally, she backed into the seat again like a cornered animal.

"Speak woman, what were you doing watching me earlier?" he asked his voice even more gruff.

"I saw nothing," she spat.

"Did you think the Police would help you?" he grinned.

"Let me go Darwin, for our children, let me go," she pleaded.

"So you can go tell what you witnessed tonight?" he asked losing his smile.

"I will tell no one I promise you, I will tell no one," she said her heart thumping.

"And what of our children? Will you not tell them what you saw?" "Leave them out of this," she said becoming defensive.

Darwin looked away, and then abruptly moved over onto the seat next to her. She instantly pressed herself into the side of the door. There was nowhere to run.

She then felt his fingers lightly caress her bare arm. She looked away not wanting to meet his eyes. His hand then gently pulled her arm down, and then moved up along her shoulder to her neck. His fingers then ran down the front of her dress caressing her breast. His touch was repulsive yet electrifying. She now knew why she had slept with the man.

"You could have had so much, I tried to make your life easy with the money," he said softly.

"But you had to leave me, turn your back on me. Force my own children to grow up not knowing who their father really was."

"Our children should have no part of your life. They will never become a murderer like you."

"I do not murder, how can you call it murder when God gives you the power to make choices?"

"God? God? You're mad Darwin to think what you have is from God. You are an evil man Darwin - evil," she spat not looking at him.

"God has forsaken you."

For a moment, Darwin sat there letting her words burn. Then abruptly, he grabbed her arm yanking her away from the door. His other hand grabbed hold of her chin squeezing tightly.

"I am Gods chosen one. I am the number one <u>Notch</u>. I, Jah-Man, nobody disobeys me - nobody!" he snarled.

"You could have had it all Evelyn, you could have been the wife of a God!"

"You are insane. I do not want your blood money!" she spat.

Her words just enraged him more, grabbing the front of her dress he tore it down exposing her breasts. Evelyn was quick; she brought her hand up digging her fingers into his face.

Darwin recoiled, his flesh tearing. Reaching up he touched his face then looked at the blood covering his fingers. Evelyn grabbed the remnants of her dress and covered herself; she could see the rage burn. His soft eyes seemed to turn black; he then looked up at her, with his lips forming a sinister smile. Seconds later his fist connected with her face.

Evelyn's world turned into a haze. She felt the warmth of her salty blood run down her face. The second blow knocked her off the car seat. She fell to the floor gasping for breath.

"Darwin, our children…don't," she croaked spitting up blood.

Seconds later she felt him grab hold of her hair yanking her back onto the seat. Then his hand locked onto her throat. She tried desperately to reach his face, possibly to gouge out his eyes but he kept out of her reach. His thumbs compressed on her larynx cutting off her air. She tried to beg, tried to plead with him but by the insane, hideous grin on his face, she saw that there was no reasoning. Spots began to dance before her eyes and her vision began to grow fuzzy. Her arms became heavy but she continued to struggle.

Darwin squeezed tighter while his teeth gnashed together. Spittle flew from his mouth, his rage consuming him. Her mouth opened and closed and she made soft croaking sounds, then her eyes rolled back. Her body became limp.

He continued to squeeze, then shook her violently; her body limp, like a broken marionette. Just as quickly, his rage began to subside, as did his grip on her throat. Staring at her lifeless body his eyes grew wide. Reaching up his hand shook while he lightly brushed the hair from her face.

"What have I done?" he said softly, as he drew her body close to his embracing his dead lover. He gently began to weep burying his face into her exposed flesh.

Then, abruptly, he let her go. Her body slipped off the leather seat crumpling to the floor in a heap. Slowly, he raised his hands looking at them. Blood covered them, her blood. Darwin felt an urgency sweep over him to cleanse his hands.

He wiped them off on his shirt smearing the blood into the fabric. That wasn't good enough; splotches of blood still remained like it was woven into his skin. Grabbing a bottle of liquor from the small wet bar within the limousine he doused his hands. Dropping the bottle, he rubbed them vigorously together wiping them repeatedly on his shirt.

Then he noticed the stains on his shirt. Panic overtook him and he ripped it off his body tossing it to the other side of the vehicle. He gazed at the lifeless body on the floor. At first, he felt an incredible loss consume him like he had just walked in on a crime. Then abruptly, he unlocked the doors and got out. His men stood around the limousine, automatic weapons in hand. Closing his eyes, he took a deep breath of the humid night air then let out a loud sigh.

"Clean up this mess," he said to one of the men.

"What do you want done with the body boss?" one of the men looked inside the vehicle.

"Throw it in the surf, let the tide take it out to sea."

His men went to work. Walking away from the vehicle, he outstretched his arms and reached to the sky as if he could grab the very stars that twinkled down at him.

He felt cleansed - he felt reborn.

Chapter 1

Five Years Later... Eve Lawson sat watching the torrents of water cascade down from the top of the waterfall into a large pool of water. This spring day was exceptionally beautiful with its brilliant blue sky and comforting hot sun. Laying back on the warm rock, she let the sun beat down on her naked body. She loved coming to this place. It offered peace and tranquility, nothing like the real daily existence she had once known.

Sadness and destitution had marked her first eighteen years. By the age of thirteen, her mama had made the choice of walking away from the family. As any normal day, her mama prepared the family breakfast, took special care in picking out her clothes and putting on her makeup but with one exception; at the end of this day, she never came home. Her brother Darrius, being the older sibling, had tried to reassure her that everything would be all right. Although doubts were clearly written on his face, he tried to remain strong and in control. Eve always provided Darrius 100% support and encouragement and thought it best not to tell him how his doubts were showing through. For two weeks, they went to the police on a daily basis trying desperately to find out if there were any leads on their mother's whereabouts but to no avail. The bottom line was – she never returned.

Their lives had been changed forever. The small home they had grown up in wasn't much but it was their home and they didn't want to leave. But without a steady income, their options of staying quickly diminished. It wasn't long before they were forced out and working full-time as Street Beggars.

One day Eve was wandering around the market keeping her eyes open for any handout opportunity when she spotted a dawta carrying a bag of fruit. The woman appeared to be not much older than she was, maybe closer to her brother's age. An incredibly beautiful woman, she was much shorter than Eve with a much heavier frame. She followed the women with determination, keeping her focus on the fruit. Eve was cautious ensuring there was no suspicion by the woman being followed or watched. The woman paid for her groceries and then headed out onto a busy Street. Eve quickly came up behind and bumped into her knocking the bag from her arms. Fruit hit the ground hard and scattered about. As quickly as possible, Eve began snatching up what she could. Immediately the woman realized what Eve was up to and acted like lightening, never giving Eve a chance to get away with her goods. The woman landed on top of Eve, making sure she couldn't run away. Simultaneously, they looked up and deep into each other's eyes. It was an experience that couldn't be explained nor did they want to try.

That day something magical occurred – a special friendship was born.

The woman, Sharon Cunnings, quickly became the older sister Eve had always wanted. Once she learned of Eve and Darrius's plight, she led them out of town and deep into the rain forest where there stood a small, rundown secluded shack. It certainly wasn't a glamorous palace but it kept out the rain and provided a place to sleep.

She also learned why Sharon kept coming to this secluded place. Her own father had died years before from a drug overdose. This was absolutely devastating, as she loved her father very much. When she saw her father slowly slipping way, she was powerless to do anything. The drug lord owned the population.

A year after her father's death, her mama met a man, Elmo Lester. He was a serious man who rarely spoke to her. One night after Sharon had gone to bed; she was rudely awakened when she felt his rough chapped hands grab onto her breasts beneath her nightshirt. Instinct had taken over and she lashed out striking the man in the groin. He toppled to the floor in pain. Sharon bounded out of bed to tell her mama, but Elmo acted quickly. Grabbing and pinning her to the bed, he explained to her that if she said anything to her mother he would make them both pay dearly.

Sharon loved her mother and she took Elmo's threat seriously thus keeping her mouth shut. But even Sharon's silence didn't stop him from trying to molest her. When he tried, she would run from the house, staying away for weeks at a time trying to figure out what she should do. Upon returning home one day, her mother announced she was pregnant. It was then that things became much more complicated.

Sharon looked at Eve and grinned. It was no secret that Steven had a crush on Eve though she never seemed to see it. Steven Winters was another orphan who never knew his parents. They had abandoned him in a church as soon as he was born. He was light skinned and took a lot of ribbing for it.

Other kids at the orphanage would constantly pick on him and alienate him. Their actions were cruel but gave Steven the determination needed never to fail. He was handsome; nearly model material and

Sharon could never understand why Eve wasn't attracted to him. His greenish brown eyes were captivating and just thinking about him made her want to know him on a more intimate basis.

But Eve had other ideas, foolish ideas. She had met a man who worked at the resort. His name was Diamond, least that's what everyone called him due to the fact embedded in one of his front teeth was an actual diamond. Nobody knew his last name or for that, matter what his real name was. Eve had fallen head over heels in love with him despite Sharon's warnings about him.

"When do the others arrive?" Eve asked.

"Day after tomorrow," Sharon said.

She was referring to the last of their little group, Ohpton Manley and Winston George III whom they called Raffie because he was always joking around. Ophton was a handsome man, quiet, always preferred observing to leading. He also came from an abused home, running away when he was just 16. Sharon had met him one day when she was going home. Two men had appeared from an alleyway making it clearly apparent what they wanted. She put up a good fight, but they managed to pin her down.

That was when Ophton stumbled upon them. His calm, quiet demeanor quickly changed and he laid into the men with a fury she had never seen before in all her life. One of the men drew a knife and inflicted a terrible wound on Ophton's arm, but he continued to fight. Soon the men had enough of Ophton's fury and ran off. From that moment on, their friendship blossomed and was bonafide.

Raffie was the one in the group whom everyone pitied the most. Though he was a prankster, it was clearly apparent his games were more of a cover. The pain he held within was deep. He came from a prominent family, his mother, father and even his grandmother where in law enforcement. They tried to clean up the island, remove the drug lord, and stop the terror that held the island in an iron vice. On his fourteenth birthday he came home from school only to find an empty house. There in the dining room the table had been set. Balloons and banners filled the room marking the party his parents had planned for him. Sitting on the table was his birthday cake with fourteen flickering candles. Raffie noticed that they appeared to have been burning for a while since the wax had melted down onto the top of the cake. Sitting beside the cake was a huge birthday present with a brilliant red bow. Raffie searched the house and thought it was odd that no one was home, especially on his birthday. Then he caught the sound of something dripping. In the quiet house it sounded like marbles hitting a wood floor. Following the sound it brought him back into the dining room. The noise was coming from the present on the table. Studying it closer he noticed something dripping from the corner of the box. Putting his finger to the edge he wiped along corner. His finger was covered with a red sticky substance.

His heart hammered in his chest and his hands shook as he pulled the small envelope from the top of the box. Opening the letter it contained two words, HAPPY BIRTHDAY. Grabbing he lid of the box his mouth was dry, his heart pounded, and he broke out in a cold sweat. Drawing back the lid, he peered inside.

To his horror, the severed heads of his parents along with his grandmother lay within; their terror-stricken faces leering up at him.

Raffie ran and ran as far and as fast as he could. He never looked back leaving everything he knew behind.

Sharon loved them all; they were her family even though they weren't blood relatives. Together they were strong. They all came from terrible drug infested pasts. This connection allowed them to share their horrors and comfort each other. They all worked for the same goal of getting enough money to get off the island. They wanted to fly to the United States and start over with a brand new life. It was a hard goal to reach but together they kept the dream alive. Over the years, the once little run down shack had been transformed into a respectable and very tastefully done house. Each one of them brought a new and different personality to the place.

They all worked during the summers at the Orion Hotel, the biggest summer resort on the island. Pooling their money, they took just what was needed to survive and the rest went into a tin can, which they buried.

The summer tourist season was soon starting and they would all be traveling to the resort, some of them would stay there, a few of them would travel back and forth from their home. Each year their jobs became more difficult since corruption was rampant at the resort. Drugs were virtually nonexistent, at least until the sun went down. As the shadows arose, so did the evil.

"Eve, why do you like this Diamond guy?" Sharon asked.

"Well, he's handsome and he's so gentle when he makes love to me. He says he's going to ask me to marry him," she smiled.

"What about our goal?"

"He can come with us!" she beamed.

"I don't trust him Eve, I get a bad feeling from this guy," Sharon pointed out.

"You're just jealous that he's spending time with me and not you!" Eve laughed.

"Eve I'm serious," Sharon said not smiling.

"Look, I know what I'm doing. Don't worry OK?" Eve giggled.

Sharon shook her head and looked at the falling water. Eve was so naive, so blind to the way of the world. She saw the horror all around her but chose not to look. She would rather look at the bright side of everything. It dosen't hurt until you step on that one pointed piece. Eve had never stepped on that sharp piece of glass. Sharon worried that when that day came, Eve might change for the worse.

Sharon also worried about Eve's brother Darrius. He was a serious and very determined young man who looked out for their little group like a father. He also harbored one hell of big chip on his shoulder. He did nothing to hide his loathing for the drug lord, freely telling people what he thought. She didn't understand why the drug lord tolerated Darrius when he did this. The drug lord, Jah-Man, was someone not to mess with. His cruelty was well known and he held their town and a good portion of the island in an iron grasp. It was even rumored that the police was on the payroll. She hated Jah-Man and it angered her that he was the one who brought the drugs freely to the people. Many people other than her father fell victim to his white powder, which every day brought them all closer to disaster. The longer they stayed on the island the more likely they would be to fall victim to Jah-Man and his power; either by direct confrontation, or being caught in the crossfire.

"When are you starting?" Sharon asked brining her attention back.

"Oh, tomorrow. In some ways, I'm looking forward to getting back to the Orion. It takes my mind off of everything else," Eve giggled.

"You mean you'll get to see Diamond more," Sharon said raising an eyebrow.

"Well of course I will, maybe this summer he'll ask me!" she said grinning.

Sharon swallowed and said nothing. She didn't like Diamond. She had heard rumors about him being a Mr. Mention. And what he did on the side for the guests. This summer she would find out the truth about this man. No matter what it took, she would find the truth for Eve and show her.

"I'm going back," Sharon said dressing.

"Back to the house?"

"No, back to my house. I must see my mother and brother before I start work," she said softly. I'm going to stay here a while and just sit back and listen to the water. Won't be able to do that once we start work," Eve said staring at the water.

Sharon said nothing and headed back to the house. The trail was well worn. Her and the others had spent much time at that waterfall. Over the years it had become one constant in their lives, next of course to their house.

She loved the house and knew the others did as well. It wasn't much when she found it, no windows and the ceiling leaked. There were so many things wrong with it but nevertheless, slowly; she began working on it as best she could. Her carpenter skills were limited but she made due with what skills she had and soon started seeing things come together. Before the others arrived she had managed to stop the leaks, find old windows to replace the broken ones and replace the rotten boards in some of the walls. Then the others came, Darrius, Raffie and Steven. Steven was very good with a saw and hammer and became the director. He was a real visionary and took what was in his mind and turned it into a reality. There were additions, porches and interior furnishings. The place really became a home and now she wouldn't trade it for the world.

When she reached the porch, she heard people talking inside. Climbing the steps, she opened the front door. Instantly Darrius and Steven, who sat in the living room with a cold beverage in their hands, greeted her.

"Sharon, I'm glad to see you!" Darrius smiled.

"Come and sit with us, tell us what you've been up to," Steven said patting the couch next to him with his hand.

For a moment Sharon stood there staring at Steven, her pulse quickened and her heart began to race. He was so handsome, so sexy, and she wanted to feel his touch so badly. More often than not, she fantasized his arms wrapping around her, his lips drawing to hers and their passion growing as they took turns slowly removing one garment after another from each other's body.

"Is something wrong?" Darrius asked. The fantasy was broken.

"No, of course not. I was just thinking I'm not yet ready to start at the Orion," she said thinking of a quick excuse.

"I don't think any of us are," Steven laughed.

"But we have to remember, the money does bring us one step closer to getting out of this place."

"The sooner the better," Darrius quickly responded.

"I fear that the longer we stay on this island the closer Jah-Man will get to dragging one of us in," Darrius said staring at the floor.

"That will only happen if we are not there for each other," Sharon quickly added. "Yes Darrius, we are all family now. We have each other and that will make us strong," Steven said reassuringly. "I have my doubts. Jah-Man is powerful and his tramp Delicia will probably make our lives miserable again this summer," Darrius said sadly.

Sharon just nodded as she agreed with him. Delicia was Jah-Man's woman; she would be a beautiful woman, in her eyes, if she didn't do everything to excess. She also had a body that would take any man's breath away and she wore outfits that revealed every curve of her body. No man would touch her and she knew it unless of course they didn't want to live to see another day. She also made all their lives miserable at the hotel treating them like peasants or ghetto trash. More often than not, she would blatantly do something that would land one of them in front of the hotel manager. What bothered her the most was the fact she was drawn to Eve. It was like the devil trying to manipulate someone for his or her soul.

"We'll just have to deal with her one day at a time," Sharon finally said.

"She does have one hell of a body," Steven grinned at Darrius.

Sharon rolled her eyes and headed for her bedroom. Men would be men; no matter how noble, how daring, how cute they still thought with their glands. Grabbing her small handbag, she began packing her clothing for what she would need at the hotel the next day. She would leave right from her home in the morning since it was closer to the hotel. She loved her mother, loved her dearly and her little brother too. However, she hated Elmo her mother's boyfriend. She only wished that she could make her mother listen and more importantly, believe. "Where are you going?" Steven said startling her from the doorway.

"Home, I have to see my brother and mama before I start work. You know I don't get much chance during the summer," she said softly.

"Look, you want me to come with you? At least stay a while in case he tries anything?" Steven asked.

"No, I'll be fine. He won't try anything while you're there anyway, he'll wait until I'm alone - that's the way he works."

"Maybe I can sleep over. That would deter him wouldn't it?" he asked.

"You'd do that for me wouldn't you?" she said turning to him. "Stupid question, of course you know I would," he smiled warmly.

For a moment she became lost in his eyes; those greenish brown eyes, they were intoxicating! Then abruptly she forced herself to look away. If she hadn't she might have thrown herself at him.

"No, that ain't necessary, I can handle Elmo on my own," she said softly.

"Are you sure? You don't sound convinced," he said moving closer to her.

"I...I...I'm sure Steven," she said her voice barely audible. She then felt his firm hand touch her bare shoulder. His touch was magically and it ran through her like a jolt of electricity. Turning she again looked into his mesmerizing eyes. Her breathing became erratic. It took all her internal strength but she pressed her finger to her lips, then reached up and pressed the same finger to his. Smiling she broke away.

"OK, I think I should but if you don't want me to..." he began to say.

"I'll see you tomorrow at work," she said her hands shaking as she zipped her bag closed.

Silence filled the room. She turned expecting him to still be standing there but instead, the room was empty. She sat on the end of the bed. It had taken all her strength, all her internal fortitude to turn away from him. Holding her hand to her chest, she felt the thumping of her heart as it beat wildly. Closing her eyes she took deep long breaths, trying to calm herself. She then grabbed her bag and headed for her other home.

By the time she arrived home, it was getting dark. Lights shone through the windows and for just a moment, she was taken back - remembering back to a time when she was little girl and her father was alive and not on drugs. Those were the happy times, the times that she longed to go back to. Their possessions were minimal but it didn't take much to make her happy. Her parents would take her to the beach and she would spend hours, building things in the sand. Other times they would take long walks together and she would ride high on her father's shoulders. They were a loving family; her heart yearned to go back to those times. Nevertheless, the darkness came, the evil darkness so tempting and provocative. The light was not enough for her father, the darkness was too tempting, too intoxicating and he turned to it, embraced it. More often than not, he would disappear for days on end.

Her mother was a strong woman, but even as a child, she could see the fear in her mother's eyes. Over time, that was what changed her from a simple child to a young woman and then into an adult. She had to be strong, strong for her mother and more importantly <u>strong for herself.</u>

When her mama met Elmo, she thought at first things had changed. He was nice. She never saw the signs, never dreamed that someone in a parent role would make an move on her. The more she was around him, the more she could see and sense the lust in his eyes. Whenever he looked at her, she <u>knew</u> he was undressing her with his eyes. He was a filthy disgusting <u>nasty naayga.</u>

Whenever she tried to talk to her mother about how she felt the subject would either quickly change or Elmo would suddenly walk in. She wondered if her mother knew, like all mothers should, that something was wrong. She loved her mother and she quickly dismissed the possibility that she knew. Her mother would never allow such a man into her bed if she knew.

Opening the front door, she stepped inside. Instantly her little brother Ronald came running up to her beaming a smile. He adored her and she loved him terribly. He had all the innocence that children should have. His short curly hair and the kind of big brown eyes that when they looked up at you, there was no way you could ever say "no." He would one day grow up to be a handsome man. With one quick bound he leapt from the floor straight into her arms hugging her tightly and she wrapped her arms around him drawing him close.

"I missed you Sis," he said with a voice that made her heart ache.

"I missed you and I love you too," she whispered softly to him.

"You're just in time, I have to go to bed," he said.

"Well come on then, I'll put you to bed and read you a story," she said squeezing him tighter.

"Aaarh! You're gonna squeeze my guts out!" he said giggling.

From around the corner her mother emerged with a bowl in her hand. When she saw the two of them she smiled warmly. Her mother was still an attractive woman, though her face had wrinkled and she had put on some weight.

Her eyes looked tired, drained and the very sight of them bothered her greatly.

"It's good that you are home," she said her voice sweet and soothing.

"I know mamma. I will be starting work tomorrow," she replied.

"I know I have seen many familiar faces in town."

"The summer crowds will be coming shortly," her mother said turning her attention to mixing what was in the bowel.

"Will you be staying long?"

"I don't know…it depends," Sharon said feeling suddenly uncomfortable.

"Awe come on Sis! Stay a while so you can play with me, take me to the beach like you promised," Ronald pleaded.

"We'll see," was all she could say.

Then from behind her mother Elmo appeared. He was a balding man with a stern face. He was wiry with a skinny small frame. When he saw her, his eyes instantly glanced down at her ample bust. She suddenly felt violated.

"Come on, time for that story," she said abruptly turning and heading for her brother's room.

"Make it a good one Sis…a real good one!" he pleaded.

It was much later that Ronald fell asleep. He had been so excited and wound up tighter than a spring at her being home. But eventually her soft voice lulled him into that dream world all children go to at night. Even though he was asleep, she continued reading the story. She kept telling herself that as soon as she stopped he would become wide-awake again. She also knew the truth, if she stopped, she would have to go into the other room where Elmo was. She also could just grab her bag and make the long walk back to the shack. She was torn; if she left tonight, again her mother would be disappointed…<u>she would be disappointed</u>. She wanted to visit with her, tell her what her and her friends were doing. However, with Elmo hanging around like a bat from the ceiling, visually peeling her clothing off as she sat, there would be no peaceful conversation. All she could hope for was by the time she finished the story, he would have drank himself into a stupor and passed out in bed. The hours wore on.

By eleven her own eyes were becoming heavy, yet she fought to keep them open while her ears strained to pick up a telltale sound from the other room. Finally, she turned the last page. For a moment she thought of starting the whole book over again but quickly decided against that idea and put it down. There was no stopping the inevitable. Getting up she walked slowly to the doorway, her legs were weak from sitting so long and she flexed them gingerly as she listened. Finally peeking out into the living room she saw her mother sitting and knitting. "Hi" she whispered softly walking out into the room. "Elmo in bed?" "Yes, went to bed a little while ago," she replied.

"He find work yet?" she said sitting down next to her.

"No, he says he's looking, maybe one of the fishing boats will sign him on," she said enthusiastically. "Mama, do you need anything?" Sharon asked.

"No, well it is nothing that you need to concern yourself with," she said focusing on her knitting.

"He's taken your money again hasn't he?" Sharon said with a bite.

"He says he needs it to get around to find a job," her mother said.

"But Mama he just comes home and drinks. What does he do all day?" she asked.

"Look for work."

"Please Mama, I want you to listen to me. There is something I have to talk to you about," Sharon said the courage to tell her about him growing. For a moment her mama continued to knit, then abruptly she stopped and let her hands rest in her lap. She didn't turn to look at her, nor did she say anything. She had waited so long for this opportunity.

"Mama" she began to say.

"What is wrong here?" a booming voice arose from the kitchen.

The voice was grating, like a person's fingernails on a chalkboard. Yet, she turned to see Elmo standing in the doorway staring intently at her.

"Is there something wrong Sharon? Something you need help with?" he said coming further into the room.

"I...I...No, nothing is wrong that I can't handle on my own," she said getting up.

"I think I best go to bed, tomorrow will be a busy day," she said heading quickly for her room.

Once there she closed the door and leaned heavily against it. The room was barren except for her bed and a small dresser containing only a few clothing items and none of her undergarments. She didn't leave many of her personal items, the thought of Elmo rummaging through her clothing. The very thought of his filthy hands on her undergarments nearly made her stomach wretch. Grabbing a small wooden chair, she propped it under the doorknob stopping anyone that might sneak into her room during the night. She hated doing it, she felt like a prisoner in her own home. If a thunderstorm brewed she would remove it. Her little brother was terrified of them and he might come running to her room like he had done in the past.

Getting undressed she neatly folded her clothes laying them on top of her suitcase. The room was hot, stuffy and she opened one of the windows to let a breath of fresh air inside. For a moment she stood there naked the night air washing in on her, then abruptly she reached up and closed the window. It was an entranceway for Elmo to get in. Reaching up to latch the window closed she noticed that the latch was gone. Where it had once been was now a clear marking and fresh wood beneath. Someone had deliberately taken the latch off. Elmo!

"Bastard" she swore to herself.

Looking around the room, she tried to think of a way to keep the window down, some way to keep Elmo out during the night. Her mind raced trying to think of a solution to her problem. Finally, she grabbed one of her dresser drawers pulling it out. Dumping the few pieces of clothing onto the bed, she took her fist and punched through the thin veneer that made up the bottom. Taking a shard of wood, she went up to the window and stuck it between the window and the frame. Then, with the heel of her shoe she pounded it down wedging it tightly. She tried to open the window. It wouldn't budge. Closing the thin drapes, she went over and pulled back the covers on her bed. Lying there she tried to let sleep take claim over her body but her eyes kept being drawn back to the window. Her imagination was running wild and she thought she could see Elmo peering through the drapes, his tongue licking his lips hungrily as he consumed her naked body with his eyes.

The thought was painful. She wanted to get up and throw some clothing on, anything to hide her body. But the room was horrendously hot. Without the window and the chance for a cool night breeze, sleeping would be miserable. Rolling onto her side, she closed her eyes tight and thought of the only thing that gave her peace...Steven.

It was late when Eve, Darrius and Steven had finished dinner. Steven, a fantastic cook had made a fabulous dinner. None of them would sleep well eating so late. Steven stood washing dishes; he loved the solitude that simple chores gave. This allowed him time to think about things such as his future; say in 10 years from now. That question had already been answered; least he and the others were working towards it. Every two weeks they would each take over half of their paycheck made and put it into the tin can. The can was their ticket out – literally, out to freedom and a new life. Over the years, they agreed that their future was waiting for them in America. However, Visas, Passports, immunizations along with transportation and other miscellaneous expenses would cost, and cost big.

At the end of each summer, they would gather around their secret burial site then recount what was saved and determine their new financial goal. Two more years to go, it was a short time to wait considering how many years had already passed, but each of them were starting to grow a bit impatient. The end of the rainbow was drawing near yet the reality that their dream was close to coming true put them all on the edge

Fate could play dirty tricks and Murphy's Law worked all over the world, not just in America. His mind then drifted; slowly he began to think about Eve. She was a beautiful woman, sexy, sultry, with a set of legs he longed to have wrapped around him. He had taken to her as soon as he laid eyes on her. She had a special way about her; so innocent yet when she smiled and her lips curled, along with her eyebrow turning up, she gave the aura of I want you...take me now. Over the years, he had tossed out little innuendoes, testing the waters to see if the interest went both ways. She noticed him, but not in the way he wanted her to. Strangely, his thoughts drifted again. This time they centered on Sharon; he admired her strength, along with her ample bust. She also had eyes that you couldn't hide from, she saw you instantly for what you were. He had thought about her before, often when he was alone. In many ways he preferred her to Eve, she was so much more than Eve could ever be but he also knew that she didn't have any interest in him. Their conversations were always straightforward, business like. They had fun together, joked from time-to-time but he never got the signals that showed she was interested. Then again, he wasn't an expert at these things.

"Going to polish that plate all night?" a voice startled him nearly causing him to drop the plate.

Turning around he came face to face with Eve. Her short blond hair and her full lips made his voice stick in his throat. With much effort though, he answered her.

"No, just lost in thought," he said. "Care to share?" she smiled grabbing another dishtowel along with another plate.

"Nothing much to share," he lied. "What about you? Ready to start the whole season off again?" he said swallowing hard.

"No, but it doesn't matter we all have to do it anyway," she teased. "I guess I am looking forward to going back, least for some reasons."

Turning she walked over and grabbed an apple from a small basket on the counter. She then went and pulled a small pairing knife from the drawer and began slicing it. Steven watched her; she wore a very loose and thin nightshirt. When she moved he could, at times, see the shape of her figure beneath, the sway of her breasts. He was getting excited. Turning he directed his attention, along with his body to the sink of dishes to dry. Maybe if he concentrated on the work he would forget the image burned into his mind.

"So do you think they'll keep you in the same area again this year?" she asked drawing closer.

"The beach? I hope so," he said not looking at her. "Hey, maybe they'll put me there too this year!"

"Wouldn't that be neat?" she mused.

"I'd like it," he said his voice soft.

"Yeah, me too. We could hang out together so I can keep all those foreign women from throwing their bodies at you," she giggled.

"Jealous?" he asked his heart thumping wildly.

"No, I just don't want to see you turn into some trashy male prostitute or something," she said eating a slice of apple.

Steven wanted to say something but the words choked in his throat. Even if he did, he knew he would sound like some babbling idiot. Suddenly, Eve dropped the remaining portion of her apple. It bounced and rolled to the side. Steven watched her as she reached down to pick it up off the floor. When she bent over, he had a clear view down the front of her shirt and of her exposed breasts. He turned his head sharply away.

"Darn" she said.

"That was a waste of a good apple," she said tossing it into the trash.

"Look, you should go to bed. I don't have much more to do and I'll be going to bed as well," he said changing the subject.

"Yes, I suppose I should, tomorrow will be a busy day," she agreed.

Turing she put the knife in the sink then headed for the door. Before she walked through, she stopped and turned.

"Steven can I ask you a personal question?" "Sure, of course you can," he
said smiling.

"Do you ever wish you had someone special in your life? I mean, someone to cuddle with at night?" she bluntly asked.

"I…I…I…err…well," he stuttered feeling embarrassment rush through him. "I guess so," he said finally choked the words out.

"So do I," she said, then abruptly turned and walked through the door.

Steven stood there his mouth hanging open. He wondered if it was an open invitation or just an innocent question. He knew in his head he prayed for the first, but his heart told him differently. Eve was innocent and naive; her question had no hidden meaning and no subtle hint. He turned back to the sink to finish the dishes.

"Going to bed?" Darrius asked watching her walk by.

"Yeah, I'm not tired though," she said stopping and talking to him.

"Steven need any help in there?" he asked.

"No, he said he'd be done soon. I wish Sharon was here, she'd stay up with me," Eve added.

"She'd tell you to hit the sack too," Darrius said.

"That's where I should be right now also," he said putting the book he was reading down taking care to only fold the very tip of the page he was on as a marker.

"Well good night," she said.

"Eve, can I ask you an important favor?" Darrius said getting up.

"Sure, I'm your sister, you can ask me for anything remember," she shrugged.

"I know that you and Delicia sometimes hang around together. She treats you better than she does the rest of us. Would you consider staying away from her? She's bad news Eve, I don't think she has your best interest in mind"

"No! I'm not a little girl anymore. I'm quite capable of choosing who my friends are and Delicia happens to be one of them. You're just angry because she's Jah-Man's girlfriend!" she snapped.

"Eve, it's more than that and you know it," he said trying to keep rational.

"No it's not! I never understood the hate you have for him. How do you know he does the things people say? How do you know that they're not just jealous of what he has? Have you personally talked to him?" she spat.

"No and I have no desire to. Stop being so blind Eve, the man is well known for being a drug lord. That is common knowledge," Darrius said his voice rising slightly.

"You blame him for Mama's disappearance, why I don't know," she ranted.

"I don't know why I blame him. I admit it's just a feeling and nothing more - a simple gut feeling," Darrius now was yelling back.

Eve had struck a raw cord in him. They argued over very little but when the topic of the Drug Lord came up it always ended in a fight. He wanted more than anything to make Eve see what he felt but he knew it would never happen.

When Jah-Man was around the hotel he was treated like a VIP although he had never seen the man doing business, least of that involving drugs. Still, he knew and felt the truth. The man was evil and he brought evil to their small community along with death.

"You don't understand, you never did," she said then stormed out of the room.

He had infuriated Eve and now there was no reasoning with her. If they continued to talk and she continued to defend Jah-Man, it would only make him angry as well. He harbored enough hate for the man as it was. He knew deep down, felt it somehow that Jah-Man had something to do with their mother's disappearance. There was no proof, not even an eyewitness that saw him even near her, yet whenever he feels the loss of his mother he has a sudden hate for the man. It could be just what he represents, nothing more. He wished his gut told him a different story. In any event, Eve was old enough to make decisions of her own although he may not like them. He also wanted to tell her that he didn't care for Diamond. That was another one of his bad gut feelings. Suddenly a thought washed over him. Was he being too overbearing? Quickly he dismissed the thought. The questions he asked her were for her own good and because he loved her – nothing more.

Suddenly Steven came into the room.

"Are you two at it?" he asked Darrius.

"Yeah, I just asked her to stay away from Delicia this summer," Darrius sighed.

"Good thought but wrong tactic," Steven said sitting down.

"I found that out already. She's a big girl now Darrius, not the same little girl you had to take care of. She's only three years younger than you remember," Steven said.

"Yes, she is…but she acts much younger!" Darrius quickly added.

"Maybe, look I don't like the woman any more than you do. She nearly got me fired last year remember?" Steven quickly added.

"So what can we do?"

"Nothing, she won't listen to you - or me or anyone else, other than perhaps, Sharon," Steven added.

"Do you think she could persuade Eve to steer clear of her?" Darrius said a shred of hope glistening in his eyes.

"Maybe, ask her tomorrow," Steven said getting up. "I'm beat, I'll see you in the morning," he said heading for his room.

Darrius sat there alone trying to think of anything he might have missed in persuading Eve from staying away from Delicia. It was a question he already knew the answer to, Eve was now grown up and he had to stop playing the father figure. The thought of her with Delicia made his skin crawl.

Steven walked down the hallway to his room. When he passed Eve's door he stood for a moment and listened. There was no sound coming from her room. He tried to imagine her laying there waiting for him, wanting him.

The thought drove him crazy.

Chapter 2

The sun was bright and glared through the side windows of the bus, which abruptly hit a pothole in the side of the road. Ohpton Manley was jostled awake by the sudden jolt. Dazed he looked around finally realizing his surroundings. He had been on the bus since early morning traveling from the other side of the island. Getting up early in the morning wasn't his favorite thing to do as he felt this was a time that should be dedicated to solitude, relaxation, and making a transition into a new day.

Starting work at the Orion again was depressing. His goals were the same as the others, plain and simple, he wanted off the island. The bus was full, yet nobody had sat next to him in the seat enabling him to put his bags on the seat and stretch out. He was thankful for the little things. Reaching over he grabbed a small bag with fruit inside. A nice banana would start the morning off nicely. Reaching into the bag he froze, his fingers touched something soft, pliable. It didn't feel like a banana. Quickly withdrawing his hand, he took a deep breath, then opened the bag and peered inside.

"Aaarh!" he screamed tossing the bag to the floor attracting much unwanted attention.

"What, what's wrong?" Raffie said looking over the top of the seat.

"There, there's a curled up snake in that bag!" he pointed to the floor where the bag was. "I hate snakes – I hate them!"

Raffie moved around the seat and poked the bag with his foot. It didn't move. Reaching down he grabbed it, then looked at Ohpton and shook it at him. Moments later he thrust his hand into the bag.

"Watch it!" Ophton exclaimed.

Seconds later, Raffie pulled out a huge rubber snake and shook it at him grinning fiercely.

"This is what was bothering you?" he said shaking it at him.

Ohpton frowned clearly showing his displeasure. Raffie had done it again, played his usual pranks. He was such a prankster. For some reason they were always directed at him. He knew he hated snakes.

"That's not funny," Ohpton, said slinking back in the seat.

"Maybe not from your perspective, but mine?" he grinned.

"Someday Raffie. You just wait, someday you'll get yours," Ohpton said softly directing his attention to the side of the road.

"Hey, you know I only do it because I care. You're my buddy and I like having fun with you," Raffie said pushing his bags over and sitting on the same seat with him.

"Sometimes your jokes aren't funny. Sometimes people get hurt by you playing them," Ohpton said not looking at him.

"OK…OK, I get the picture, I'm sorry. I didn't mean for the rubber snake in your bag to be a mean joke." Raffie said trying not to laugh.

"I think you of all people would hate finding things inside bags and boxes," Ohpton said snidely.

Raffie stared at him; the meaning of what he said cutting sharply. He was referring to the death of his family at the hands of the drug lord. Though there was no direct evidence to prove the drug lord was connected, all indicators pointed to him. His parent's work to try to bring him to justice was enough in his eyes to prove guilt. What the others never truly grasped was the reason why he played the pranks. He used the laughter to hide his pain and anger. There was nowhere to direct it and slowly day-by-day it consumed him. Then, more as a defense mechanism than anything else, he started playing practical jokes. He loved the others though and he didn't lie when he said he cared. Darrius, Steven, Ohpton, Sharon, and Eve had all become his family and he would do anything for them…anything at all.

"I said I'm sorry."

"I'll tell you one thing, I'm not looking forward to working with the tourist crowds again this summer," Ohpton said shaking his head.

"I don't think any of us really are, but I don't mind it though," he smiled.

"That's because you have one of the best jobs, seeing all those sexy women in evening gowns. Heck, I'd like that," he grinned.

"Yes, I have to admit my job does have incentives, but it has it's downfalls too," Raffie added.

"Yeah, like what?"

"You can't touch any of it," he beamed.

"Besides, you must see your share of attractive women too," he implied.

"Yeah, from a grounds cart and only when they walk by," Ohpton shook his head.

"Well the important thing is to remember why we even do it," Raffie added.

"How close are we?" Ohpton asked.

"I do not know, we still have to go through our usual ritual of counting," Raffie explained.

"We must be close though."

"Think about it, all of us getting on that plane, going to the United States, living the good life," Ohpton fantasized.

"You do know that it will not be that easy there either. We will have to work there too, the grass will not be much different there than here," Raffie pointed out.

"True, but the grass is much fuller there. We will all have opportunities, can we say the same here?"

"Of course not, all I'm pointing out is that it is not going to be easy. None of us have extensive college backgrounds. Finding high paying jobs might not be an option for some time," Raffie explained.

"You're depressing me," Ohpton frowned.

"Sorry, remember I came from a fairly prominent family and now look what I have," he pointed out.

"But you lost it because of the drug lord, not your own choosing. If your parents were still around you wouldn't be coming with us," Ophton added.

"Possibly, my parents might have sent me to America anyway…maybe even to go to college," Raffie said staring down at the floor. "It's rough isn't it?"

"You know it is. Funny thing how fate throws us curves.

"Think about it this way, if events hadn't occurred the way they did none of us would have ever met. Our lives would have been so different," Raffie said softly.

"I try to forget my past because it's too depressing," Ophton shook his head.

"Yeah mine too," Raffie, added.

"Hey, check that out."

Ophton followed Raffie's finger; he was pointing to a woman three seats up from them. She was a pretty woman with dark succulent skin and very short curly hair. From where they sat, they could only see a profile of her face but a very good view along the side of her shirt. She was fairly well endowed.

"You wouldn't stand a chance," Ophton said softly.

"Watch" Raffie grinned.

Standing, he moved up the isle to the woman. Even though the distance was short, Ophton couldn't hear what he was saying to the woman. He did watch her reaction though. She looked up at him, then grinned sliding across the seat. Raffie sat down next to her, then abruptly turned and looked at him winking. Ophton sighed, sometimes things never changed. It was mid morning when the bus finally came to a stop outside the gates of the Orion, a huge multilevel resort. The entire complex was constructed in Spanish architecture, though it had a display of modern conveniences. As resorts go, it was top-notch sporting every luxury a person could want. It was not geared to children and none were present. It did cater to the rich and excessively wealthy. The staff comprised of hundreds, mostly local residents except for management, which were brought in from someplace else. What kept everyone coming back of course was the money.

"Well here we go," Raffie said grabbing his bag and heading up the long path to the main house.

Tourists hadn't begun to arrive yet. The facility had been closed down for two weeks during annual maintenance and to provide adequate time for the summer staff to arrive and settle in. There was still new equipment waiting to be validated, tested and installed in preparation to handle new customer requests and orders all for one purpose – to provide the customer luxury.

When they reached the main building, they both stopped and looked around for the manager's office so they could report in. During their check-in process, they would be able to find out what their assignment for the summer would be. Usually everyone kept the same assignment from summer to summer unless there had been a problem or a person was inept. It was then that the manager would try to find a better-suited assignment for that person.

"Hey you two!" a voice yelled to them.

Turning they saw Eve waving her arm and grinning from ear to ear. She quickly rushed over to them.

"Just Arrive?" she asked.

"Yeah" Raffie said.

"Me too, the others are around here somewhere," she said looking around.

"They still got you working the boutique?" Ophton asked.

"Sure do, what about you two?" she smiled.

"Don't know yet, we haven't checked in," Raffie explained.

"Well come with me, I'll show you where the new office is," she motioned to them.

Steven stood waist deep in the pool adjusting the jets on the pump. He not only was a lifeguard on the beach but also managed the pool and hot tubs. It was a job he somewhat liked. Angling the flow of the jets, he made sure the pumps were discharging correctly.

"Make sure there's a good strong flow," a voice called from behind him. Turning he felt his breath catch in his throat. Delicia stood staring intently down at him. She was a ravishing woman, browning with long flowing black hair.

She had a body that screamed unadulterated lust, she liked to display it more as a tease than anything else. For a moment he couldn't help himself, his eyes went from hers down her luscious body. She wore a scant two-piece bathing suit the fabric barely covering her breasts and the lower portion leaving little to the imagination. She was a walking pheromone. She was also Jah-Man's woman.

"So? Don't you have anything to say?" she said breaking his concentration on her body.

"Huh...no," he said then diverted his attention back to his work.

"Well that's rude," she snapped.

"I am a year-round guest here you know. You're job is to make my stay pleasurable."

"We haven't reopened yet," he said not looking up at her.

"Are you even supposed to be here?"

"Of course I am, I'm overseeing the opening. Just remember who has a lot financial interest in this place," she said with an evil grin.

It was no secret; Jah-Man had a major financial interest in the resort. He spent alot for the upkeep among other things and was frequently seen walking the grounds. Steven tried to keep the realization that Jah-Man's money more than likely also paid his paycheck. The thought made him nauseous.

"I haven't forgotten," he said softly.

"You better not or you'll be selling trinkets on the beach someplace," she snapped.

"What do you want?" he said changing the subject.

"Nothing - maybe later though… You are a cute one," she gave him an evil smile.

"Jah-Man wouldn't like to hear you say that."

"I am his woman but he doesn't own me," she snapped her anger seething.

"I can have what I want, anything I want."

"I suppose money buys anything," he said sarcastically.

"Yes it does…and if I want you it will buy me that too," she snapped.

Steven sighed, there was only one way out of this conversation. Agree with her then avoid her. He had to admit, if she were a different person than who she was and had a different attitude, he wouldn't think twice about hopping into bed with her. That was of course if she took all the cargo off.

He wondered how she supported all that stuff, diamonds, gold chains, and wristbands that went halfway up her arms. She even had toe rings. There was so much, it actually detracted from her perfect body.

"So how much extra will I make?" he asked taking a different tact.

"That's better," she smiled.

"We can talk about that one later," she beamed then abruptly turned and walked away.

He watched her bare bottom sway back and forth, the cut of the thong barely visible. Her high heels made a clicking noise on the slate that surrounded the pool. She also knew he was watching her and made every effort to swing her butt from side to side and bounce her breasts. It was pathetic.

Sharon glanced around the room; there really wasn't much to set up where she worked as the resort's Salon was pretty well stocked. Two other girls worked with her and due to her talents as a hairdresser she was in high demand during the summer months. Out of the entire group, by far she pulled in the most money. Wealthy women tipped big and she knew exactly what topics of conversation to discuss with them. When they walked out, they felt like a million bucks. It was also taxing and at the end of the day, she was exhausted. The rich, arrogant attitude was sometimes more than she could take. They had odd tastes and sometimes very odd behaviors. Most of her customers were very nice, polite and fun to talk with but it only takes one or two to spoil the day.

"Hey how's it going?" Eve called from the doorway.

"Same ordinary ting," Sharon sighed.

"Raffie and Ohpton are here. Ohpton is bummed, he got the grounds job again," she said.

"Steven is doing the beach again and Darrius is behind the counter this year," Sharon added.

"Ooh…Darrius was hoping to be put behind the desk this year so he should like that." she smiled.

"Might not be too bad of a season - we might actually have some fun."

"Yeah, maybe all this is one step closer to you know what," she pointed out.

"You have to look at things differently, make the best of it, try and enjoy the work for once!" Eve beamed.

"You're an optimist," Sharon scowled.

"Thank you" Eve grinned even more.

"What are you doing for dinner?" Sharon asked.

"Don't know yet. Guests are due to arrive tonight sometime, early arrivals and all. Delicia wants to get together sometime too," Eve said.

"Eve…" Sharon began to say.

"I know, I know. I can look out for myself remember," Eve quickly said.

"She's trouble."

"She's rich!" Eve beamed.

"Yes with Jah-Man's money and…"

Sharon's words were cut off. Behind Eve, Delicia came strolling in wearing a thin wrap covering her scandalous bathing suit. Eve turned and smiled at her and she smiled back, then directed her attention to Sharon and frowned. It was no secret that they hated each other. More than once Delicia had tried to get her fired; only the high volume of compliments from other guests had saved her. They were also her only protection from Delicia.

"I do not know why you waste your time with her," Delicia said to Eve.
"She isn't your caliber."

"She's my friend," Eve pointed out innocently.

"That's something we'll have to work on this summer," Delicia added.

"What can I do for you?" Sharon asked her anger seething.

"I want you to do my hair, this afternoon," Delicia said running her hand through her long hair.

"We're not officially open until tomorrow," Sharon added.

"I know, but you'll just have to find time this afternoon. There is a big welcoming party in the ballroom tonight," she sighed "Party?" Eve turned to her.

"Yes, Jah-Man wanted to welcome all the regular guests that are arriving today," she explained.

"I also want you to come with me tonight," she said to Eve.

"M…me?" Eve looked shocked.

"Of course, you need to see how the other side works honey," Delicia gloated.

"I'm not allowed to attend functions like that, it's prohibited," Eve exclaimed.

"Not if you're with me."

"What do I wear?" Eve stuttered.

"We'll take care of that too, as soon as she gets done with my hair we'll go and find you a dress," Delicia said giving Sharon and evil grin.

The anger Sharon felt was overwhelming. It was so blatantly obvious that she was trying to impress Eve, tempt her with things that in reality were out of reach. Delicia was also doing it to spite her, she knew how close Eve and her were. Anything that she could do to divide them and strike a wedge into their friendship Delicia would try. Sharon also knew that Delicia didn't give a damn about Eve.

"Well then, better come right over here and sit down," Sharon said forcing a smile.

"So meet me here in an hour and we'll go shopping," Delicia said to Eve who nodded and left the salon.

"So what do you want?" Sharon asked grabbing a protective cover from the cabinet.

"Oh I want just a slight trim, nothing much, maybe feather the sides. A good wash and dry also," Delicia said glancing at herself in the mirror.

"Why not cut it short, less to take care of, cooler in the summer heat," Sharon suggested.

"Because, short hair would take away from my perfect body," Delicia said obviously not joking.

"Oh brother," Sharon muttered under her breath.

"What was that?" Delicia said her ears perking like a rabid dog.

"You're right, it would only make you look fatter," she lied.

"Just get to work," Delicia said.

Darrius was busy behind the desk in the lobby. Unknown to everyone, Guests were already arriving. They were the regulars, the ones who squatted and stayed most of the summer. Many of them he recognized from years past, some he had never seen before. Most of the people who arrived were couples, but there were also a few single people. A majority of these singles were men, but there were a few women. Every one reeked of money.

The staff had to scramble to prepare the suites in time. It was a busy afternoon. He liked it behind the desk; he was the first person they saw when they came. He had the personality for the job too, his smile was intoxicating and management knew it. He had a magical way of making people feel welcomed and the company was comfortable that this was the first person people would be greeted by.

A young couple walked through the huge revolving doors in the lobby. He gave them a quick glance, and then had to take a second longer look. They contrasted greatly to one another. The male was oriental, most likely Japanese. He was short, with short dark hair and a very stern, serious face. He also wore a very expensive tailored suit. Walking beside him was a woman, American he guessed. She was tall, towering nearly a foot over him. Her long blond hair hit about the middle of her back. She had full lips and her high cheekbones contrasted with her crystal blue eyes. She wore a pale blue halter dress that came to just above her knees. When she moved, it was clear that she wore no bra beneath.

For a moment, they stood and looked around, then directed their attention in his direction. As they approached, Darrius grinned and tried his best to keep from watching the woman's breasts jiggle.

"Welcome to the Orion, are we expecting you?" he asked politely.

"Tsai" the man said his voice stern.

Darrius quickly scanned the computer finding his name. Smiling he turned and grabbed one of the suite keys and placed it on the counter.

"Have you stayed with us before Mr. Tsai?" he asked.

"No, this is our first time," he responded without a smile.

"We have a suite set up for you and…," Darrius said catching his choice of words. "…and your lovely young lady," he smiled.

"Is it private?" the man asked.

"Yes Sir, very" Darrius smiled.

"Do you have anything open and airy?" the woman spoke up her voice soft and sexy.

"Let me see," Darrius said checking the computer.

"Yes, we can change your room to the crystal chalet. I must warn you though that much of it is comprised of glass," he explained.

"That would be lovely," she smiled back.

Darrius changed the keys and for a moment, he thought he saw the man crack a smile. As with all guests there had to be more to these two than what he saw.

"Follow this map, it will lead you directly to the chalet. There is also a formal dinner being served in the ballroom at 8:00 p.m. tonight. Do you wish me to reserve a table for you?" he asked.

"Of course," the man added his expression resuming its cold glare.

Moments later they walked off, a valet carrying their bags. Darrius watched as the couple walked away, keeping his gaze on the sleek shape of the curves her butt made in the dress. Then to his astonishment, the woman turned catching him staring. Darrius felt his face flush, but the woman smiled then winked at him seductively.

"Who are they?" the other clerk asked.

"New, his name is Tsai, from Japan," Darrius said glancing at the computer.

Then something caught his attention. A man walked through the revolving glass doors. The man was excessively short yet his physique was exceptionally muscular his hair dangled with light brown locks. He had a light complexion, his face stern and commanding. His movements were direct and regal. His clothing was of the finest make and multiple gold chains dangled from his neck. He was definitely Hitey Titey. On his right hand, he wore two black onyx rings. Four other men strode close behind him. They were much taller than he was and built just as rugged. One of the men carried a briefcase handcuffed to his wrist. They all wore baggy light suits. It was apparent that they all were carrying some form of weapon. For a moment, they all stood looking around, and then abruptly moved in his direction. Jah-Man had entered the building.

Darrius felt his body suddenly go numb as he watched the man draw closer. Then Jah-Man locked eyes with him rooting him further. Darrius's rage burned fiercely within him. He hated the Man-God, hated what he represented, hated the way he controlled people even hated how he looked. It took all his internal strength not to launch himself over the desk and strangle the life from the man. His anger was strong but his reasoning was stronger. There was no doubt that as soon as he made a move towards the man his bodyguards would draw their weapons and quickly cut him down.

"C...can I help you?" Darrius croaked out.

"Of course you can Mr. Lawson," Jah-Man said, the corner of his mouth turning up in a smile.

"Have all my guests arrived?"

"We've had many check-ins," Darrius said his voice cracking.

"Let me see the book," Jah-Man demanded.

"There is no book as everything is computerized," Darrius said softly.

"Then show me," he asked.

"Come around the side," Darrius pointed to the end of the counter.

Jah-Man quickly yet methodically walked to the end of the counter then lifted the wooden divide, stepping behind the counter. Darrius watched him approach, this would have been the perfect opportunity to attack the man, end his evil. Fear rooted him.

"Show me," Jah-Man ordered.

Darrius used the mouse and scrolled through the guest log showing him who had arrived and who hadn't.

"You work well with these things. Do you like working with them?" he asked Darrius.

For a moment, Darrius was taken back at his pleasant nature and curiosity. He had very little dealings with the man and only in passing had JahMan even acknowledged him. Now the man was talking directly to him. It took him by surprise; it was something he wasn't ready for.

"Yes, I enjoy working with them," Darrius said softly.

"Then you are in a good position here. I will keep my eye on you, maybe you would like to make much more money than you do here?" Jah-Man asked.

"I...I..." Darrius stuttered.

"Do not worry about it now, we will talk later. How is your sister?" he asked quickly changing the subject.

"Eve?" Darrius said sounding stupid.

"Yes, Eve your sister. You do have a sister do you not?" Jah-Man said raising an eyebrow.

"Yes. She's fine," Darrius said.

"That's good. You will make sure that every table has fresh flowers," JahMan said turning to leave. "I can count on you to accomplish this?" he stopped then turned and looked at him.

"Of course," Darrius said feeling stupid.

"Good, good," he said moving out from behind the counter.

"How are things shaping up around here?"

"I do not know, you would have to ask the manager," Darrius quickly said.

Jah-Man nodded saying nothing. He then quickly walked off disappearing around the counter along with his four thugs.

"Man that guy scares me," the other desk clerk whispered to Darrius.

"He is dangerous, very dangerous," Darrius replied.

"He seems to have taken to you. Maybe you will get a really good job working for him," the clerk said slightly elbowing him.

"I DO NOT want to work for him," Darrius said.

"Why not? You'll make a hundred times more than you do here," the clerk pointed out.

"Blood money" Darrius replied.

"So what? You know Darrius you worry too much about the past and other people. Maybe you should try worrying about you for a change," the clerk said walking off.

Darrius felt his rage return, it abandoned him earlier, pushed aside by a fear he never realized he had. Inside he felt ashamed, belittled and tainted by even associating with the man. Now, for some strange reason, the drug lord had taken an interest in him. Suddenly without warning, a man rounded the corner and quickly approached the desk.

"Darrius Lawson?" the man said. "Yes?" Darrius replied.

The man handed him an envelope then as quickly as he appeared he was gone. Darrius looked at the front of the envelope it was blank. Tearing it open he pulled out the card within. Opening it he read...

You and a guest are cordially invited to attend the gathering in the main ballroom tonight. Festivities start at 8:00 p.m. sharp. Purchase whatever attire you wish and charge it to the Resort.

Darrius stared at the message letting the words burn deeply into him. He was being sucked into the drug lord's world quicker than he expected. He was being roped in. With one swift crunch he crumbled the card into a ball and tossed it into the trashcan next to his feet. There was no way he would attend; he would ignore the invitation completely. Suddenly a thought crept into his mind, one so staggering that he had to grip the counter to keep steady. He realized that he had to go, he had no choice in the matter. Jah-Man had asked specifically about Eve. If he did anything that would anger that man, he might take it out on her. He couldn't ever allow that to happen.

Reaching deep within the trashcan, he snatched the balled up paper and unfolded it glaring at the words. What was happening? They were all so close, so very close to having enough money to get off the island. Why now had the drug lord taken an interest with Eve and him? Why would he invite him to go to one of these functions? He wasn't even close to the caliber of people that would be invited. He and his friends grew up in poverty, despair, and at times, hadn't even had food to eat. Why would Jah-Man choose to invite one such as he? He was totally baffled.

Although having never attended anything like this before, he did know enough that a tuxedo from one of the pavilion shops in the resort would need to be rented. He also needed to find someone to go with. He could ask his sister and she would enjoy it for what it was and not see the real reason for being invited.

"Could you watch the counter?" he asked the other clerk.

The man nodded and Darrius quickly left the counter and began looking for Eve to tell her the news. She too would have to find the proper attire. Hesitating, he thought of where she would be. She worked in the Boutique so that would be the first place to start.

The Boutique was large and very well stocked with everything from evening gowns to lingerie. It was actually the perfect place for Eve to work, it was a way for Eve to be close to the things she desired in life, even if she couldn't have them. Darrius quickly went to the back of the store where the counter was.

Tisha was a very attractive oriental that was quick to smile and had a warm personality. She was one of the few off islanders that came for the summer.
She was also the manager of the boutique.

"Tisha, have you seen my sister?" Darrius asked.

"She was here a minute ago, she said something about going to the Salon to meet Delicia," Tisha said smiling warmly.

"You ready to open?" he asked not wanting to be rude and just walk off.

"Oh yes, we were ready hours ago," she grinned.

"I hear you were placed at the front desk this summer?"

"Yes, I like it very much also. Well I must find my sister, maybe later we can get together for a cool drink," he smiled warmly back.

"That would be divine!" she beamed.

When he reached the salon, he came face to face with Eve and Delicia. Locking eyes with Delicia they both frowned showing their mutual disgust for each other. He then turned his attention to Eve.

"Eve, I have been invited to the party this evening. I can bring a guest and would like you to go with me," he asked.

"No" she grinned then looked at Delicia.

"No? Why not I thought…" he began to say.

"Because she is already going with me," Delicia said coldly.

"Y…you?" he said surprised.

"Yes, do you have a problem with that?" she snapped.

"No, I was just wondering…" he said stopping.

"Wondering what?" Delicia growled.

"Nothing"

"There better not be, come on Eve let's go find you a simply exquisite evening gown," Delicia said holding out her hand.

Darrius watched them both walk off. Then his nagging voice that questioned everything began to scream. Why her? Had Jah-Man told Delicia to bring Eve? The plot thickened.

"I'd like to push her in front of a truck," Sharon said walking up to him.

"You and me both. She sure is taking a liking to my sister," he frowned.

"I know, I tried to warn her but you know how she gets when someone tries to tell her what to do," Sharon pointed out.

"What about you?" he turned to her.

"What about me?" she asked.

"Would you like to go and hobnob with the filthy rich for an evening?" he asked.

"I'd go just to spite Delicia. I don't however, have the proper attire, unless of course what they want us there for is servants," she said raising an eyebrow.

"No, this is for real. I got the invitation from Jah-Man himself," Darrius said softly.

"Jah-Man? You?" Sharon looked at him with surprise.

"My thoughts exactly," he added.

"Why would…"

"I've been trying to figure that one out myself, it doesn't make sense," he shook his head.

"Seems pretty weird that both Eve and I get an invitation."

"Well Eve's doesn't surprise me, she invited her to try and throw a wedge between Eve and I," Sharon stated.

"She's stupid if she thinks she will. Eve adores you, I don't think there is anything that could come between you two," Darrius said trying to reassure her.

"So, you want to go?"

"Only if we talk with Uncle William first, I think we both need some pointers on social etiquette."

"I have to wear a stupid monkey suit," he added.

"Yeah who's picking up the tab for the clothes?" she asked.

Darrius handed her the crumpled note. Sharon looked at it and then looked up at him.

"Time to take advantage of the situation," she grinned.

Uncle William sat drinking a cup of tea out on one of the three large verandas. In his other hand was the islands newspaper, which he enjoyed reading from front to back. He was the assistant manager of the Resort a position his brother had obtained for him years ago. He loved the position and was very good at it. Years ago he had gotten both Eve and Darrius jobs and as their little group enlarged he found employment for each of them. They all looked at him with affection and called him Uncle William. Eve loved him with some of her earliest and fondest memories being of Uncle William. He wasn't actually their uncle just a close friend of their mother and was fi real.

Over the years he came to their little house and helped with repairs and whatever they needed. He would also take them to the beach or for long walks. Even after their mother disappeared he still tried to take care of them, he showed up and hung around them more and more as if looking out for them. At one point he even wanted them both to come and live with him. Darrius had taken charge though, and his pride wouldn't allow him to take a handout from anyone, not even people whom he considered family.

Taking another sip of his tea he noticed movement out of the corner of his eye. Darrius and Sharon approached him smiling.

"And how are you two this afternoon?" he asked returning their smile.

"We're doing fine. We have a little problem though Uncle," Darrius said sitting down opposite from him.

Reaching into his pocket he produced the invitation and handed it over to him. Uncle William adjusted his glasses and read the note. He then looked up at them, his face showing more concern than surprise.

"What do you need?" he asked.

"We need to learn how to act, you know, how to be formal. None of us know how to do this. We've never been exposed to it before." Sharon pointed out.

"That won't be a problem, I can show you in a very short time what you need to know. Why though, do you want to go to this?" he asked the obvious question.

"Jah-Man wishes that I be there," Darrius said.

"Why?"

"We don't know, but he must have some reason. Jah-Man does not do anything without a purpose," Sharon added.

"Well, maybe you should look at this differently. Go, enjoy yourselves, eat, drink, dance and have a good time," he said his frown suddenly turning into a smile.

"Come let me show you what you need to know."

It was going on 2:00 p.m. when Uncle William finished. He sent them on their way, then folding the newspaper neatly, he got up and headed into the main building. Stopping one of the caretakers he inquired where Jah-Man was. Moments later he entered one of the textured gardens. Benches sat scattered all around for guests to sit and enjoy the sights and smells of the surrounding garden.

Jah-Man sat talking with a burly white man who was overly dressed for the mid-afternoon heat. He sweated profusely and repeatedly blotted the perspiration from his forehead with a handkerchief. Jah-Man sat in his usual regal manner giving the impression that the man was beneath him. William knew well enough never to interfere when his brother was with a client. He was family, that was true but Jah-Man had a temper that transcended blood ties. Pushed far enough he would kill him too.

Waiting for nearly half an hour, he watched the caretakers work at the other end of the huge garden. If only they knew that a short distance away from them drug deals were being made, that peoples lives were being changed. He hated what his brother had become, hated to see the way he controlled and dominated people. He could only turn his back, walk away from the horror that surrounded him. That still made him an accessory though; still dirtied his hands right along side his brothers. He might not have made the exchange, took the money or pulled the trigger, but he might as well have. Keeping quiet about everything was just as wrong and he knew it. He also loved his brother dearly.

"Brother, it is good to see you again," Jah-Man, said startling him.

"It is good to see you too brother. We do not spend as much time together as we should," William said.

"Times are difficult these days, I am wanted in so many places as you are. Maybe we should take the time brother - make the time," Jah-Man smiled.

William smiled back, he knew his brother well enough that nothing would come of it. Life would go on just as it always had.

"I would like that very much brother," William gave him a false smile.

"What did you want to see me about?" Jah-Man said in a business tone.

"Why have you invited Darrius and Eve to the festival tonight?"

"Oh that," Jah-Man said softly then turned and sat down on the nearest bench.

"Darrius came to me today, wanted me to teach him <u>culture</u>, so he could fit into your world better and not make a fool of himself," William said sitting down next to him.

"For too many years I have stayed away, for too many years I have watched them grow, grow without me by their side," Jah-Man said softly.

"Those times much change, Darrius is a strong man, a man worthy of taking my place when I grow too old."

"And Eve?"

"Eve, Eve - I did not invite her. That was Delicia's doing. She has taken a fancy to her and wishes to spend more time with her." "Does that bother you?" William asked.

"Eve bothers me. She reminds me, well she reminds me of her mother," Jah-Man said softly.

"What are your plans for Darrius?" William said quickly changing the subject.

He could see the change in Jah-Man; the murder of their mother Evelyn had a profound impact on him. The mention of her name could drive him to utter rage; he did not want to see this conversation head in that direction."I must slowly, very slowly bring him closer to me. Allow him to become accustomed to being around me and my business," Jah-Man said. "Are you going to tell him the truth?"

For a split second Jah-Man's gaze shot up and stared into his brother's eyes. The madness had returned, there was no stopping it.

"Are you going to tell him that you are his father?" he quickly said rephrasing the question.

"No, not yet. The truth would drive him away from me and I do not, will not do that," he said shaking his head.

"What of the others?" William asked.

"Others?"

"His friends, the small group that he spends most of his time with," William asked.

"That is of no concern to me unless of course they get in my way and my reputation is enough to keep them from not defying me. If I must, I will illuminate them all."

William was going to laugh, tell Jah-Man that he was being a fool, but he didn't. He loved his brother that was true, but not enough to help him commit murder. He didn't understand his children, for too long he wanted no part in their lives, trying to forget what he had done to their mother. Now, he expected Darrius to eventually embrace him, take over his business of drugs and death. He knew Darrius well enough to know that he loathed Jah-Man, loathed his business and everything about him and he knew that if Darrius found out that Jah-Man was responsible for their mother's death… He didn't want to think of what would happen if that secret came out.

"So there is nothing in particular that you want with them tonight?" William asked.

"Not yet, I will just observe him and learn more about him that is where I must start."

"And Eve?"

"She is still my daughter. I will allow Delicia to deal with her. I do not want her involved in my business, that is a job for a son, not a daughter."

William just nodded even though he didn't agree with him. Jah-Man in many ways was still a dinosaur when it came to modern thinking. Hanging around the kids, watching them grow together he had learned much. The most important thing – a woman can be just as deadly as a man - sometime even deadlier.

It was well after 6:00 p.m., the waning sunlight added a new aura to the island. It was truly a tropical paradise, the reds the yellows mixing with the blue sky was breathtaking.

Darrius fumbled with his bow tie, which was part of the tuxedo he rented at Jah-Man's expense. He had never worn one, had no desire to wear one and couldn't wait to be out of it. The clothing was constricting and the bow tie had become one of his greatest challenges, which he was losing.

"Having problems?" Raffie asked listening to him struggle.

"How are these things tied? What good are they anyway? Why do people press themselves into these monkey suits?" he said his anger flaring.

"They do it to stand out from the others and from people like us," he explained.

"Why us?" Darrius frowned.

"We represent what they loath, and what they will never be - poor." "Doesn't it bother you?" Darrius asked him.

"What?"

"You came from a prominent, fairly well-to-do family. Doesn't it bother you to be living day to day, nothing substantial, no money to burn?"

"I have you guys, to me that's more important than all the money in the world. Someday we will have it all, when we get to America," he said working on Darrius's tie.

"It seems so far off, so distant, like we'll never get there," Darrius sighed.

"We'll get there, together or not at all. That is what I believe my friend. You know what I want to know?" he grinned.

"What?"

"Why Jah-Man wanted you to go to this gathering. He has never taken interest in any of us, at least not one on one. Delicia seems to like your sister though," he pointed out.

"Don't remind me," he frowned.

"I don't know why he wants me there. Who knows, maybe to offer me a new job or something," he speculated.

"Or something - the things that Jah-Man offers comes with a price tag. Please remember that my friend," Raffie said finishing his tie.

"I know and you know that out of all of us I hate Jah-Man the worse, I still believe he had something to do with my mama's disappearance," Darrius said looking in the small mirror hanging on the inside of the closet door.

"Maybe not out of us all..."

Darrius turned to see the somber expression on Raffie's face. His usual beaming grin had turned in the other direction. It was like the man had transformed before his eyes and the person now standing before him was someone entirely different. He understood though and that was all that mattered.

"I am really going now to look after Eve, that's my main purpose," Darrius said patting Raffie on the shoulder.

"I hope so."

"I need to see if Sharon is ready, it is going to be a long walk to the resort," he said changing the subject.

"You're not going to have to worry about that," Ohpton said coming into the room.

"Huh?"

"Seems there is a limousine waiting at the center of town," he thumbed over his shoulder.

"Jah-Man" Raffie said softly.

"Only one that owns a limousine around here," Ohpton added.

"Great" Darrius said exhaling loudly.

"Hey, take it for what it is. You won't have to walk all that way," Ohpton said casually.

For a moment Darrius felt a sudden rage, then just a quickly it subsided, Ohpton was right, if Jah-Man wanted to waste the time and gas to send a car for them, then that was his loss.

Entering the living room he saw Steven sitting on the couch reading a book, he was an avid reader and loved to immerse himself in thrillers. When they entered, he looked up at Darrius and grinned. "Shut up," Darrius frowned.

"Sorry, Mr. trash an' ready."

"Shut up," he said. "Where is she?"

"Right here, don't get your feathers in an uproar," Sharon said from the hallway.

Sharon emerged from the hallway. Steven glanced up then went back to his book, then abruptly looked up again his mouth hanging open. Ohpton, Raffie and even Darrius stood there staring in mute silence.

"What are you all gaping at? My God you'd think none of you have ever seen a woman before," she shook her head feeling embarrassed.

She wore a long emerald green gown that glittered with sequins. The top formed a halter exposing her shoulders and displaying slightly, her rather ample cleavage. The side of the dress was open to her knee exposing her supple leg. She wore fake pearls around her neck and round green earrings. Her hair was tucked up, two strands flowing from the sides along her cheeks. She finished the outfit off with a pair of green high heels.

"I said stop gaping! You look like a penguin," she said pointing to Darrius.

She locked eyes with Steven who stared intently at her. If she wanted to impress anyone, it was him.

"You better get going," Raffie said glancing at his watch.

"Where's Eve?" Steven asked.

"She decided to get ready at the resort with Delicia," Sharon said a bite in her voice.

Darrius suddenly felt worried, he had thought Eve was getting ready with Sharon. He shot a worried look to her, of which she acknowledged.

"There's not much we can do about it now or for that matter even later.
She has to learn about Delicia the hard way," Sharon shrugged.

"If it helps, I hate it just as much as you do."

He said nothing and just opened the door for them. Stepping out into the humid night air the others watched them walk off the porch and into the shadows of the approaching night. They quickly slipped out of sight heading down the long winding trail that led to town.

"I hate trying to walk on soft ground with heels," she said angrily.

"Take them off," Darrius replied.

"Yeah, then my feet will end up dirty. No thank you, I'll just suffer for the rest of the walk," she said.

"Suit yourself," he shrugged.

It was growing considerably dark by the time they broke off their trail and headed up the road a short ways to town. They talked and joked along the way until they drew close. The sight of the small town always bothered them. It was run down, with dilapidated buildings that needed to be torn down instead of repaired. It was in stark contrast to where they all worked, which was styled for the tourist. People didn't have much in this small community, most lived from hand to mouth and some, not even that. Suddenly, Sharon stopped. She stood still and motionless her eyes gazing at the town before her. Darrius didn't notice until he had walked a few steps ahead. When he did, he turned and looked at her.

"Come on, we do not want to be late," he reminded her.

"Yeah, I'm coming," she said not moving.

"What's wrong?" he asked walking up to her.

"Nothing, it's just a feeling that washed over me whenever I come here. It is a distinct reminder of all our goals, to get off this island," she said softly.

"We'll do it, you watch. We will get off the island," he reassured her.

"I know we will, I feel it," she said finally looking at him.

Continuing into the town there were few people out, those that were, paid no attention to them. At the center of town, there was an eight-sided gazebo. It was put there by Jah-Man for when he visited to do business. The structure looked out of place, it was clean, white. It was a rose in the middle of a garbage dump. Sitting alongside was a stretch limousine, the engine idling softly. The windows were tinted stopping them from seeing either the driver or who sat in back.

They approached the car cautiously. Suddenly the driver's door opened and a clean-cut and very burly man stepped out. He walked casually around to the opposite side of the car and opened the door. Sharon tilted her head trying to see if anyone was inside but they weren't close enough. She then suddenly had an odd feeling. She was beginning to feel like a fly that had just been caught in a spider's web.

Chapter 3

The ride into Montego Bay was quiet. The interior of the limousine was immaculate and like nothing Sharon or Darrius had ever seen. There was a bar, television, and cellular telephone just to name a few things. Although totally intrigued, neither touched anything. They both felt if they were to touch something, they might catch some disease by being exposed to something JahMan had touched. Being in fear of the driver overhearing anything said, they chose to ride in complete silence.

A large city sporting a wide variety of industries, Montego Bay was also known for being one of the primary stops for weary winter tourists, travelers from all over the globe venture to this nook for rest and relaxation. The city being one of the primary junctions for both port and rail in Jamaica offered a variety of produced goods exported to other countries such as coffee, sugar, bananas, and yes, even drugs.

This city meant activity, a bustling hub that sat in stark contrast to the depressed communities all around it. Sharon's family lived the closest to it; more often than not, she looked forward to the times she lived at the shack with the others. Darrius on the other hand, hadn't grown up in a city; he was enthralled by the activity, good and bad, looking forward to the times when he could interact with it. The only one in the group who had exposure to the city was Raffie.

His prominent family had ties deeply into law and government. There were times at the shack she could see his frustration with rural living while the others never missed what they didn't know.

The air conditioning inside the limousine felt so refreshing – you just wanted to stay immersed in its wonderful soothing coolness. Usually though, air conditioning made you feel washed out and sick, when you had to step out of it and back into the oppressive heat. The driver pulled up through the massive gates leading to the main house of the Resort. When the car came to a stop, he was quick to get out and open the door on the other side. Sharon and Darrius stepped out not giving the man the slightest thank you. He was more than likely one of Jah-Man's killers.

They both knew exactly where they were going, as they headed toward a door guarded by two robust guards. An oriental woman smiled warmly at them extending her hand. Darrius handed her his invitation. She glanced down at it and then back up at him.

"Table 34 please," she said motioning them to enter.

The ballroom was massive with a huge cathedral ceiling spanning above. The Spanish architecture was designed with elaborate scrollwork and pillars. The floor was mahogany; polished to a high sheen so brilliant you could easily cast a reflection. In the far corner of the room, a large Reggae band played. Tables were scattered all around room except for a large open area toward the front where guests could dance if they chose.

Behind the dance floor was a small raised podium with a microphone. The lighting was dim yet light enough to eat, drink, and dance.

Sharon took Darrius' extended arm as they walked into the room. There were dozens of people scattered about the room talking. Some they recognized as regular patrons, others they had never seen before. Sharon eyed them as they headed for their table, the men looked rough, tough and very businesslike. The women where beautiful and stunning with bodies they were not afraid to display in scant dresses. She was beginning to worry. She then noticed a table on the far side of the room containing various people whom she recognized as elected cabinet ministers. Sitting next to them was another table full of magistrates. Why had Jah-Man invited elected officials to a resort opening for guests? Was the corruption so deep that leaders in this part of Jamaica was under Jah-Man's thumb? The thoughts danced about in her mind as she continued to walk.

Table 34 sat right in the middle of the room. It was centermost so that anyone sitting there could chat and mix with other tables. A serious knot was beginning to form in her stomach. Darrius pulled the chair out for her and she sat down under many watchful eyes. As she sat down, she noticed that there were four other place settings at the table. She wondered who would be sitting with them.

"I don't like this," she whispered to Darrius.

"You think I do?" he said looking around nervously.

"I wonder who else is going to be sitting here," she added.

"Hopefully Eve so we can keep an eye on her."

They didn't have to wait long to find out. Walking between the rows of tables was Jah-Man followed closely by Delicia, Eve, and Diamond. Sharon held back a gasp; she didn't want to look so obvious as they stared. Jah-Man was dressed in a finely tailored suit; his light brown locks tied back. Darrius hadn't noticed it before, but the man wore a pair of thin black gloves. He also smiled warmly as he approached the table.

"Darrius, it is good to see that you came. I was hoping you wouldn't turn down my invitation."

"T…thank you for inviting me…us," he replied standing.

"And who do you have here?" Jah-Man asked turning his attention to Sharon.

"This is my friend, Sharon Cunnings," he said introducing her.

"Ah! A beautiful delicate flower, you look exceptionally lovely my dear," he said with a seductive grin.

"Thank you, so do you," she replied undaunted.

"I am assuming you already know Delicia and Diamond," he motioned to them.

Darrius and Sharon only nodded. Delicia's dress was long, white and exceptionally sheer. She wore no undergarments and when the light cast on her from a certain angle, nothing of herself was hidden from anyone. She also wore enough chains and jewelry to weigh down an elephant, along with her excessive make up, which made her face look like a mask.

Eve was dressed more conservatively; her gown was dark blue satin and hugged her figure tightly. She also wore makeup; too excessive like Delicia's.

Diamond was handsomely dressed in a black tuxedo. He was tall with a good built and exceptionally strong features. He didn't say anything, just nodded to them. He also didn't pull Eve's chair out. Darrius felt his rage building; he had no desire to sit with Jah-Man or his hired help Diamond, which he would rather bludgeon to death than watch his sister direct her misguided affections to. Under the table, he felt Sharon's hand grasp his giving him reassurance and strength to keep his mouth shut.

"Have you waited long?" Eve asked them smiling.

"Just got here," Sharon replied.

"You look beautiful," Eve, grinned at her.

"Thanks," she replied feeling very bashy.

"So what do you think?" Eve said extending her arms displaying her dress. "You look nice too,"

Sharon said forcing a smile.

"It was all Delicia's doing, she's an expert at these sorts of things," she beamed.

"Yeah, I bet," Sharon, said softly.

"You really need more makeup dear. Your complexion…well…you look all washed out!" Delicia said overhearing their conversation being the fire bun she was.

Darrius gripped Sharon's hand this time squeezing it hard. It was taking all of her composure to keep from throttling Delicia.

Jah-Man watched, saying nothing. The silence was deafening. Finally, Jah-Man let out a loud and very distinct laugh. He then directed his attention to Delicia.

"Keep our guests happy my dear, I must get the festivities going." "Isn't this exciting?" Eve beamed.

"Ball of laughs," Darrius said softly watching Jah-Man get up and head for the podium.

The man carried himself well, though he was short, his build was impressive and it clearly strained in places against his finely tailored suit. He also had an aura of power about him. It seemed to seethe from every pore in his body. Everyone watched as he approached the microphone. When he tapped the end, it made a vibrating noise. This was the band's queue to stop playing.

"I first want to thank all of you for coming here tonight. I realize how busy your schedules are, just as mine. Nevertheless, this gathering is meant as a thank you for all your support and business. It has been a profitable year and I wish to share my good fortune with each and every one of you. The bar is open, the band will play whatever you wish, and food will be brought out shortly. Please enjoy yourselves," he said grinning.

Everyone showed approval with a huge round of applause. He seemed to bathe in the admiration drawing energy off the guest's physical action. To watch him was mesmerizing, he knew exactly what to say and how to say it to gain maximum effect from the crowd. It was nauseating.

Darrius turned keeping an eye on Eve. She was lost in all this, the money and the excitement. It was like a drug in itself and he was afraid that when she was tossed back into the real world she would be devastated. Suddenly, she leaned over giggling and pecked Diamond on the cheek. He smiled at her and returned her kiss. Darrius then felt his fingers being crushed. Sharon had noticed it also and was now squeezing his hand until it hurt. All he could do was grit his teeth and take it.

"So, when do you two start your petty jobs?" Delicia gave them an evil grin.

"Tomorrow" Darrius quickly responded with a smile.

"You know Sharon honey, you really did a so-so job on my hair today. I think maybe next time I'll let one of the other girls do it. I'm sure someone has to be good in that salon," Delicia prodded.

"Just come in anytime. I'm sure one of the other girls will be delighted to help you," Sharon said with a bite in her voice.

"That dress - that dress is so…plain," she jabbed, again casting judgment.

"I think it looks fabulous on her!" Eve exclaimed.

"Look at her breasts. You would think she would be more apt to show them if she had them. That dress makes it look like they're full of padding, or tissue," Delicia grinned.

Darrius wanted to scream his hand hurt so much. Instead, he just continued to smile and look around like a person doped up on sedatives. Sharon's grin quickly faded, she was losing her temper and loosing it fast.

"Maybe I should have worn a see-through dress like yours?" she tried to jab back.

"Heck honey, if you got it, flaunt it."

At that point, she realized there would be no insult she could dish out that would affect Delicia. The woman was a slut, a tramp and very crazy.

"What do you think Darrius?" Delicia said leaning back in her chair and holding her arms out.

"W…what?" he said not paying attention.

"What do you think of my dress? Does it bother you?" she asked making sure he got a clear look at the dark ovals of her breasts.

"Well actually…" he began to say.

There came an audible cracking sound as Sharon squeezed his hand even tighter popping one of his knuckles.

"You can see right through it," he quickly said.

"But do you like what you see?" she asked.

"I…Ouch!" he said trying to draw his hand away from Sharon.

"I'll take that as a yes," Delicia grinned.

"I tried to get Eve to wear something more revealing but I think she's too shy."

"I don't want every guy gawking over my body," she said smiling at Delicia.

"Why not? Ask Diamond there if he minds gawking over a woman's body."

Diamond quickly looked around the table, he was being put on the spot and that was something he didn't care for. He liked to keep a low profile, stay out of the limelight.

"Only if it's someone I'm interested in," he said quickly.

"Better only be me!" Eve said turning to him.

"Of course only you," he smiled.

"Do you care to dance?" Darrius said turning to Sharon.

"Oh yes, I'd be delighted," she nodded.

He led her out onto the dance floor and she wrapped her arms around him. At the exact same time, they both let out a deep sigh of relief.

"I don't know how much more of this I can take," she said softly.

"Yeah, me too, I'm ready to crack Diamond in the side of the head. Do you believe that guy?" Darrius exclaimed.

"Do you believe her dress?"

"Well, if you put a paper bag over her head to hide the makeup" he stated.

"Don't say it, please don't say it," Sharon pleaded.

"Now I want to know why Jah-Man invited me. Why we're sitting at his exclusive table, why there are very few guests here and why the ones who are here look more like thugs or drug dealers."

"Is there anyway we can get out of here and take Eve with us?" she asked.

"I don't know, if we do something we could find ourselves floating in the surf," he shook his head.

"I wish the others were here too," she said softy.

"Yeah, I could use some more moral support," he agreed.

Abruptly, Sharon felt something tap her on the shoulder. Both her and Darrius looked over, Delicia stood there, an evil grin broadening her face. "Mind if I cut in?"

Sharon looked at Darrius; she wanted to tell the woman to bug off. Actually she wanted to <u>haul off</u> and punch her lights out. Instead, she kept the peace; this wasn't the time or place for it. They needed to learn what Jah-Man wanted from Darrius first. She let go of him allowing Delicia to take her place. The woman nearly pushed her out of the way, as she wrapped her arms around him tightly. Darrius wasn't prepared; she drew her body up against his. He could feel her breasts squash against his chest and the sleekness of her thigh as she pressed his leg against her. She was so <u>boasie</u>.

Sharon reached out but then abruptly stopped. She had to get out of here – now! Turning she went back to the table and sat down sulking.

"She's incredible isn't she?" Eve said resting her chin in her palm as she watched them dance.

"Eve, we're best friends right?" Sharon blurted out.

"Of course, nothing will ever change that," she said turning her attention to Sharon.

"What do you see in her?"

"She's got class, she does what she wants and gets what she wants. She has money."

"Jah-Man's money," Sharon professed.

"Yes…but."

"Did someone mention my name?" Jah-Man said sitting down, he then directed his attention to Darrius and Delicia as they danced.

Sharon felt a chill wash through her; Jah-Man was not a person to cross especially with his woman. Though it was purely Delicia pressing her body against Darrius, she made it appear as though it was he who was initiating things.

"They dance well together, Delicia is a fine dancer," he said to Sharon's surprise.

"Would you dance with me?" he asked looking at Sharon.

The words sounded hollow, far away. She reached up and touched the side of her face because she knew her jaw must have been hanging open. It wasn't though and she just nodded.

Darrius felt Delicia's breath on the side of his neck. He could also feel her grind against him. She was provoking him, trying to arouse him. Turning he came face-to-face with Sharon in the arms of Jah-Man.

"Ouch!" Delicia said. To his surprise, he accidentally stepped on her foot. "Sorry" he said swallowing hard.

Jah-Man wasn't much taller than Sharon, yet his powerful arms gripped her and drew her close. His body pressed against hers, his hand sliding down and resting on the top of her butt. Her breasts were crushed against his hard muscular chest, his other hand lightly rubbed along her bare back. Her mind reeled as he guided her across the floor. Others cleared a path as he danced back and forth with her. She stared over his shoulder at the far wall. She didn't want to meet his eyes; if she had, he would have seen the truth. She was becoming aroused.

Deep down she knew how evil the man was, how he polluted the island with drugs, how he controlled peoples lives with the simple wave of a hand. She had also never been close to him. She found him to be handsome and very sexually arousing. She felt like a small animal being charmed by a hideous snake that at any moment would strike her down.

Darrius tried to break away from Delicia but she hung onto him. She was becoming irritated that he showed no interest in her body and kept glancing over at Jah-Man and Sharon.

Finally, she did something extremely direct - she pushed her pelvis against his. That got his attention.

"That's more like it," she grinned.

"I'd rather you didn't," he said frowning.

"I do as I please," she continued to grin.

"You are Jah-Man's woman and he can easily find another you ," Darrius coldly said.

Something clicked in Delicia; her grin quickly faded turning into a frown. Her once warm eyes grew chilled as they stabbed at him. She then quickly released him heading back to the table. Stopping abruptly, she turned, looked at him and threatened,

"You'll get yours."

Darrius stood there for a moment more stunned at her sudden outburst. Fortunately it hadn't been loud enough to draw attention from the other guests and more importantly, from Jah-Man. Darrius knew what he had to do. Walking over he tapped Jah-Man on the shoulder.

"May I cut in?" he said.

At first Jah-Man shot him an angry stare, and then he smiled and released his hold on Sharon.

"Of course you can," he said walking casually back to the table.

Darrius resumed dancing with Sharon. He half expected her to say something but she remained quiet.

"Are you OK?" he finally broke the silence.

"Yes, I am fine," she replied.

"We need to get out of here," he said. "Let's use working tomorrow as an excuse." "OK" Sharon said softly.

They went back to the table. Everyone's eyes were upon them as they stood there. Darrius expected Sharon to say something but she didn't. He finally found the courage to speak.

"We appreciate the invitation, but we will have to take our leave. We both have to be at work early tomorrow, including Eve," Darrius pointed out.

"But we haven't even had dinner," Eve blurted out.

"Yes, stop being rude and sit down!" Delicia snorted.

"Now, now, if they wish to retire we must respect their wishes," Jah-Man said not smiling.

"If Eve wishes to stay, I will be happy to return her after the gathering is over," he said turning to her.

She just grinned and nodded her head. Sharon shot Darrius a quick look. She did not want Eve showing the drug lord where their little cabin was, that was out of the question. Pulling out her chair, she sat back down.

"I am hungry," she smiled feeling embarrassed.

"Good, good, you won't be disappointed," Jah-Man said smiling. "Darrius?"

"I...I suppose I could eat," he said sitting back down.

It was going on 10 p.m. and both Sharon and Darrius were both tired. All they wanted was to go home and get a good nights rest. Jah-Man had wandered off chatting with his guests. Delicia had convinced Eve to go back to her room to look at all her jewelry she carried in her case. Diamond remained and he kept a watchful eye on some of the guests, mainly the women. At one point, a woman approached him asking him to dance.

Sharon watched him and the woman as they moved out onto the dance floor. As they danced, they talked but between the music and the distance, she couldn't make out what they were saying. When the song ended, the woman took hold of his hand pressing something firmly into it.

"Did you see that?" Sharon blurted out.

"What?" Darrius said sluggishly.

"That woman. That woman gave Diamond her room key!" "She what?" he said

becoming more alert.

Diamond returned to the table sitting down he took a sip of his drink and again directed his attention to guests around him.

"Did that woman give you her room key?" Sharon asked him bluntly.

"What? What are you talking about?" he shot her a stern look.

"Simple question stupid, did that woman give you her room key?" she asked again.

"No, she just wants me to play golf with her husband tomorrow," he quickly said.

Sharon pursed her lips; she couldn't continue to confront him, least not here. It was true though, at times he would be requested to play golf with some of the guests. She couldn't prove anything, though her gut told her different.

"You don't like me do you?" Diamond said leaning closer to her.

"Does it show? My, maybe I should try to hide it better," Sharon snapped.

"Why don't you care for me?" he asked.

"Because I don't think you have Eve's best interests at heart," Darrius cut in.

"I'm not talking to you," Diamond said coldly.

"You'd better because if you hurt my sister then you'll be answering to me!" Darrius said his anger flaring.

"You're sister is old enough to make her own decisions. She doesn't need big brother to help choose who she sleeps with," Diamond said grinning.

"You better not have..." Darrius said his voice raising.

"And what business is it of yours?"

"This is not the time or place for this you two," Sharon cut in stopping the escalation.

"You best keep a set of eyes in the back of your head," Diamond grinned pointing two fingers at his eyes.

"I said this is not the time or place for this. But rest assured..."she looked at Diamond.

" If I find out you've hurt Eve in any way, any way, you'll be answering to me also."

"Oh! I feel scared!" he all but laughed at her.

Darrius came out of his chair his fists clenched tightly ready to strike. Sharon grabbed his arm trying to stop him. At that moment Jah-Man returned, his eyes glancing from Darrius to Diamond.

"Is there something wrong?" Jah-Man asked.

"Nothing" Darrius said directing his attention away from Diamond.

"We have to go."

"I want to thank you for attending, I will have a limousine bring you home," Jah-Man said.

"That is not necessary, we would rather walk," Darrius sharply said.

"You will arrive late, you said you have to work in the morning," Jah-Man pointed out.

"We're not that tired," Sharon added.

"I think you two are just being modest, why don't I arrange for a room tonight, then you can have breakfast with me in the morning?"

"I...I...don't have any of my work clothing here," Sharon pointed out.

"I will buy you a new one," he smiled.

"I appreciate your gesture, but I think we would rather go home," Darrius said sternly.

"I do not think you understood my offer! <u>I would rather you stay tonight</u>," Jah-Man said coldly.

"I don't think..." Darrius started to say.

"I don't think we would mind at all," Sharon said finishing his sentence.

"Then it's settled, I will have a room prepared for you two tonight, you do not mind sharing a room, do you?" he looked at Sharon his eyebrow raising.

"While that is being done I will have whatever clothing shop opened so you can choose what you will need for tomorrow. Is that satisfactory?"

Both Darrius and Sharon nodded. What could they say; they were both too terrified to defy the man. They watched as he snapped his fingers, quickly one of his thugs came over. He told him to prepare a room and to have another man open whatever clothing shops they wanted. Then he smiled at them.

"Please go with this man, he will attend to whatever you wish, tis <u>cook & curry</u>," Jah-Man said.

"Breakfast is at 7:00 a.m."

They both reeled from the way Jah-Man was acting towards them. They chose their clothing, everything right down to their shoes. The burly guards said nothing as they closed the stores behind them. They were then ushered into the elevator, one of the guards then handed Darrius a room key. The man looked at Sharon, then Darrius and grinned showing a large gap between his two front teeth.

"Have a good night," he said in husky voice, then left.

Darrius opened the door and turned on the light. It was a basic room, but fortunately had two beds. He looked in each area of the room partially expecting to find another of Jah-Man's guards. Instead, he found a bottle of chilled champagne.

"What is going on here?" Darrius said showing Sharon the bottle.

"It's pretty plain to me," she began to say.

"What is?" Darrius said putting the bottle back in its chiller.

"Jah-Man seems to think that you and I...are...well...you know," Sharon said raising an eyebrow.

"He obviously doesn't know we're just friends. He must have thought - put two and two together, that because I brought you..." "Exactly" Sharon mused.

"What does he want though?" Darrius said sitting on the end of the other bed.

"There is no doubt, no doubt in my mind that he has something in mind for you," she said.

"I figured that much out on my own. But what?"

"The others are going to be worried," she shook her head.

"Especially, when we don't return home tonight," she pointed out.

"We could always just leave the key here and walk home, then come back in the morning to meet him for breakfast," Darrius said.

"It's going on 11:00 p.m. now. It would take an hour to get home on foot and then another hour back. You may have boundless energy but I'm pooped. Especially from being in these heels," she said reaching down and unclasping the thin strap that held them on.

"So what about the others?" Darrius asked.

"If you have the energy, why don't you head out there and let them know, then come back?" she said.

"I'm going to stay right here."

"You sure you're going to be OK?" he said grabbing his new clothes.

"Of course," she said tossing her heels against the dresser.

"You gonna to let me in when I get back?" he grinned.

"If I'm awake," she grinned.

"Try to find Eve for me?" he asked.

"You know I will. Now go before it gets too late," she said.

Darrius changed into his new clothes. Leaving the tuxedo he headed quickly for the elevator. It would be a couple of hours before he made it back. He would also have to wake up the others if they were asleep to let them know what was going on. The heat had abated and a cool breeze blew in from the ocean. The walk would at least be pleasant; he quickly headed off into the night.

Sharon continued to sit on the end of the bed. The room suddenly felt cold and empty as she sat there alone. Getting up she unzipped her dress letting it fall to the floor. Since she didn't have a hanger, she folded it as neatly as she could. Slipping out of the rest of her clothing, she went into the bathroom turning on the light. There was a large shower, toilet and a double vanity sink with a huge mirror. She stood there staring into it, her eyes glancing down at her naked body. Delicia's words had bitten deeply. It was true that she was heavier than Delicia, but her breasts were bigger, that was obvious.

"Darn you!" she said aloud.

"Why am I letting that stupid women get to me? Why am I being such a red eye?"

Leaving the bathroom, she grabbed her clothes for tomorrow and quickly dressed. She was going to find Eve, hopefully not with Diamond or Delicia.

Grabbing her room key, she locked the door and quickly headed down the hallway. She tried to think of where Delicia or Diamond would be. It would prove to be a long search.

Diamond slipped the key into the lock. He looked around as if he was trying to rob a bank and at any moment, someone would catch him. Slipping into the room he was bathed in darkness, quickly he closed the door behind him and locked it. Standing there, he listened. Suddenly a light came on temporarily blinding him. When his eyes adjusted, he could see the woman he had danced with earlier. She lay on the bed, the covers drawn down. One arm was propped up under her and she stared intently at him an evil grin forming on her face. She was also very naked.

"Well its about time, I thought you were going to stand me up," she whispered to him lying down on her back.

"I couldn't get away that easily," he said tossing the key on the dresser.

"What from that little twit?" she asked.

"Yeah, she was clinging a little too hard tonight," he said unbuttoning his shirt.

"What are you doing with her anyway? What does she have that I don't?" the woman said running her fingers down between her breasts.

"Nothing" he said watching her.

"I hang around her because Jah-Man wants me to." "What does he want with her?" the woman asked.

"I don't know nor do I care. I just do what I'm told," he said removing the rest of his clothes.

"Is that so?" the woman grinned.

"Then come over here and give me some <u>wuk</u>," she ordered.

Diamond walked over to the bed his excitement clearly showing. Her eyes looked at his naked body taking in his well-formed and very tight frame. He then reached over and turned off the light.

Sharon had spent at least an hour searching the entire grounds for Eve. She was about to give up and go back to her room when she heard Eve's distinctive giggle. Following the sound, she walked through the garden then diverted off the footpath onto the grass. The path wasn't lit nor was the moon bright, but she could make out Eve and Delicia walking along the path. They both held her high heels in their hands as they walked. Sharon tried her best to avoid being seen, the bushes all around her provided excellent cover.

"So what do you think of my idea?" Delicia said her voice barely audible.

"I don't know, it's a big decision. I would like some time to think about it if that's alright with you?" she asked.

"Certainly, take all the time you need. I understand that decisions like this can't be made quickly. But it's a great opportunity remember that," Delicia pointed out.

"I know, I know I won't take too long I promise," Eve added.

"Where are you staying tonight?" Delicia asked.

"I was going to walk home," she said.

"What, back to that shack you told me about?" Delicia asked.

Sharon felt a rush at the mention of their home. No one except the group knew about it or where it was located. She couldn't believe that Eve would confide such an important secret, especially to Delicia who would blab about it to everyone.

"That place is my home. It's been my home for some time now," Eve pointed out.

"Yes but wouldn't you rather have <u>a real home</u>? A home where you <u>don't</u> <u>have to share things</u>?" Delicia said her voice changing to sound more persuasive. "But…"

"Look honey, I want you to seriously consider my offer," Delicia added.

"I already told you I would," Eve cut in.

"Well, you can stay at my place tonight," Delicia said changing the subject.

"You mean with you and Jah-Man?" Eve said surprised.

"No silly, I have a room here at the hotel that <u>Jah-Man keeps for me</u>," she laughed.

"Oh" Eve said.

Sharon tried to hear more but they had walked past and now all she could make out were a few words, most everything else sounded like a mumble. What had Delicia offered Eve? Sharon continued to crouch her mind reeling with the possibilities. It was obvious that Delicia was charming Eve to get back at her. She also tried to figure a way to tell Darrius when he came back; he would be very upset just to learn she was staying in Delicia's room. There would be no way to tell if Diamond was going to stay there also, she knew Delicia though, if she could arrange it…she would.

She waited until they were completely out of sight then quickly returned to her room. It was getting late and Darrius still hadn't returned. There was nothing more she could do. Slipping out of her clothes she tried to decide what she could wear as a nightshirt, there was nothing. Shrugging she pulled back the covers of one bed and slipped between the cool sheets. The bed felt much softer compared to her well-worn bed at the shack. Though the room was dark, she stared up at the dark ceiling her mind reeling with possibilities. So much had happened tonight, so much she was worried about too. Darrius hated Jah-Man, he was also very vocal about it and Jah-Man must have heard too. He had eyes and ears everywhere. Not much slipped by the man.

Her thoughts then shifted to Jah-Man. Though he was older than she was, he was very, very handsome. He was not like she had envisioned him. She also remembered how aroused she had become and how she had felt like clay in his hands as they danced. Closing her eyes, she tried to envision the man making love to her. She couldn't.

The face that kept slipping in place of his was Stevens. She was more aroused by him than Jah-Man. It was easy to get lost in his greenish brown eyes and just as easy, she hoped to get lost in his arms. She wished though, that he would notice her instead of Eve. More than once she had wanted to talk with him about her, or them, but when she approached him, she lost the courage.

He also confided in her about his love for Eve. Their closeness was something she wouldn't jeopardize; she would contain her feelings for him.   Sleep was not going to come easy for her.

The road was dark, nearly to the point where he couldn't see. Darrius knew it well though and traversed it with ease. The stillness of the night was calming, reassuring. It blanketed him hiding all his hidden fears. This night was not something he wished to repeat; having any association with Jah-Man was disturbing. For some reason, he still blamed the man for his mother's disappearance. He might have had nothing to do with it, but a little voice kept nagging at him fueling his anger whenever the man was around.

His mother was not the only reason either, Jah-Man ruined many lives over the years. Lives of families he knew, lives that now were gone. People were murdered without the killer being found, others just disappeared without a trace. Nobody questioned, fear was omnipresent, and it controlled people's lives. Even his and the rest of the groups lives were affected. They all worked at the resort, a resort primarily owned by Jah-Man, a feared and ranking man. Their lives were somewhat in his hands; with a snap of a finger, he could order one of them to be killed without reason. The group of men that surrounded him was also alarming. They were all armed to the hilt and known professional killers.

They were a stark contrast to Jah-Man's easy going personality. The man was manipulative. He got what he wanted, when he wanted it, no matter what. He also was a compulsive person. He washed his hands continually, scrubbing them until almost raw. More than often he wore black silk gloves to protect him from the surrounding environment that he encountered every day. Though he had never experienced it, he had also heard that Jah-Man quoted scripture, as if saying the words of God made him one also or brought him closer to being a God.

Rumor had it that Jah-Man had worked at the Bayside years ago, back when there were more yardie's. He had a way about him and gained favor with the other drug lords. Over time, he gained more power and then slowly and methodically had each eliminated. Before long, he was the only one left - the supreme power. That power went straight to his head.

Over the years, Jah-Man had been seen with other women, but Delicia seemed to be a constant. More of a figure head for him, or a pet.

When he finally reached the outskirts of town he directed himself to the trail that led to the shack. Turning, something caught his attention. Two tiny shadows moved between two buildings. At first, he thought it must have been his mind playing games, or his tired eyes tricking him. However, there was also the audible sound of footfalls. Then came the very soft, but very distinct giggling.

The sound rooted him where he stood sending a chill up his spine. It sounded like a very young child. Nevertheless, what child was out this late at night? Despite his little voice yelling at him to continue up the trail he turned and as quietly as possible headed for town. His heart beat and thumped wildly. He didn't understand his sudden fear; it numbed his limbs and made his mouth dry and pasty. His eyes darted back and forth from building to building trying not to miss anything. The shadows of night had suddenly become his enemy. The protection they provided earlier was now the place that harbored a hidden threat. His mind raced as though at any moment something would jump out at him with malicious intent. Then came another soft yet distinct giggle.

It sounded more distant than the one previous but still as terrifying. He was not one to scare easily, however at this moment his body quaked with chills. Suddenly memories flooded in on him, memories of when he was a child and his mother would tell him scary stories, stories of duppies and goblins that haunted the night. He loved them as a child, but now for some reason he felt as though they were alive and somehow he was part of it all.

Suddenly something moved in the shadows at the very edge of his vision. Was it an animal? Maybe someone who couldn't sleep coming out for fresh air? At first, he wanted to call out and pray that whomever it was would respond, but fear kept him silent. If it were a duppy or goblin, he would attract attention to himself.

Dashing across the street he headed for where he saw the movement. When he reached the spot there was nothing, just a few vegetable crates propped up next to a building.

"What in the hell am I doing?" he said softly to himself.

Without warning, a hand clasped over his mouth and an arm wrapped tightly around his neck. Darrius let out a muffled cry but it sounded more like a burst of air from a balloon.

"Quiet" a voice whispered to him.

Both hands quickly released him and he spun around coming face to face with Raffie.

"What?" he said trying to keep his voice low.

"Listen" the voice said.

They both stood there listening, straining their ears to pick up any unnatural sounds. All Darrius could hear was his heart thumping in his chest. Then another giggle, more distinct and this time closer.

"Where is that coming from?" Darrius breathed softly.

"Sounds like over there," Raffie pointed to the other side of the street where Darrius had just been.

"I was just there. I thought I had saw something," Darrius said.

"Probably was just me," Raffie said his eyes straining to see in the darkness.

"What are you…"

Suddenly there was another giggle and the pitter-patter of tiny shoes on the dirt street. Both of them became rooted, their senses on high alert trying to figure out where the sound had come from.

"Duppies" Darrius said.

"Something." Raffie added.

"We could always dash out there and confront them," Darrius exclaimed.

"My gut tells me that isn't a good idea," Raffie replied. "Come on, let's sneak along the next two houses, maybe we can see something."

They both dashed out from the side of the building moving as quickly as possible in the darkness. They went from house to house stopping at each one and listening.

"What are we doing anyway?" Darrius asked.

"You heard that too, wherever that came from we have to find it," Raffie said his attention drawn to the street.

Again, there was movement on the opposite side of the street between two buildings.

"There!" Raffie pointed, then dashed out from the shadows running directly to where he had seen the movement.

"Hey wait up!" Darrius said following him.

Raffie moved as quickly as his legs would carry him. When he reached the spot there was nothing, it was like whatever had been there had disappeared in a wisp of smoke. Then came another giggle so close that he spun around expecting whatever was making the sound to be standing there waiting. Darrius heard the sound and froze halfway in the middle of the street. He suddenly felt vulnerable, exposed. He also didn't want to continue for fear of missing another sound, another clue as to where the duppies were.

Raffie's eyes darted from side to side as another giggle erupted from the opposite direction. Then another one from a different angle, then another and another. The sounds were all around him, surrounding him ready to pounce at any moment. Darrius heard the multiple sounds also and he forced himself to continue if not belay his fears, but to save a friend that he felt was in gave danger.

Raffie wheeled around just as Darrius reached him. They both turned and gazed into the shadows waiting for the next sound. It didn't happen, the silence of the night returned.

"Where was it coming from?" Darrius asked.

"It sounded like it was all around me, moving steadily in a circle," Raffie replied.

"It sounds like children," Darrius said.

"Yes, but where and why?"

"Children of the damned," Darrius said.

"What? What gave you that idea?" Raffie asked trying to keep from chuckling.

"A story my mother told me when I was a child. It was a story about a ship, hundreds of years ago that ran aground off the coast during a powerful hurricane. The ship contained many families, families with many, many children. Well, there were only a few lifeboats and they decided that the children should get off first. Therefore, they loaded the boat up with children and launched it. It was never seen again."

"Tall tale," Raffie grinned.

"It is said that on certain nights the children roam the island in search of their parents. They laugh and play as they search," Darrius explained.

"You mean giggle?" Raffie continued to smile.

"Yes"

"Scary story," Raffie added.

Suddenly there came a blood-curling scream.

Chapter 4

The night had become deadly silent. The only sound to be heard was that of Darrius' pounding heart. Never before had he heard it so distinctly, it rang in his ears and he fought to control it. His ears strained to pick up any sounds, either normal or unnatural. He was terrified.

"What direction did that come from?" Raffie asked his voice but a whisper.

"Not sure, why do you want to know that?" Darrius questioned.

"Because, I want to find out what happened," Raffie said then abruptly sprinted back across the street.

"Awe man," Darrius said shaking his head and following.

The shadows crept in swallowing Raffie causing him to disappear from sight. Darrius stopped his eyes from struggling to find his friend or whoever else might be lingering in the darkness.

"Raffie?" he called out softly.

No answer.

"Raffie?" he called again.

"Over here. Stop yelling or you'll scare away whoever is over there," he called back.

Darrius followed the soft voice into the shadows. Raffie was much farther away than he expected and he had to reach out and feel along the wall of a building to keep his bearing. Finally, he came to his friend who was crouched down peering across the street at a small run down home.

"I think it came from over there," Raffie pointed to the house.

"How can you be sure?"

"I can't, but I just saw something move on the porch," Raffie said.

"What?"

"I can't be sure but whatever it was, it was small," Raffie said softly.

"Come on, let's get <u>Babylon</u> and let them do their job," Darrius said grabbing Raffie's arm.

"Forget them, you know as well as I do, they're probably on Jah-Man's payroll," he said. "Anyway, aren't you curious?"

"What, to be the next person who screams?" Darrius said.

"Look, head back to the shack. I'll be along shortly as soon as I figure out what's going on here," Raffie said.

"You know I'm not going to leave you out here alone. What's gotten into you? Have you become some detective or something?" "Or something," he grinned.

"Raffie, you work at a hotel, you don't go chasing criminals. I realize that it might be in your blood with your family and all…but…"

His words trailed as his eyes cast upon something more ominous. The house across the street was a small one story dwelling with a tiny wrap around porch. The boards were rotten in many places leaving huge gaps and in the darkness; those gaps looked evil, foreboding. Most of the paint had peeled and what was left hung in tatters like an unshaven face. There were no lights on in any of the windows, yet what he saw made a chill dance up his spine.

Moving rapidly across the porch was what appeared to be a little girl, a <u>schooler</u>. She wore a very flowing white dress. What unnerved him was that the <u>dress appeared to glow</u> in the dark. As quickly as she appeared, she disappeared around the opposite corner of the porch - gone from sight. Then, breaking the stillness of the night came a very distinct <u>and playful</u> giggle.

"My God it's true!" Darrius choked. "The legend is true!"

"Come on, we need to check out that house," Raffie said darting from their protective cover.

"What for? Why are you so insistent on sticking your neck out?" Darrius said following.

Raffie was cautious as he stepped onto the first stair leading onto the porch. He wasn't sure how firm the wood was or how rotten. He didn't need to break an ankle. As he placed his weight onto the next step it let out a loud and clearly audible creaking sound.

"Damn" he breathed taking the next step quicker.

Darrius followed being much more cautious. He made sure he didn't step where Raffie had made noise. He kept his eye on him though and wouldn't allow him to leave his line of sight for an instant. He had a bad feeling about all this.

Raffie moved quickly along the porch keeping his body pressed firmly against the wall. When he reached the area where he had seen the little girl disappear he cautiously peered around the corner half expecting someone to be standing there waiting for him. The porch was empty.

"What's there?" Darrius asked coming up behind him.

"Nothing"

"Where's that <u>duppy</u>?" he asked.

"Don't see her," Raffie said scanning his surroundings.

"Good, time to go home. Remember, we both have to work tomorrow," Darrius reminded him.

"I'm going to check the house out," Raffie said moving to the front door.

"Why? Come on Raffie, enough is enough, it's time to go home," Darrius said with irritation as he watched Raffie disappear back around the corner.

Letting out an audible sigh, he followed. The front door was wide open. Raffie had a small flashlight that he illuminated the inside with. When Darrius entered the room, he became rooted. The sight that greeted him suddenly made him nauseous.

The room was <u>chaka chaka</u>. Chairs were overturned, books scattered around the room, and things were strewn all about. It looked like a whirlwind had blown into the house through a window and back out again.

"What happened here?" Darrius breathed.

"Don't know, come on let's check the other rooms," Raffie motioned to him.

The kitchen was in much the same shape; pots, dishes, and cups were strewn everywhere. They quickly moved to the only other room in the house, the bedroom. Raffie was the first through the small doorway. His hand then quickly reached back stopping Darrius.

"What?" Darrius asked.

"I think I found something," he said.

"Well let me see," Darrius said with irritation.

"It's messy," Raffie said.

"You dragged me all this way, I might as well see whatever it is," Darrius said pushing past him.

The sight was gristly; Raffie kept his flashlight focused onto one area. Two people, a woman and man lay half naked on the bed. They appeared young, healthy, except for the deep and hideous gashes across their throats. Their lifeless eyes peered intently at the dingy yellow ceiling. The bedding they lay on had huge dark, crimson stains.

"I think I'm going to be sick," Darrius said holding his hand to his mouth.

"No sign of struggle, whatever killed them was quick and quiet," Raffie said.

"Must have been, look at their hands," Darrius pointed out.

Raffie shined the light on the couple's hands; they were entwined like they had both grabbed each other's hand <u>before they died.</u>

"Suicide?" Darrius asked.

"Who cuts their own throat in a suicide?" Raffie said pointing the flashlight at him.

"Hey, what's that?" Darrius said pointing to something against the wall.

The beam of light turned abruptly and cast upon a small beat up dresser and mirror. The wood had seen better days but the mirror was still intact and it was what drew their attention. Written in blood on the glass were two words, the Osirus, below them were two tiny handprints. The whole thing looked like a child's finger painting. Raffie quickly moved from the side of the bed and examined the message. He then turned and headed for the door.

"We better go," he said to Darrius.

When they emerged onto the porch they both suddenly stopped dead in their tracks. Three vehicles sat parked their headlights illuminating the house and chasing away the duppies. There were also men crouched low pointing pistols at them.

"Get your hands in the air where we can see them," one of the men called out.

Both Raffie and Darrius complied raising their hands. They were then directed to lie down on the porch keeping their hands and legs outstretched. One of the officers entered the house while two others kept their guns trained on them.

When the man emerged, he roughed grabbed Darrius's arm pinning it behind his back.

"Officer, we did nothing wrong," Darrius pleaded as he felt the handcuffs slip around his wrists.

"You are under arrest for murder," the officer said sternly.

"We didn't kill them. We saw a child run along the porch. We figured we would see if she was lost," Raffie pointed out.

"Sure, sure, get your stories straight before we throw the book at you," another officer said.

"But officer, we found them like that - look at the mirror!" Darrius said straining at the cuffs.

"Trying to blame it on children heh?" one officer asked.

"No. We told you we found a child running along the porch," Darrius explained.

"And where is this child? Why is a child running around when it's near midnight?" the man barked.

"I don't know. I'm just telling you what we saw," Darrius said.

"Save it," an officer snapped then roughly hauled them to their feet.

"You can think about it a little more when the bars of the cage close you in."

Raffie could see the fear in his friend's eyes. They were going to jail, which were stinking rotten holes that undesirables were thrown. He had seen enough jails over the years, he only wished he had been more cautious about letting Darrius follow him. Now his friend was in hot water along with him.

Sharon saw the plane; it was gleaming silver with two huge props. The side door was open and she could see the Ohpton standing next to it waving frantically to her.

There were three small windows along the fuselage. In them, she could see the rest of her surrogate family. What struck her as odd was that they looked sad, withdrawn. She had never seen them so sullen, depressed. She couldn't understand why they were that way; this was it the time they all waited for. Their trip to America, their freedom was beginning. Worry began to creep into her and she began to feel anxious, she moved towards the plane but with every step, she seemed to go nowhere. She began to run.

Ohpton climbed into the plane and closed the door, moments later the huge props began to churn, slowly at first then with increasing speed. Though she was running, she was no closer to the plane. The silver hulk began to move the tiny tail section swinging around. She screamed, screamed at the top of her lungs for it to wait but no one heard her. Within seconds, the plane was airborne. It banked to the right as if letting the occupants take one final look. Stopping, she raised her hand waving goodbye.

Her family was gone.

Sharon sat upright gasping for breath her hand clutched to the center of her chest. Perspiration glistened over her naked body even though the air conditioning had chilled the room. For a moment, she was disoriented and she looked around at the unfamiliar surroundings. The dream had been vivid, so real to her and it frightened her tremendously. The thought of losing them, Eve, Darrius, Ohpton, Raffie and most importantly Steven, tore at her heart. All the years they had worked hard, saved every penny so they could start a new life in America, for them all, including her, somehow something had gone wrong.

"It's just a dream, that's all it was, a dream," she said aloud trying to convince herself.

It was then she glanced to the bed next to hers and realized that the covers had not been turned down. Darrius had not come back last night. A new worry seeped into her mind. People had a way of disappearing on the island, people who had done nothing to anyone else, others who voiced their opinion. It was common knowledge that Darrius disliked the drug lord, he voiced it enough in front of people whom he should have kept his mouth shut around. Her fear turned to panic.

Bounding out of bed she glanced at the clock on the wall, it was going on 6:30 a.m. There was still time for him to show before her breakfast with the JahMan. Stepping quickly into the shower, before long Sharon had her clothing from the night before tucked in a bag and was out the door heading for the lobby. When she got to the desk, she asked if Darrius had come through this morning. The person just shook his head no.

Going quickly to the salon, she fumbled with her keys and finally opened the door. She tossed her bag in one of the chairs and rushed over to the wall where they had a radio. Turning it on she adjusted the dial so she could hear the announcer when she spoke. All she could do was listen, listen to the news and pray.

"Hey what's going on?" a voice called from behind startling her.

Sharon turned to see Steven walk through the door. He wore a pair of shorts and a resort shirt, which was required by all employees that didn't work in shops. As he walked towards her, she watched his perfect body and for a moment the world went away…but, only for a moment.

"Oh Steven. Did Darrius come home last night?" she quickly asked.

"No, I didn't see him and I was up late too," he said his smile quickly fading.

"What's wrong?"

She explained the night's events to him and her soon to happen breakfast with Jah-Man. She also explained her fears, Steven's brow creased and he sat down in the nearest chair as if absorbing all her new information had suddenly made him tired.

"Raffie was gone also," he added.

"He left just about 10:00 p.m. last night. Wouldn't tell me where or why, he just grinned. You know, a grin like he was setting up to play one of his pranks?"

"What can we do?" she asked.

"Nothing, you need to go to breakfast with Jah-Man, if you don't show up it might enrage him," Steven said.

"I'll check around, see what I can dig up before work starts," he said getting up out of the chair.

"Steven" Sharon said drawing up close to him. "I'm worried, something is wrong I can feel it," she said her hand pressed firmly against his chest.

For an instant, they both locked eyes. Her hand against his chest felt reassuring, sensual and it calmed him. Her eyes were warm, wanton; it was something he had never seen in her. He found himself becoming aroused.

"Let me check things out," he said forcing himself away from her.

Sharon watched him leave and felt like a fool. She had nearly thrown herself at him, her desire and the feeling of security he gave was something she needed. If she had done what she had wanted or felt, she would have ripped his clothes off and given herself to him. They would have made sweet tender love right here on the floor, their bodies entwined, their hands exploring the most intimate parts of each other's bodies.

Sharon shook her head tossing the pleasing fantasy from her mind. Sometimes she couldn't help herself around him. It took all her strength to control her hormones. She also realized why she allowed herself to fantasize, it took the worry away, and the panic she was now experiencing for Darrius and now Raffie. Turning she walked over to the mirror and began preparing herself for her breakfast with Jah-Man.

It wasn't her idea of a good time, and the thought of explaining to him why Darrius wasn't with her, angered her.

Darrius rolled over then fell to the hard concrete floor with a thud. It was filthy and the choking stench of mold wafted into his nostrils. He coughed and nearly gagged.

"You okay?" the familiar sound of Raffie's voice called to him.

"Yeah, yeah, I think so," he said pulling himself from the floor.

The Police had thrown them both in the same, rank and very filthy jail cell. There were two rusted iron cots and a toilet in the corner that was plugged and had backed up. The odor was offensive it hung in the air and never dissipated.

"What time is it?" Darrius asked sitting on the edge of the bed rubbing the back of his head.

"Going on 7:00 a.m.," Raffie said glancing at his watch.

"I think we're going to miss work this morning."

"We'll lose our jobs if we don't show up. I'm also suppose to have breakfast with Jah-Man," he said letting out a sigh. "Jah-Man?" Raffie said his interest peaked.

Darrius explained the evening events telling him of Jah-Man's interest in him. Raffie stared at him in disbelief.

"Why is he suddenly taking an interest in you?" Raffie asked.

"You're guess is as good as mine," Darrius said.

"I hate the man."

"Well that much I've known for years. He gives you a new position at the resort, then ask you to one of his parties and then breakfast. It sounds like he has plans for you!" Raffie grinned.

"Yeah, and how do I tell him to shove his plans." his words trailed.

"Go with the flow bro, take what the man gives you and use it for your own interests," Raffie said.

"I wish I was having breakfast with the man."

"Why? You hate him as much as I do," Darrius asked.

"Oh, maybe I would like to study him, learn his quirks so I could use it against him later," Raffie grinned.

"You mean you'd like to unscrew the caps on the salt and pepper shakers before he gets there," Darrius grinned.

"Yeah, that too," Raffie gave him an evil grin.

For a moment, the silence was deafening between them. Neither of them wanted to talk about Jah-Man and the stench was so overpowering that they feared opening their mouths for fear of tasting the smell.

"What about last night?" Darrius finally broke the silence.

"We won't stay here long, they don't have any evidence to keep us here," Raffie explained.

"Maybe not, but that doesn't mean we won't rot here for a few days." "I want to know what we saw last night," Raffie said softly.

"Duppy"

"You don't believe that do you?" Raffie asked.

"You tell me what you saw, that was a little girl, maybe 7 or 8 years old. She glowed Raffie - she glowed!"

"Could have been a trick of light or something," he speculated.

"It was dark, very dark. Where was the light coming from? Look I don't know what you think, but what I saw was a duppy child." "You sound ridiculous," Raffie laughed.

"Oh I do, do I?" Darrius said his voice growing stern.

"What about the mirror, the bloody message on the mirror? What did it say, the Osirus?"

"Yes, it did say that but keep in mind someone had to write it out. Do <u>duppies</u> write?" Raffie asked.

"The Osirus was the ship, the same ship where those children lost their lives. What more proof do you need? You saw her too and saw the message, come on, how can you be a skeptic." Darrius said with irritation.

"Okay, yes I saw the same things you did, but that doesn't mean that we're dealing with <u>duppies</u> here. There are number of explanations that would explain the things we saw, a number of them!" he said defending his opinion.

"Yeah? Like what?" Darrius pushed.

"Look, what <u>duppy</u> uses a knife to cut someone's throat? Don't they just <u>scare</u> person to death?"

"This is so strange, <u>Babylon</u> are not going to believe us," Darrius shook his head.

"No kidding."

Sharon changed clothes again. She remembered that she kept a change of clothing in the back of the salon. She wore a flowering skirt that came to just above her knees and a halter-top that followed the well-defined shape of her breasts. It was almost too revealing for her, but she wore it anyway. When she was through with her hair she slipped her keys into her pocket and locked the salon behind her.

It didn't take long to reach the dining room. When she did, a waiter was already expecting her and ushered her out onto the large veranda that overlooked the water. There were many tables and chairs but only one table had someone sitting at it. Jah-Man sat with his elbow on the edge of the table and his hand rubbing his chin as he stared out at the water. He wore a dark tunic, the front open exposing his chest and the few gold chains that hung around his neck. When she approached the table the waiter helped her with her chair. Jah-Man turned, for an instant, he looked at her and her body - his expression serious.

Then, as if someone had flipped on a light switch the man broke out in a huge beaming grin. He wore pair of <u>darkers</u> that he kept on the end of his nose, reaching up he drew them off setting them on the table.

"Good morning, my, you are very ravishing young woman," he said grinning.

Sharon felt like a caged animal with nowhere to go. He was like a wolf in sheep's clothing and she was the unsuspecting sheep. At any moment, he would toss off his disguise and pounce upon her. He was also quite handsome.

"And where is Mr. Lawson?"

"I do not know, he had an errand to run last night and he never returned," she said truthfully.

Jah-Man's face lost its jovial expression and turned instantly to a frown. The change was so dramatic that she suddenly felt threatened even sitting across from him. He looked like he would at any moment fly into a rage. Instantly he grabbed his cellular phone and pressed a button. He began talking but very soft, so soft that even at their close proximity across the table she couldn't make out what he was saying. The conversation was brief; he snapped the cover on the phone in place and set it on the table next to his cappuccino. He then grinned at her again, another sudden change washing over him.

"I trust that you and Darrius had a good evening last night?" he asked.

"Splendid" she replied.

"And after? Was the room and privacy adequate for you two?" he asked probing.

For a moment, Sharon was bewildered at his question. Then, slowly, it began to dawn on her what he was getting at. He assumed that they were a couple and couples had sex.

"He went on his errand just after we got to the room," she explained.

"Oh, so you spent the night alone?"

"Yes"

"How long have you known him?" Jah-Man asked.

"Quite a few years, we met shortly after his mama disappeared," she explained.

Jah-Man's expression again fell, his eyes suddenly looked hollow, distant. Sharon felt fear, she also felt like she was on a roller coaster with a broken car and at any moment the car would fly off the tracks. Her eyes pulled away from his and they cast upon his hands, which were covered in silk gloves.

"Is there something wrong?" she said not believing she had the courage to ask.

"Nothing my dear, nothing at all. The past has a way of coming back to haunt you. Memories seem to open doors that are best left shut," he said softly.

"I take it you knew her?"

"Whom my dear?" he asked.

"Evelyn Lawson, Eve and Darrius's mama," Sharon asked.

"I knew of her as she worked here at the resort. She was a very, very beautiful woman," he said looking out at the water.

"She had a voice that was calm. At least that's what I heard."

"Did anyone ever figure out where she went? I mean to abandon two children…" Sharon pointed out.

"She abandoned no one!" Jah-Man snapped suddenly flying into a rage.

Sharon drew back, for many years she had listened to Darrius express his thoughts about his mother, thoughts that included the possibility that Jah-Man was at the center of her disappearance. At this particular moment, she would have to agree with Darrius, that somehow Jah-Man was involved. His cellular phone rang.

Again, she couldn't hear what he was saying and just as quickly he put it down drawing his attention back to her.

"I have found your lover, he will be here shortly," Jah-Man said smiling.

"He's not…" she began to say, then caught herself and kept her mouth shut.

"I have plans for him you know," Jah-Man beamed.

"He's is a very bright young man. His father must be very proud of him," he said as a waiter wheeled a cart close to the table.

"I wouldn't know and neither would he or Eve, they never knew their father," she said watching the waiter.

The man pulled each silver lid off each platter, beneath was an array of different breakfast foods. Jah-Man pointed to what he wanted and the man filled his plate.

He then turned his attention to her. Sharon stared at the food, she had no appetite but given the mood swings she had witnessed from Jah-Man, she reluctantly chose the scrambled eggs and toast.

"Where was he?" she asked lightly salting her eggs.

"Indisposed of for the evening," Jah-Man said directing his attention to the poached eggs on his plate.

"You mentioned you had plans for him, do you care to elaborate on that?" she questioned.

"All in good time. I am glad though, that you keep his interests in mind. That is the mark of a good, faithful woman," he smiled warmly.

Again, Sharon wanted to tell him that Darrius was not what he thought, that they were just good friends, like brother and sister. She didn't though, partly because she didn't want to see his mood again shift to the dark side. The other reason was that she didn't know what else to say to the man.

She ate her breakfast.

"Do you like it here?" he asked.

"You mean working at the resort?" she said between bites.

"Of course, does it provide what you need?"

"More money would help, I sometimes feel awkward around so many rich people," she said.

"Do you feel that way around me?" he said giving her that same seductive and sinister smile he did the night before.

"Sometimes" she said wiping her lips.

"That is something I would very much like to change.

"There is too much sadness on this island, too much suffering," he said extending his arm.

"And what do you propose to do to change that?" she asked.

"I have lain at night pondering the answer and it eludes me. I treat <u>my</u> <u>people</u> very well; I provide for them and give to them what they need. Sometimes though they stray from the path I have laid out before them," he said sadly.

Sharon stared at the man and a chill washed through her body. He was talking like; well like he was a God and the people of the island were his children. He was the <u>Don Dada</u> and his eyes had gone hollow again and his mood shifted. He now grew very quiet and he stared down into the creamy whiteness of his coffee cup.

"Those that stray must be punished, they must be set as examples for others to see. Others must know the price of straying away from me," he said.

"You understand, don't you?" he asked looking up at her.

"Of course," she lied not knowing what else to do.

"You are a bright woman Sharon Cunnings, a bright woman indeed."

Steven glanced at his watch; it was nearly 9:00 a.m. Asking around he had found out both Raffie and Darrius were arrested during the night. When he reached the police station he opened the door and nearly collided with them as they were coming out.

"What happened?" he stood staring at them.

"We're out of here, the police for some strange reason, dropped all charges against us," Darrius smiled.

"They really had nothing on us anyway."

"I'd like to know the sudden change in heart though," Raffie explained.

"How did you find out?" Darrius asked Steven.

"You know how the buzz is around here. Not much happens without everyone finding out. Sharon is worried sick, she explained to me what happened last night." Steven said as they headed back down the street towards the resort.

"What could I do, I couldn't telephone her," Darrius shrugged.

"So who supposedly did you murder?" Steven asked raising an eyebrow.

"I don't know who they were, a woman and man, young too," Darrius explained.

"Don't forget our little <u>duppy</u>," Raffie winked at Darrius.

"<u>Duppy</u>?" Steven took notice.

"We saw...well, it was a little girl in a glowing white dress. We watched her run down the porch and disappear around the corner." Darrius explained.

"The lifeboat legend?" Steven asked.

"Yeah, that's what Darrius here thinks," Raffie scoffed.

"What else could it have been? Think about it, us seeing a little girl running around after midnight? Doesn't that sound odd to you? Then add that couple with their throat cut from ear to ear," Darrius said defending his belief.

"Look, we can talk about this later tonight, we all have to get to work, that is if we still have jobs," Steven said glancing again at his watch.

The day bore on in its usual humdrum of activity. Guests were arriving every hour and before long the resort was nearly at capacity. People golfed, sailed and did a variety of activities. Some just lay on lawn chairs enjoying the rich and brilliant sunlight that made Jamaica one of the best vacation spots on the globe.

Ohpton was working on the hedges with an electric trimmer. It had become a very hot and brutal day. He was exhausted and wanted nothing more than to sit back with a cool drink and do nothing. Working the grounds was hard labor but he liked it. He did his own thing and most of the time had very little contact with guests.

Suddenly he heard the grass swish behind him. Turning he glanced over his shoulder. Two girls stood staring at him, they were in their mid twenties. One had flowing black hair that accented her dark skin well. She had high cheekbones and long eyelashes that she batted repeatedly at him. The other was a white girl with blond hair and hazel colored eyes. Both wore bikini bathing suits that left little to the imagination. The blond also had the biggest breasts he had ever seen on a woman. He smiled and shut the trimmer off.

"Can I help you with something?" he asked politely.

"No, not really," the dark hair girl said.

"We've been just watching you for a while," she smiled shyly.

"Oh" he smiled back.

"My friend here is too shy to talk to you," the girl thumbed to the blond next to her.

"We were both wondering, if...well...you know what they say about men with large feet?" the girl said smiling while the blond blushed.

"That it's directly proportional to..." he began to say.

"To the size of his cock," the blond blurted out.

"Okay, is there something else you girls would like to know that isn't so personal?" he asked trying to change the subject.

More often than not, he was kidded about having large feet and that large feet meant a large cock. He never, until this day though, had a strange woman ask him that question.

"Well?" the blond said with a beaming smile.

"Of course it is," he said humoring them.

"I'd like to find out - we'd like to find out," the blond asked.

"It's prohibited for me to fraternize with guests, I could loose my job," he explained.

"Well, if you change your mind," the dark haired girl said putting her room key in his hand.

"Just come on in.," she said seductively.

He watched the two girls walk off; he had also broken out in a sweat. It wasn't the first time he had a woman approach him. However, never until now, had two at once approached him. It would make an interesting experience.

Suddenly something caught his eye. Setting the trimmer down he followed the hedge, in the distance he noticed Jah-Man walking casually through one of the resorts many gardens. His arms were behind him and his gate was slow and casual. A small case sat on the stone path a few steps away from him.

From the other end of garden, he watched a woman enter. She wore a short dress with a plunging neckline; she was Hispanic with long straight hair and a light complexion. Her high heels clicked on the stone as she walked and there was no mistaking that she was beautiful. Ohpton watched the woman, her legs were long, supple, her breasts bouncing with every step she took. In her hand though, was a slim briefcase.

Jah-Man turned when he heard the clicking of her heels. He already knew who it was; he was expecting her nearly an hour earlier. As she approached, her straight face turned into a broad smile.

"Mr. Stone" she said setting the briefcase down next to her leg.

"Ms. Jones" he said not smiling.

"You are late and I don't like waiting," he said his glare intense.

"My apologies. I was detained at the airport," she said.

"Do you wish to do business here?" she asked looking around.

"Yes, is there a problem?" he asked.

"It's rather open and visible, how do you know we're not being watched or videotaped?" she said as she looked over her shoulder.

"Ms. Jones, this is Jamaica not Mexico or the United States. Everything has a place here. Everyone knows their place also. They will not defy me," he gave her an evil grin.

"We do not have federal agencies looking to squeeze their fingers into the pie," he explained.

"You buy them off?" she asked.

"Yes, or kill them," he smiled.

"So shall we conclude our business?" his warm demeanor returning.

She just nodded and picked up the briefcase. Walking over she set it down on the marble bench seat and opened it.

"As we agreed, 1.5 million," she said.

"All in U.S. currency, non traceable."

Jah-Man walked over, grabbed a random coil and thumbed the bills back making sure they were all currency and not a trick. He then returned the money to the case and closed it. Walking over he grabbed his own case and set it down next to hers, he then motioned her to open it.

"We have increased the yield and will be able to provide more with better quality," he said to her.

"But the price will go up."

"How much?" she said testing the quality of the cocaine.

"10%, that is to cover operating costs," he explained.

"I will have to inform my superiors. I will notify you with our decision," she said holding the test tube up to the sky, then shook it slightly.

"Do not wait too long Ms. Jones, there are many others that I can sell to. I am giving you and your organization exclusive rights because we have done much business in the past. But that will change if I feel the profit is better elsewhere," he said sternly.

"We will inform you by this evening. Your quality has improved…greatly," she smiled.

"That should help convince them, but how much can you produce? We are looking for a big order," she continued to smile.

"How big?" he asked.

"At least 125 tons," she said.

"That's a lot."

"Yes, and if we decide to pay you the extra 10% we would expect no delays in shipment," she said.

"I can provide what you need," he reassured her.

"Good, I will be in touch with you this evening," she said taking the case containing the cocaine.

Ohpton watched her disappear into the garden where she had entered. JahMan grabbed his case of money and walked in the opposite direction. For a moment Ophton felt shock, he had never seen that much money in one place before. There was enough money there to buy them all trips to the United States and much more. He also knew that he had just witnessed a drug deal. If Jah-Man had known he was there he would make him disappear quickly. In a few hours his work would end, he wanted to find the others, tell them what he saw. More importantly, he wanted to tell them about the case of money.

Eve locked the door to the boutique, it had been a long day and she was excessively tired. The high life from the night before had gotten to her, she wasn't use to the constant flurry of activity and she longed for a quiet night back at the shack. Turning she nearly bumped into Delicia.

"Oh, excuse me I didn't hear you," she apologized.

"No matter honey, I was just coming to see you anyway," she gave her an evil grin.

"Really?" Eve perked up.

"Yes, I was wondering if you wanted to go out tonight. There is a nightclub in town that I've been dying to check out!" she said excitedly.

"I'd like to but I'm really tired. It's been a long day and I didn't get much sleep last night," she said softly.

"Sleep? Who needs sleep?" Delicia grinned. "You need a stiff drink and a hard body next to you in bed." "I'd really like to but…"

"Now I won't take no for an answer," Delicia said sternly.

"Well I need to tell my brother so he won't worry," she sighed.

"Good, go tell him and then meet me up at my room. You can change there," she said adjusting the many spirals of chains that surrounded her wrists.

"Delicia…" Eve began to say.

"What honey?"

"What do you see in me? I mean, why are you so nice to me but dislike my friends so?" she bluntly asked.

Delicia's face turned into a <u>screw</u>. It was clear to Eve that the woman didn't like talking about serious matters.

"You have potential honey. The others are just riffraffs with no class. Peasant types," she snapped.

"My brother too?" she winced.

"He's the only one of that mangy group, that may make something of him if he lets Jah-Man help him," she said.

"Jah-Man wants to help my brother?" she blinked with surprise.

"Why?"

"Every so often, Jah-Man sees something in someone, something he knows he can make flourish. He takes that person under his wing and well, helps them," she smiled.

"But everything I heard about him, all the rumors about drugs, killings…"

"Just rumors honey, just rumors. Jah-Man is a kind, compassionate sexy man," she said not smiling.

"What about you and Diamond?" she asked changing the subject.

"Oh, I don't know. He says he loves me but yet he avoids me too," she said sadly.

"Men are strange honey, you just have to get to know them better. Maybe you and him need to spend a weekend together - alone," she suggested.

"I don't know," she said looking up at her.

"I could arrange it you know," Delicia grinned.

"Look, go tell your brother and I'll meet you up at the room."

Before Eve could say anything, Delicia walked off swishing her hips as she walked. Before she disappeared into the elevator, she wanted to call out to her and tell her that she would rather pass on going out tonight. However, she didn't.

It was going on 7:00 p.m. when Sharon finally climbed the last knoll to the shack. The place looked wonderful to her, so serene, so inviting. It was more of a home than she ever had. She loved her mother and brother but this was hers. It was someplace that she felt comfortable. Entering the shack she looked around, there was nobody around. She went from room to room wondering where the others were; she then shrugged and grabbed her towel. Slipping out of her clothes, she wrapped the towel around her and headed up the winding path behind the shack. A quiet night dip in the hot springs would do her tired body good.

When she got to the top of the hill she heard voices. Turning she saw the others in the group standing at the base of a tree. It was not just any tree either; it was their special tree, the tree where they buried all their money. As she approached, she noticed that everyone was there except for Eve.

"Wha'ppen" she said softly.

"We were wondering when you'd get here," Ohpton smiled.

"We decided that tonight was the night, to come up here and check how much more we needed," Steven said holding the metal container.

"Where's Eve?" She asked.

"Delicia again," Darrius scowled.

"What!" Sharon snapped.

"Why does she hang around with her?"

"Eve is different, we all know that. She sees things from a different perspective than we do," Raffie explained.

"Yeah, screwed up," Ohpton breathed.

"Look I don't like it anymore than the rest of you but she's my sister remember. She's also 18 and can make decisions for herself," Darrius said defending her.

"Like what I heard you and Raffie did?" Sharon asked.

"We were just at the wrong place at the wrong time," Darrius frowned.

"I still want to know who killed those people," Raffie said rubbing his chin.

"Rumor has it that it was you two," Ohpton said.

"Least that's what's going around at the Orion."

"I'd also like to know who bailed us out. If the police had such a firm case on us, why set us free with no charges?" Raffie speculated.

"Jah-Man" Sharon breathed.

"What?" Darrius shot her a cold look.

"It was Jah-Man who bailed you two out. I was having breakfast with him, remember? Well his telephone rang, after he mentioned that he had found out where you were and you would be arriving shortly."

"I think I would have rather rot in jail," Darrius said hanging his head.

"Why is he taking a particular interest in you anyway?" Steven asked.

"He said he has big plans for you," Sharon added.

"Oh brother," Darrius howled.

"Like I said earlier, take what you can get and then run," Ohpton smiled. "That brings up another topic I want to talk with everyone about."

The whole crowd became silent wondering what Ohpton was going to say. The man usually kept relatively quiet. Now for some reason he was jubilant and excited.

"I watched Jah-Man this afternoon. He had a meeting with a woman, they exchanged cases."

"Drugs" Raffie added.

"Yes, that was in one case. The other, well the other contained stacks of money! American dollars from what I could see," he grinned.

"So?" Steven asked.

"So? Do you realize that with one, just one of those cases we could all be on a plane out of here tomorrow? We wouldn't have to worry about money, ever again!" he beamed.

"No, we'd just have to worry about getting a knife or bullet in the back," Raffie shook his head.

"What are you getting at?" Darrius asked.

"Why don't we figure out a way to get one of those cases, then, run like hell!" he grinned.

"You're nuts," Steven shook his head.

"Why? For trying to think of a way to get us all out of here quicker?" he said defensively.

"You're idea will get us killed," Sharon added.

"Though, it does sound appealing."

"Look, I'm not asking any of you to decide on this tonight, but give it some thought," he said trying to regain some enthusiasm.

"How much is in the can?" Raffie said changing the subject.

Steven unlatched the small hook and opened the watertight military can. Inside there were coils, along with a sheet of paper. For the next hour they all sat there watching him count the money, then sadly he looked up at them.

"Ballpark, we're at least a thousand shy," he breathed.

"We could possibly make it up this summer," Darrius added.

"Yeah, that would buy us our passports and the plane ride. But what do we do when we get there? We have to have some money to eat and find a place to start from," Sharon added.

"We can easily find jobs," Ohpton said.

"That's what we hear now but what about when we get there and find work isn't as plentiful as we thought?" Sharon asked.

"We'll find a way, we always do," Darrius smiled.

"All of us have been through our share of troubles, what's a few more?" "We need more than that," Sharon said flatly.

"How much more?" Steven asked.

"I don't know, enough to find us a place to stay and food," she said.

"Maybe a year from now," Steven sadly added.

"No, we've waited so long. Another year is so terribly far away," Ohpton scowled.

"After all these years, what's a few more?" Darrius added.

"Hell" Ohpton said.

Sharon said nothing; she turned and walked a few feet away then stopped. Turning she looked at the small group, she loved them all dearly. She wanted to go to the United States just as bad as the rest of them. She wished she had a better solution, one that would get them off the island this year, however, she didn't.

"Any of you want to go for a swim?" she asked.

"I'll go," Raffie grinned. "Me too!" Steven added.

"I will once we bury the can again," Darrius said.

"Ohpton?" She asked.

"I'm tired. I think I'm just going to go back to the shack and hit the sack early," he said softly.

Sharon watched him walk down the path leading to the shack. At first she wanted to stop him, console him. She knew, no actually, she felt how badly he wanted to get off the island. How badly he wanted them all to get off the island.

Instead, she just let him go, then turned and headed for the hot springs. Before the others arrived, she slipped the towel off and let the hot water envelope her naked body. The springs churned the water blocking her nudity from the others. She didn't care though, they had seen her naked before, just as she had seen them. There was very little they hid from each other and that was what she attributed to their getting along so well.

When the others arrived, she watched as they slipped off their clothing. They were all handsome men, Steven most of all. She tried to divert her eyes from his naked form but found she couldn't stop looking up at him. He was well built in all the right areas. Raffie was ordinary, nothing spectacular; he was the first in the water. Darrius had a strapping physique that would turn any woman's head. Her eyes though, kept going to Steven and for an instant; she wished the others had opted not to swim. That would have left her alone with him. Maybe, she fantasized, he would take her into his arms, and their lips would touch in a tender sweet kiss. His hands would squeeze and fondle her breasts as she became limp in his arms.

"Hey is it me or is this water hotter today?" Raffie called out.

Sharon frowned at him; he had destroyed her fantasy, her daydream. It was gone now; the rapid pounding of her heart had subsided. She watched Steven slip into the water, he glanced over at her and smiled and she smiled warmly back.

Watching him, she suddenly felt sad. She realized that his fantasies probably included Eve and not her. She wanted him though, wanted him badly.

"What's gotten into Ohpton?" Darrius asked sitting next to her.

"I don't know, I've never seen an outburst like that. Something is eating away at him," she said softly.

"Maybe he's right," Darrius said watching Raffie slip beneath the water.

"About?"

"The money, think about it Sharon. If we could get hold of one, just one briefcase that contained his drug money we could be out of here before the end of the season."

"It's dangerous thinking Darrius, thinking that might get one of us killed."

"Possibly, but compared to the hardships we've all been through..." "And are still going through,"

she added.

"Exactly, we would just need to plan it out, watch the man, find patterns in what he does," Darrius said.

"You sound convinced," she said.

"No, not yet, I wouldn't do this unless we all agree to it," he said shaking his head.

"I'm concerned about Eve," she blurted out.

Darrius suddenly grew quiet. He felt the same worry as she did. He didn't care for Delicia, didn't care for the way she was trying to manipulate Eve. He loved his sister though and just as Sharon did, wanted her to be happy. Over the years, he watched a special relationship develop between Eve and Sharon, a friendship that would never be broken. Now that Delicia was worming her way between them, he felt a confrontation was on the horizon. A nasty war was developing between the two women and he hoped that Jah-Man would keep his influence out of it. Jah-Man had also had taken a keen interest in Sharon for some reason.

At first, he thought it was just him, but now he realized that she also played a part in Jah-Man's thinking. Now they were thinking of stealing from him, stealing a great deal of money - blood money.

Suddenly he wondered if death lay ahead for them all instead of a plane that would take them to freedom.

Chapter 5

Delicia stepped into the shower; the water was hot, just the way she liked it. It beat down on her body. The massage action soothing her tired muscles. She had left Eve in her room at the resort. She needed to come back and she needed to be here when Jah-Man arrived. Despite her socially whirlwind lifestyle, she still had responsibilities. One she dared not take lightly was to be where Jah-Man expected her to be. Shortly, she stepped from the shower and quickly dried off.

When she emerged from the bathroom wisps of steam rose spilling out into the cool bedroom. She hadn't noticed it at first, but out of the corner of her eye, she saw something move. Startled she jumped nearly loosing the towel covering her body.

William Stone sat in one of the plush chairs on the other side of the room.
He tapped his fingers together slowly but continuously as he stared at her.

"What are you doing here?" she snapped her anger flaring.

He said nothing, his eyes were locked on her and he continued to tap his fingers together.

"Did you suddenly go deaf? I asked you a question, <u>what are you doing in Jah-Man's bedroom?</u>" she spat.

"Looking for you," he said softly.

"That doesn't give you the right to enter my bedroom," she said wrapping her arms tightly around herself.

"I am Jah-Man's brother, that gives me <u>all</u> the right," he gave her an evil grin.

"What do you want?" she said the cool room air chilling her.

"I've noticed you've taken a shine to Eve Lawson," he said.

"What are you up to?"

"I happen to like her. I am simply showing her a world she would never, ever, experience by hanging around with that riffraff bunch she calls friends." "And?" he asked.

"And what?" she shot back.

"What else Delicia? I've watched you for some time; you don't do anything unless you have an ulterior motive. My gut tells me that you don't have
Eve's best intentions in mind."

"What I do is none of your business," she snarled.

"Be careful Delicia, you are playing a dangerous game. If you do anything to harm Eve or Darrius there will be nowhere on this planet you can hide from me," he said his voice deep, stern.

Delicia stared at the man; he was not acting himself. He was a docile man, warm, friendly. Now the man that sat before her was cold, calculating, giving her much the same stare as Jah-Man did.

William got up and walked to the door, for an instant he hesitated then turned to her.

"Walk away from this Delicia, keep your nose out of it," he said, and then left the room.

Delicia went into the bathroom letting the towel fall to the floor. She stared at herself in the mirror and began applying the multitude of makeup. The words that William had spoken burned in her mind. They rolled around and around causing her to become angry.

"To hell with you," she said aloud.

Suddenly, she jumped with fear. Two hands slipped over her thighs and up around her breasts. Looking into the mirror, she saw Jah-Man behind her grinning.

"You startled me!" she said into the mirror.

"How could you not see me, with a mirror as big as this one?" he smiled.

"I was thinking, not paying attention," she said.

"Did you have a good day?" she asked changing the subject.

"Same as always," he said fondling her breasts his fingers rubbing her nipples.

She closed her eyes letting his hands work; she knew what was coming next. This was just another of her responsibilities. When Jah-Man wanted her, he took her.

His strong arms reached down and scooped her off her feet. Though he was short, his strength was plainly apparent. Carrying her to the bed he placed her down, then slowly took his clothes off. The arousal of his buddy was apparent, like a hawk descending on hapless prey he took her. Together, they would fuck intensely. Ravaging her body she submitted to his sexual ferocity, her own desires peaked many times before he finally released collapsing into her arms.

They lay there saying nothing, her hand lightly stroking the length of his back.

"What was William doing here?" he asked softly.

"Nothing, looking for you," she lied.

"Is that all?" he asked again.

"He was concerned about my relationship with Eve Lawson," she admitted.

"Eve Lawson?" he asked.

Delicia suddenly felt his muscles stiffen. Something about Eve Lawson had affected him.

"Yes, Eve Lawson," she said softly.

"What was he concerned about?" he asked.

"He was worried that I didn't have her best intentions in mind," she said.

"Do you?" he asked.

"She is a way to get to the others, you know how much I despise that little group."

"So you're using her?" he asked.

"No, I actually like her," she said sensing a sudden change in him.

"I forbid you to hurt her Delicia - forbid it," he said suddenly.

"She's trash Jah-Man, just trash," Delicia said.

Jah-Man rose up on his arms, he was still deeply inside her. Delicia stared up at his face, the passion that was there a minute ago, was now gone, replaced with hate, anger.

Her mouth opened to say something but before she could he slapped her, his hand coming down hard against the side of her face.

"Heed my words Delicia. Do not harm Eve Lawson ever," he spat withdrawing from her.

She heard him go into the bathroom and slam the door. She rolled over feeling her stinging cheek, a tear rolled down her cheek and she fought to control her emotions. Curling up into a fetal position she closed her eyes and lay there listening. She could hear the water running hard in the bathroom sink. He was washing his hands; he always washed his hands, over and over.

For some reason he was obsessed with clean hands, like he was trying to wash something away that wasn't there. Reaching up she lightly touched her cheek then looked at her fingers to see if they were covered in blood, they weren't

There were only two other times that he had struck her, both times, she reasoned, had been her fault, just like this time. She suddenly became curious, why was the mention of Eve's name having such an effect on him? Why was he so bent on protecting her? Why was William so interested in both Eve and Darrius? The thoughts rolled around and around their importance numbing her stinging cheek. She heard the bathroom sink shut off then door opened. She closed her ey

Jah-Man stared at her naked body. For an instant, as he stared at her, he thought he saw Evelyn. He was suddenly overcome with pity for the woman. It was so strong he reached out and gripped the dresser for fear of falling over. The moment was brief though and it quickly passed leaving only Delicia. Walking over he knelt next to the bed.

"Delicia, promise me you will not harm Eve or Darrius Lawson?" he softly asked.

"Why Jah-Man? Why does the mention of their names bother you so?" she asked as another tear streaked down her face.

"It does and that should suffice for an answer," he stated.

"Promise me…now!"

Delicia knew that if she didn't agree, his anger would again flare and she would take the brunt of it. Slowly, she closed her eyes and nodded. The only thing he had done was to ignite her curiosity. She would figure out his and William's secret. Sooner or later she would know the truth.

Sharon was quiet as she walked the long trip into town. Odd things were happening, fate was throwing obstacles in front of them. She felt a twinge of fear, the words Darrius spoke echoing over and over in her mind. He was right though; one of those briefcases would be enough to set all of them up for life. If they decided to act on their idea it would be like playing one hand of poker with the Devil…and it was a hand they couldn't afford to lose. As she entered town she was suddenly overcome with another dread feeling. Go home.

She wanted to see her little brother and her mother. She loved them both dearly and prayed that Elmo wasn't there. Glancing down she cursed; she hadn't given her clothing a thought. She wore a pair of batty riders and a T-shirt that showed ever curve of her breasts. Elmo's eyes would be peeling her clothing off before she got two steps into the house. Maybe though, she could make it to her bedroom before anyone saw her, there she could put something a little less revealing on.

Rounding the corner she saw her house, it was getting dark again and she could see lights shining through the windows. Going up to the front door she hesitated, she could always turn around and go back to the shack. It was a long walk one that she wasn't prepared to make right now. She opened the door and stepped in. Her eyes shot around the room casting upon the grinning face of her brother who was always overjoyed to see her.

"Sis!" he said bounding to his feet.

"Hi Ronald," she smiled warmly back giving him a big hug.

"Why don't you come in the kitchen and eat? her mother called from the kitchen.

Sharon walked hesitantly to the kitchen; there she half expected to see Elmo sitting at the table smoking a cigarette while her mother did the dishes.
Instead, only her mother stood by the sink, Elmo was nowhere in sight.

"Hello Mama," she said kissing her cheek.

"Are you hungry?" she asked again.

"Yes, I could definitely nyam some food ," she smiled. "Where's Elmo?"

"Oh he had to go out for the evening, said he wouldn't be back till late," she said grabbing a plate and filling it with food.

"So how is work going?"

"Fine, fine, we just opened so the season hasn't really started yet," she said.

"Any nice boys working there this summer?" her mother asked.

"Oh mama! Why are you so concerned about my love life?" she said picking at her plate of food.

 "Because pumpkin, you look so sad and lonely," Leeann said.

"Yeah, I suppose I am," Sharon said staring at her food.

"What's troubling you? You can't hide it from your mama you know," she asked.

"I really don't want to talk about it," Sharon said softly.

"Is it work?" she asked.

"No"

"What then?" she pushed.

"You're not going to leave me alone on this are you?" Sharon asked looking up at her.

"I wouldn't be your mama if I did," she smiled showing her missing tooth.

"Mama, it's Elmo," she said her eyes falling back to her plate again.

"Why won't you believe me about him?"

"Because you don't like him. You've never liked him, nuh" Leeann stated.

"But Mama, he's tried…" she began to say.

"I don't want to hear those lies!" her mother became stern her eyebrows turning down.

"He provides for us. He keeps your brother in clothes, kept you in them too before you decided to leave for weeks on end."

"Mama, I leave because he tries to touch me," she said feeling a lump grow in her throat.

"Lies, all lies!" Leeann said getting up.

Sharon pushed the plate of food away from her. Getting up she went quickly to her room her tears falling in streams down her cheeks. She didn't know what to do, didn't know what to say to her mother to convince her about Elmo. She also didn't understand why her mother sided with him; he was only her boyfriend, they weren't even married. She was her daughter, her flesh and blood. How could her mother choose him over her?

The thought only made her cry more. She loved her mother, loved her brother but totally hated to come home. The feelings were things she tried to hide.
She wanted to keep them buried deep and just totally forget they existed. She wanted to run, run so far that the world she grew up in would disappear. Slowly she let thoughts of America seep in, they were pleasant thoughts, happy thoughts and she welcomed their peacefulness.

Something caused her to stir, at first she thought she was dreaming but her senses began to scream. Her eyes bolted open. Elmo sat on the edge of her bed, his hand under her shirt gripping firmly onto her bare breast. His other hand came firmly up and clamped over her mouth.

"Now sweetie, don't you say a word, not one word or I'll make sure your little brother has an accident," he whispered.

"Understand?"

All she could do was nod her head. His body was leaning against hers pinning her down, his breath reeked of alcohol and his clothes of cigar smoke. She had forgot to prop a chair under the doorknob before she went to sleep.

"It's been a long time hasn't it sweetie? I've been chasing you for so long, very long. You're breasts are so big and firm. You like the way I feel them don't you?" he breathed leaning closer to her.

Sharon felt fear, so intense, so consuming that it made her stomach wretch. She wanted to puke but she fought the feeling. His hand fondled her right breast, and then moved to her left.

"Now we'll do what we <u>both</u> wanted to do for so long, right?" he said slurring his words.

She then felt his hand slid down her stomach, he grabbed the top of her pants and tugged at the button holding them. Sharon panicked, with all her might she swung her fist up and boxed him hard against the side of his head. Elmo, not ready for the attack reeled back falling off the bed with at thud. Dazed he sat there for a moment then looked up at Sharon his expression full of anger.

"You better be ready to do more of that because when I get to my feet..." he grumbled and rolled onto his hands and knees.

Sharon wasted no time; she bound from the bed, grabbed her shoes and coat and dashed for the door. Fumbling with the handle she was about to open the door when Elmo's huge hand slammed it shut.

"What are you afraid of sweetie, you might like it," he breathed his rancid breath against her.

"Let me go!" she spat.

"Sharon? Is that you honey?" her mother called from down the hall.

"You better not answer her or I'll make sure none of you see tomorrow," Elmo grinned.

"Better keep your mouth shut too sweetie...or you know what will happen," he winked at her then released the door.

Sharon bolted for the front door. She swung it open and dashed out into the night. Elmo walked behind her and closed the door locking it.

"Sharon?" her mother called out again.

"No honey, just me," he called to her then headed to bed.

The night air was humid. Sharon ran as fast as her legs could carry her. She didn't know where she was going, she didn't care the only thing that mattered was putting distance between herself and Elmo. When she finally stopped, she found she was at the beach the waves licking softly against the white sand. Her stomach churned, then she leaned over and heaved. Sobbing she grabbed her shirt and pulled it off, then her shorts slipped down. Moments later she was naked and running for the water. She wanted to clean herself, wash his filthy touch from her body.

Once she was in the water she scrubbed her breasts violently, her sobs echoing out into the night. She felt so violated, so dirty, he had never come so close as he did tonight. She had been careless in leaving her door unlocked, if she hadn't found the courage to hit him.

The thought made her heave again; her anger was now replacing her fear, anger so intense it gave her strength. Walking out of the water she realized that she was totally naked. It was also, a public beach. Glancing in both directions she looked to see if anyone had seen her. The beach was desolate, quiet, only the moonlight bounced off the small waves as they crawled their way in onto the sand.

Casually she walked up and grabbed her clothes. Finding a small spot between two palms she pulled her shorts on and sat down staring at the ocean beyond. Moments later she pulled on her shirt, and then curled up onto her side praying sleep would quickly claim her.

Eve slipped into the tight dress then walked over and stared into the fulllength mirror. The dress was soft velvet, burgundy in color that came to above her knees. Turning from side to side she grinned, then squealed with delight. She felt really bashy. Delicia had been right when she bought the dress for her, it did fit her well. She only hoped Diamond would be as impressed. She had a surprise for him though, reaching up she adjusted her breasts, and without a bra, every movement was magnified. Turning her back to the mirror she bent slightly over and glanced into the mirror wondering if her bare backside would be visible. When she was satisfied, that all her body parts were covered she walked over and slipped her feet into a pair of matching high heels. Delicia was teaching her well.

Then there came a distinct knock on the door. Walking over she opened the door slightly; Delicia stood on the other side.

"Open up," she said without smiling.

"Is everything okay?" Eve took notice of her intense look.

"Fine, fine, you ready to go?" she said.

"Sure am, what do you think?" she said spinning around for her to see.

"Million bucks, you look like a million buck honey," Delicia forced a smile.

"You're dress is better though," Eve said staring at her.

Delicia wore an extremely short dress; the front was halter style and came down in narrow strips in the front barely covering her breasts. Delicia was definitely a skettel.

She wore dark stockings and black heels to match. Her hair was pulled up exposing her neck and shoulders. When she moved Eve could tell she also wasn't wearing anything beneath her dress.

"I told Diamond to meet us at the club," Delicia said.

"Come on or we'll be late."

The limousine pulled in front of one of the top nightclubs Jamaica had to offer. Many locals came to the spot, least those that had money, along with tourists and uptowners looking for a good time. Delicia took Eve by the hand and led her past the huge gruff looking bouncers and the familiar sound of a Reggae band playing loudly inside. Everyone knew who she was and who owned her. She was never asked to pay, nor did any man ever hit on her. They feared whom she represented - feared it with their lives.

The inside of the nightclub was bustling with people; many were on the dance floor while others sat around small tables. Dim lights were strung from one end of the room to the other; small plastic sleeves in the shape of seashells covering the lights. A thick pall of smoke hung in the air and Eve waved her hand repeatedly in front of her face in a frugal attempt to sweep it away. The band played, their tunes reverberating from the four massive speakers at the end of the stage and along the back wall of the nightclub.

The singer seemed oblivious to the crowd, his eyes closed as he weaved passion into his music. Eve was overwhelmed; she had never been to a nightclub before. There was so much activity, so many people and so much happening that she felt small and insignificant.

She suddenly wished she had worn something beneath her dress. Delicia's mannerism changed and moments later she thrust a glass into her hand her grin telling Eve that she was in her environment.

"What's this?" Eve asked staring at the glass.

"Special drink I had made, one that they drink in America," Delicia beamed.

"What is it?" Eve asked holding the drink up.

"It's called a Long Island Ice Tea," she grinned. "You like the taste of tea?" "Very much," Eve said.

"Then try it," Delicia grinned.

Eve took a sip of the drink, then another. It tasted just like ice tea, only with a slight sweetness. She then grinned and nodded to Delicia.

"Where's Diamond?" Eve asked.

"Don't know yet, let's get a table first. I want to talk with you," Delicia said grabbing her hand.

They found a small table in the corner of the nightclub; it was far enough away from the speakers where they didn't have to yell. Sitting down, Eve took a few more sips from her drink then noticed Delicia staring at her.

"Something wrong?" Eve asked.

"No honey, nothings wrong," Delicia grinned.

"How does Sharon like you spending time with me?" Delicia asked.

"She doesn't. You know that. I can't seem to get her to understand how nice you really are. I don't think she likes you Delicia," Eve said taking another sip.

"Jealously, that's all it is, plain jealously," she waved a hand at her.

"What about the others in your small group?"

"Well my brother feels the same way as Sharon does. But he doesn't tell me what to do anymore. It's not like when we were growing up you know," she said.

"Do you remember much of your childhood?" Delicia asked.

"Of course I do, don't you?" she gave her a surprised look.

"Yes, I do too, but what about you? How was your childhood, I know this is something we never talked about," Delicia said with growing interest.

"Well what do you want to know?" Eve said taking another long sip draining half the glass.

"What was your mama like?" she asked, and then motioned to the waiter to bring another drink.

"Mama? She was sweet; she worked so hard, so very hard and gave us as much as she could, at night I used to wait up for her to come home from the resort, it was late you know. Well she knew I was awake, she always knew and she would sit on the side of my bed and sing to me. Her voice was sweet, so very sweet and it put me right to sleep."

"Where is she now? Do you go and see her much?" Delicia asked.

"Mama disappeared many years ago one night when she was coming home from work. We woke the next morning to find her missing. At first, we thought maybe she had to stay and work overnight but when Uncle William came to the door that morning. We both knew something bad had happened." "What did happen?" Delicia prodded.

"I don't know, Babylon never found her and she was listed as a missing person. She just didn't come home," Eve said sadly.

"What about your father?" Delicia asked.

"Never had one, least one that I ever met. Mama never talked about him - never said a word about who he was or what he was like. He had to be handsome, I know that much," Eve grinned.

"Why?"

"Because, Mama was a beautiful woman and handsome men always took a shine to her. I can remember going into town and how she would turn their heads as we walked, or when we went to the beach," she grinned.

"That's how I know."

"So after your mama disappeared...what did you do then?" Delicia asked.

"Well, not long after is when I bumped into Sharon...literally. We became friends right off, she's a good friend too," Eve smiled.

"The others, well our little group slowly grew. We're all orphans you know," Eve pointed out.

"I know, I also know that Sharon is the only one who still has a family," Delicia said.

"Yeah, we all kind of get jealous because she still does. But we have each other, what more family do you need?" Eve smiled.

"What about Jah-Man? When did you meet him?" Delicia asked.

"At the resort, just like everyone else," Eve said.

"What?"

"What about Uncle William?"

"He's not our <u>real</u> Uncle you know. For some reason over the years he's just taken to us, he knew mama from work and she's the one who told us to call him that. He was so friendly and used to take us out to play. I'm glad Mama had at least one good friend," Eve added.

"Drink up," Delicia said as the waiter brought the drink.

"These are real good," she said taking another long swallow.

Delicia could feel that somehow there was a connection. Were Eve and Darrius Jah-Man's children? She quickly dismissed this thought, if they had been she would have known by now. For the years she had been with him, he never mentioned nor took any particular liking to them at the resort, until now. There had to be another connection, something she was overlooking. Still though, Eve was her key to the mystery and she knew the perfect tool to use.

"Come on honey, drink up I'll get you another," Delicia said getting up.

"These are good too, not much booze by the way they taste," Eve said grinning.

"You wait here, I'll get you another," Delicia winked. Long Island Ice Teas were potent drinks, they tasted just like ice tea and went down just as easy as ice tea...but when they hit they would take you right off your feet. Delicia walked up to the bar and ordered another drink for Eve.

Then Delicia spied the person she was looking for at the other end of the bar. Diamond leaned on one arm his face drawn close to another woman with long black hair who smiled at whatever he was saying. Within the next instant, he leaned closer and nuzzled her ear, the woman closing her eyes and smiling more broadly. Diamond was actually a good name for him; he was like a shining jewel something that was irresistible. Women flocked to him taken by his good looks, well kept body, and his reputation for being a <u>stamina daddy</u>. He also had the right equipment, she had seen that personally. His real name though should have been <u>snake or cobra.</u> His flex was cold, calculating and he was a total womanizer.
He was perfect for what she had in mind.

Grabbing the drink, she walked over to the end of the bar next to the woman who sat there completely under his trance. Diamond noticed her and frowned, Delicia smiled and winked at him.

"Who's she?" the woman asked.

"Me? Oh I'm the woman he slept with last night," Delicia grinned.

"Oh honey, our five children would very much like to see their father one of these weeks or months," Delicia said gleefully.

The woman shot him a cold look of surprise, then slipped off the barstool and disappeared quickly into the crowd ever so often glancing back the same shocked look on her face.

"I could have made a huge mass on that one," he said taking a sip of his own drink.

"What do you want Delicia?"

"I have a skank for you," she said losing her smile.

"I sleep with you and I find I don't wake up in the morning," he said coldly.

"I don't want to sleep with you numb skull, but there is someone who I want you to sleep with," she said.

"How much?" he said with ice in his voice.

"We can talk price later. Who and what is more important," she said drawing closer to him.

Eve watched the couple dancing, many looked so happy together. She wondered if someday she would be just as happy. Then thoughts creep into her head, thoughts about her past. Delicia had dug up memories she had wanted to keep buried, memories that caused her much anguish over the years. Glancing down at her tall glass, she noticed it was empty. Then suddenly, another drink was thrust next to her empty glass.

Looking up she saw two Delicia's grinning and two exceptionally handsome Diamond's standing next to her.

"Care to dance?" he said holding out his hand.

"I'd love to!" she beamed getting up.

Delicia watched as a much-hammered Eve walked between the tables to the dance floor. Diamond turned and winked at her his grin showing pure evil. Soon she would have the information she wanted.

Eve felt so carefree in Diamond's strong arms. She loved the man, loved him so deeply that her heart ached. He was so handsome, so strong that his touch filled her with electricity. She had met him last summer at the resort, he appeared out of nowhere and as soon as she saw him, she fell quickly under his spell. At first he didn't notice her, wouldn't even give her the time of day. Then, suddenly, he took a shine to her, talking and making more effort to be around her. When they first kissed, she felt like dying, she wanted to give herself to him then and there, but he wouldn't take her. More than once she had wanted to make love to him but he wouldn't and when she asked why he always avoided the question. She took this as an honorable act; he was saving himself for her, for them.

His hands slipped down along her back until they rested firmly on her buttocks. He then pulled her closer to him until she could feel his excitement for her. His hot breath glided from her shoulder up the length of her neck sending a chill rumbling through her pelvis. She felt like clay in his arm, clay that he could mold in any form he wished. She was also fiercely aroused.

When the band stopped playing they stood there for a moment, maybe longer but she couldn't tell for sure. All she knew is that she wanted the time to last forever.

"Come on, let's go back to the table," he whispered to her.

She said nothing allowing him to lead her back. She felt so lightheaded, the sounds around her magnified to immense proportions. Sitting down she took another long hard swill off the glass draining half of it.

"Go easy honey or you're going to get sick," Delicia laughed. "Can I have another one?" she said giggling.

"Of course you can," Delicia said waving to the waiter.

Diamond sat next to her, his body so close to hers that she could smell his cologne. The smell was arousing and intoxicating and she struggled to keep all her senses from jumbling up. Then she tensed, on her knee she felt his hand his fingers were warm, pleasing, and poignant. Then ever so slowly, ever so lightly they moved up along the inside of her thigh. By the time they reached the bottom of her dress her heart was hammering, her mouth was dry and the room had suddenly become excessively hot.

Delicia watched her and Diamond; she had to admit the man had a way about him. The girl was like a doll in his hands, anything he wanted her to do she would obey. Eve was so innocent, so childish in many ways that what she wanted Diamond to do was almost criminal.

The waiter came, set Eve's drink down, and quickly disappeared again. Eve's hands shook as she grabbed the long tall glass in both hands. Diamonds hand had reached his objective, touching her ever so lightly. Her body tensed as he worked methodically over her. Delicia grinned at her and she didn't understand why. She then realized that her mouth was hanging open.

"Everything okay honey?" Delicia asked.

"F…f…fine," Eve stuttered.

Diamond kept his eyes moving about the crowd as he touched her. He knew he was having the desired affect on her. He could feel her moistness, feel her passion as it built. He had wanted to do this for some time, wanted to take this girl. Only he never wanted the excess baggage that went with it. He wasn't out for a relationship, didn't want a girl on his arm all the time. He wanted to make money using his body, the one thing he had going for him. There were plenty of women who wanted his particular services. They looked for one night of passion and paid handsomely for it too. Some were women he knew from the year before, they had become his regulars.

Eve jerked and pulled the glass to her lips taking a long drink. Her body quaked as he methodically and rhythmically stroked her. Her passion was building, building to the point where she felt like she was going to explode. Never before had she felt like this, paralyzed by a simple touch. She began to perspire and her eyes darting out into the crowded room wondering if anyone noticed - none paid attention. He then quickly withdrew his hand.

"Oh" she burst out.

"Something wrong honey?" Delicia asked.

"Oh…oh…nothing," Eve said trying to regain her composure. "This place is getting stuffy," Diamond said looking around. "Maybe you two should take the limousine and get a bit of fresh air?" Delicia offered.

"What do you think, do you feel like getting out of here?" Diamond asked turning to Eve.

All she could do was nod her head in agreement. The lump hadn't cleared from her throat yet and she realized that she must look like a fool to Delicia. Diamond helped her up guiding her through the crowd to the entrance of the nightclub. She was extremely intoxicated. Once they were outside, Eve took a long breath letting the clean air fill her lungs, all it did though, was make everything move in a blur. Diamond waved his hand for the limousine driver to pick them up. Within moments, they were speeding away from the nightclub.

"Where would you like to go?" he asked her.

"Anywhere you'd like," she smiled cooing softly to him.

Grabbing the telephone, he picked it up, as did the driver.

"Bring us back to the resort," he said then hung the receiver up.

His arm was tightly wrapped around her as he guided her into the elevator and up to Delicia's room. Reaching into his pocket, he withdrew the key and opened the door. As soon as the door closed, Eve turned to him and in a frenzy of passion; they began tearing at each other's clothing. Diamond led her to the bed where he pulled her heels off, for a moment he stared at her naked body, the nipples taunt, the wanton look of desire in her eyes. It was stimulating, exciting him tremendously as he climbed onto the bed with her.

Eve felt him press against her, felt his lips hungrily grope at her breasts. She wanted this man, wanted him so incredibly much. She was also scared, this was not how she expected her first time would be. She expected it to be slow and tender, not rough and frenzied.

"Please, go slow," she breathed to him.

"Is this your first time?" he asked as he pushed against her.

"Yes" she said softly.

"My first."

Her words only filled him with more lust, he had very few virgins in his time and this one he would make the most of, he might, he thought even give Delicia her money back.

Sharon awoke then sputtered and spit the sand from the side of her mouth. The sun was bright yet no one had ventured down to the beach yet. Wiping the sand from the side of her face, she sat up and again stared at the ocean beyond. Her body was sore and she was tired. Sleeping out on the beach was not a very smart way to get a good nights rest. Hauling herself to her feet she walked casually back to her house. Again, she hesitated, and then reluctantly entered through the kitchen door. Her mother was busy making breakfast while Ronald and Elmo sat at the table. Ronald gave her a beaming smile, he was always overjoyed to see her, but Elmo gave her an intense stare one that cut right through her.

"Are you going to stay for breakfast?" her mother asked as she continued to cut open a melon.

"No, I have to be at work soon, I'm just going to grab some things and going," she said softly.

"You really should eat honey, I don't think you take very good care of yourself," Leeann said with concern.

"Yes, maybe you should stay around here more often," Elmo added his voice deep and stern.

"I have to be at work soon," Sharon said quickly moving through the kitchen and down the hallway to her room.

As soon as she entered her room, she quickly shut the door and shoved a chair under the handle. She felt so humiliated, so violated from the night before. She also feared Elmo, feared not what he would do to her but for her mother and little brother. They meant so much to her, so very much. Slipping out of her clothes, she quickly changed then pulled the chair out and headed back to the kitchen.

"Are you going to be home for dinner tonight?" her mother asked.

"No mama, not for a few nights," she said quickly heading for the door.

As soon as she closed it behind her, she leaned heavily against the wall. Just being in the same room as him drained her of energy. She could feel his eyes undressing her; feel his hot rancid breath against her neck.

Forcing herself away from the house, she tried to think of something else that would take the darkness from her life.

Steven, he was the one thing that could do that. The thought of him brought her spirits up, gave her hope and brought a smile to her face. He made her feel as though all fruits were ripe. Then she thought about Eve, worried about her was more the right word. She wondered how the evening went, how Delicia had corrupted her and how much she changed in the short time since she last saw her. That would be her first stop when she got to the resort, she would check on Eve. As she walked along the street more than one car full of men offered to give her a ride, she shooed them away. Her mind also began to wander, the previous night she had toyed with Ohpton's idea. It was exciting and dangerous. But he was right, it would change all their lives, change it together. It was a foolish idea; one that might get one or more of them killed. Jah-Man was well known for his temper. Any person who wanted to live knew better than to cross Jah-Man.

Guests busied about, going to the dining hall for breakfast or were already on the tennis courts and bicycles. When she got to the salon, it was already open and two guests were already being worked on.

"Glad to see you could make it," one of the girls called to her, a frown on her face.

"Sorry, it was a miserable night," Sharon said not wanting to remember. "Who's ready for me?"

"Mrs. Gillmore is waiting for a permanent, and you have two more scheduled for this morning," the other girl said as she worked.

Sharon went into the waiting room and smiled she escorted Mrs. Gillmore to the only open chair. She wanted to go find Eve, but now she would have to wait until at least mid morning.

Steven tossed his towel down on one of the paddleboats; it was going to be another long hot day. Crowds were already beginning to form on the beaches. Sitting out on the water were two big-wheeled paddleboats already moving about. Glancing at his watch, it was after nine and his first lesson hadn't arrived yet. It was going to be one of those days.

"Well it's about time you arrived," Delicia said walking up to him.

Steven turned his eyes going from her stern face to her scantily clad body. The bathing suit she wore had tiny patches that just covered her nipples; the bottoms were high cut forming a thong in the rear. Still though, she wore a mass of cargo around her neck and along both her wrists and ankles.

"What do you want?" he said forcing his eyes away from her.

"My lesson," she smiled.

"I signed up for sailing lessons and personally requested you," she beamed.

Steven frowned; he didn't need this right now. His day he was confident, was going to be a disaster. Now, he was positive of it.

"Well?" she demanded.

Steven nodded then motioned for her to follow. He led her down the beach to one of the resorts many catamarans. There were small 14 footers with two narrow hulls and a very comfortable trampoline deck between. They were fast in light air and would scream when the wind began to blow. He began the lesson, telling her what the parts were, what they did and how to control them. He couldn't help but stare at her body, it was perfect in every sense and it took all his willpower to keep things focused on the lesson.

"Enough with the lesson, just take me for a sail," she demanded.

Steven glanced along the beach; he then spotted another woman strolling along the white sand. Waving, he attracted her attention and she walked up to him.

"I'm taking this young lady out on a sail, would you like to join us for an hour?" he asked praying.

"I'd love to," the woman grinned.

"This is a private lesson," Delicia scowled.

"If you just want me to take you for a sail, then this isn't a lesson," Steven pointed out.

"Am I getting between something here?" the woman asked.

"No, not at all," Steven said.

"Please climb aboard and I'll push us out."

Delicia presented one of her looks of sheer anger. Steven tried not to look at her and focused his attention on the boat. There was no way he was going to take Delicia out on a sail by himself, she could make up any story to tell Jah-Man, then his life would be worthless.

From the balcony, Jah-Man watched Steven push the boat out into the water. He was beginning to feel rage until the other woman joined them.

Snapping his fingers, a man quickly came to his side.

"Yes sir," the man asked.

"See that man taking that boat out?" he pointed to the beach.

"Find out all you can about him."

"Yes sir," the man said and quickly departed.

Just then the telephone rang; it rang three times before another man picked it up. Moments later he handed the receiver to Jah-Man.

"Yush?" he spoke.

"As a preliminary trial, we would like to acquire two tons of material. If all goes well then we can talk about a much larger shipment," a definite female voice spoke on the other end of the line.

"Where and when?" he asked.

"Let's say day after tomorrow – 11 p.m.?" the woman asked.

"I will also be coming to stay at the resort, to watch your operation more closely."

"Please come, I will entertain you in the ways of Jamaica," he said his voice almost seductive.

"Good, I will arrive later today and make the arrangements," she said then abruptly hung up. He then motioned to the man who brought the telephone to him.

"A guest will be arriving later today, make sure Delicia stays in her room here at the resort, tell her to entertain herself until I call for her."

The man nodded taking the telephone and disappeared into the next room. Jah-Man again raised his binoculars and stared as the boat danced across the water. Delicia was a beautiful woman, but she was only a woman. Business came first and she would have to wait, and if he found out that she was sleeping with the man sailing the boat, he would have him killed before her eyes as an example. Then, abruptly, another thought entered his mind. Walking quickly from the balcony, he grabbed the telephone off the stand and dialed the desk.

"Yes, I would like you to send Darrius Lawson to my room as soon as he arrives," he ordered.

Darrius checked to make sure his tie was straight then slipped behind the counter of the front desk. No sooner had he done this than his partner handed him a piece of paper. Reading it, his early morning optimistic attitude quickly faded, crumpling the paper he slipped from behind the desk and into the elevator.

Two guards stood outside the door automatic weapons in hand. They eyed him as he approached the door. Saying nothing one of the men opened it allowing him into the room then quickly closed the door behind him. Darrius looked around, he had never been in Jah-Man's personal room, it was plush beyond belief with every convenience he could imagine. Everything was so cris. The room reeked money. He even wondered if the mattress or cushions on the couch were stuffed with money. His gaze then fell on Jah-Man sitting out on the veranda. His first impulse was to grab the tiny man and haul him over the edge leaving him to drop twelve stories to the concrete below. Instead, he walked up saying nothing. Jah-Man smiled warmly as Darrius walked through the sliding glass doors.

"Please, come and sit down. Have you eaten breakfast this morning?" JahMan said warmly.

"No, I'm not hungry thank you," Darrius said.

"You are still a growing man, you need to keep your strength up." JahMan said trying to coax him into eating.

"I have no appetite - thank you," Darrius said again only more sternly.

"Suit yourself, suit yourself," Jah-Man said.

"Why have you called for me?" Darrius said becoming bolder.

"First off I said for you to sit!" Jah-Man said his own voice raising.

Darrius could see the warmth the man portrayed suddenly vanish. Pulling out the chair, he sat down trying not to act so obedient. As soon as he did though, the warm glow came quickly back to Jah-Man's face.

"That is better, now I have a <u>bly</u> for you. A very important job, I have a client that will be arriving later today. She is to be wined and dined, no expense spared. I want you to provide for her <u>anything</u> she wants, I mean <u>anything</u>!" he said with force.

"But sir, what about my job responsibilities?" Darrius said trying to figure a way out.

"I will have you temporarily removed from you responsibilities. I can not stress to you enough how important this client is."

"If this client is so important why don't you wine and dine her?" Darrius blurted out.

"Because I have other responsibilities that need to be carried out," he stated.

"I like you Darrius, you have a keen eye and a good head on your shoulders. I don't think I made a mistake asking you." "What about expenses?" Darrius asked.

"No expense spared. Take her around and show her everything but no matter what, make sure she has a good time." He ordered.

"Here," he said throwing manila envelope down in front of him.

Darrius picked up the envelope and sheered off its outer layer. Inside he found two large stacks of money. Quickly he shot a look at Jah-Man who took particular notice.

"Wine and dine her is that understood?" he asked.

Darrius said nothing and quickly left the room. As soon as he did, he sighed heavily and stared at the bundle of money in the envelope.

There was enough there to pay half of their tickets to the United States. He came to another realization also, if Jah-Man had enough money to toss about and waste, then taking one of his briefcases would be easy enough.

Chapter 6

The little bell on the door dinged as it opened. Two small <u>schoolers</u>, a girl and boy ran up to a small counter. Sitting next to it was an old wooden box; they both knew exactly what to do. Raising their little legs they climbed up onto the box. It was there to provide them enough height to peer into the glass container; smiles quickly broadened their face. Behind the glass were rows and rows of shapes and colorful candy. Most were handmade, but many had been specially shipped in. The little boy grinned at his sister who smiled showing her missing front teeth.

"I know what I'm gonna get!" the boy beamed.

"Me too!" the little girl squealed.

In the back of the room was a doorway leading to the rest of the house. A thick heavy curtain hung down instead of a door. A wrinkled old hand pushed the curtain to the side. It hovered there for nearly a minute as the person watched the children gazing with satisfaction at the candy. Mama Rose emerged beaming a youthful grin. She loved them, loved them all within the community and anywhere else. She was in her twilight years, her short hair a mix of gray and black, but mostly gray. She was an adorable mampi and moved across the room with much labor, mostly though, due to her arthritic joints. When she got to the counter she looked over and smiled down upon the children.

"Hi Mama Rose!" the little girl gleamed at her.

"Hello Devilia, I think you've grown a few inches since the last time I saw you!"

Mama Rose shined causing her face to wrinkle more.

"A few more weeks and you'll be catching up to your brother Delvin!" "She'll never be as tall as me!" he teased.

"Yes I will! Mama Rose says so!" Devilia said poking at her brother.

"So, what would you children like today?" Mama Rose asked grabbing a small paper bag and opening it.

The children pointed to what they wanted and she filled the bag with candy. The boy put his <u>mass</u> on the counter, a few hard-earned cents from doing chores either at home or for other people. The little girl put what she had, though it was considerably less.

"That's not enough Sis," the boy pointed out.

The little girl looked at her brother, the money on the counter, then to Mama Rose, the warm sweet smile she had quickly falling.

"I think it's just the right amount," Mama Rose beamed handing the bag to the little girl who again responded with a loveable smile.

"Thank you, Mama Rose!" the little girl said hopping off the box, the boy quickly following.

"Don't eat all that at once or it will spoil your dinner," she called to them as they dashed from her little candy shop.

As she watched them run and play she felt a surge of youthful vigor rush through her. She loved them all so, the innocent expressions untouched by the harsh world they lived in. Life to them was playtime; every day was new and refreshing. It had been that way for her once too, though life had decided to deal her a bad set of cards. It was times like these, watching other children, that she missed her own. She had two sons, one who just turned 20 and a younger boy who <u>would have</u> been 16. Jaco had been a good boy; he never disappointed her and went out of his way to help around the little candy shop she ran. He had dreams, dreams of one day going to America and becoming a doctor or lawyer. He was always cheery; smiling and never letting their poverty get him down.

His older brother, nicknamed Junior, was cynical and a <u>nasty naayga</u>. He had a deep involvement in the drug business that dominated the island. He always treated the others in the community badly, looking down on them because he had money and he was full of <u>badness</u>. It was one night; Junior had to make a drug run. He had to pick up a shipment down on the beach and had asked Jaco for his help. At first Jaco was reluctant to help. His sense of right and wrong told him what his brother did was wrong, but, being the kind, caring person he was, he agreed to help. The drug run went bad, someone pulled a gun and bullets flew. After the carnage ended Junior went looking for his brother, he found him floating face down in the surf, his body riddled with bullets.

From that day on, Mama Rose blamed Junior for Jaco's death. She grieved every day for the loss of her son, and every day her relationship with Junior became worse. Junior also became colder, arguing with his mother over the most trivial of things.

He had lost his ability to care for anyone, least anyone within the small poverty stricken community. All he cared about was his money and his personal possessions. One day he had even tried to give her money, lots of money to show that he still cared. She became enraged like he had never seen her before and threw the money back in his face screaming that it was <u>blood money</u>.

Mama Rose walked slowly back through the curtain to her small kitchen where she sat down and continued to drink her herbal tea. She had to keep active, had to think about other things. If she let herself relax then her mind would open the door to all the hurt she felt, all the pain she tried desperately to keep hidden, the failure she was as a mother.

"The children, have to keep thinking about the children," she mused to herself.

Suddenly she heard, the door opened again the little bell dinging. Setting her cup down she laboriously got up and walked back out into the next room. She half hoped that another group of children would be standing there grinning, waiting for the tasty delights she kept within the glass box. Instead, Junior stood there. He was a short man, with short hair and an even shorter temper. He was lanky, thin, wiry, and of average looks. For a moment he stood there staring at her as if he expected her to say something, then he remembered that it was he, who had entered the shop.

"Hello Mama," he said softly.

"Hello Junior," Mama Rose said softly, then turned and headed back into the kitchen leaving Junior standing by the door.

For a moment he watched her walk stiffly out of the room, then he followed. By the time he parted the curtain she was again sitting at the table drinking her tea.

"What is it you want?" she said not looking at him.

"Mama I've come to talk with you," he said pulling out another chair, reversing it, then sat down.

"What do we have to discuss?" she said.

"Haven't we talked enough? Hasn't there been enough pain?" "I am worried Mama, worried about you," he said softly.

"You need not worry about me, I've been around far longer than you have," she said.

"But Mama, you are getting old, you have trouble moving about," he said.

"I do just fine," she said.

"No, you don't. Look how slow you moved just getting from the other room to here!" he pointed out.

"You have to start facing reality Mama."

"What? The same reality you face?" she shot back to him.

"At least I am looking out for my future. I will have enough money to take care of me when I get old," he stated.

"Just as you took care Jaco?" she said with a jab.

"Mama…"

"Will all your money, all your blood money bring him back?" she snarled.

"No. It won't bring him back or stop what happened and I can't change that. But I can help you if you'll let me," he said.

"With your blood money? How many others have to die before you realize that what you are doing is wrong?" she frowned.

"I do what I have to in order to survive," he said his voice raising.

"And at what cost Junior, what cost?"

"I am not ashamed of what I am or what I do! If you want to live like - like this!" he spat pointing to her dingy surroundings.

"Then you go right ahead and live like this," he spat getting up.

He kicked the chair away; it slid across the floor tipping over with a crash. When he reached the doorway, he hesitated his hand lightly touching the curtain. Mama Rose stared down at her tea; she could hear a ringing in her ears. Her blood pressure was up.

"When will you stop blaming me for Jaco's death? When and how can I ever redeem myself to you?" Junior said softly.

"When you grow up Junior and do the right thing. When you stop hurting people," she said bluntly.

"I do what I must," he said.

"If that is the case Junior, then never - never,"

He continued out through the curtain and headed for the door. If he had stayed, if he had looked back at his mama's face, he would have seen the wetness on her cheeks and the pain in her eyes. Mama Rose wiped the tears away. She had shed enough tears over the years, more than any mother should have. Yes, she had been dealt a terrible hand of cards, a terrible one indeed.

Junior walked quickly down the street oblivious to everything around him. He hated going to see his mother, hated the way she put Jaco above him, even after he was dead. She never understood that he loved his brother also and when Jaco died, he hurt too. However, deep down he was also glad. Jaco always received the best of everything. In his Mama's eyes, he was always the best, the do-gooder. Stopping, he leaned heavily against the side of a house. Guilt washed over him, guilt so intense that he quickly felt sick to his stomach. The feeling quickly passed, he couldn't afford to harbor feelings like guilt - it was beneath him. He didn't hear the wheels, but a small rusty compact car pulled up. There were dents all over it and the windows were smudged and dirty. Junior looked at it for a moment as if trying to remember where he had seen it before. The side window rolled down, an intense and very ugly man looked out. His nose was bulbous with deep pot marks, a scar ran the length of his face as if the man had been flayed open by a machete. Strangely though, his eyes were very deep blue, something Junior couldn't stop staring at. It looked so unnatural.

"Get in," the man said in a husky voice.

At first Junior hesitated, and then walked around to the side of the car sliding into the passenger seat. The man was tall and muscular his arms showing many scars. Staring at him he wondered how the man had even managed to get into the car. He dwarfed the seat, the steering wheel looking tiny before him.

Before the door even closed, the man sped the car off down the road. The vehicle turned up clouds of dust creating a brown cloud behind it. Junior looked at the man whose attention was directed to keep the tiny vehicle on the road. It was as if he hadn't even gotten into the car.

"What do you want?" he said to the man.

The man said nothing as he turned the car off onto another road that seemed more like a trail. Vegetation beat in through the windows causing Junior to move closer to the man, who didn't budge. Finally the car broke out into a clearing, a white and desolate sandy beach sat in the distance, beyond that was the clear aqua marine blue of the ocean. Junior's eyes locked onto something else though, sitting nearly 300 yards off the beach was a huge white yacht. The rear of the yacht was open, a large swim platform jutting out. There were people onboard, but they were too far away to make out any details or features.

The husky man turned the car onto the pointed blades of grass heading for the edge where it dropped off onto the beach. When he finally stopped, he shut the car off pocketing the keys, then looked over at him with a mean expression.

"Get out."

Junior obeyed the man, partly because he was curious, mostly because of fear. He watched the man get out of the car, when he did; he towered over it like a huge golem. Then suddenly, he reached inside the car and pressed on the horn. The noise it made was sickening. It howled with a high pitch and a load of crackling noises. It was most irritating.

"What's this all about?" Junior again questioned the husky man.

He said nothing and just stared out at the yacht his arms folded, waiting.

"Look, either tell me what you people want, who you people are, or I'm walking," Junior said gaining some courage.

"You move and I will kill you," the man said not looking at him.

Junior winced at what the man said; something was going on, something that gave him chills. Then another sound reached his ears drawing his attention back to the yacht. A small rubber inflatable skimmed across the water toward the beach. Two men sat on either side. Moments later they slid up onto the beach.

"Move" the man growled.

Junior walked down the steep slope to the beach. He looked over his shoulder half expecting the man to be following close; instead, he remained next to the car his arms still folded, his stare unwavering. The two men remained in the raft. They were both stern looking with deep dark skin and both wore darkers hiding their eyes. When he reached the raft, he stopped and glanced back looking for the man. He was gone.

"Get in" one of the men said.

Moments later the raft was heading back to the yacht. Junior felt his blood run cold. What was going on? Who were these people? What did they want with him?

Round and round ideas flooded into his mind, most of them causing him to be fearfully terrified. As they approached the back of the yacht, he could see two more men standing on the swim platform waiting. Seconds later one of the men in the raft tossed out a line to a man on the platform. The rafts outboard motor ceased. As the raft was being tied up, something else caught his attention.

Emerging from the water was a woman; she climbed the swim ladder and stepped up onto the platform.

Junior's breath was instantly taken away. The woman was completely nude; water droplets cascaded down her supple form. Taking both hands, she swept her long hair from her face, then turned and looked directly at him smiling.

"Get on board," one of the men barked at him drawing his attention back.

Junior stepped out of the raft and onto the swim platform next to where the girl stood. He couldn't take his eyes from her; she was beautiful her body perfect like it had been sculpted from a mold.

A gentle shove from behind turned his attention back to the matter at hand. He stepped onto the transom of the yacht and was met by another man who motioned him towards the two large doors going into the cabin. His attention was draw quickly away though, other women, all nude, were scattered about either lying in the sun or going about some chore. All were exotic and beautiful and none seemed to mind his staring. He was beginning to think things were okay when he entered the cabin and came face to face with another man.

The man was white with thick graying hair, at least in his fifties. He wore a loose fitting shirt with the front open displaying his well-groomed body and the mass of cargo hanging from his neck. His face was stern, sharp cut with a nose that looked more like a beak. His eyes were dark, almost black, giving him a look of a man without a soul. Junior was instantly chilled by his stare.

"Come in, please sit down," the man said with a thick French accent. "Would you care for a drink?"

"I…huh…sure…whiskey?" Junior said softly.

The man snapped his fingers, a pale naked redhead bounded off the couch and over to the bar where she began to get his drink. Junior stared at her; actually, he stared at her overly large breasts.

"Please be seated," the Frenchman motioned to him.

Junior sat down in the nearest chair, his eyes darting around the room staring at the half naked women and because he expected a knife to come out of nowhere. The redhead came up next to him handing him his glass of whiskey and a napkin. She smiled warmly as he took it then resumed her position on the couch. None of the women said a word.

The Frenchman fixed himself a drink then walked over and sat next to the redhead his hand reaching out stroking her long supple leg. Taking a sip of his drink, he turned his attention to Junior.

"They are beautiful are they not?" he said bringing his hand up and lightly touching the woman's breast. She smiled giggling softly.

"Yes, yes they are, all of them," Junior said taking a swill from his drink.

"Do you know who I am?" the Frenchman asked.

Junior just shook his head his eyes going from the Frenchman to the redhead.

"My name is unimportant, you will not need to know it. What you do need to know is that I am a supplier," he said.

"A supplier?" Junior said playing stupid.

"Do not insult me," the Frenchman spat.

"You work for Jah-Man do you not?"

"I do not know what you are talking about," Junior tried to lie.

"We are not the police Junior, you are not in trouble," the man said giving him a ghostly smile.

"Than why am I here?" Junior asked.

"Because we want to make you an offer," the Frenchman said leaning closer to him.

"An offer?" Junior looked dumbfounded.

"Yes, dolt an offer. We know that Jah-Man has agreed to an order to Cuba through a new supplier. We also know that this order is a big one - a really big shipment. What we want is this; you are employed by Jah-Man and have information to his shipments and material. We need to know where this shipment is being stored and when it's going to move," the Frenchman said jiggling the ice in his glass.

"Are you Babylon?" Junior gasped.

"No, I said we are just competitors, nothing more," he said continuing to spin the liquid.

"Why?" Junior blurted out.

"Simple, we would like Jah-Man to be dealing with us and not them," the man said.

"Then why do you not just ask him?" Junior asked.

"We have, but it would seem that someone else made him a better offer," the Frenchman said glancing at the redhead who grinned back.

"So? Go after the competition then?" Junior said as if nobody else had the brains to come up with the idea.

"That is pointless, we could eliminate the competition, but there would be others there always are. No, we want to show Jah-Man that dealing with me is the only choice he has."

"What you ask is much. No one betrays Jah-Man and lives," Junior blurted out.

"Why do you people look at him as thought he is God? He is just a man like every other man, nothing more," the Frenchman frowned.

"Jah-Man is a living God. He is very powerful" Junior pointed out.

"He is but a man, flesh, blood, and nothing more," the Frenchman became irritated.

"We are prepared to compensate you very…very well." "How well?" Junior's ears

picked up.

"Let us say, 10% of what the shipment is?" the Frenchman grinned.

"That would make you a very, very wealthy man."

Junior didn't skip a breath; he coldly looked at the Frenchman.

"50%"

"50%, you're mad!" the Frenchman scoffed.

"I will go as high as 25%, no more. Take it or <u>leave it,"</u> the Frenchman laughed.

"I will accept your proposal," Junior said extending his hand.

The Frenchman never even noticed. He turned his attention back to the redhead his fingers rubbing over her swollen nipple. He did that for nearly a minute before turning his gaze back towards Junior.

"Do not, do not think of double crossing us. We will find out. We know you can not hide from us, wherever you go we will be close behind."

Junior nodded his head in acceptance. His blood was cold at the prospect of betraying Jah-Man. If he told him about the Frenchman, he most likely wouldn't believe him. In addition, 25% of a whole shipment would end up as a massive amount of money. Money that would enable him to buy anything, go anywhere. That was of course if he lived.

"Now, now that we have that settled I have a little surprise for you," he said breaking away from the redhead.

Getting up he ushered Junior out of his chair. He followed the Frenchman down a long narrow corridor to one of the staterooms.

"This is a little token of our appreciation. We know how difficult is to make the choice," he said motioning with his hand to the stateroom door.

"Enjoy!" he muse then walked back down the hallway.

Junior watched the Frenchman disappear, then reached out and opened the door. Instantly his eyes locked on the bed. Lying sprawled out naked was the girl he had seen on the swim platform earlier. Slowly she shifted, exposing herself more, and then licked her lips seductively. Junior grinned, entered the stateroom and closed the door. Maybe betrayal wasn't so bad after all.

Jah-Man sat in the air-conditioned limousine. The noonday sun had gotten excessively hot, hotter than he liked. Inside the limousine, it was a cool 75 degrees, and he thought of making it colder still. Staring out the tinted glass windows he watched as a twin engine Comanche aircraft dipped down out of the sky. The tail portion tilted to the side and the wheels finally touched the pavement. The pilots reversed the engines while applying the brakes to stop the aircraft. The Comanche was one of only a few airplanes that could land on a short runway. All large aircraft could only use Jamaica's two major airfields. The propellers began to slow until they finally came to rest. Then the side door opened, dropping down into a set of stairs for the passengers to disembark.

At first two men stepped off then another couple that looked like honeymooners. Finally, a lone woman emerged. She was short with long jet-black hair, her complexion was pale, and her body was small. She was obviously Oriental, possibly Japanese, Korean, or maybe even Chinese. She wore a pair of tan slacks with a black silk top tucked into them. The cut of her shirt revealed the well-rounded shape of her breasts. She also wore tiny-mirrored darkers hiding her eyes. In her hand was a small suitcase, which she carried with ease.

The limousine driver got out and walked over offering to take her bag, she refused opting to keep it close to her side. He led her back to the limousine where he opened the back door for her.

Jah-Man scowled as the hot humid air rushed in, sucking the cool air conditioning out. The woman stepped in and the driver closed the door behind her. After she seated herself, she turned her attention to Jah-Man.

"The pre-shipment will arrive tonight," she spoke with a soft seductive tone.

"What time and where?" he asked not introducing himself.

"Midnight, down at the docks," she said.

"The docks? Is that not a ridiculous place to ship drugs out from?" he grinned.

"Maybe for you it is, but for us it doesn't make a difference, dockworkers can be bought just as anyone else can," she pointed out.

"Your bosses take many risks, risks that are not necessary," Jah-Man stated.

"We run a business, nothing more. Are you incapable of working under those conditions?" she asked.

"No I am not, I have learned over the many years of trade that it is best to keep a low profile in regards to shipping. We are much closer to the Americans than the Columbians are," he pointed out.

"The Colombians are weak fools, are you Jah-Man?" she said with a bite.

For a moment Jah-Man's temper flared, he wanted to box her hard across the face for her remark. Instead, he smiled warmly but never took his eyes off her.

"In consideration for our business dealings, I will forget that remark and allow you to live. Please remove your glasses so that I may see your eyes, they will tell me how truthful a messenger your bosses have sent," he said his voice grating.

The woman did nothing at first then reluctantly she reached up and withdrew the glasses. The woman had pale ice blue eyes with long dark lashes. They were cold eyes, determined eyes. This was the first woman whose stare gave him a chill. They also told him she was telling him the truth.

"What is your name?" he asked.

"You can call me Yashi," she said.

"A determined name with much honor," he smiled at her.

She didn't smile back.

When they arrived at the resort Jah-Man escorted her inside. The place was full of tourists who went about minding their own business. Jah-Man went up to the lobby desk. Darrius had seen them come in, seen the woman that he was suppose to entertain. She was beautiful, but anything even remotely associated with Jah-Man was dangerous. He still hated Jah-Man, hated him more because for some reason he had shown interest in him. He felt coddled by a killer.

"Miss Yashi, I will leave you with an escort for the day. I have much I need to attend to. He will show you to your room and escort you anywhere you wish to go," Jah-Man said politely.

"It's Ms. Yashi and I expected to be following you around," she said sliding her mirrored glasses to the end of her nose.

"As I said, I have other engagements. We will meet later this evening when the time is appropriate," he said not smiling, then abruptly turned and walked away.

The woman watched him walk through the doors; she then turned her attention back to Darrius.

"Well?" she said with a bite.

Darrius fumbled with her room key then slipped from behind the counter. He ushered her to the elevator and finally to her room.

"I hope you find things to your liking," he said politely.

Yashi tossed her bag onto the small couch and looked around the room. It was one of the resorts suites; the view of the ocean beyond was spectacular. She went to each room, looking inside before finally coming back to where Darrius was.

"It'll do," she breathed.

"Now go away," she said making a shooing motion with her hand.

"Huh, excuse me. I was asked to escort you, to show you around," he said feeling a lump form in his throat.

"You have to show me nothing, go away little boy," she scoffed nearly ignoring him.

"I...huh...Jah-Man will be very disappointed with me if I do not," he explained.

"So?" she said opening her small bag.

"People around these parts do not disappoint him if you know what I mean," he said.

"Why should I care?" she said.

"Well, maybe my life doesn't mean much to you but it does to me," he said with a bite.

"I don't particularly like you." "Feeling is mutual," she said.

"What is it with all you whacked out criminals?" he blurted out.

"Criminals? Criminals?" she said turning to him the rage clear on her face. "How dare you call me a criminal! We are business people and nothing more." She snapped walking swiftly over to him.

"Dealing drugs isn't criminal?" he stood his ground.

Yashi hesitated, then turned and went back to her bag.

"Maybe it is," she said softly.

"Look, I'll allow you to show me around and take me where I want to go okay?"

"Sure, fine by me," Darrius replied.

"Now let me go change into something cooler," she said grabbing some clothing and heading for the bedroom.

It was nearly noontime when Sharon managed to break free from the salon. She was so tired and sore from sleeping on the ground that every move was an effort, yet she quickly rushed down the long hallway towards the Boutique where Eve worked.

Customers milled about, pulling clothing off the racks and holding it at arms length or close to their bodies. Moving between the isles she went to the register in the middle of the store. Tisha was taking the money from a customer, she looked tired, a flock of her long flowing dark hair hanging limply along her cheek.

"Tisha, where is Eve?" Sharon blurted out, watching the couple walk away.

"Good question, she never came in today for work. I've been here by myself and I have to go to the bathroom," she sighed.

"Really not like her."

"Call the Salon if she happens to come in okay?" Sharon said as she turned racing from the boutique.

Standing in the hallway, she wondered where Eve could be. There was only one person to check with - Delicia. She went quickly to the nearest elevator and pressed the button for the top floor, that was where Jah-Man had bought Delicia a room. Moments later she stood on the other side of the door. Knocking with her hand she waited, nothing, she knocked again. Standing there she listened, she heard nothing. She was about to turn and leave when she heard someone cough. She again knocked on the door, though this time it sounded more like she was pounding.

"Eve? Eve are you in there?" she called out.

Moments later the door opened, Eve stood in a red silk bathrobe. The front was open slightly and she could see that she wore nothing beneath it. She could also see that she had been crying. Backing up into the room, she allowed Sharon to step inside.

"Eve, what happened?" Sharon asked worried.

"Oh nothing," she said as tears began to fall from her puffy eyes.

"Come on Eve, you and I are best friends. If you can't talk to me then who can you talk to?" Sharon pointed out.

"You are a good friend aren't you?" she said trying to force a smile.

"Yes. So what happened? What has Delicia done to you?" "Delicia? Delicia has done nothing. Diamond…" she began to say.

"What! What has he done to you?" Sharon yelled feeling her anger swell.

Eve cradled her head in her hands and began to weep uncontrollably. Sharon reached out and gently put a hand on her shoulder.

"I...I gave him everything," she said gasping between sobs.

"What has he done to you Eve. Did he, did he rape you?" she said the words tender and biting even to herself as she remembered Elmo's advances.

"No! No, I gave myself to him freely - totally. We made love all night long. I have never felt such ecstasy it was incredible!" she exclaimed.

"Oh God," Sharon thought to herself.

"What has she done now?"

As if on cue, Eve began wailing again her grief overtaking her. Sharon quickly went into the bathroom and cold soaked a washcloth bringing it back to Eve.

"Here, put this on your eyes, it will help reduce the puffing. Here's some tissues too," she said grabbing the box off the coffee table.

"If you liked it, then why the tears?"

"Liked it, liked it? I loved it!" she yelled.

"But this morning he got up, dressed then told me told me that he didn't want to see me anymore!" she said as tears fell repeatedly.

"I love him Sharon. I love him so much!"

Sharon had the urge to point out to Eve that she and the others had told her to avoid Diamond. Instead, she just reached out and cradled Eve in her arms letting her sob the hurt away.

The catamaran bounded once, then twice as it rode the surf onto the beach. Steven guided the sailboat up onto the sand of a small and very secluded beach up the coast from the resort. It was a common spot he brought couples that wanted to sail, but just go along for the ride. More often than not, he would spend hours on the beach by himself while the tourists would follow his directions and hike into the woods a short ways to a waterfall. Even on the beach he could hear them making love, sound traveled in open areas, reverberating, magnified by the water and leaves. This time though, he had brought Delicia and another woman, Janelle.

After he pulled the boat a little way up onto the beach, the two girls slipped off the sides. Janelle was a much older woman; at least in her mid 30's, she wore a one piece and very conservative bathing suit. Her long blond hair was tied up with a wooden holder keeping it in place. She was intrigued by his description of the waterfall and wanted to see it. He volunteered to take her, he needed to take her, cause he had no desire to be left alone with Delicia.

"Come on, it is only a short way from here," he motioned to Janelle.

"Why don't you let her go on her own? I'm sure you and I could find something to do," Delicia said seductively.

"Are you two sure I'm not intruding on anything here?" Janelle said looking first to Delicia then Steven.

"No, you're not!" Steven blurted out.

"She already has a boyfriend, a very powerful boyfriend."

"Oh really?" Janelle asked looking at Delicia who now looked embarrassed.

"Yes I do," she said with a tone like she had been whipped.

"But he doesn't control my life," she added with defiance.

"Yeah, well he scares the hell out of mine!" Steven said, then turned and pushed away the fronds as he entered the trail.

"Well, whatever floats your boat!" Janelle shrugged as she followed, Delicia closely behind.

Steven stayed quite a ways ahead; he had no desire to continue the conversation. He knew his job was to entertain the guests, but Delicia's type of entertainment was going to get him killed or worse.

"He is extremely cute isn't he?" Janelle whispered to Delicia.

"More than cute. Look at the way he fills out those shorts," she replied.

"So what's the scoop with this other guy?" Janelle asked.

"He's the most powerful man on the island," she sighed.

"I love him but in a different way," she said.

"Older huh?" Janelle breathed.

"Yeah, nearly 19 years." she said.

"My I guess that's older!" Janelle said with surprise.

"Don't get me wrong, he's good to me; the best actually. But I…" she said letting her words trail.

"But you're a little hottie eh?" Janelle giggled.

"You could say that," Delicia nodded.

"Well then, you're not married to this guy right?" she asked.

Delicia shook her head, which was the one thing that bothered her about Jah-Man. He had never asked for her hand. She also knew he never would. When she got older, maybe not too much more than she was now, he would lose interest in her. Another woman, more beautiful would take her place. She knew this was going to happen eventually. She just wanted to come out of it with more than just memories; she wanted a fat bank account that she could live on. She also had desires she never shared with him, more than once she had approached him to make love and he had spurned her his anger flaring causing her to run and hide.

"Well then, if you like what you see there…" she pointed to Steven's butt. " Then go for it!"

Steven could hear the two girls chuckling behind him, which wasn't a good sign. Pushing aside some large vegetation, it opened up into a large pool of water. In the distance was an extremely large waterfall. The sound of the water falling and slapping the rocks as it plummeted made it hard to hear.

"Oh wow!" Janelle said upon seeing it.

Delicia sighed again, she had seen it before, she knew the islands like the back of her hand. This was just another waterfall, one of many on the island. Janelle yelled as she dove off the rock into the cool water leaving Delicia and Steven alone.

"This is romantic," she whispered to him drawing close.

"This is insane!" he replied, then dove off the rock into the water.

Delicia stood there for a minute, then dove into the crisp cool water. When she came up, she noticed that Janelle had climbed up onto one of the rocks and was heading into the dense underbrush.

"Do you want to head back?" Steven called to her.

"No, not yet, just answering the call of nature," she said winking at Delicia.

As soon as she disappeared into the underbrush, Delicia reached down slipping her bathing suit off. Tossing it up onto a rock, she swam swiftly over to where Steven was on the other side of the pool. She then quietly slipped beneath the water.

Steven had come up and was wiping the water from his face when he felt a sudden tugging on his swim shorts. At first, the tugging had pulled him beneath the water and he accidentally gulped in a mouthful of water. Rising to the top, he was more concerned with breathing than what was happening with his shorts. Before he could do anything, they were gone.

Delicia surfaced not too far away gulping in a lung full of air. She swiftly turned around and yelled hoisting Steven's shorts high into the air.

"Delicia what are you doing?" he said frantically.

"What do you think?" she said swinging them around on the end of her finger.

"Give me my shorts back! This isn't funny, it's dangerous," he said his eyes showing the terror he felt.

"Why are you worrying so much?" she said moving steadily away from him.

"Because, you are Jah-Man's woman, because of that you're taking my life and tossing it away!" he spat.

"But don't you find me attractive?"

"Delicia, you're a very attractive woman but you're Jah-Man's woman!" he exclaimed.

"That may be so but that doesn't mean I don't have feelings for someone else!" she said tossing his shorts onto a rock next to her own bathing suit.

"Delicia, answer me this, why are you coming on to me? You hate my friends, and me why this, here, why now?" he snapped.

"I don't hate the others," she lied.

"I just pick on them because I like them," she smiled.

"That's why last year half of us, me included, got into trouble? You nearly cost us our jobs!" he growled.

"None of you would have lost your jobs. Remember, Jah-Man owns the resort?" she pointed out.

"Yeah, so half us could have been found floating in the surf," he said shaking his head.

"Okay, okay, maybe I've been a little mean to you all but I do like everyone, you especially," she said slowly moving closer to him.

"This isn't right Delicia," he breathed softly.

"Why? Is the thought of fucking me so horrible?" she breathed moving closer.

"I don't want to make love to you Delicia."

"Why not? Whom are you saving yourself for?" she said not more than a foot from him.

"No one," he said, not being able to take his eyes from her.

"Who is it Steven? Is it Eve?" she said softly.

Steven swallowed hard as he felt her hand softly touch him beneath the water. He was excited, that was obvious and he was thinking about Eve...but there was more. For some strange reason, Sharon kept popping into his mind. He wanted images of Eve to flood into his mind, but instead those images turned to Sharon.

"Feel how excited you are for me Steven?" she said her hand gently working over his buddy.

"Delicia, please I Do.... Don't," he stuttered.

"You're a virgin? Do you mean - are you really?" she gasped with excitement.

"I don't want you," he breathed her hand working feverishly over him.

"You'd rather have Eve?" she said with a bite.

"Why do you want her when she's in love with Diamond? She doesn't want you Steven."

"That doesn't mean..." he said trying to pull away but found he couldn't.

"Doesn't mean what? Did you know they spent last night together? Did you know that they made love all night long?" she said.

"Please stop." he pleaded. He hated her boasie behavior.

"Doesn't that bother you?" she said sliding her body up against his, her breasts squashing against him.

"Or could there be someone else?"

"Delicia remember Jah-Man. Please he'll kill me if he find us like this," Steven pleaded.

"Who else Steven - who could turn you on more than I?" she said drawing her lips to his neck.

"Sharon," he blurted out astonished he had said her name.

At the mention of Sharon's name Delicia released him. The soft seductive look on her face had turned to insane rage. She hated Sharon, hated her so bad she wished she were dead. Turning she moved over to where her bathing suit was, Steven quickly followed to grab his own swim trunks.

Suddenly, something rustled in the bushes close to them. It was large enough to draw his attention. Delicia kept going for her bathing suit. Steven came up behind her as she drew her body half out of the water. His eyes stared at her supple, yet exotic body his hormones screaming at what he had turned down. Then, without warning Delicia lost her footing and fell backwards. Steven, reacting out of instinct, grabbed her, his arms sliding around her feeling the smoothness of her breasts. His body pressed against hers and for a moment, they both stood there, then abruptly she pulled away from him.

She then bounded up onto another rock grabbing her bathing suit. He didn't follow her out of the water, instead he just watched her as she slipped the scant fabric over her most intimate parts. She said nothing, when she was done she bounded into the underbrush disappearing from sight. Steven paused, then climbed up onto the rock, and then grabbed his bathing suit.

Again, from behind the foliage there was a rustling. At first, he thought it might be Janelle, but she had gone into the bush on the other side of the pool.

"You're just jumpy, probably a wild pig or something," he scoffed at his own insecurity.

Grabbing his trunks, he quickly slipped them on then followed the trail back to the beach. As he walked he wondered where Janelle had gone, he hoped she hadn't wandered off and gotten lost. Another couple had gotten lost, it took him nearly three hours to find them. Other thoughts crept into his mind, he had blurted out Sharon's name. Was he attracted to her and never realized it? Was what Delicia said about Eve true? Sharon was a beautiful woman; he had known that since he first met her, her long eyelashes, that cute mole above her right lip and her large firm breasts. The thought made him stop dead in his tracks, he was getting excited. Ten minutes later, he broke through onto the beach.

Delicia and Janelle were sitting on one of the catamaran's hulls their legs dangling into the water. As he approached, Janelle looked up at him and grinned. "We were going to send out a search party for you," she laughed.

"Huh, you two ready to head back?" he said diverting his eyes from Delicia.

"Of course we are why do you think we've been sitting here?" Delicia snapped the anger clear in her voice.

It became clear to him that her words earlier had been lies. She hated him and hated the group. As he already suspected, she was a manipulator and gravalicious. She would use every resource available to achieve her goals, even if the resource was her own body.

Pushing the catamaran out, he turned it around then hopped aboard letting the wind catch the sails. The late afternoon breeze had picked up, which meant the ride home was going to be brisk. The catamaran moved swiftly through the water spray skimming up along the hulls. The wind pushed hard against the sail forcing the slim hull to slide gracefully out of the water. They all hung on exhilarated by the sheer speed of the boat.

Steven, caught up in the moment hadn't noticed the small powerboat that cut through the water just a little ways away from the cove they were in. If he had, he would have noticed the man in the bow holding a video camera.

Raffie straightened his tie as he headed to the dining room, in less than an hour seating would begin for dinner. He had chores to do and paperwork to fill out before any of the guests arrived. He followed the walkway toward the dining room smiling at guests as he passed them.

"Hey Raffie," a voice called out to him.

Stopping he looked to see if he could find where the voice had come from. He quickly locked eyes with Ohpton.

"I haven't got much time. I have so much to do before dinner begins," he explained then glanced at his watch.

"Have you seen Steven?" he asked.

"Not since we left the shack this morning. Why?" Raffie asked.

"I'm not sure, I saw him earlier this morning pushing a boat out. There were two women on it with him, one I think was Delicia," Ohpton said softly as he rested his arm on his rake.

"So? That's his job to entertain the guests, even Delicia," Raffie said still not impressed with what Ohpton was explaining.

"Yeah, that might be his job but after they took off I saw another boat with three of Jah-Man's thugs heading out right behind them." "Are you sure?" Raffie was now interested.

"Of course I'm sure. Remember I see things around here, things nobody else sees," Ohpton reminded him.

"They haven't come back yet?"

"Look, I've been trying to hang around the beach area for most of the afternoon and I haven't seen them or the other boat."

"Well, there's nothing we can do from here but just keep an eye out and pray that there's nothing wrong. I think everything is okay anyway," he said smiling.

"How can you be sure?" Ohpton frowned.

"Remember, Delicia is with him along with some other woman, JahMan's thugs wouldn't try anything with witnesses," Raffie explained.

"But how can you be sure?" Ohpton asked.

"I can't."

Chapter 7

The sun began to set leaving red crimson with purple hues along the horizon. It was beautiful and a picture-perfect setting in paradise. At least it was for the tourists.

Ohpton gently tossed more bark mulch around the hedges lining the gardens. The gardens sat high overlooking the horseshoe shaped beach. There were a few tourists still swimming, lovers mostly. They usually came out late, after the bulk of the crowds had retired to their rooms to prepare for dinner. It gave them their privacy, yet they didn't seem to mind the few other couples that shared the beach. They were in their own world, consumed by their passion, and lost in their emotions. Pawing, groping and kissing, he half expected them to make love right out in the open. It wouldn't be the first time either; just last year, a couple began making love right there on the beach. Bathing suits were tossed; they didn't care who watched because they were just lost in their passion. Nobody stopped them either.

As he occasionally glanced at the couples, his eyes drew more to the water. Steven still hadn't come back, nor that mysterious power boat wielding Jah-Man's thugs. He was worried and he had good reason to be. Jah-Man was powerful, even Delicia wasn't beyond his control. Unlike Raffie, he wouldn't put it past the man to have Steven and another woman disappear, even if Delicia was involved. Something caught his eye, slipping into the small cove was a catamaran. The sail fluttered as the boat tacked to a different side trying to catch the dying evening wind. Straining his eyes, he tried to make out who was onboard. He could make out three people. Steven, Delicia and the other woman he had seen earlier when the boat slipped out of the harbor. He glanced at the edge of the cove to see if the powerboat was following, nothing was there. Quickly he rounded his lawn equipment up and headed back to the main building.

Steven was exhausted; the sail back had been laborious. The wind had died off much sooner than he had expected. Probably because a low front was headed in their direction, promising bad weather for the next few days. Delicia and Janelle were restless. They chatted and laughed all the way back, Delicia keeping a keen eye on him. On more than one occasion, he caught her staring at him. He could see the passion in her eyes; the lust that he saw earlier was still there. Nevertheless, there was something more too, he saw hate. It was obvious that she despised Sharon, hated her was a better word. They were too different people with different ideas. Sharon represented all that Delicia wanted to be as a woman, yet would never attain. Delicia represented money, money that Sharon would never have. His thoughts quickly turned to Eve, for many years, he had taken a liking to her, yet she showed no interest. She always treated him like a bedren, not a potential boyfriend. Yet, it wasn't until today that he realized it was Sharon that interested him. Eve had an hourglass shape and a smile that spelled out lust. Sharon was heavier, yet still extremely sexy in her own way. She had gorgeous black hair with eyes you couldn't hide from. She had the sexiest legs he had ever seen on woman. The years they had spent up at the shack, the years they had spent skinny dipping in the hot springs and by the waterfall, all those years he had never noticed just how incredibility sexy she actually was. Not until now that is.

"So Steven, what does the help do at night around here?" Janelle asked breaking his concentration.

"Huh? Well, we go home and try to rest for the next onslaught of tourists tomorrow," he said half jokingly.

"You don't, I mean you don't socialize at all?" she asked.

"It is forbidden for the help to socialize, unless of course management permits it," Delicia said raising an eyebrow.

"So, if I found out who your boss was and I could get permission to have you, say, have dinner with me?" Janelle smiled.

"Yes, I suppose you could. But it's been a rather long day and I'm really bushed. I would rather just go home and get a good nights sleep," Steven said as politely as possible.

"I couldn't persuade you to change your mind?" Janelle asked.

"Forget it honey, he's got his eye on some other slut," Delicia blurted out.

Steven shot her a cold stare, one that Delicia fully acknowledged as angry. She had crossed the line with him and dissed Sharon. Delicia knew exactly how to light his fire and get him in trouble. She would be damned if the woman she hated the most would end up between the sheets with him if she couldn't first.

"I really don't understand what you see in her, she's plain, ordinary, and overweight," Delicia jabbed.

Steven steered the boat in trying to focus his attention on anything other than Delicia's words. She was looking for a reaction, something to let her know that what she said was eating at him, tearing him apart.

"She wears clothes that are so big, probably from a tent maker, probably to hide her overly large breasts that sag to her waist," she continued to jab.

Steven was at the boiling point; he gritted his teeth but focused. When he was a child growing up in the orphanage, he was continually picked on and humiliated because of his fair skin. In time, he learned to accept the ridicule, shrug it off like water droplets. However, when the ridicule was directed at someone he loved, that became a completely different story.

"She doesn't wear any makeup, nothing, she looks like a commoner-a working class girl with no class," Delicia sighed.

"She probably whores herself to make a buck."

The last straw on the camel's back quickly broke.

"Shut up! Shut up!" he blurted out not able to contain himself.

"If you were half the woman she was, just _half_! And as for a whore, take a look in the mirror," he snarled.

Delicia was shocked at his outburst; she clutched her hand to her chest and gasped. Then drew her attention to Janelle who was also astonished by his actions. He blew it.

"My, is this how you treat guests? I will not stand to hear abuse like this!" Delicia snorted.

"Shove it," Steven growled knowing that he was in serious hot water.

The catamaran slid up onto the beach. Hopping out he pulled it further up then lowered the sail as the girls stepped off. Janelle said nothing and quickly walked towards the resort.

Delicia stood there for a moment staring intently at Steven as he went about his work. She then casually strode up to him an evil grin broadening on her face.

"Steven?" she said soft and seductive.

"What?" he snapped not bothering to look up at her.

"I can be persuaded to forget the whole matter. That is, if you care for some extra activity," she said her voice barely audible.

"Forget it," he snapped.

"You do realize that I can get you kicked out of here, you can lose your job?" she asked.

"Look Delicia, if you want to take my job then you take it! You will not hold anything over my head to get me into your bed. You are Jah-Man's woman and I don't mess with that," he said finally looking at her.

"How do you think you would fare if I told him what you did today?" "I tried nothing, nothing you can say to him will make him believe you. Just your words would be enough to infuriate him to kill you on the spot!" she said her eyebrows now turned down making her look more like a possessed demon than a beautiful woman.

"Just leave me alone," he said binding the sail.

"Don't bother coming to work tomorrow - you won't have a job," she said, then sharply turned and walked up the beach.

Steven watched her nearly bare bottom as she headed back to the resort. His future had just ended, there was no way he would be able to contribute to the fund, he couldn't pull his weight and he wouldn't allow the others to do it for him. His outburst had cost him his freedom.

Darrius started the Jeep; he had taken Yashi for a drive showing her Montego Bay's finest spots. He had ended his tour taking her up the coast a ways where she could watch the Sunset. She seemed to enjoy the day; she said little in the way of conversation but spent much time asking questions about Jah-Man. Most of which he couldn't answer.

"We should be getting back," he said.

"What is your opinion of the man?" she asked then reached over turning the Jeep off.

"What do you mean?" he asked feeling uncomfortable.

"It's a simple question, what is your opinion of Jah-Man?" she asked more slowly this time as if he hadn't heard what she said.

"My opinion is mute, he is what he is," Darrius said trying to skirt the question.

"Oh come now, don't go simple on me. Tell me the truth. What do you think of the man?" she said blinking her long eyelashes at him.

"He's corrupt, a killer, a pusher, a true ginnal and I don't really like him much," Darrius said staring at the steering wheel.

"Why do you work for him then if you feel that way?" she asked softly.

"I work at the resort and nothing more," he said.

"For some reason he has taken an interest in me and my sister," Darrius said softly.

"So you're not part of his organization?" Yashi asked.

"No"

"I suspected as much, you don't seem the type that Jah-Man would have around.

"You don't look or act like a killer nor a thug." "What do I look like?" he asked looking at her.

Yashi turned and stared at him. Her hair was tied in a ponytail; her lips were glossy red and looked even more so in the dimming sunlight. She wore a white, very thin jumpsuit that was low cut enough in the front to allow a slight view of her braless breasts. Her legs were supple and smooth, she wore white sandals that laced up her calves.

"I see, I see a bright and very sexy young man. A man who's holding back a lot of pain for some reason, a pain that he wants desperately to let out. I also see a man who not content with life as he has it, who wants more than this island can give," she said softly.

"Close?"

"Right on the money and thanks for the sexy part. I don't get a lot of women saying that to me," he smiled warmly.

"So what is your scoop with Jah-Man?" she asked directing her attention to the setting Sun.

"How do you fit into his world? You don't seem the ruthless type, what are you doing with him?" Darrius quickly changed the direction of the conversation.

"I'm a scout," she smiled.

"You don't mean like what the American's call a Girl Scout?" he looked at her bewildered.

"No, not that type of scout. I test potential suppliers, find out who they are, what they're about and whether or not they can be trusted. When you talk millions, if not billions of dollars, you make sure you can trust the people you work with." she explained.

"You're American?" he asked.

"Some what, yes. I am an American citizen, but I was born in Tokyo," she said.

"Someday I will be going back, someday," she said softly.

"Miss your family?"

"Of course I do, don't you at times?" she asked.

"I have no family. I never knew my father and my mama disappeared," he said solemnly.

"So you and your sister live on your own?" Yashi asked.

"We are old enough you know. I'm 21," he frowned.

"Sorry, you look younger than you are," she smiled.

"What about you? How old are you?" he asked.

"That Darrius, is one thing you do not ask a woman," she shook her finger at him.

"So, you don't know where Jah-Man conducts most of his business?"

"That's obvious, he most likely does his business at the resort, he does own it you know," Darrius explained.

"Do you have someone special?" Yashi asked not looking at him.

"You mean a girlfriend?" he looked at her with surprise.

"Yes, a girlfriend. Do you have someone special waiting for you?"

"No, just my friends. We all live together and share the expenses and all," he said.

"Then you wouldn't mind having dinner with me tonight?" "I…no…not at all," he said.

"I want you to show me around the resort, show me where you think JahMan does most of his work," she asked.

"You can do that can't you?"

"Yes, I suppose I can," he said starting the Jeep again.

"But first, drive out onto the beach, I want to take a ride along the water," she pointed out to the beach.

Darrius nodded and slipped the Jeep into four-wheel drive, he then edged the vehicle out through the palms then down along the sand until he reached the beach. They would only be able to go a few miles before the beach ended and an outcropping of rock jutted its jagged form out into the water. Occasionally, he looked over at her the wind blowing her hair, the fabric of her clothing fluttering, exposing more of her breasts. She was different somehow, not like he expected a criminal in the drug world would be. She acted almost like an ordinary ting. Maybe it was because she was an American; maybe all American's acted a certain way. Maybe he and the others would someday act the same - someday.

Delicia slipped the lock into the door and opened it. Her first sight was of Sharon and Eve sitting on the couch talking. At first, she was astounded that Sharon was even there, then her astonishment turned to rage.

"What are you doing here?" she spat.

"Look, I just came here to see Eve and nothing more," Sharon, said instantly going on the defensive.

"Well get out. This isn't your place I never want to see you in here again!" she pointed to the door.

Sharon padded Eve on the leg and got up heading for the door. Eve at first watched her, then got up and quickly followed.

"Where are you going Eve?" Delicia asked.

"I wanted her here, I guess that was wrong, I'm sorry Delicia, but Sharon is my friend too and I want to spend some time with her," Eve said.

"She's only going to hurt you," Delicia said trying to sound convincing.

"I am already hurt by Diamond," she added.

"Diamond? What did he do to you?" Delicia asked surprised.

"He used me. I still love him but he used me," she said sadly.

"Well, that isn't nice. I will have a talk with him and straighten him out!" Delicia said with a bite in her voice while secretly acting wicked..

"You'd do that for me?" Eve looked astonished.

"Of course I would dear, sometimes us women have to put our feet down and tell our men what's right, and what's wrong, put them on the right track again."

"Is that what we're suppose to do?" Eve blinked smiling.

"Of course, now you go along. Tomorrow check in with me, that will give me time to have a woman to man talk with him," she said shooing her towards the door.

"Thank you Delicia. Thank you so much!" Eve said excitedly.

Sharon waited in the elevator her arm outstretched holding the doors open. She watched Eve quickly run down the hallway a beaming smile on her face. It was a sudden and stark contrast to the girl she had talked with most of the afternoon.

"Why are you so happy?" Sharon had to ask.

"Delicia is going to talk some sense into Diamond, put him on the right track again!" she blurted out barely able to contain her excitement.

"But Eve..." Sharon began to say.

"Oh isn't it wonderful Sharon! Tomorrow Diamond will come back to me and we can be together," she sang.

Sharon let the doors go allowing them to close. A chill washed over her as she stared at Eve's jubilant attitude. Delicia was playing hardball. She was playing for keeps and she wondered just what was up her sleeve. She wanted to tell Eve that Diamond was no good for her and that he was just out to use her - nothing more. Instead, she decided to hol' it dung and just keep her mouth shut. Whatever Delicia had told her was enough to drag her out of the pit of despair and make the clouds part for her again. She wouldn't ruin it just yet. She would try to ease Eve down before someone pulled the rug out from under her.

Yashi and Darrius ate dinner in the main dining room. He introduced her to Raffie who seated them in one of the many tables with a superb view of the ocean. He was sure that Raffie would be surprised with the fact he was eating in the dining room, hired help never ate in the dining room, even under special circumstances. He would explain everything later. The more he sat with Yashi the more he liked her, she was humorous and not the cold hearted woman he had met earlier. He had put on the only suit he had, it was old but still fit him well. When he met Yashi at her room, he was astonished. She wore a very flowing gown that hugged every curve of her body so well it left little to the imagination. Her hair was pulled up and she wore just enough makeup to accent her exotic Oriental features.

They ate dinner and chatted about everything except why she was there. Suddenly out of nowhere, Jah-Man appeared wearing a finely tailored suit. He approached the table his face stern and business like. When they both looked up at him, it suddenly changed into a broad smile.

"I trust you had a good day?" he said to Yashi.

"Very enjoyable, very," she said glancing at Darrius.

"I am sorry to interrupt your dinner, but it is time for us to go," Jah-Man said.

"Good enough," she said placing her napkin on the table.

"I must go and change first though," she said getting up.

"I will escort you to your room," Jah-Man said smiling.

"Please excuse me, will you be around later?" she asked Darrius.

"It is late, tomorrow will be another long day," Darrius said.

Yashi stared for a moment then leaned over and lightly pecked him on the cheek. She then headed out of the dining room followed closely by Jah-Man. Darrius watched them then felt something odd in his jacket. Reaching into his jacket pocket, he produced a room key - Yashi's room key.

Raffie stood outside, it was well after 10 p.m., the night was dark and foreboding. He was sure the others had already left on the long walk back to the shack. He wished he could have gone with them, but his responsibilities at the resort didn't allow him to. Many of the guests preferred late dinners and the dining room was open until well after 9 p.m. Fortunately after the last guest left, he could leave. He wasn't in charge of the kitchen staff; he only had control over the waiters and waitresses.

"Putting in a late night?" a voice called from behind him.

Raffie turned to see Uncle William; he had just come through the revolving doors. He stood with his hands in his pockets and for a moment, Raffie thought he looked like a cop.

"Yes, working in the dining room always means late nights, it comes with the territory."

"Are things well for you and the others?" he asked.

"As good as can be expected, more money would be nice," Raffie said politely.

"Well, we all must make do with what is given. I am sure that you all will succeed in whatever you plan," he smiled warmly.

"I'm sure we will too," he grinned.

"Well have a good evening Winston, please tell the others that I am thinking about them," Uncle William said as he headed down the marble stairs.

"Can I ask you a question?" Raffie called out to him.

Uncle William stopped then turned around and nodded to him. Raffie stepped down the few stairs to meet him.

"Who was that girl with Darrius tonight?" he asked.

"And what does she have to do with Jah-Man?"

"I do not know and even if I did, these are things that are better left alone. Winston they can be dangerous," Uncle William said patting him on the shoulder.

Moments later he disappeared in the darkness as he walked the path away from the resort.

"Hey, you still hanging around here?" another voice called to him.

Turning he saw a smiling Eve followed closely by Sharon coming out from the main building.

"It's late, what are you two doing here?" he asked surprised.

"Detained, had to clean up a mess from earlier," Sharon pointed out. "You heading home?"

"I was thinking about it, I really don't want to stay here tonight, even though it's late," he said looking up at the dark night sky.

"It might rain too."

"Well then, we might as well walk together!" Eve beamed taking Raffie by the arm.

It would be well after midnight before they arrived at the shack. He sometimes hated the walk, especially on nights when he got out of work late. The air was humid, there were no stars shining and wind was picking up again. A storm was brewing.

By the time, they arrived at the beginning of the trail a few flashes of lightning streaked through the sky lighting up everything for a split second. Any moment it would begin raining, probably before they could get to the shack. Stepping onto the trail something caught Raffie's eye. Turning, he saw something white dash from one house to another. A chill ran through him. It was the dupies again.

"You two go on up to the shack. I will follow shortly," he said softy to Eve and Sharon.

"Why? What's wrong?" Sharon asked sensing a radical change in him.

"Nothing, I just need to check on something. You two go back..." his words trailed.

Darting between two more houses, this time closer, was a little girl dressed all in white. Even on this hideously dark stormy night, her dress seemed to radiate and glow. All three of them watched the little girl dash between the two houses. Then, abruptly, there was a giggle, it wasn't the giggle of a happy child it was more evil, foreboding.

"Someone please tell me I didn't see what I just saw," Sharon whispered.

"The Osirus children, the legend is true!" Eve blurted out with fear through her voice.

"That's just a legend and nothing more, there are no such things as dupies," Raffie flatly stated.

"If that's true then someone tell me what we just saw?" Eve countered.

"I don't know," he admitted.

At that moment, a sprinkle of rain began to fall. The storm was coming in fast and the deluge of rain that usually accompanied a storm would soon begin.

"Look, you two go on to the shack, I'm going to check out this so called duppy," Raffie said heading off towards the town.

"What are you doing? If that is one of the Osirus children…" Eve said with fear in her voice.

"There is no such thing as duppy children," Raffie added.

"Look, if you're going in there, what if one of them gets you?" Sharon asked.

"They're just kids, plain and simple kids," Raffie said with laugh.

"And what if they're not?" Eve pointed out.

It was dark but he turned towards her as if he could see her. Silence grew between them until finally he couldn't stand it anymore.

"Okay, you two want to come along, then come on," he said softly.

They moved quickly back into town their hearts hammering in their chests and their eyes moving about expecting anything at any moment.

"This is down right scary!" Sharon breathed.

"Maybe this wasn't such a good idea," Eve added.

Suddenly a movement made them all jump. A little boy dressed all in white, his clothing aglow jumped off the nearest porch. He was far enough away where they couldn't make out his face, but they all knew he was standing there staring at them. Their eyes were locked on the apparition and they were wondering what would happen next. Eve heard a sound from behind her; slowly she diverted her eyes then wheeled around. Standing directly behind them was the little girl; her dress radiated, masking her features. Nevertheless, it wasn't enough to keep her from seeing that the little girl's eyes were red and gleamed back at her with devilish intent. Then, suddenly the girl outstretched her arms. In her left hand was a large butcher knife poised ready to plunge down.

Eve screamed and fell back. The others, their attention snapped away from the little boy turned to Eve.

"What's wrong?" Sharon said frantically.

"The little girl, she had a knife!" Eve pointed to where the little girl had been.

Only darkness greeted them. The little girl had disappeared like a wisp of smoke.

"The other kid is gone too," Raffie said looking back to where the boy was.

"What's happening here?" Sharon asked bewildered.

"They were the same kids we saw the other night when we found those two people with their throats cut," Raffie breathed.

"The little girl had a big butcher knife!" Eve said her fear unabated.

"Did you tell the Police this?" Sharon said to Raffie.

"What about duppy kids? I mentioned I saw a little girl, but not a duppy kid," he said.

Sharon said looking around her.

"I suppose we'll find out soon enough!" Raffie sighed.

"Maybe, maybe it was us!" Eve said frantically.

"I don't think so. If they wanted to kill us they could have easily along the road while we walked. Also for what reason?"

"Did they have a reason with those other people?" Eve asked.

"I don't know, I don't know who they were. I've seen them around the town but I never knew them personally," Raffie shook his head.

At that moment, there was another burst of laughter from the darkness. It sounded so close that it seemed on top of them. Then another came from the darkness opposite them, then another and another. The laughter seemed to radiate from every direction, taunting them like a cat does with a trapped mouse.

"We better get out of here!" Sharon pointed out.

"Get a grip on yourself. There is no such thing as duppies - no such thing!" Raffie said softly to himself.

Alma Francis Heyliger

Suddenly the laughter faded and the normal sounds of the night returned. They slowly moved to the middle of the street and headed for the outskirts of town. They had enough for one night.

When they arrived at the shack, all three of them were quiet, brooding. None wanted to sleep. Steven sat in the living room chair his head pressed against the palm of his hand. He seemed to have been sitting there a while. Ohpton was already in bed, snoring as if nothing mattered.

"Steven?" Sharon said lightly touching his arm.

"Huh…what? Oh you guys just getting in?" he said yawning.

"Yeah, we had a rather terrifying ordeal in town!" Eve blurted out.

Steven sat up taking notice to the fact they all seemed nervous. His eyes then shot to Sharon who seemed the calmest of the three.

"What happened?" he asked.

Raffie explained what had happened and he could see the concern form on Steven's face. When he was done silence again filled the room.

"I have more news," Steven said then recited what had happened between Delicia and him, making sure to leave out his newfound affection for Sharon. Now wasn't the time, he wanted to make sure what he felt was a two way street. "Have they fired you yet?" Raffie asked.

"Not yet, then again I'm almost scared to death to go to work tomorrow. Who knows what lies Delicia will spin to Jah-Man. My head may end up on a pike somewhere," he fearfully mused.

"Delicia is not bad Steven," Eve said her voice scolding.

"What are you nuts?" Raffie shot her a sharp look.

"She just assume hang us all!"

"You're all wrong about her, totally wrong. She's only misunderstood that's all, she actually likes us," Eve blurted out.

"Yeah, that's why she tried to get in my pants earlier right?" Steven said making a whistling noise.

"Where's Darrius?" Eve asked changing the subject.

"He didn't come home tonight," Steven added.

"Last I saw him was in the dining room with some Oriental woman that was dealing with Jah-Man," Raffie added.

"Why has Jah-Man taken to Darrius for?" Sharon asked.

"Delicia says he likes him, says he has a lot of potential. I guess he's trying to take him under his wing or something," Eve shrugged.

"Or something…" Sharon said worried.

"Look, nothing is going to get accomplished tonight. It's late and we all have to work tomorrow including you Steven. Until they fire you I'd continue to do your job," Raffie said.

"Yeah, I suppose you're right," he nodded.

"I'm going to bed," Eve yawned.

"Me too," Sharon said.

Raffie said nothing and headed off for his own room leaving Steven by himself. The room was quiet, tranquil, very peaceful. He loved sitting for hours enjoying the silence all around him. He could think clearly, that was the thing he loved so much about the shack. His thoughts then shifted to Sharon, he had wanted to tell her the other part of the story, tell her how much he cared for her.

Getting up he was determined to let his feeling out. He walked down the hallway to Sharon's room, the door was slightly ajar and he reached out pushing it open further.

His heart caught instantly in his throat.

Sharon sat on the end of the bed; she was completely nude and drew a nightshirt over her head. She hadn't seen him and he felt ashamed for standing there staring at her body. It was exquisite though, the curve of her breasts, the taunt shape of the nipples.

He was becoming aroused. Sharon drew the shirt down over her head, and then realized that Steven was standing there staring at her.

"Oh, I didn't realize you were there," she said with surprise.

"I apologize, I didn't mean to stare…it's just…well," he stuttered.

"What Steven? Why don't you come in here and sit down?" she patted the bed beside her.

Steven was reluctant; she still fiercely aroused him and getting that close, that quick, he hoped his hormones wouldn't do the talking for him. Still though, he stepped into the room and closed the door behind him. Sitting on the edge of the bed next to her, he felt his heart beat wildly.

"What did you want to talk about?" she said softly as to not disturb the others.

"I...I..." he stuttered the words failing him.

"Is there something wrong?" she said concerned.

"No, nothing wrong I guess. It's just, well," he tried again.

Turning he looked into her eyes, they were so soft, so sweet. He felt he could easily get lost in them forever.

Then, abruptly, he leaned over and kissed her on the lips. It was tender, soft yet stimulating. Just as quick, he pulled away and bolted for the door.

"Steven wait!" Sharon called out her own heart racing.

It was too late though; he was already out of the room disappearing into the darkness of the hallway. Sharon went quickly after him, they never locked their doors to one another, and it was just something that was understood between them, yet this time Steven's door was locked.

"Steven?" she whispered to him.

There came no answer.

"Steven please open the door," she again asked.

Waiting she heard nothing on the other side. She then slowly headed back to her room. Her heart was still beating wildly in her chest as she slipped beneath the covers on her bed. She lay there wide-awake staring at the ceiling. There was a flash of lightning, it seemed to light the room up, then, within a few moments, a boom of thunder followed. Torrents of rain beat down on the roof with such force that she was surprised the water didn't find a way in. Her thoughts didn't stay long on the storm; instead, they quickly drifted to Steven.

"Did he feel the same way about her as she felt about him?" the thoughts ran through her mind.

His kiss was so soft, so electrifying she didn't want it to end. Her body went instantly numb with the thought that he had watched her slip her nightshirt on. He had seen her naked before but never until now had he noticed her! For a moment she wanted to get up and try his door again, maybe he unlocked it after he thought she had left. She would slip into his room, undress and slid along side his naked form.

Erotic thoughts danced through her mind, thoughts of their lovemaking, their passion as they explored every part of each other. The dreams were comforting and they relaxed her until the beating of the rain lulled her into sleep.

Steven lay wide-awake; he cursed himself repeatedly for what he did. He shouldn't have kissed her; it was foolish for him to assume that she felt the same way as he did. His childish behavior had probably cost him the one thing he desired most. Rolling over onto his side he watched the rain beat down against the window. More flashes of lightning glared in through the glass and booms of thunder rattled the weak panes.

His life was coming apart again. Things were a chaotic mess and he wondered how he let it all happen. It was unlike him, he was a planner, a thinker always one step ahead of everyone. His desire to succeed in life was now hindering him. He needed to get back on track. In the few brief seconds between lightning flashes, he had made the decision that starting tomorrow he would change things; start to put his life back on track. His renewed confidence was enough to allow him the peace of sleep.

Darrius heard the lock on the door click, then it opened and in the dim light from the hallway, he could make out Yashi's silhouette. She hesitated upon entering the room, then quickly closed the door and latched the deadbolt. The room was dark and only the flashes of light that burst through from the storm gave him any bearing as to where she was. He listened intently, there was a rustling sound, then moments later he felt the covers pull back. Yashi's smooth hand glided up his chest, then her lips locked onto his neck moving steadily up to his ear. He could feel her nakedness against him, her nipples against his stomach, her pelvis against his thigh.

"I'm glad you're here," she whispered, then locked her lips to his.

Darrius wrapped his arms around her drawing her close; he was excited by her touch, aroused by her sensuality. It was going to be a short night.

Dawn broke with brilliant sunshine; the storm had quickly passed as most storms do in Jamaica leaving low humidity and clear blue skies. Sharon awoke and looked at the small wind up alarm clock on the small stand next to her bed. It was going on 6:00 a.m. she still had another hour she could sleep before getting up for work. Instead, she slipped the covers back and quietly went back down the hallway to Steven's room. The feel of his lips still lingered on her memory.

Reaching out she tried the doorknob...it turned. "Steven?" her voice but a whisper.

Opening the door, she noticed that the covers on the bed were turned down but the bed was empty. Steven wasn't in his room. She quickly went through the house, finally ending up on the porch where she half expected him to be. Instead, it was empty; he had disappeared probably going back into town early. Sighing she went back to her room and grabbed a towel, then headed up to the hot springs. It would relax her to lie in the warm water and listen to the forest sounds around her. When she got up there, she found Steven already sitting in the warm water leaning back against one of the smooth rocks that lined the pool. His eyes were closed and he hadn't heard her yet.

Sharon smiled then as silently as possible pulled her nightshirt off then slipped into the steaming hot water. As she submerged her body, Steven's eyes burst open and locked onto hers.

"Good morning," she smiled.

"Hi" he said softly.

"Seems we had the same thing in mind," she said drawing closer to him.

"Yeah" he said not looking into her eyes.

"Steven…" she began to say.

"Sharon, about last night I'm sorry, I shouldn't have been that forward," he blurted out.

"It's okay. You did nothing wrong," she said smiling.

"I kind of liked it," she smiled.

"I…well my life is kind of screwed up right now," he said feeling ashamed.

"How so? We still have the same goal of getting to America, we all still work at the resort," she added.

"But for how long? Jah-Man could already want my head," he said.

"Maybe Delicia said nothing, maybe she will do the right thing this time," she lied knowing that more than likely she would hang him. "Steven, I have to ask this. What about Eve?" "What about her?" he said.

"I thought, well I thought that you were, well sweet on her," Sharon said softly.

"I was."

"Hey, did someone mention my name?" Eve said coming up to the pool.

Sharon sighed, she loved Eve, but right now, she wanted to be alone with Steven. She wanted to find out if what he felt was the same. Instead, Eve slipped out of her long nightgown and tossed it to the side. She then slipped into the warm water on the other side of Steven.

Steven looked from Eve to Sharon; he then quickly got up and climbed from the pool. Sharon watched his naked form, he was plainly aroused, and he just as quickly wrapped the towel around his waist hiding it. Her gaze turned to Eve who stared wantonly at him. He then abruptly turned and headed down the path to the shack.

"He is handsome isn't he?" Eve sighed.

"So?" Sharon asked.

"Are you interested in him instead of Diamond now?" Sharon asked with a bite in her voice.

"No way," Eve frowned at her.

"Look, I didn't mean to snap. I just have a lot on my mind that's all," Sharon said looking away.

"Anything I can help with?" Eve optimistically said smiling.

"No, these are things I need to work out on my own," Sharon added.

"Wow weren't those <u>duppies</u> last night exciting!" Eve beamed.

"One of those duppies was carrying a knife remember?" Sharon point out. "Yeah but if it was only a duppy knife?"

"I'm going to go talk to Mama Rose today after work, you want to come with me?" Sharon asked.

"No, I promised Delicia I would eat dinner with her tonight."

"You're spending a lot of time with her. Do you think that is a good thing?" Sharon asked.

"Yeah sure, what's wrong with that?" Eve shrugged. "She's my friend."

"Is she?" Sharon asked.

"Yes she is, what are you going to start giving me a lecture like Raffie? Why can't any of you look beyond the shell and see what's inside like I do?" Eve said.

"Maybe because we haven't forgotten the last few years of all the torment she's given us. Remember Eve when she accused you and turned you in for stealing clothes?" Sharon pointed out.

"I haven't forgotten but people change Sharon. Time can change people and often times for the better," she quickly said.

"And you?"

"What about me?" Eve asked.

"How have you changed Eve?" Sharon asked.

"I don't think I've changed at all except I'm not a virgin anymore," she smiled.

"You and I used to spend much time together and now you spend all that time with Delicia," Sharon said.

"You're just <u>red eye</u>," Eve scoffed.

"Yes Eve, I am," Sharon nodded.

"I have to get ready for work."

Sharon slipped from the hot water and grabbed her nightshirt. Eve watched her until she disappeared into the woods. She was right, she was now spending much of her time with Delicia. Delicia represented a world she longed and dreamed for. She too wanted the <u>tek life</u>. She wanted very much to be part of it - even if it was a small part.

Darrius rolled over expecting Yashi to be snuggled close to him. Instead, the bed was empty. Opening his eyes he yawned and looked around the room, he then slipped from beneath the covers and went to the bathroom.

"Yashi?" he called softly.

There came no reply, he then looked around the room and went into the small sitting room. The curtains on the large sliding glass doors billowed in; walking over he peaked out onto the small private balcony. Yashi stood naked leaning on the wrought iron railing. Her hair blew in the light breeze as she stared out at the open ocean. His eyes searched her supple body from head to foot. She was beautiful, exotic and the night before had been the best sex of his life.

"Yashi?" he said softly.

"Yes Darrius?" she replied not turning to him.

"Is everything all right?" he asked, not really wanting to know the answer. "Everything is fine."

He reached out and lightly ran his hand down the small of her back. He felt her tense, and then she relaxed. She then every so slowly looked over at him, her expression was not like the night before. It was blank, emotionless and Darrius upon seeing it, hesitated.

"What's wrong?" he asked again.

"You're a nice guy Darrius and someone to chat bout between the sheets," she said not smiling.

"And you're point?"

"You're a nice guy. But in my line of work, nice guys get squashed," she said bluntly.

"So what does that have to do with you and I?" he questioned.

"Darrius, you don't belong here. You should have nothing to do with JahMan, he is trouble for you," she said.

"I know that. I don't want to be around him either, unless it's with my hands around his throat," Darrius added.

"You hate him that much?" she asked.

"More than you will know," he said his smile fading.

"What if I told you there was a way to take him down?"" she asked.

"I'd say add me to the list," he grinned again.

"I trust you Darrius, I trust you because what we just talked about could cost me my life if it got back to Jah-Man," she breathed softly.

"Who are you?" he asked.

"A friend," she quickly said.

"All I can tell you is that there is more going on than you know."

"You and your bosses are going to take him down aren't you?" Darrius beamed.

"No, least not like that," she laughed.

"Then…" his words trailed.

"Look, come back inside with me and make love to me before the day begins," she said taking his arm leading him back into the room.

Jah-Man sat on the fine leather couch; his hand was drawn up to his lips with his eyes glued to the television set. His breathing was erratic. His eyes flaring open wide then relaxing.

Suddenly blood began to leak from his finger. His teeth bit down hard on the flesh cutting it open. Unexpectedly, he bounded to his feet. Reaching out he grasped the nearest object, which happened to be a bust of Venus. With raw unchecked rage, he smashed the statue down hard against the clear glass coffee table shattering the glass in millions of fragments. He then swung the remainder of the statue with such force that it flew across the room slamming into a large glass framed painting. His rage wasn't quelled.

Grabbing a heavy hardwood stand, he hefted it clean off the floor tossing it against his bar on the other side of the room. He went berserk. Anything within reach became airborne slamming against other objects and shattering them. He wailed, screaming as he tore through the room. When he was done, the only thing left intact was the television. Moving swiftly to the door, he yanked it open.
Beyond two guards stood with their automatic weapons.

"Bring me Delicia, <u>NOW!</u>" he snarled.

Delicia was roused from her bed. She put on her silken bathrobe and slippers and followed the guard out of the room and into the elevator. Moments later her senses went on high alert as she entered the shattered room. Jah-Man stood amongst the carnage his back to her as he watched the television. Moving further into the room the guard closed the door behind her leaving her with JahMan.

It wasn't until she moved closer to the man did she noticed what he was staring at. On the large wide-screen television was an image of her naked. Behind her was Steven who too was naked. Someone had seen them at the spring and had videotaped them. When she stumbled getting out of the spring, Steven had caught her but by looking at the television, it looked like he was trying to have sex with her. She felt her blood drain from her body. Jah-Man turned, the insane rage that broadened his face made her gasp. She had never seen him so insane with rage.

"Why, why did you not tell me about this?" he spat pointing to the television.

"I did not want to cause you problems," she feigned.

"Who is this man?" he snarled.

"Did he...did he..." he snarled his body shaking with rage.

"No...no he didn't. He tried but I wouldn't let him," she lied. "<u>Who is he?</u>"

"He works on the beach and teaches sailing and swimming," she quickly said as he drew closer.

"How did your bathing suit come off?" he asked his face now inches away from hers.

"He pulled it off when we were swimming," she quickly said.

"Are you sure he didn't harm you in any way?" Jah-Man spat.

"No he didn't have a chance," she shook her head.

"I will find this man and rip his heart out!" Jah-Man snarled shaking his fist as the television.

"He is a dead man - <u>a dead man!</u>"

Chapter 8

Steven slipped into his swim trunks and grabbed his towel. He had lifeguard duty down at the beach; it was going to be another hot and humid day. He passed no one in the men's locker room, which wasn't too odd for 8:30 a.m. By the time he got to the beach, there were already three couples lying on the sand. Walking up onto the ramp of the lifeguard hut he hesitated. There were noises within the hut, bamboo shades hung down covering the windows keeping him from seeing who was inside. His heart thumped, was it some of Jah-Man's thugs? Was it Jah-Man himself? His mind raced with possibilities as he drew nearer the hut. Reaching out he drew aside the large bamboo shade covering the door. His eyes instantly locked on Delicia, her face was drawn, serious, and her eyes were red and puffy.

"Steven..." she began to say.

"You should not be here Delicia, I already told you yesterday," he said softly.

"No Steven. I am here to warn you," she said drawing close.

"Warn me?" he said his attention now locked on her.

"Yes. There was someone, I did not know but there was someone in the woods yesterday. They videotaped us when we were in the spring together - naked!" she said frantically.

"What? My God Delicia, do you realize what you've done?" he blurted out in panic.

"Steven, Jah-Man saw the tape. He thinks, he thinks you were trying to have your way with me," she said.

"Me, why? Why would he think that? It was you Delicia. It was totally you, not me! Did you tell him that?" Steven snapped.

"He would have beat me or worse. He thinks it was you Steven, you!"

"I've got to explain things and try to reason with him, let him know that it wasn't me," he said turning away from her.

"Steven I am so sorry. He asked how my bathing suit came off and I told him you took it off," she said softly.

"What? Dear God Delicia, do you realize what you've done?" Steven said with instant fear on his face.

"He says he'll find you and kill you," she said looking away.

"I don't believe what you've done. I don't believe it! I've got to get out of here, get away and hide!" he said turning to the door.

"Steven, I'm sorry. I didn't mean for it to get this far out of hand! I was attracted to you, truly," she blurted out.

"You're attraction has cost me my life Delicia, my life!" he snapped then bolted through the bamboo door.

Hesitating, Steven looked around to see if anyone was looking for him. With any luck, maybe, just maybe he could get away and hide.

Darrius arrived at the front desk beaming a smile. The other person with whom he worked with took one look at him and then another. It was so unlike him to come to work grinning from ear to ear.

"What are you so happy about?" the coworker asked.

"Oh nothing. I just woke up on the right side of the bed for once," he grinned.

"You look like you came into a lot of money or got laid," the coworker smiled.

"Yeah something like that," Darrius said losing his smile.

"Hey don't stop on account of me. You have a message here for you anyway," the coworker said handing him a note.

Darrius took it, opened the thin piece of paper and read what was inside. The note was from Jah-Man requesting that he have breakfast with him and Yashi. Instantly the thought of Yashi even being around Jah-Man made his blood boil. The man was like a disease, once you were touched, the infection spread and you were consumed by it.

"I have to go on an appointment," Darrius said.

"What now, another meeting with Jah-Man?" the coworker asked. "It must be nice that the guy's taken a shine to you." "The shine ain't mutual," Darrius said frowning.

"Sure, you can tell me all about it when you get back, if you come back," the coworker said waving his hand.

Darrius said nothing and headed for the veranda. Jah-Man always ate breakfast on the veranda; it was private and away from all the other guests. As he approached the sliding glass doors, he noticed Yashi taking a sip from her coffee cup. He pushed the door opened and stepped out onto the veranda.

"Darrius, why are you here?" she asked with surprise.

"I could say the same for you, Jah-Man wanted me here," Darrius said.

"Have you seen him?" she asked.

"No, I thought he would be here waiting," Darrius said sitting down next to her.

"I've noticed that he is interested in you. Do you know why?" she asked taking another sip from her cup.

"Your guess is as good as mine. I've never done anything for him over the years, just my job, nothing more," Darrius shrugged.

"Nothing?" she asked again.

"No, not unless expressing my distaste for him publicly means anything," Darrius said.

"Well, that might put a new slant on things. Have you ever heard the expression keep your friends close but keep your enemies even closer?" she asked.

"Never heard of it," he smiled. "Makes sense though. Yashi.

Why do you do what you do? I mean, you're really special. Why get tangled up with Jah-Man and drugs?"

"It's not that straight forward Darrius. Like I said earlier, there is much you do not know about me," she said softly.

"I'd like to know," he smiled.

"I also said nice guys get squashed." "Doesn't have to happen that way,"
he grinned.

"Darrius, I really think you're special, but don't make more of us than what we shared, okay?" she said reaching out and gently touching the side of his face.

His expression fell. He had thought she felt the same way as he did.
Instead, it was all a job for her and nothing more.

"I am sorry Yashi. I'm sorry that I felt the way I did," he said getting up.

"Darrius…" she said watching him turn to leave.

Suddenly, Darrius looked up, Jah-Man emerged through the sliding glass doors. His expression was stern, drawn and his eyes were piercing.

"I must apologize for my tardiness," he said his expression suddenly changing into a beaming smile.
"Have either of you eaten?"

Both Yashi and Darrius shook their heads. Darrius returned to his seat, his senses on high alert. He felt uncomfortable, awkward sitting there with them.

"Well, shall we order then?" Jah-Man smiled looking over the menu.

The waiter came and took their order. Yashi ordered an English muffin and a juice; Darrius ordered an omelet and more coffee. Jah-Man, on the other hand, ordered a large steak and egg breakfast.

"I trust my associate took good care of you yesterday?" Jah-Man asked Yashi.

"Yes, very much so," she smiled back.

"I was shown much of the island."

"You were pleased also with our business dealings last night?" he asked her.

"Not totally, you showed me the merchandise but you never showed me how you could deliver the quantity asked," she said bluntly.

Darrius said nothing, he was numb, and he couldn't believe that Jah-Man was conducting business in front of him. It was something he had never done before, least to his knowledge. He also took notice of the sudden change in JahMan's expression, Yashi had struck a raw cord in the man.

"You have my word that I can deliver what I promise," Jah-Man smiled again.

"You will not show me?" she asked.

"That is none of your concern, nor is it any of your associates concern either," Jah-Man said his voice growing raw.

"Then our business agreement will have to be changed," she said.

"Terms will have to be different," she pointed out.

"The terms will remain the same," Jah-Man said his voice barely audible.

" I can inform my superiors but I can already tell you what they'll say," she said calmly.

"You tell your people, you tell them that if they do not like my terms and they can deal with someone else," he said sternly.

"That will most likely be their answer. What we require is not worth losing us as a buyer Jah-Man," she pointed out.

"That may be so, but loyalty well, <u>trust</u> is more important than money," he said not smiling.

"Like I said, my people will not approve your terms," she said frankly.

"Maybe they need a message, something they will not forget," he said rubbing his chin.

"Jah-Man, our organization does not revolve around you," she pointed out. "<u>Maybe you need the lesson more?</u>" he gave her a sinister stare.

Darrius became attentive at Jah-Man's threat to Yashi. He suddenly had images flash through his mind, images so graphic, so vivid that he shuddered at them. Images of his hands locked around Jah-Man's throat squeezing the life from his body, avenging his mother and others that had been eliminated by him.

"I do not think we need to come to violence," Yashi said.

"Let me go to my people and talk with them and see what I can work out."

"No deals. Either accept my terms or find another supplier," Jah-Man stated.

"There are always room for deals Mr. Stone, always," Yashi said calling him by his real name.

"Perhaps. I want some insurance also. Being as you dealt with Darrius so well yesterday I wish that he accompany you when you negotiate with your people."

"That is not acceptable, he is not part of our deal nor is he aware of your actions," she said sharply.

"That makes him even more ideal for the job," Jah-Man grinned.

Yashi stared at Jah-Man trying to second-guess his next move. She couldn't, he was distant, and the truth behind his eyes was well concealed. She finally nodded.

"Okay, but I want two days," she said.

"Acceptable" he said not smiling.

Yashi got up; she then directed her attention to Darrius. For a moment, they stared at each other saying nothing. Then she looked away and left just as the waiter brought breakfast. Darrius got up also hoping to leave behind her.

"Darrius, please sit down and eat your breakfast," Jah-Man motioned to the chair.

"I have duties to perform," Darrius said trying to excuse himself.

"Sit. I will have someone take over your duties," Jah-Man said in a deep voice.

Reluctantly, Darrius sat back down. The waiter placed the food in front of him; Jah-Man immediately grabbed his knife and cut off a piece of the steak. Taking the first bite, he closed his eyes savoring the taste.

"There is nothing like a big breakfast, it guides how the rest of the day will turn out. Don't you agree?" Jah-Man asked cutting another slice of steak.

"I usually don't eat breakfast. No time and no money," Darrius said staring at his omelet, the sight of the food suddenly making him feel sick.

"You've had a hard life have you not?" Jah-Man asked.

"It has had its ups and downs," he replied.

"You know I have been watching you for some time now. You are not afraid to take charge, you have great determination," Jah-Man said pointing the steak knife at him.

"Look, I really must get back to work," Darrius said tossing his napkin on the table.

"Sit"

Darrius looked over at him, his face was stern, cold, in the last few moments the man's demeanor had quickly changed. He envisioned the man drawing the steak knife up and plunging it down into his chest. "What do you want of me?" Darrius blurted out.

"As I said, I see great potential in you, potential that can be nurtured and allowed to grow," Jah-Man said.

"You have much to learn and I wish to teach it to you."

"Why me? Why not someone else that has just as much potential?" Darrius said pushing his luck.

Jah-Man staring intently at Darrius now was not the proper time to tell him - tell him that he was his father.

"I like you Darrius," Jah-Man said giving him a cold smile.

"What if I choose not to?" he asked

"That would not be advisable. I do not think it would be in your best interests," Jah-Man pointed out.

Darrius swallowed hard, he was pushing his luck. Now wasn't the time to defy the man, Yashi had done that already and two people defying the man was dangerous.

"Okay, so what do you want me to do?"

"Simple, I want you to watch her. Watch her people then tell me what you've seen. That is all I want you to do," Jah-Man said continuing to eat.

"I have no desire to be involved in the drug trade Jah-Man," Darrius said his stomach doing flip-flops.

"You have no choice," Jah-Man said not looking up from his food.

"I understand," Darrius said feeling his anger boil.

"Good. There is one more thing I need from you," Jah-Man said wiping his mouth. Grabbing a moist cleaning towel, he wiped his hands vigorously then reached over and opened his briefcase. Darrius watched him remove a folder and rifle through it; he then pulled a photograph out and tossed it in front of him.

"Do you know this man?" Jah-Man asked.

Darrius looked down at the black and white photograph. His breath instantly caught in his throat. The photograph was a picture of Steven.

Junior yanked on the pull starter, the small single cylinder engine puttered at first then spewed a puff of black smoke and roared to life. Sitting down he angled the small boat away from the dock. He had just come from a meeting with Jah-Man's people; there he found out that Jah-Man was dealing with another source and that a large shipment was due in. It didn't take him long to reach the yacht, one of the Frenchman's thugs tied his line and he bounded out of the boat and onto the rear swim platform. As before, half naked and very naked women walked about totally ignoring him. One of the thugs led him into the yacht, there he found the Frenchman submerged in a hot tub, two naked women, a blond and brunette sat on ether side working a soft sponge over his arms. "Sir?" Junior spoke aloud.

"What is it, what do you want?" the Frenchman said not opening his eyes. "I've learned that Jah Man has planned for a shipment to be sent tonight."

"A shipment? A shipment to whom?" the Frenchman said sitting up taking notice.

"I do not know the buyer - he did not mention it. I did learn though, where this will all take place," Junior added.

"Where?"

"There is a small bay down the coast, it is quiet and no one goes there, not even the tourists," Junior pointed out.

"Good. We will have a reception for him when he arrives," the Frenchman said pushing one of the women away.

"Is there anything more you wish of me?" Junior added.

"Nothing yet but do not disappear though, something may come up along the way."

Junior nodded then turned and quickly headed back to his small boat. He could taste the money. Soon he would have a fat bank account, then nobody would ever tell him what to do - nobody.

Ohpton skimmed the trimmer over the hedges, by the time he awoke that morning everyone had left for work. He wanted to walk in with them, he usually did, but he also liked to sleep in and those few extra minutes were worth walking in alone. As he worked, he watched guests mill back and forth going about their business. Most ignored him, a few cute women smiled and winked at him but other than that it was another boring day.

"Ohpton" a voice called to him, barely audible over the sound whirling sound of the trimmer.

Ohpton shut the trimmer off and stood there listening. Again, the voice called out to him, this time he pinpointed where the voice had come from. Setting the trimmer down he walked around the hedge. Steven sat crouched, his body hugging the hedge as close as possible.

"Steven? What are you doing?" Ohpton asked.

"Listen to me, I need you to do something - something important," Steven said looking around.

"Sure, what do you need?"

"I need you to run interference for me and find a clear path out of this place," Steven softly said.

"What in the <u>blood fire</u> is going on?" "I think there is a price on my
head," he sighed. "What? A price? For what?"

"If you had stayed up long enough last night you would have heard me explain it to the others, it's a long story. Just find a clear path out of here for me okay?" Steven asked.

Ohpton walked casually towards the Orion's entrance. Steven followed as close as he could without drawing attention to himself. He used buildings, shrubs or anything else that would hide him. He wasn't sure where he would go once he was out. He couldn't go back to the shack it would endanger the others. He would have to go someplace else, someplace where Jah-Man couldn't find him.

Darrius stared at the picture of Steven; he felt a cold chill wash through him. What did Jah-Man have a picture of Steven for? A multitude of scenarios bombarded his thoughts. He was also being quiet for too long.

"Do you know this man?" Jah-Man asked again.

"I've seen him about," Darrius said softly, hoping he wouldn't let the cat out of the bag.

"He is not associated with you and your little group?" Jah-Man bluntly asked.

Darrius was caught in a difficult situation, he wanted to lie, tell Jah-Man he had never seen him before. Then there was Delicia, she would spill the fact she had seen them together.

It was now time, time for him to make a choice, either to play the game or defy the man whom he hated. He decided to lie.

"No, he isn't associated with me or my friends," Darrius said.

"That is good because if I found out he was there could be serious consequences for your friends," Jah-Man said not meeting his eyes.

"What did he do?" Darrius asked.

"That is of no concern to you," Jah-Man quickly replied.

"Something to do with Delicia?" Darrius said taking a wild guess.

Jah-Man's eyes shot up, they were filled with uncontrollable rage. It was something Darrius had never seen in the man and he wondered if his mother had seen the same the night she disappeared. "What do you know of Delicia?" "Not much," he lied again.

"I only hear what my sister tells me, I guess they're friends," Darrius shrugged.

"Does that bother you?" Jah-Man asked.

"What, that my sister is friends with Delicia?" Darrius acted stupid.

"Of course."

"She is old enough to make her own decisions but I do not think Delicia has my sisters best interests in mind," Darrius said taking a jab at her.

"What do you think of me Darrius?" Jah-Man said again looking away.

"I...do not know you," Darrius replied not knowing what to say.

"I have heard that you dislike me, is this true?" Jah-Man asked his voice growing lower.

"I...like I said..." his words trailed thinking how he had no <u>rispeck</u> for the man.

"Do not lie to me Darrius. I despise liars and I hate cowards who are unable to speak their minds. I do not think you are one of those are you Darrius?"

"No I am not and yes you are correct, I do not like you," Darrius said suddenly finding courage.

"Why don't you care for me Darrius?" Jah-Man asked.

"What you do. The drugs and the manipulation of people, it is wrong," Darrius spat.

"I rule an empire Darrius, from where you stand you can not see the top or the big picture. From where I am, things must be done, decisions made to ensure the operation continues," Jah-Man explained.

"So why then do you not rule your empire with honesty and integrity?"

"I rule my empire with the resources God has given me. He would not have given me nor placed me in the position to rule if I was not intended to be there," Jah-Man casually said.

"So killing people is God's way?" Darrius pushed.

"I do not kill Darrius. I simply <u>remove</u>," he said giving him a sharp look. "You have much to learn, much indeed. That will require that I spend more time with you to teach you what you will need to know," Jah-Man smiled an evil grin.

"Why? Why have you shown interest in me especially if I dislike you so?" Darrius asked a chill running through him.

"I see potential among other reasons," Jah-Man continued to grin.

His demeanor chilled Darrius, yes, maybe he had potential but what else was he to the man? There was a reason for Jah-Man to keep him close, a reason he hadn't divulged. He also worried about Steven, something had happened between him and Delicia to enrage Jah-Man, enrage him to the point where there might be a price on his head.

"So, are you sure you have nothing to do with this man?" Jah-Man again pushed the picture at him.

"Sure" Darrius said not looking at it.

"There is something else I want you to remember, keep an eye on Yashi and her people; report to me when you get back," Jah-Man shook a finger at him.

"Is that understood?"

Darrius just nodded and quickly got up, he couldn't leave the veranda quick enough. He needed to find any of the others. They had to warn Steven of Jah-Man's intent.

"What's the hurry?" Yashi called to him.

"I must attend to something before I can go with you," he said his voice laden with fear.

"What is wrong Darrius? What did Jah-Man tell you in there after I left?" she asked.

"Nothing" he lied to her.

Yashi nodded, if anything Darrius was a miserable liar. His face told her the opposite of what his voice spoke. She watched him turn and quickly head off towards the elevator. Reaching into her leather purse, she produced a cellular telephone. Moments later she listened as a person on the other end picked up.

"Is it set?" the voice asked.

"Not entirely, he is suspicious," she said.

"This is not good. Everything could easily blow up in our faces," the distinct male voice said.

"I am suppose to discuss with you his terms but there is another problem," she began to say.

"What now?"

"He has put someone with me to watch and listen. This person is not in his organization, least not from what I can tell," she said.

"How can you be sure?" the voice asked.

"Just a feeling, just a feeling," she softly said.

"Anyway, we'll be arriving later tonight."

"Keep this person close. You may trust him but we can't take that chance since there is too much is riding on this," the voice quickly said.

"I didn't say I trusted him," she quickly added then hung up.

Sharon took the woman's money and returned her change. The day had been long and extremely busy. One of the other girls had called in sick and she ended up taking over her appointments. Sitting down in one of the chairs, she leaned heavily back and closed her eyes.

Not getting any sleep the night before didn't help matters either. She was still shocked by the events from the night before, she somewhat believed in duppies and what she saw was terrifying to say the least. Yet, the very thought of an actual duppy fascinated her. She had remembered her mother telling her about the duppy children, but she hadn't remembered any time growing up that she could remember anyone seeing them. Why now? Was Raffie right? Could there be some other explanation?

"Sharon!" she heard Darrius's excited voice call to her.

As he came into the salon, she could see he was agitated by something, which was not like him. It was enough to make her sit up in her chair.

"What's wrong?" she asked.

Darrius explained everything that he knew; he could see Sharon's face turn to dread. She then held her hand to her mouth in disbelief. "Does anyone know where he is?" she asked. "Yes, Ohpton said he helped him get out of the resort." "Thank God for that!" she exclaimed.

"We all need to get together later and discuss this to try to figure out what we can do."

"You'll have to do it without me. Jah-Man has me tagging along with Yashi," he said.

"Yashi?" Sharon frowned.

"One, I think, one of his contacts," he said.

"In any event I have to go with her to keep an eye on her for him." "Where do you think he would go?" Sharon asked.

"We both know that he won't go back to the shack, not if Jah-Man's men are looking for him," Darrius explained.

"Then where?" Sharon asked.

"Where would you turn if you didn't have anyplace else to go?" Darrius said grinning.

"Mama Rose!" Sharon grinned.

Mama Rose watched as three schoolers left her little candy shop. When they were gone, she walked slowly over and pulled the shade down on the door. That was her way of saying she was closed for the day.

Her legs were bothering her and she leaned heavily against various pieces of furniture as she made her way back to the kitchen. She was old and she knew it.

"Keep moving, just keep moving before you wake up one day and find you can't," she said to herself.

Upon reaching the kitchen, she put a teapot on the small stove and waited for the steam to rise. There was a soft clicking noise, nothing she paid attention to at first but when it got louder she looked up and around the kitchen. Her old eyes immediately locked on the kitchen door. With much effort she quickly got up went over opening it.

"Steven! This is a surprise," she said drawing him into her arms.

Steven gasped as her hug squeezed the air right out of his lungs. Mama Rose was a strong woman, much stronger than she looked.

"Please come in. I am making a pot of tea would you like some?" she asked moving over to the stove.

"Huh? Yes, a cup of tea would be nice," he said peeking through the other doorways.

"What are you looking for?" she asked.

"Are you alone here?" he asked.

"Of course, I just closed the shop for the night. Steven what is wrong?" she said concerned.

Steven recited what had happened the day before with Delicia and the trouble he was now apparently in. When he was done, the room grew silent. Mama Rose had a frown on her face, which made the crease in her brow more apparent. It also took that sweet innocent look away.

"Now you know you can't go back with the others right?" she asked.

"If they find me with them, they all could be in trouble. Even you could be in trouble if they found me here!" he pointed out.

"I just didn't know where else to turn."

"I am not worried about Jah-Man. He does not scare me. His magic is false. He uses others to do his bidding and his crimes. Deep down he is a coward," she said tapping her finger on the table.

"Well I wouldn't want to be the one to tell him that to his face," Steven shook his head.

"You did the right thing coming here Steven. I will hide you until we can come up with a way to deal with all this," she nodded reassuringly.

"There's more too. I have lost my job at the Orion. Without that job, I cannot continue to add my share to help get us off the island and to America. I have become a prisoner here.

I have trapped myself. If only I had kept my mouth shut!" he shook his head.

"It is hard to do that when someone speaks harshly of someone we love," she stated.

Steven quickly looked up at her. How did she know? How could she know that he was in love with Sharon?

"H...how?" he blurted out.

"Steven when you are my age you see the world much differently. I may be old and wrinkled but these eyes still notice things," she winked at him. "Does she know how you feel?" "No, not yet," he said softly.

"I haven't had the courage to talk to her. I tried the other night but I couldn't," he shook his head.

"It will come in time. Things always have a way of working themselves out," she smiled warmly.

"What about Junior?" Steven asked.

"If he finds me here, it could go right back to Jah-Man."

"Junior only comes by every so often, and lately that has been every few weeks," she replied.

"If only my boy could have been more like you or one of the others," she said sadly shaking her head.

"I'm sorry Mama Rose," Steven said putting his hand over hers.

"That is all right. Like I said, things always have a way of working out," she said patting his hand.

At that moment, there was a sharp knock on the door. Mama Rose looked at Steven and raised an eyebrow. Not too many people came to the front door when the shade was pulled down.

"You wait right here," she said then slowly stood up from her chair.

Steven watched as she left the room. He loved Mama Rose, and they all did. Over the years, she had always been there for them. She had virtually watched them grow and when they need the guidance, she was always there for them. He then shuddered wondering if it was wise to have even come to her. He could be putting her life in danger.

Moments later he noticed the curtain part. Sharon stood in the doorway staring at him her face showing the concern and fear that was welling up within him. Seconds later they flew into each other's arms.

"Oh Steven, I was so worried!" she said kissing his face.

Steven hugged her tightly and returned her kisses. Suddenly they both stopped and stared into each other's eyes. He then let her go.

"Well it is good to see you two are happy to be together," Mama Rose said hobbling into the kitchen.

"We're sorry, we did not intend to act that way in your home," Sharon said embarrassed.

"Sorry for what? Being in love with each other?" she frowned.

Sharon looked up at her with surprise; she then turned her attention to Steven who just shrugged.

"Have you heard anything?" Steven asked her.

"Darrius warned me. He said something about Jah-Man questioning him about you. I'm so sorry Steven, I should have believed you last night when you were so worried," she said shaking her head.

"It's okay Sharon. Now I just have to figure out a way to get off this island in one piece," he said sitting down.

"That alone could be very dangerous," Mama Rose said resting back in her chair.

"What else can I do?" he looked at her.

"I do not know. Have you heard about the killings?" Mama Rose asked.

"I heard the story about Raffie and Darrius finding that couple with their throats cut," Steven said.

"Was there more?" Sharon became attentive.

"Last night," Mama Rose began.

"Last night a man was stabbed in his bed, nobody knows how the murderer got inside the house."

Sharon looked over at Steven; he knew exactly what she was thinking after her encounter the night before.

"Duppy children," Sharon said softly.

"Duppy children?" Mama Rose asked raising an eyebrow.

"Last night, Raffie, Eve and I saw two duppy children. One of them had a large butcher knife in her hand."

"Really?" Mama Rose said shifting in her chair.

"Yes, they taunted us and at one point I thought they were going to attack us and then they just disappeared."

"Do you remember what the children looked like?" she asked.

"None of us saw their faces, their clothing almost seemed to glow in the dark. We did notice one other thing though, they had glowing red eyes," Sharon said shuddering.

"Red eyes! My that is horrifying!" she gasped.

"And you said they just left you alone?"

"Yes, they seemed to becoming right for us, then they disappeared into thin air," Sharon made a gesture with her hands.

"Did you actually watch them disappear?" Mama Rose asked.

"Well, no. One of them distracted us then when we looked back they were gone," she said.

"You three must have been terrified!"

"Yes, you could say that. I still get goose bumps thinking about it," she said rubbing her arms.

"You remember the tale I told you about the duppy children don't you?" Mama Rose asked.

"They could be coming back for some reason."

"But duppies killing people with butcher knives? Scaring them to death yes, but knives?" Steven scowled.

"The spirit world works in many different ways Steven," Mama Rose shook her finger at him.

"You would be safer not to dispute that it exists. It is clear that some form of evil as infected our little community. How long it remains we can only guess, who it comes to claim next…"

"I have to be going. If I don't get home soon, the others will be worried," Sharon said getting up. She then directed her attention to Steven.

"Will you be okay here?" she asked him already knowing the answer.

"Of course, but if you come back here and find me gone then you know that Mama Rose was being put in danger and I will not stay here if that happens," he stated.

"I understand," she nodded.

"Sharon, there is one more thing I need to mention to you," he said taking a deep breath.

"I know that I no longer have my job and that means that I can't contribute to our fund. I know that we all wanted to go together, but as you can plainly see that won't be happening," he said softly.

"That doesn't mean though, that any of you should remain behind worrying about me."

"Steven, I don't want to talk about this right now. Let's worry about one problem before we dump the whole cart load on our heads, okay?" Sharon quickly said, then headed for the door.

"Good night honey," Mama Rose called to her.

"I will be back as soon as I can," she said then abruptly left the room.

Arriving back at the shack, Raffie, Ohpton waited patiently for her to change her clothes. The three of them then sat in the living room, they were quiet as she told them about Steven. Darrius had found each of them and filled them in. She also told them about Darrius not being able to come home tonight and about Eve spending time with Delicia.

"What is happening to us?" Ohpton said shaking his head in disgust.

"We used to be so close, now the closer we get to getting off this island, the more we begin to fall apart."

"Steven is a dead man," Raffie shook his head.

"There has to be another alternative," Sharon said softly feeling her stomach tighten at his words.

"Yeah, kill Jah-Man before he kills Steven or us," Raffie blurted out.

"That would make us no different than he is - a cold blooded killer," she stated.

"What other choice do we have?" Raffie shrugged.

"I am not going to kill the man in cold blood!" she stated flatly.

"We could always go with my idea," Ohpton said casually.

"Which is?" Sharon asked.

"Plan on robbing him," Ohpton said half expecting them to instantly scoff at the idea. Instead, the room grew silence.

"That would give us enough money to get all of us off the island, easily," Raffie pointed out.

"I would be also excessively dangerous," she said.

"It would require much planning, much planning. We would have to watch Jah-Man like a hawk. Determine if the man has any routines that we could utilize to our benefit," Raffie added.

"And what happens if we fail?" Ohpton added.

"We won't!" Sharon said with confidence.

"We also have to get everyone on board for this. This is something we all have to agree to do it because it's going to require all of us working together to pull it off," Ohpton added.

"And if one of us gets caught?" she asked.

"Then we deny the existence of the others...and...well," Raffie's words trailed.

"Take the bullet like a man?" Sharon scoffed at him.

"There has to be more alternatives," she said.

"A very elaborate con," Ohpton smiled.

"What happens if something goes wrong?" she asked.

"Then we have to have multiple options and contingencies."

"And a way off the island before any of this goes down," Raffie added.

"I've noticed in the past Jah-Man making exchanges, the briefcase he is always given contains cash, that I'm sure of," Ohpton smiled.

"So it's a matter of getting the briefcase away from him without him seeing us or figuring out he's missing it," Sharon added.

"I didn't say it was going to be easy," Ohpton shook his head.

"Or dangerous." Raffie said.

Silently a boat glided along the water, it ran no lights not even navigational lights. An electric motor pushed it silently through the water. Sitting in the bow, Junior peered out into the darkness. He could hear the small waves crash along the shoreline but couldn't make out the whiteness of their forms. Behind him were four other heavily armed men. One of them steered the boat while the others hung onto their weapons as if they were going to use them at any moment.

"How much further?" one of the men whispered to Junior.

"Not much further, just around the point. Tell him not to steer too close to the shore, we don't need to get stuck or slice open the bottom of the boat on the coral," Junior pointed out.

"I hope you are right about Jah-Man's men. I would hate to end up in the middle of a few dozen men with automatic weapons," another man added.

"He keeps a low profile. I know, I've delivered for him," Junior added.

"I'd like to see the look on his face when he discovers that his shipment has been hijacked," one of the men softly laughed.

Junior just grinned; he would rather ignore the man's comment. These men didn't understand the type of wrath Jah-Man would inflict when he found out that his shipment had been hijacked.

The little boat rounded the next point; in the distance, they could make out the dim lights shining on the beach. All looked quiet and serene. There appeared to be nothing going on.

"So? What's the problem, did we miss the whole show?" one of the men asked.

"No, it was suppose to happen at 10:30 p.m. Jah-Man is rather punctual in regards to doing business," Junior whispered.

The beach was quiet, small wavelets licked along the sand then receded disappearing from sight. Small lanterns shown back casting devilish shadows along the sand making the whole beach look like a medieval dungeon. The boat drifted casually up onto the sand. The four men jumped out onto the sand, crouching low to keep their bodies hidden in the shadows. Junior followed, the cold metal of the maggy he was given was wet with sweat. Anyone they would come across would have to die, if anybody saw his face and reported it back to Jah-Man, his life would instantly become worthless. There wouldn't be enough money in the world to hide away from him.

A lone guard strode along the sand heading back to a small shack. He never saw the man that crept along behind him. With a swiftness that astounded him, Junior watched the guard let out a garbled cry then collapse to the ground dead. They raced along the sand expecting hoards of Jah-Man's men to descend upon them. Instead, it was quiet and calm.

"So, where it is?" one of the men grabbed Junior by the arm.

"I don't know, maybe in one of the small shacks," he stuttered.

"Something tells me you've been duped," another man added.

"That's impossible, my sources are exact," Junior said with irritation.

"Yeah, so where are they?" another asked.

"Maybe they just didn't arrive yet," he explained. "This isn't good," another man breathed.

"Maybe you brought us to the wrong cove?" one of the men snapped at Junior.

"This is the right cove, I'm positive of it," he said.

In the distance, the small shack was aglow with candlelight. Through the old weak windowpanes, they could see a dim glow and shadows of the people inside. The small group moved cautiously along the sand until the reached the outside of the shack; one of the men moved to the nearest window and peered inside. Six men sat around a table playing cards, the room was basic with bunk beds along the rear wall. A small dirty sink sat against the opposite wall. One of the guards got up from the table and went over to the sink, moments later he splashed water over his face. He said something that none of them could hear, laughed, then returned back to the table.

"There's nothing else in there, just the guards," one of the men said to Junior.

"Maybe the shipment hasn't come yet. Maybe the delivery was postponed till later?" Junior speculated.

"Maybe you're a liar," another of the men spoke up.

"Could be a trap too," another man chimed in.

"Look, there must have been a change of plans, the shipment was suppose to be delivered here," Junior shrugged.

"Let's get out of here before we're discovered," another of the men suggested.

"Just give it a little more time," Junior asked.

"I think we've given it enough time as it is," one of the men glanced at his watch.

The men were quick; they darted back along the sand towards the shoreline where their boat waited. Junior hesitated, and then followed. He didn't know how he would explain this blunder. He was just happy he wasn't caught.

Suddenly, a whistle blew.

"Come on move people, move!" a man asked as he raced across the sand.

The men in the shack bolted through the door their automatic weapons ready to fire. Junior raced as fast as his legs would carry him. Gunfire erupted from behind him and he half expected to feel the searing hot pain as a bullet tore into his chest. Instead, he plunged into the water and climbed aboard the boat that was now being turned around.

Looking back, he noticed one of the men had been captured. He was on the ground his hand being forced behind his back, automatic weapons pressed against his body. Junior watched as they hauled him to his feet, they would torture and eventually kill the man.

He wished that he had a high caliber rifle. He would shoot the man before they had the chance to interrogate him. He also wondered if that was what was in store for him once the Frenchman found out.

Chapter 9

Darrius was nervous as he stepped aboard the twin-engine airplane. Yashi was in front of him and occasionally looked back at him smiling. It was the only reassurance he had. In his hand, he carried a small overnight bag, which was worn and old, but still practical. He noticed something else too, the way he was dressed was different. His clothing was practical, comfortable and more <u>casco</u>. Yashi's was designer cut and reeked money. He felt like a peasant.

The inside of the aircraft was custom tailored to the owners, which he assumed were Yashi's bosses and drug smugglers. There were high back leather captains chairs, a full bar with a small kitchenette and everything was carpeted and plush. He thought of asking her if she wanted him to ride with the luggage. Instead, she motioned him to sit in one of the chairs; she sat directly across from him and smiled warmly at him. She was so different, not like he expected a drug dealer to be, she was warm, sensuous and very businesslike.

It didn't take them long to get into the air. Darrius had never flown before and at first was very nervous, but once the plane smoothed out he relaxed some.

"Never flown before have you?" she asked smiling.

"Never" he breathed, glancing out the small side window.

"What was your childhood like?" she asked.

Darrius looked away from the window and into her eyes. Not many people had ever asked him that question. For the poor of Jamaica it was not good to bring up things you tried to forget.

"I don't know, I guess it was okay," he shrugged.

"What were your fondest memories?" she asked.

"The times my mother would take Eve and I to the beach, we would sometimes get a treat on the way," he smiled.

"What was she like?" Yashi asked.

"You really want to know this stuff?" Darrius frowned.

"Yes I do," she replied.

"Well, my mother was so pretty; least that's what I remember," he began. "She worked at the Resort also. She started out cleaning and quickly

worked her way up to front end manager," he said.

"What happened to her? Did she die when you were young?" Yashi asked.

"I don't know, when I was 16 she went to work one day and then never came home again," he said sadly.

"So she might be alive still?"

"My mother would never have run out on us, never," he said sternly.

"What did the Police say?"

"Nothing. Like I said she was a very beautiful woman. They told us that she probably ran off with some rich tourist."

"I'm sorry Darrius, that must have been very hard to deal with," Yashi said softly.

"Yeah, I had Eve to look out for so I had to keep a level head," he explained.

"What do you think happened to her?"

For a moment, Darrius stared at her; nobody had ever asked that question either for he knew deep down what had happened to her.

"Jah-Man killed her," he said.

"What makes you think that?"

"It's just a hunch that somehow maybe she saw something she shouldn't have, maybe something else happened, I don't know. But my gut tells me he's the one who killed her,"

"But they never found a body so she might still be alive," Yashi pointed out.

"She's dead. Like I said, she would have never left us," he shook his head.

"That would explain why you dislike Jah-Man so much," Yashi added.

"More than you know - more than you know," he nodded.

"Can I ask you where we're going?"

"Florida. Would you like a drink?" she asked getting up.

Darrius watched her; she wore a short navy blue skirt and a white silk blouse. As her body moved he was quickly reminded of the night of passion they shared. When she caught him staring, he smiled and looked away.

"Sure, anything will do," he said softly.

His thoughts then drifted to their destination and they left him with an intense feeling of guilt. They were heading to the United States, Florida the home of Mickey Mouse and Disney World - the home of freedom. It was where he and the others were trying to reach.

They had agreed that Florida would be their first stop before heading someplace else, maybe Virginia. Now he was going to be the first of their group to set foot in the States. The feeling made him nauseous. For too many years they had worked towards a common goal, now that he was reaching it first, he felt like he was jilting the others. He felt chuh.

"What's wrong?" Yashi asked handing him a beer.

"Oh nothing," he lied.

"Still thinking about your mother?" she asked sitting back down.

"Always, but that's not what's bothering me," he said taking a sip of his beer.

"Then what?" she asked.

"Come on, you must know by now that you can trus mi?"

"You deal in drugs Yashi and Jah-Man deals in drugs - I don't," he said. "What you are doing is criminal, it's wrong. I've spent my life trying to do the right things, working hard, saving my money to try to improve my life. Being here is wrong..." he added.

"Not everything is what it seems you know," she smiled at him. "Does that make you like me less?"

"No, you already know that. The line of business you're in can get you killed; it can get me killed too. Do you know that?"

"Of course, so can walking across the street. What's the big deal?" she shrugged.

"People get hurt from what you do and people that don't deserve to get hurt," he tried to explain.

"We all die some day Darrius, what we do with our lives is what's important," she replied. "What do you want out of life?"

"Me, but there's more than just me," he began to say.

"Yes I know. There's also your sister," Yashi nodded.

"No, there are others too."

"Who else? I thought it was just you and your sister."

"The years after my mother didn't come back we met others, a bunch of us, all orphans in one way or the other, got together. We all live together even now and we all work for the same goal." "Which is?" Yashi asked.

"We are all trying to save enough money to get passports and a plane to bring us to the United States. We all want new lives, not the poor desolation that Jamaica offers people without money."

"Wow, you sound determined. Do all the others feel the same way?"

"Yes"

"How close are you all to succeeding?" she asked.

"Very, this year would have been our last. We would have had enough to squeak by. But now there are complications," Darrius said looking back out the window.

"What?"

"Jah-Man, well he has taken a liking to me and it has become increasingly hard to avoid him. Plus my sister seems to be making the wrong choices lately in regards to her friends."

"Jah-Man does seem to like you doesn't he?" she added.

"Even I noticed that."

"I'd like to kill him," Darrius said his anger flaring.

"I'm sorry Darrius," she softly said.

"For what?"

"I'm sorry you got tangled up in the middle of all this. You're right, this isn't your world and you don't belong in it, just promise me one thing though." "What?"

"Promise me that you won't judge a book by it's cover and that you'll try to not form opinions until you know all the facts," she asked.

"I'll try," he said then drew his attention back out the window.

Delicia sat in the room Jah-Man had wreaked. In her hand was a remote control and her eyes were glued to the large television set in front of her. She watched intently the video that was taken of her and Steven. When it ended, she rewound it and played the tape again, stopping the picture at various scenes. Mostly, they were of Steven, his naked body and where she fell against him. The more she watched it the more aroused she became. He was so handsome, his body so perfect.

She knew Jah-Man would kill him if he found him, she also knew he'd beat her if he caught her watching the video.

There suddenly came a gentle knock on the door. Delicia quickly stopped the tape and shut the television off. She quickly got up the <u>mass of cargo</u> dangling around her neck clinking together. Opening the door she came face to face with Diamond.

"Oh it's you," she said standing back and allowing him to enter.

"Who else were you expecting?" he said coming into the room.

"Nice décor," he added surveying the wreaked room.

"What do you want," she asked irritated.

"My <u>mass</u>. Remember our agreement?" he said turning to her.

"I haven't forgotten. What did you find out?" she asked.

"She talked a lot about her mother and how she disappeared," he began to say.

"What was her name?" Delicia asked.

"Evelyn - Evelyn Lawson," he replied.

"She used to work at the Orion, then one night - Poof! She just disappeared," he said making a gesture with his hand.

"What else?" Delicia asked obviously not impressed with Diamonds theatrics.

"Well, her brother Darrius seems to hate Jah-Man, which of course is no big deal, except for the fact he blames him for the death of his mother," he added.

"See what else you can find out from her, she is quite smitten with you, first love and all that," Delicia said with an evil grin.

"Yeah, I gathered that from the other night. Look Delicia, I don't want any excess baggage hanging onto my arm and that's exactly what Eve is, excess baggage."

"Look at her as well, employment," Delicia said raising an eyebrow.

"It is already effecting my current clients. Everywhere I turn she's there, drooling and going gaga over me. How am I suppose to work?" he asked.

"You'll find a way," she said walking over to her purse.

"Delicia, I don't know what you're cooking up here but when I start to lose money that's when I call it quits. If she happens to discover me with a client, so be it, her bubble can burst for all I care," he said.

"This should cover any lost clients," she said handing him an envelope. "There's more where this comes from. Just play the game right."

Diamond opened the envelope and glanced at the wad of bills inside. He then looked up at Delicia grinning. Nodding, he turned and headed for the door. Hesitating he turned to her.

"Are you going to cover any additional expenses, remember dating costs?" he grinned.

Delicia frowned at him, and then withdrew a few more large bills from her purse handing it to him.

"Make sure you deliver or Jah-Man will find out where his money is going," she said her threat blunt and very clear.

Diamond quickly lost his grin, snatching the bills he opened the door and slammed it behind him. Delicia stood staring at the door trying to put together what he had said. Her next course of action was to dig up information on Evelyn Lawson. Turning she went back to the television and turned it on. Pressing the remote, she again began to watch the video. Maybe with some luck she could find Steven before Jah-Man did.

Jah-Man slipped from the air-conditioned vehicle. Beyond lay a white sandy beach, the glistening ocean beyond that. The beauty of the scene was quickly taken away though by the gristly sight on the beach. Babylon stood over the crumpled body of a man; the sand around his head was dark and saturated with blood.

"What happened here?" he asked turning to William.

"Someone attacked one of your guards last night," William said.

"The police have no idea who did it or why."

"There is nothing here to steal nor nothing worth killing the man for," JahMan added walking down the slope to the beach.

As he drew closer to the body and the police, he pulled a pair of white gloves out from his pocket and slipped them on. He felt filthy even getting this close to the body. He was disgusted; he would have to shower after to remove any of the filth that might get on him.

Looking down at the body, the man's eyes were wide and an expression of fear was frozen onto his face from the moment of death. The cut around his throat was deep and very clean. Jah-Man had seen such a cut before; whoever had done it was a professional killer. Someone was trying to move in on his territory.

"Brother, was this not the site you were suppose to be at last night?" William asked.

"It is, that was before my discussion with our client," he said looking out over the water.

"Let us leave this place, I can smell the filth."

William nodded, Jah-Man was quick to turn and head back to the limousine. When they were inside and the doors were closed. William turned to him.

"You know someone is trying to muscle into your territory?" he said.

"I know brother. This has never happened before. Am I getting too soft? Has my methods of terror not been enough?" Jah-Man spat shaking a clenched fist.

"I can do some checking to find out who is new on the island," William added.

"Yes, bring me a list and I will find whoever is behind this. I will find them and crush them!" Jah-Man snarled.

"Don't forget something else brother," William said calmly.

"Somehow the people who did this knew about your meeting. There's a <u>labba</u> within your organization."

Jah-Man's rage quickly faded and he turned to William a surprised look on his face. The one thing Jah-Man demanded from his people was loyalty. The thought of one of his subjects breaking that trust was like a hot dagger into his back. As William stared at him, he almost wished he never brought the subject up. He could see the insane rage in his brother's eyes - the wonton lust for murder. It scared the hell out of him.

"Brother what is this I heard about Delicia?" William asked trying to change the subject.

"One of my son's friends, one from that little ragtag group tried to have my woman!" Jah-Man snarled even louder.

"He is just a young man, not unlike your son. Maybe he didn't realize who she was?" William speculated.

"He works for me at the resort. Everyone knows that Delicia is my woman, I mean everyone!" he snarled.

"I will find him and when I do, I will tear his beating heart from his chest!"

"I assume he is not at the resort anymore or you would have already found him. Why do you not just forget the matter? If he's smart is probably scared out of his mind knowing you're after him. Is that terror not enough?"

"Delicia told me how he removed her clothing and how he tried to have his way with her. There is a video," Jah-Man said his teeth grating together.

"Brother there is more things to worry about than this."

"No! I will have his life. If I allow him to walk away then I will be looked at as soft and weak. That is something I can not allow ever."

"Darwin, he is your son's friend."

"My son says he doesn't know him. He lied to me William, lied to my face!" Jah-Man snarled.

"He then told me he didn't like me and didn't like what I am."

"He doesn't know <u>who you really are</u> does he?"

"No and I have no intention of allowing him to find out. I must gain his trust without him knowing that," Jah-Man said confidently.

"What about your daughter?"

"She is more accepting. I do not think when she finds out that I am her father she will mind."

"What of Delicia? Does she know that Eve and Darrius are your children?" William asked.

"No. She has no need to know either, my patience is wearing thin with her William."

"She is young brother," William smiled.

"When you were young you made some bad choices also."

"She can be replaced easily enough, there are enough women that would like to be at my side," he said softly.

"Yes there are Darwin but none will ever be like Evelyn was," William said.

"Do not ever, ever mention her name!" Jah-Man said instantly flying into a rage.

"You are my brother and the only person I truly trust. You are as much at fault as I am."

"I am not the one who strangled her to death," William frowned.

"As with everyone else, remember your place brother. I would hate to see bad luck befall you."

William stared at him his face showing astonishment. Never before had Jah-Man threatened him, specifically threatened him with death. Something had changed in him, something in his mind had snapped. At that moment, William knew that his brother was ill, mentally ill. He had to be careful now, Jah-Man was powerful and his threats were not idle babble. He just nodded.

"Good, now we must figure out who the <u>labba</u> is; who is leaking information, who is a traitor."

William said nothing, he wondered if there was anyone truly leaking information or had Jah-Man now just convinced himself that there was.

Junior was led into the large stateroom by two huge thugs. The stateroom was massive and lined heavily in teakwood. A large round bed sat in the middle of the room. The covers were turned down; sitting in the middle of the bed swathed in a dark green silk bathrobe was the Frenchman. Lying on both sides of him were two women, one a beautiful blond and a very stunning brunette. They were both naked; the blond appeared to be asleep. For a moment, Junior wondered where this man acquired such stunningly beautiful women. They seemed to pop out of the woodwork to do his every bidding, both as servants and whores. For a brief moment, he was jealous.

"You will explain what occurred?" the Frenchman asked.

"The exchange never took place. Something must have changed," Junior shrugged.

"We have now alerted Jah-Man, he is not stupid. He will realize that someone else is involved," the Frenchman said his expression stern.

"It was your man that decided to kill one of Jah-Man's men," Junior said.

"He would not have had to if your information had been accurate."

"These changes happen, something changed and I was unaware of it," Junior shrugged.

"You will go back, find out when the actual shipment will be exchanged. If another such disaster happens, I will hold you personally responsible. Is that understood?" the Frenchman said sternly.

Junior just nodded, defying this man was not an option. He had his own agenda anyway, one that would eliminate Jah-Man along with the Frenchman at the same time. With Jah-Man on edge, getting close to him would not be easy. He would be suspicious of everyone, except William, his brother.

Raffie slipped into the office behind the lobbies counter. Darrius was gone leaving one person behind the counter. The office was plain, but it contained the one thing he was looking for, a computer.

Out of them all he was the only one trained in computer operation. His parents had used one extensively and over the years he was taught how to operate one.

Hacking into the Orion's computer system was fairly easy, he just hoped that the information he needed would be there. He began working the keys staring intently at the computer screen, watching window after window open as he dug deeper into the resorts system. Every so often he would glance at the door just in case someone decided to come in and question why he was on the computer.

Finding records on Jah-Man's operation would not be easy. The man wasn't stupid and he most likely hired the best people to cover their tracks well.

After nearly an hour he leaned back in the chair and sighed. There was nothing in the resorts computers that lead to Jah-Man's drug business. He didn't actually expect there would be. Jah-Man would not keep things so obvious. His job had just gotten harder, he would have to get into Jah-Man's residence, which would be the only place he would have his files and information on his business. If they were going to rob the man of one of his payments, they would need information.

"Did you find anything?" Ohpton asked.

Raffie jumped in his seat, then shut the computer off and got up.

"Nothing"

"The information has be someplace," Ohpton whispered.

"Oh it is, I just have to get into Jah-Man's house to get it," he raised an eyebrow.

"What are you nuts?"

"You have a better idea?" Raffie asked.

"You get caught in there and you're a dead man. Jah-Man will put two and two together and the rest of us will end up floating in the surf!" Ohpton pointed out.

"You didn't think this would come to us on a silver platter did you?" Raffie asked.

"No, but I don't expect one of us to get killed doing it either."

"We start messing with Jah-Man and we mess with death. Remember what happened to my family?" he asked.

"Raffie, there has to be…"

"My parents…" Raffie said then suddenly sat back down in his chair.

"My parents Ohpton, that's the answer, my parents!" he beamed.

"I don't get it," Ohpton shook his head.

"My parents, before they were killed they were trying to shut down JahMan, shut down the drug trade. They had extensive files on him – I mean extensive!" Raffie said excitedly.

"But that was years ago, many years ago," Ohpton added.

"Yes and remember how I mentioned that my house was burned down?" Raffie asked.

"Yeah, so what?"

"Well, I remember where my parents kept dual files! We just have to go through the place and see if we can find it," he smiled.

"What if someone decided to use the land bulldoze the foundation, build a new house or something?" Ohpton asked.

"It's a chance we'll have to take. If only we could find it!" he grinned. "I'll talk with Sharon, see if we can get a Jeep from the resort."

Ohpton nodded and they both left the room, Ohpton went back to his landscaping work and Raffie quickly went to the elevator. Within moments he was in the salon, Sharon was working on a customer. The woman was over 50 and by the way she wanted her hair styled she was trying to look 30. Around her neck was a plastic cover that draped down keeping her clothes clean, he would bet that her clothing were much the same as her hair - old body, young styled clothing. In any event, he motioned to Sharon that he was there and sat down to wait. Glancing at his watch he had a few hours before he needed to begin the afternoon preparation for dinner.

Finally, Sharon finished with the woman and took off the plastic cover. Sure enough, the woman was dressed like a tramp or, Delicia's twin. She wore an abundance of jewelry along with an outfit that jutted and exposed most of her breasts. She looked horrible. But, she was obviously pleased with Sharon's work. Reaching into her purse she paid for the work, then handed her a large bill as a tip. As she passed Raffie, she glanced at him and smiled invitingly. He did what he always did, smile back, all the while hoping she wouldn't proposition him.

"What's going on?" Sharon asked.

"Not here," he said grabbing her arm and leading her out of the salon.

He led her from the hallway out into the adjacent garden and when he was sure that nobody else was around he began to talk.

"We need to learn more about Jah-Man's business right? Well, at first I thought that I would have to get inside his house to get information," he began to say. "What are you nuts?" Sharon gasped.

"That's exactly what Ohpton said," he grinned.

"Anyway, I found another alternative. My parents kept very detailed files on Jah-Man - very detailed files. They also kept duel copies of everything, I'm sure of it."

"Raffie that was years ago, after your place burned down who's to say even if you find the information it will still be useable?" she asked.

"It's worth a shot, right?" he shrugged.

"I'm going to try and get a Jeep for tonight, I was thinking that the three of us could go and look."

"You know the resort doesn't allow vehicles for personal use," she shook her head.

"No, I know that. But what if I had to pick up some things for tomorrow?" he asked.

"At 10 p.m.?"

"No, just in the morning on my way in," he smiled.

"Bet you didn't realize how crafty I really was?" he smiled shaking a finger at her.

"Okay, if you can get the wheels we can go and look. I'll hang around with Ohpton till you get off work," she said.

"Speaking of which, I have to get back to my own."

He watched her head back into the resort. He always admired her, she was so determined, so strong. Their group had a lot going for it, they were all so different, but she was the cement that bound them together. Turning, his next job was to get the Jeep.

Eve took the money and returned the change to the woman who had just purchased an armload of clothing. The woman was new and had never been to the island before, a typical tourist.

"Hey, it's going on 4:00 p.m., do you mind if I go and get something to drink?" Tisha asked coming up to Eve.

"No, I can watch things. We'll be closing soon anyway," Eve sighed.

"You sound depressed, what's wrong?" Tisha asked.

"Oh nothing…"

"Come on now, you're horrible at fooling people, you don't have the face for it," Tisha smiled.

"So what's wrong?"

"Diamond"

"Oh, I should have guessed. I don't know what you see in him anyway," Tisha shook her head.

"I thought he loved me - I thought."

Eve's words were cut short when through the doorway walked Diamond. Her breath stuck in her throat as she watched him walk through the store towards her.

"Hi babe," he smiled at her.

"And what am I chopped meat?" Tisha frowned at him.

"Yeah, hi to you too," he said not even looking at her.

"You want anything?" Tisha asked as she turned to leave.

"No. Well grab me a soda?" Eve asked as Tisha walked away.

"Sure thing, later," Tisha waved.

"So, do you have any plans for tonight?" Diamond asked.

"Nothing much, I was just going home and have a quiet evening," Eve smiled not meeting his eyes.

"What do you say I take you out to dinner tonight and then maybe a walk on the beach. Then…" he said jingling a set of keys.

"What do they go to?" she asked.

"I bumped into Delicia earlier, asked her if we could use her place again. We had so much fun the other night," he smiled.

Eve held her hand to her mouth with surprise, and then burst out in a grin. She felt embarrassed, and she looked around to make sure there was nobody around.

"It was that good?" she sese'd to him.

"The best," he leaned forward whispering back.

Eve grinned and nodded.

Tisha decided to take a shortcut through the gardens. The café was on the other side of the resort and she could shave off a few minutes. She hated leaving Eve alone in the store with Diamond, she didn't like the man and had heard too many bad things about him. Things of course she couldn't prove and that if she mentioned them to Eve, they would end up in a massive argument. She was seeing with innocent eyes, eyes that only saw the good and not the bad.

Following the stone pathway she hurried as much as possible. Turning left she stopped, the pathway didn't look familiar to her. She knew that there had been extensive work done during the winter, but she didn't expect them to change the layout of the garden. Continuing on, she rounded another hedge into a small alcove where a park bench sat. She was literally stopped in her tracks as she saw two men sitting on the bench, neither whom she recognized. However, she did recognize what they were doing.

One man was testing the quality of cocaine, the other man, obviously, the supplier, watched. Then one of the men happened to glance her way and he saw her. Tisha turned, bolting as fear consumed her as she heard one of the men yell. Trying to remember which way she had come, she made a right-hand turn, then left through the hedges. Her heart beat wildly in her chest as she stopped for a moment and listened. There was crashing coming from the right of her, which was where they must be coming from.

Turning she dashed again through the labyrinth of hedges, they all looked the same, they all turned and twisted, she was becoming increasingly disoriented. Then she broke out into another opening with another park bench. Her eyes locked on the slim leather case sitting on the edge. It was the same one; she had gone completely in a circle.

"Dear God how do I get out of here?" she muttered softly, and then dashed for the other entrance. Again, more crashing through the hedges, this time though, they were directly in front of her.

Like a small scared animal, she instantly went to ground. At the edge of the hedges where they met, were bushes of other flowering plants and rose bushes. At first, she hesitated staring at the bushes but then she bit down hard on her lower lip and pushed her way into the middle of them. The sharp thorns tore and cut her bare arms and punctured through her thin dress.

They were like hideous arms entrapping her, imprisoning her never to let her free again. Then she saw them, from within the rose bush she watched the men hesitate as they tried to determine which way she could have gone.

The pain was unbearable, she could feel blood run down her arms, feel it snake down her legs. As she watched them she continued to bite down hard on her lip, it was the only way to control the pain. Why didn't they just move on? Why did they just stand there? Thoughts rolled into her mind repeatedly as she watched them.

Then, slowly, the two men moved back into the small alcove where she had seen them before. She still couldn't move, couldn't free herself from her safe, but costly hiding place. If she moved, they would hear her and they would pounce upon her like a hawk on its prey. She had to remain still and completely and silent until she was sure they were gone.

She had no idea how long had passed but she continually strained to hear any sound, any crunch, or single syllable that would let her know they were still there. There was nothing. Her limbs were stiff as she slowly moved them, the thorns as if in protest to her leaving, bite into her with more vicious intent. Tears streamed out of her eyes as the pain washed through her, for a moment she thought she would pass out as a surge of hot searing pain washed up her legs.

When she was free, she fell to her hands and knees trying to pull herself back together again. Then with much effort, she forced herself to her feet and walked slowly towards the edge of the hedge. Peeking around the corner, she was relieved to find the alcove empty. The thin leather briefcase was gone along with the two men, probably frightened off after they didn't catch her earlier.

Looking at her arms and legs she was covered in her own blood, bits of thorn protruded from her flesh, her dress was torn with spots of dried crimson dotted along the edges where the fabric touched her legs. She was a mess and late, Eve would be worried.

Turning she was about to head back into the maze of hedges when she felt something wrap tightly around her throat. A thin cord bit deeply into her flesh cutting off her supply of air. Grabbing it with her hands, she tried to pull the cord away from her throat but the thin wire was taunt and cut into her fingers with equal force. Terrified she tried to scream but could only mutter a garbled wheeze. She then felt the hot breath against her ear; the air seemed to slide down her neck chilling her.

"You saw too much honey, too much," a voice whispered into her ear.

Spots formed before her eyes and they moved as if they had a life of their own. They dashed left, and then right and their tiny acrobatics lulled her. Then, slowly, her vision dimmed, sounds grew distant until she could only hear the beating of her heart.

Eve glanced at the clock on the wall, it was going on 6 p.m. and Tisha hadn't come back yet. It was unlike her to be gone long; she had never done it before. There hadn't been many customers, only a couple, and they didn't buy anything. Suddenly Diamond came in the front door his hands outstretched.

"So, what's going on here?" he asked obviously irritated.

"Look I'm sorry, but Tisha never came back. I was waiting for her," Eve explained.

"Maybe you misunderstood her, did she say she was coming back?"

"I don't remember. I thought she said she was because I asked her for a soda. But, maybe I misunderstood her, maybe she wanted me to close," Eve said pursing her lips.

"There, see? Why else would she not show up?" Diamond smiled at her.

"Okay, can you give me a few minutes? I need to cash out then bring the money to the vault," Eve said sliding off her chair.

"No problem babe, no problem at all," Diamond said looking at some of the women's clothing.

Eve hurried as she cashed out, making sure that the books matched what was in the register. If they didn't, Tisha would have a fit in the morning when she came in. When she was done, she zipped the bag closed.

"Hey, you wear any of this stuff?" Diamond said holding a very sheer negligee.

"I would like to, but I can't afford them, but yes I do like them," she said embarrassed.

"This one wouldn't look good on you," he said holding it higher.

"What would you like to see me in?" she asked not believing her own words.

"Well let me see here," he said hanging the garment back on the rack. He then began to rifle through them until he came to what he was looking for.

"Now, this would do you justice!" he beamed pulling the garment from the rack.

Eve held her breath, she already knew what he was going to hold up and it wasn't very conservative as clothing went. The boutique had a rack or two of very risqué clothing styles that were only found in catalogs from Hollywood California. The item he chose was a tight piece of leather that was bound tightly around her waist. It pushed up on the breasts exposing them and making them look much bigger than they were and there was no bottom.

"Well, what do you think?" he beamed raising an eyebrow.

"You would like to see me in that?" she said softly.

"Oh yeah, all night long," he said with an evil grin.

"It's too expensive. I can not afford such clothing," she said feeling relieved that she found an excuse.

"Well I'll tell you what. Why don't we take this one for tonight and you can bring it back in the morning?" he said softly.

"But that's - that's stealing," she shook her head.

"Of come off it, it's only borrowing, right?" he shook it in his hand. "You're going to bring it back tomorrow."

"Diamond, I don't know, it's wrong," she sighed.

"Look, it's going on 7 p.m. now and you're going to be back before 9 a.m."

tomorrow. That's not too long from now and you're going to be staying here at the hotel anyway," he said trying to sound convincing.

"It's still stealing…"

"And boy would I like to see you in this tonight!" he added.

Eve stared at the skimpy negligee and then back at Diamond who smiled warmly at her. She wanted to do anything for him, anything to make him happy. Slowly, she nodded her head in resignation.

"Great! Come on; let's go get some dinner and then we'll take that walk on the beach. Then…" he said dangling the leather garment.

"Here, at least put it in a bag," she said tossing him a small plastic bag.

Locking the main doors, they quickly headed out through the front lobby to an awaiting limousine, compliments of Delicia. Diamond glanced from side to side, he tried to usher Eve as quickly as possible to the car. He didn't want any of his other women recognizing him, and then trying to set up various nights.

"Oh Diamond?" a voice called out.

Eve stopped upon hearing Diamond's name. She watched a woman quickly approach them. The women was in her late 40's and had a slightly plump shape that she had crammed into a skirt and blouse obviously too small for her. Although her hair was graying, her eyes were vibrant and youthful. She apparently knew Diamond as well.

"Well where do you think you're going?" the woman beamed coming up to him.

"Out with a date," he said casually.

"Oh you devil!" she smiled looking at Eve.

"Like them young now, Huh?" "Who are you?" Eve butted in.

"Well honey, I'm…"

"She's my aunt from the other side of the island," Diamond quickly blurted out.

"I, well, yes I'm his Auntie V from the other side of the island. I was here for a few days and wanted to stop in and say hi," she said giving Diamond a hard stare.

"Are you staying here?" he asked the woman.

"Absolutely, are you going to be free any time soon?" she asked.

"I'm booked up for tonight, but tomorrow I should have no problem finding time," he said.

"Look, why don't you visit with your Aunt tonight and we can go out tomorrow night instead?" Eve asked.

"Isn't she sweet," the woman smiled at Eve.

"No, I promised you a night out and I keep my promises. I'll spend tomorrow night with my Aunt," he nodded to her.

"Good enough, I'm staying in 314," she said then gave him a kiss on the cheek.

Diamond breathed a sigh of relief as he watched the woman walk away. This was getting out of hand. After they were in the limousine, he nervously stared out the side window. He could tell that Eve was watching him, watching him close.

"Your Aunt seems nice enough," she said breaking the silence.

"Yeah, she knows me like a book," he said not turning to her.

"She seems to really like you," Eve added.

"Yeah I know. She likes everything about me too."

"It's nice to have family. You should feel lucky, I wish I had Aunts and Uncles," Eve said sadly.

"It's not all what it's cracked up to be," he shook his head.

"Yes maybe, but at least you have family."

Diamond finally turned to her and for a brief instant, he felt an intense pang of guilt for what he was doing to her. The moment quickly passed though, like he had told Delicia it was business, just business.

The plane touched down and quickly came to a stop. Darrius was more nervous landing than taking off. One of the pilots came out from the cockpit and lowered the door. Late afternoon sunshine streamed in along with hot humid air. Yashi smiled at him and motioned him to grab his bag. Following her off the plane, he noticed a waiting black limousine. The windows were tinted making it impossible for him to see who was inside. Moving quickly in front of Yashi he opened the door for her then followed her inside. He was surprised that nobody was waiting for them.

"I thought…" he began to say.

"Not here, never here," she said crossing her legs.

"How long before you meet with your people?" he asked.

"Why are you concerned?" she asked. "Unless you do care about Jah-

Man's business." "Never" he frowned.

"Maybe I was wondering how much time we would have together."

"Oh, I see what you're getting at," she smiled glancing at her watch.

"We have a few hours before dinner, then all evening and all night together, how's that?"

"I like that just fine!" he smiled.

"We will have to leave early in the morning though," she added.

"So, where are we going now?" he asked.

"Hotel"

The limousine pulled into a very small hotel that sat right on the beach. Grabbing their bags, he followed her inside. Ceiling fans rotated sucking warm air down from the ceiling making the air around them seem hotter. The hotel was shabby compared to the Orion and he was surprised that Yashi had come here. He expected something much more lavish, plush, men running around with fully automatic weapons. Not a run down hotel sitting on the beach with nobody around.

"Room 40, that's down the hallway, last room on the back facing the beach," the man behind the counter said tossing the key down for them.

"Could we get a wake up call for 6 a.m.?" she asked.

"What, do you think I'm going to be up then?" the man looked at her nearly laughing.

"It was a thought," she shrugged.

Darrius said nothing and just followed her out of the office and down the corridor to their room. The inside was small, quaint but clean. There was one large king size bed and he sat down on the edge testing the springs.

"Hope they don't squeak," she said opening her suitcase.

"Quiet as a mouse," he smiled.

"Want to take a quick swim?" she asked.

"Sure, do we have time?"

"I wouldn't have asked if we didn't," she said grabbing her bathing suit.

Together they walked down to the beach, there were a few other couples wandering around and the first thing that rooted him in his tracks was that all the women were topless.

"Never been to a topless beach?" she asked tossing her towel down on the sand.

"Nope" he said softly.

"I could have taken mine off but I'm not into public display," she said tying her hair back.

"That's good," he said trying not to stare at other women.

She took his hand and moments later they were in the water together. To Darrius the world along with the topless women ceased to exist. All that existed was Yashi. All he wanted to exist at this moment was the blissful fun they were sharing, which he never wanted to end.

Eve took her high heels off and grabbed hold of Diamonds hand. The night sky was illuminated by a beautiful full moon that glinted off the water. They ate dinner not saying much and she thought that odd compared to other dinners they shared. Maybe he was concerned about his Aunt? In any event, the sand was cool on their toes as they walked along the wet sand, the water rushing up over their ankles then just as quickly rushing away back to the sea.

"Diamond?" she asked softly.

"What?" he replied.

"Tell me the truth, please. How do you feel about me?" she asked.

"What do you mean?" he said.

"How do you feel about being with me? Am I special to you?" she asked.

"Eve, you're the most wonderful woman I've ever known," he began to say. "You're sexy - damn sexy!"

"You're just saying that," she smiled.

"No I'm not," he said stopping her.

"I really mean it, you are the most sexy woman I know," he said looking into her eyes.

"Do you want me to prove it to you?"

She said nothing and just nodded. Standing right at the water's edge he slowly began to remove her clothing until she stood before him naked. He then removed his own, tossing them down at their feet. Eve felt embarrassed and covered her breasts with her arms. She was worried that someone would chance upon them, her without her clothes. It also excited her terribly.

His hands were soft as they guided her down to their pile of clothes. She could feel his cock press against her as his lips gently yet firmly caressed her ear and then her neck. Between the beating of her own heart, all she could hear was the water as it slid in and out along the sand.

Nearly an hour later they were again walking along the sand, though she was wobblier on her feet than he was. He had taken her like never before whispering his love to her as he did. Her world was never better, it was perfect and she wanted the events of this night to be repeated until the dawn of the new morning sun.

"I love you," she breathed to him as she rested her head against his arm.

"I love you too," he replied.

Something caught her eye ahead in the water. The gentle movement of the waves sucked it out, then back in again to embed itself on the sand. It was a dark lump; one that was large for the distance they were at.

"What's that?" she pointed to the lump.

"I don't know, let's look," he added.

As they drew closer, he could feel Eve's hands tighten on his arm. The dark lump that moved back and forth along the sand was a body. The waves swung the arm back and forth giving it a grotesque image of it waving to them.

"Eve, stay here," Diamond said stopping her.

"No, I don't want to be alone," she said following him.

The body was that of a woman, her saturated dress clung tightly to her body. Reaching out Diamond gently and cautiously turned the body onto its back. Staring blankly up at the full moon was Tisha, her eyes bulging and her mouth agape with a sand crab hanging from the corner. The skin around her throat was white the thin outline of a cut that ran the length of her throat. Diamond let go of her body and it rolled back onto its side, all he could hear was Eve screaming repeatedly.

Chapter 10

The Land Rover bounced along the bumpy dirt road, its headlights lighting the roadside. The lush landscape looked ominous at night, and the lights caused it to look even more so. Raffie drove, Ohpton sat next to him and Sharon hung on in the back. It was a long trip to the suburbs of Kingston where Raffie had lived, which would mean it would be early morning before they arrived back at the Orion.

"Wake me when you want someone to switch time with you at the wheel," Sharon said yawning.

"You should get some sleep too," Raffie said to Ohpton.

"Hard to sleep when we're doing something dangerous. I'm also worried about Steven, I know Mama Rose will take good care of him, but," Ohpton began to say.

"Yes, I feel the same way. Jah-Man is relentless and he'll go from house to house in order to find him."

"That makes what we're doing that much more important," Sharon said from the back.

"I hope we're not getting in over our heads," Ohpton breathed softly.

"Your idea," Sharon added.

"Look, we just need to keep our wits about us, no mistakes, no problems," Raffie said trying to give them hope.

"What about Darrius and Eve?" Ohpton asked.

"Jah-Man has something in mind for them."

"Yes he does and I feel that the woman Jah-Man has Darrius escorting is not what she seems either," Raffie added.

"How so?" Sharon asked.

"If she is a buyer, why is she spending so much time with Darrius?" Raffie asked.

"Because Jah-Man wants it that way," Ohpton added.

"No, she doesn't have to do what Jah-Man wants yet she spends much of her time with Darrius. He doesn't fit into the equation at all. That's what bothers me," Raffie said.

"Maybe she's more civil, not like Jah-Man and the rest of his flunkies," Sharon speculated.

"Maybe but I doubt it. I hope that whatever goes down that Darrius isn't caught in the middle of it all," Raffie said tapping the steering wheel with his finger.

"Eve bothers me too."

"You're telling me. Delicia is pushing hard on her. She has Eve's head so screwed up regarding Diamond that she won't listen to me or anyone else," Sharon explained.

"Why?" Raffie asked.

"Doesn't it seem odd to you that Jah-Man and Delicia have taken an interest in Eve and Darrius, who are sister and brother?" Ohpton said cocking his head around to look at Sharon.

"I don't have any answers," Sharon shook her head.

"And what about these duppy children?" Raffie said.

"That might be a whole other matter, something that's not related to JahMan and the others," Sharon said.

"I found out something else today while I was digging. There's been someone snooping around the resort, asking questions about Jah-Man," Raffie said.

"Babylon, maybe drug enforcement?" Ohpton added.

"I doubt it, Jah-Man has the police and every other agency on the island in his hip pocket. He pays them off handsomely for their services. No, I think there is someone else entering the picture," Raffie said softly.

"I've also had a lot of women, really beautiful women in the salon in the last couple of days. No men hanging around, which is odd anyway, but I overheard them talking to each other. They said something about some guy called the Frenchman and how they hoped he stayed on the island for a while longer," Sharon added.

"That would explain the yacht, supposedly a big, I mean big yacht came in about three days ago. South American registry," Raffie said.

"I'd bet my teeth's eye that it's his."

"How do you find this stuff out?" Ohpton grinned.

"You forget, my parents were the law," Raffie beamed.

"You two should try to get some sleep."

Sharon said nothing and just closed her eyes; sleep wouldn't come easy to her.

Steven lay out on the small bunk in the back of Mama Rose's place. It was going on two days since he left work, two days since Jah-Man had more than likely put a price on his head. He worried about the others, worried much more for Sharon. He couldn't take his mind off her. He saw her every time he closed his eyes, the simplest things reminded him of her, and he wanted nothing more than to be at her side. Yet, now he was hiding, hiding like a scared animal. Sitting up on the bunk, he became determined not to hide. He was determined to face life like a man, like he had done for so many years in the orphanage. It was the only way to face your problems.

"That is not a good idea," a soft voice spoke from the shadows.

Looking up he saw the large frame silhouette of Mama Rose. When she knew he had seen her she hobbled into the room and sat down on the bed next to him.

"This isn't the way either," he said softly.

"Maybe not, but it is the way you need to follow right now," she said rubbing his back.

"I'm worried about the others, worried that they'll pay the price to protect me," he said.

"They are strong willed, just like you are and they are not stupid either. You see Steven, one of you alone is vulnerable but all of you together?"

"But this is my problem, not theirs. I'm the one that got into trouble," he shook his head.

"No, you didn't. You defended Sharon so you did nothing wrong," she said.

"I spoke when I should have kept my mouth shut," he said.

"No, Delicia is to blame, she is the one who lied. She caused Jah-Man to put a price on you. She's the Dibi Dibi," she said.

"How am I going to get out of this?" he said rubbing his hands over his face.

"Solutions always come, you have got to have faith, and believe in the higher good," she softly said.

"I can't just sit here, I can't."

"You must, if you leave you risk endangering the others," she said. "Sometimes the toughest burdens are the ones we least expect."

Patting him on the back she wearily got to her feet. Steven watched her leave the room, her words filled with wisdom, he understood that much of her intention. Lying back on the bunk he stared at the ceiling. He was fighting what he felt, fighting it with all his might. A little voice inside of him screamed, screamed for him to find a solution on his own. His mind held back the voice but it was quickly losing ground.

He had no idea how much time had passed but an idea came to him.
Maybe he could reason with Delicia, maybe he could persuade her to talk to JahMan, make him understand it had nothing to do with him. It was a logical solution to a terrible problem, at this time at night though,

where would she be? Was she with Jah-Man or was she at the Orion? He was sure of one thing, the only way he was going to find out was to go there.

Getting up he tiptoed as quietly as possible to the front door. Opening the door the bell above it jingled slightly, he was quick though and snatched the bell with his hand preventing it from sounding. Moments later he was outside, the night air feeling refreshing on his face.

Inside Mama Rose lay awake; she knew that Steven had left. She knew the feelings of turmoil inside of him had won over logic. She could do nothing to stop him from leaving; she had already tried. He was following his own destiny; she only prayed that it wasn't death that was close behind.

William sat on the darkened porch overlooking the ocean. It was quiet and he didn't have a single light on. The star filled sky was beautiful, especially the way it glinted off the water.

His discussion earlier in the day with Darwin had alarmed him. Repeatedly, he had tried to fathom his brother's reasoning behind his threat. Why would he think that he was dangerous to him? There was much going on, was it possible that Jah-Man had felt threatened and had lashed out at the nearest person?

The possibilities were endless; he loved his brother though and worried much about him. He knew it was Steven that was involved with Delicia; he also knew that Steven wouldn't have put a hand on her ever. Delicia was playing a dangerous game one that he still hadn't figured out. There was something up her sleeve, something that involved Eve, he was sure though, that if she knew that Eve and Darrius were Jah-Man's children she would back off…way off.

William sighed; he also knew that if Eve and Darrius ever found out that their father had killed their mother.

A rustling in the bushes next to his house alerted him. He was jumpy after talking with Darwin.

"Mr. Stone?" a voice whispered from the bushes.

"Yes, who is there?" he called back.

From the shadows emerged Junior, for a moment, he stood there, staring at William then quickly walked around the front of the house and climbed the stairs. William knew Junior since he was a schooler, knew Mama Rose when she was young and he was there when they buried Jaco. Junior never understood what he had done that fateful night; never accepted the blame for his brother's death.

"What brings you out here this late at night Junior?"

"I wish to talk with you about your brother," Junior said.

"May I sit?"

William motioned with his hand; Junior pulled one of the heavy wooden chairs closer to him and sat down.

"Your brother Jah-Man is powerful. We both know that, but have you noticed any changes in him lately?" Junior asked.

"My brother's business is his own and is no concern of mine," William lied.

"You say that but do you actually believe it?" Junior pushed.

"I've worked for him for many years now. He has done me well and I am very loyal to him. I have also heard many rumors lately," Junior said sighing heavily.

"Rumors, gossip, they are the breeders of lies," William said.

"Tell me truths."

"I have heard that Jah-Man refuses to deal with certain clients, that he is actively seeking or in the process of seeking a new client to sell to," Junior said softly. "Is this true?"

"Like I said, his business is his own and of no concern of yours, or mine" William said.

"I have also heard that his old suppliers are not happy with him or his dealings with others. I have heard them making threats; threats to him and the people closest to him," Junior explained.

William frowned at Junior's words. The night was cloudless, the moon full and Junior could see William's expression of concern.

"Who Jah-Man deals with is his business," William reaffirmed.

"Even it costs him his life?" Junior pointed out.

"Why do you not go directly to Jah-Man? Why come to me with this information?"

"Because you are close to him, because he would take your words seriously while he would scoff at mine," Junior stated.

"Do you have names of those who are displeased with him?" William asked.

"No names yet, but I will keep my ears open and see what I can find out. I did hear though that they were planning on hitting him during his next big shipment."

"Is that so?" William said softly.

"They have someone inside, someone close to Jah-Man," Junior said.

"We already know this," William nodded.

"Yes, you might, but we can flush out this person also," Junior stated.

"How?"

"I can give these people false information and set a trap for them. Where and when was Jah-Man's next big shipment?"

"Soon"

"If I knew then I can pass along bogus information, throw them off his trail," Junior added.

"You have been under Jah-Man long enough to know that this type of information is not talked about," William pointed out.

"I understand completely, I just want to make sure that we put a stop to this as soon as possible," Junior said.

"That is something I will have to think about, I will let you know soon if I choose to," William said.

"Do not wait too long, if Jah-Man's enemies are getting close to him, we will have to move quickly," Junior said getting up.

"How is your mama?" William said changing the subject.

"My mama is my mama. Her ideas are old fashioned - ancient," he said slightly rattled at the mention of her name.

"They maybe old fashioned but her heart is in the right place," William said.

"She is old and foolish," he retorted.

"She is your mama and family is important Junior, I would have thought after your brother..."

"I must be leaving, there is much to do," he said and quickly bounded down the porch stairs.

"If you see her, tell her I was thinking about her," he said watching Junior disappear into the underbrush.

He did not care for Junior; the boy had no respect for his elders. Family meant nothing to him, only money and power. If though, what he said were true it would explain many things. The man who was killed on the beach was an example; someone was trying to crowd in on Jah-Man's territory. They were challenging him for control of his empire.

Suddenly another chill washed through him with intense force. If what Junior said was true, a war was brewing, a war that could have profound impact on all their lives.

It was close to 1 a.m. when Ohpton pulled the Land Rover off the road per Raffie's directions. In the beam of their headlights was a very tight pathway through the grove. They had passed the spot once before, the vegetation had grown in so much that even Raffie had trouble locating the road.

"How far?" Sharon asked.

"300, maybe 400 feet," Raffie said.

"Stuff is pretty thick in there, you think we should drive through it?" Ohpton asked.

"We scratch this thing up and our butts are going to be in a sling." "You mean <u>my butt</u>?" Raffie said softly.

"Yeah, your butt," Ohpton said staring out at the thick foliage.

"We could just walk it," Sharon said.

"Won't take us long, we have flashlights," she said pulling them from the bag they brought.

Both Raffie and Ohpton looked at each other and shrugged. They got out of the vehicle; he locked the doors and slipped the key into his pocket. Sharon handed each of them a flashlight. Moments later three small beams of light shone back and forth, as they walked down the dense road.

Sharon suddenly felt uneasy, she stopped and turned the flashlight to the trees around her. She had the intense feeling that someone was watching them. Her imagination was running wild as she expected the flashlight to reveal two glowing red eyes connected to some hideous beast. The Moon was full and the light it cast only added to the scary atmosphere.

"What's wrong?" Ohpton whispered to her.

"I don't know. I just have this feeling like someone is watching us," she said darting the light back and forth.

"This late at night, I highly doubt anyone is watching us. I don't know if you noticed, but there weren't many other houses on the way here. This place is remote!" Ohpton said darting his light around them.

"Come on you two, if we want to get back to the Orion in time we have to keep moving," Raffie called to them his flashlight the only indication of where he was.

They kept moving, the distance seemed much further than any of them expected. Sharon still felt uneasy and she occasionally swung her flashlight directly behind her as if she expected some demon to be waiting to pounce on her.

Instead all that greeted her was the empty and very dense road they had just traversed.

"How much further? We must have gone double what you expected already!" Ohpton said.

"Are you sure this was the right road?" Sharon asked.

"Maybe I just brought you two out here because in disguise I am a violent ax murderer," Raffie said solemnly.

"Yeah right," Ohpton nearly laughed.

Suddenly, Raffie swung around directing the beam of light beneath his chin. The effect made him look hideous and gruesome and he growled at the same moment. Ohpton caught unaware, fell backwards onto the hard dirt road. Sharon startled, let out a scream that was more frightening than Raffie's prank.

"Damn you! That wasn't funny. This is no time for one of your pranks Raffie!" Sharon snapped.

"Sometimes I don't get you," Ohpton said picking himself up off the ground.

"Hey come on you two, it took the tension off things didn't it?" Raffie chuckled.

"I should box you," Sharon said pursing her lips.

"I think my house was right over there," Raffie pointed into the darkness. "Look for anything that resembles a small square 3.5 inch computer disk."

Sharon and Ohpton said nothing; they just followed Raffie, only this time not as closely. He was correct, looming out of the darkness and clearly visible in the bright moonlight was a humongous pile of rubble.

Raffie stood quietly staring at the huge pile, he didn't want to tell the others but just being here brought torrents of memories back. Some good but many of them traumatic like his last few days at the mansion. His eyes darted back and forth as if he half expected the boxes containing his parent's heads to be still strewn amongst the rubble.

"Are you all right?" Sharon said softly coming up behind him.

"I can still see them like it was yesterday, the blood and the expressions," he said his voice barely audible.

"They're no longer here Raffie. They're gone, long ago," she said trying to help him.

"I know that, but it doesn't make it any easier. I've tried to put this place out of my mind for years now, but I knew that someday I would come back."

"We better start looking," Ohpton said as he moved to the opposite side of the debris pile.

Raffie said nothing and began sifting through the debris. Sharon felt sorry for him; she could only imagine the horror of what he went through.
Concentrating on the task, she began looking for the disks.

The night wore on and they began to tire. Ohpton and Raffie had begun to move some of the heavier charred beams and debris while Sharon continued to search. They had come across many things that were personal to Raffie, things from his childhood, things his parents owned. He was surprised that looters hadn't picked the site clean.

Suddenly, Sharon spied something beneath another large timber. She tried to move the dirt from around it but the timber was wedged tightly above it.

"I think I found something," she said casting the light for the others to see.

"Looks like a metal storage box," Ohpton said.

"Those fireproof types."

"We have to get it out," Raffie said.

"Maybe we can use a lever and pry the beam up enough for Sharon to pull the box out."

Searching with their flashlights, Ohpton found another beam capable of wedging beneath the large beam that covered the box. With all their might, they both pulled down on the lever. The larger beam groaned and moved slightly. Sharon tried to wiggle it free but it was still too tight.

"A little more, just a little more," she said yanking on the box.

Without warning, from the dense brush around the ruined house came an ear-shattering scream. It was so intense, it sounded like a woman or child was being tortured. The three of them froze the hair all over them standing on-end.

"What in the blood fire was that?" Sharon muttered.

"I don't know, let's just get that box and get out of here!" Raffie said pressing down on the lever with all his might.

The beam moved an inch further, it was just enough for Sharon to wiggle the box free from its earthly tomb. No sooner had she pulled the box free than a child's giggle broke the stillness of the night.

"Oh no, don't tell me," she said looking in the direction the sound had come from.

At the edge of the tree line a dimly, yet glowing form skirted from behind a tree only to disappear out of sight behind another.

"What are they doing here?" Raffie stuttered.

"They must have followed us, but why?" Sharon said.

"Is that what you two saw the other night?" Ohpton said watching the dark woods where the child disappeared.

"Yes it is, but what are they doing here now?" Raffie asked.

"They must have followed us," Sharon said again.

"But why?" Ohpton added.

"To kill us," Raffie said his eyes darting from side to side.

"I knew something was watching us…I could feel it!" Sharon said.

"Something tells me we should clear out of here right now!" Raffie said the urgency in his voice.

Again, the subtle yet chilling giggle and again the figure darted from behind a palm only to disappear again. All their hearts beat wildly as they tried frantically to find the ghostly apparition.

A chilling voice of a child rang out from the thicket.

"You're all going to die – your going to die!" They sang almost like a nursery rhyme.

"Oh brother, this is getting scary," Sharon said her mouth dry and pasty.

"Yeah, mainly because the last few times I saw them they didn't speak," Raffie breathed his eyes focused on the thick forest.

"Look, grab something, anything to defend yourself with," Ohpton said casting his light into the rubble.

"How do you fight a duppy?" Sharon said doing the same.

"Remember, there were two of them," Raffie said grabbing a thin broken metal pipe.

"Come on, let's get out of here, Ohpton, you keep your flashlight focused behind us, Sharon you watch the sides and I'll keep us clear ahead," Raffie said heading for the road.

"And what happens if I see one of them?" Sharon said following.

"Yell" Raffie said.

"Oh that'll help," Ohpton added.

They began moving back down the road as quickly as they could. Their flashlight beams darted back and forth in rapid secession. Their ears strained to hear any movement around them, the frightening giggle, or a blood-curling scream, anything that would give them direction as to where the duppies were.

Suddenly, Ohpton caught something out of the corner of his eye, the duppy of the little girl dashed across the road.

"One of them is back here!" he yelled.

At that instant something slammed hard into the side of his head. The world around him spun and quickly became distorted. He could hear Sharon yelling but it sounded so distant and far away.

Seconds later he collapsed to the ground.

"Raffie! Something happened to Ohpton!" Sharon yelled dashing to Ohpton's side.

Rolling him over she quickly felt this neck, his pulse was strong but he was just unconscious. The side of his head was covered in blood caused by a nasty gash running along his hairline to the side of his right temple.

"A rock," Raffie said from above her.

"He's just out cold," she said softly.

"Why would duppies use rocks?" Raffie asked casting his flashlight into the woods.

"Does it matter? We need to get out of here and fast," she said.

"Can you carry him?"

"I can try, he's nearly double my size you know," Raffie sighed handing Sharon his flashlight.

"Well we're not leaving him." "No kidding," Raffie said.

With considerable effort Raffie managed to get Ohpton up off the ground and onto his back. He grunted and strained as he carried the dead weight of Ohpton. Every step was a struggle and he shuffled along like a drunken man. Sharon kept the flashlight beams dancing along the road, in front, in back, in all directions. Her palms were sweaty, her skin clammy, she was terrified.

Casting the light forward the beam came upon the shiny body of the Land Rover. The vehicle never looked so good and she noticed that even Raffie was trying to move quicker to reach it.

When they reached the wheels, Sharon opened the door and Raffie set him on the back seat. Breathing hard, Raffie leaned against the side of the vehicle.

"You know that duppies can't throw rocks," he said.

"Why not? If they were using guns I'd tend to believe you," Sharon said putting the small box on the floor of the vehicle. She was going to shut the flashlight off when her beam cast upon the vehicle.

"Oh sweet Jesus!" Raffie breathed softly.

Sharon's light cast upon the front tire of the Rover, it was flat. Quickly she moved the beam to each tire - they were all intact.

"We only have one spare. only one," Raffie said.

"I'm in serious trouble."

"We all will be if we don't get back by morning," Sharon added.

"At least they didn't flatten all the tires."

Raffie quickly moved to change the tire. They would have to try and get the spare fixed before they brought the Rover back, and that would mean it would be morning before they could get it fixed.

Sharon tried to keep the light focused on changing the spare tire but she occasionally directed it into the dark forest around them.

"I need the light. I can't change this tire in the dark," he said struggling with the lug nuts.

"Sorry but I can't help but think they're watching us and waiting for some reason," she said looking around them.

"They're out there all right, the quicker we change this tire the quicker we can be out of here," Raffie said.

When he was done he tossed the flat tire and the tools into the back, opting not to put them where they belong. He slipped behind the wheel and Sharon slid into the passenger seat. No sooner had they closed their doors than rocks began to rain down on them. They were small, but deadly enough.

The first one cracked the windshield leaving a spider web pattern; the others beat against the body with unusual frequency.

"Hurry get us out of here!" Sharon yelled.

Raffie spun the vehicle backwards spewing up a cloud of dust, and then pushed the accelerator to the floor. The rover lurched to the right, then left before straightening out. Sharon reached behind the seat trying to keep Ohpton from bouncing off onto the floorboards. Raffie drove like the devil himself was chasing him. "You can slow down, slow down Raffie," Sharon said her grip on Ohpton's arm tight.

Slowly, Raffie eased off the accelerator until they were traveling at a comfortable speed. His mouth was dry, parched and beads of sweat trickled down his face.

"W...what happened?" Ohpton said waking.

Sitting up he blinked, then held his hand to the side of his head wincing. Sharon grabbed a few napkins that were in the glove box and handed them to him. He held them to the side of his head then rolled his eyes.

"Ouch!" he said softly.

"You got one nasty bump on the side of your head," Sharon said.

"What happened?" he asked.

"Those duppy children threw a rock and struck you," Raffie said.

"I knew your head was hard though," he smiled.

"No, what happened to the windshield?"

Raffie's smile quickly faded when his eyes glanced up at the fractured glass. He then quickly pulled the rover to the side of the road. Grabbing a flashlight he got out and walked all around the vehicle. Sharon was going to do the same, but in the dim light of the flashlight she could see Raffie's expression. It was grim.

When he got back into the car he clicked the flashlight off and sat there staring at the dash. He then looked over at Sharon his face showing serious concern.

"It's dented - dented all over," he breathed.

"How bad? Is it something we can pull out before we get back to the Orion?" Ohpton said softly.

"Forget it, the dents are too small. It chipped a bunch of paint off too and then add the windshield to it," he said shaking his head.

"We'll deal with it when we get back," Sharon tried to sound optimistic.

"It's over and you both know it is. When they get wind of this damage, my job is gone," Raffie shook his head.

"You don't know that," Ohpton added.

"Come off it. Do you think they're just going to forget this?" Raffie snapped.

"So what? So what if you get fired," Sharon shot back.

"So what? How can you say that? I want to get off this island as much as the rest of us! Without my job, without adding to our fund then I'm stuck here!" he shot back.

"Cool down Raffie and just think for a moment will you?" Ohpton said grabbing his shoulder.

"You might get fired and then again you might not, either way we didn't come here for our health," he said.

"Yes he's right," Sharon added.

"We're doing this to get information on Jah-Man so we can take his drug money, right?"

Raffie nodded not looking at them. They hadn't done this for their health, but now they had just committed themselves to their plan. With Steven out of work, now him, getting hold of Jah-Man's money had now become a priority. It would be the only way for any of them to get off the island. Raffie slipped the transmission into drive and pulled the rover back out onto the road.

Eve sat huddled in Delicia's arms, she wept uncontrollably. After finding Tisha's body on the beach they had, per Diamond's request, called the Babylon anonymously. They then went to Delicia's where they found her just about ready to leave.

"It's okay Eve, it's okay," Delicia said stroking her hair.

"She, she was my friend! Why and who?" she wailed.

"There's nothing you can do now, what's done is done," Delicia said looking at Diamond.

Diamond stood leaning against the window frame, in his hand was a tall glass of whiskey. He seemed unaffected by what had happened, almost impatient.

"What am I going to do?" Eve cried.

"Nothing honey, nothing at all," she said.

"You need to get some sleep. Come on, let's put you to bed," Delicia said guiding her to the bedroom.

A short time later Delicia emerged closing the bedroom door behind her. Diamond continued to stare out the window at the dark ocean beyond.

"What really happened?" she asked him.

"Don't know what you're talking about, we found her in the surf," he shrugged.

"You didn't kill her?" Delicia asked.

"Me?" he asked laughing.

"Why would I want to kill her?"

"Because maybe she found out about your true intentions with Eve?" "She had no idea, nobody does," he shook his head.

"Are you sure?"

"Positive"

"Then who killed her?" Delicia asked.

"Why don't you ask your boyfriend? He's the logical place to start," Diamond said setting his glass down.

"Jah-Man doesn't kill kids," she snapped.

"You're kidding me right? Jah-Man has killed kids before. Maybe not directly but he gives the order to do so," Diamond pointed out.

"I don't believe it!" she shook her head.

"Are you that much of a fool? He uses children now to do his dirty work!"

Delicia shot him a cold look, she had her suspicions, had seen things that she couldn't explain but she just didn't want to believe it.

"You find out anything more from Eve?" she asked changing the subject.

"Maybe I would have if the night had ended up the way I planned. A dead body in the surf kind of throws off the sexual urge if you know what I mean?" "Well, keep trying. Maybe in the next few days," she said.

"Yeah, maybe," he said glancing at his watch.

"I have to go, if I leave now I can still make a little corn," he smiled heading for the door.

"You really enjoy selling your body don't you?" Delicia said following him to the door.

"They flock to you, why?"

"Ha! There are worse things for a guy to do in life you know, and I'm just good at what I do," he winked at her.

"Maybe someday I'll give you a freebie."

Delicia said nothing and just closed the door behind him. She went back into the bedroom, for a moment she stood and stared at Eve. She had given her a sedative; she would be asleep the whole night. As she watched her sleep she felt a pang of jealously. There had been a time in her own life that she too had been innocent and free. She had been a different person then, she looked at life through very different eyes. Then she had met Jah-Man and her life changed.

Slipping out of her clothes she hung them up and grabbed a silk nightgown. She then grabbed a blanket and went out into the living room. Tossing the blanket on the couch she hesitated. She wondered if she should have gone to Jah-Man and spent the night there. He would undoubtedly still be upset with her with what he saw on the video. No, it was better that she allow him to cool down. Holding her hand to her face she remembered how he had struck her before. Indeed her life had changed and she wondered if it had been for the better.

Unfolding the blanket she curled up on the couch, reaching up she turned the light out and let the darkness close in around her.

There came a soft knock on the door. For a moment she thought it was something else but the soft rapping came again. Sitting up she frowned, had JahMan come looking for her? This she quickly dispelled, he would have just walked in - he had a key anyway. Turning the light back on she walked over and slipped the chain on the door. Opening it slightly she saw Steven standing on the other side. He was looking from side to side nervously.

"Delicia, I need to talk to you," he whispered.

Delicia quickly unlatched the chain and opened the door. Steven came in and she closed it, putting both the chain and the deadbolt in place. She then quickly went over and closed the drapes keeping any outside eyes from prying.

Steven watched her; she wore a very short silk nightgown. It barely covered her bottom. When she turned to him he noticed that the front was a mesh lace and displayed her breasts openly. He looked away.

"Why have you come here? Do you know how much danger you're in? Do you know how much danger you put me in?" she snarled softly.

"Delicia I had to come. I have to try and straighten this out and the only person that can do that is you," he said.

"Me? What makes you think I can change anything?" she shook her head.

"Because you're the reason I'm in this situation," he pointed out.

"You need to tell him the truth - tell him what really happened."

"He has a video Steven, a video of us naked," she said feeling her heart race as she remembered the video.

"But if you tell him the truth, tell him that it didn't happen, that the video was a lie," he pleaded.

"None of it would have happened if you had, if you had just..." she began to say.

"You would have lied if I had? That would have made the difference?" he frowned.

Delicia turned and began to pace, she thumbed and played with the mass of gold chains around her neck. Thoughts ran through her mind, thoughts of how she could send a knife through Sharon's heart. Turning she looked at Steven. "Yes, I would have lied to Jah-Man, I would have if only you had made love to me," she said softly.

"But Delicia," he said his eyes growing wide.

"...and I will <u>now</u> if you do," she said.

Steven ran his hands through his hair; he was again faced with a choice. If he made love to Delicia, if he forced himself to make love to her, she would get Jah-Man off his back. He could recoup his life without living in fear. He would also be saving the others from Jah-Man.

"The choice is yours Steven. I'll wait for your answer. I promise I will keep my end of the deal," she said.

"Delicia. Why can't you help me out without doing it this way?" his voice nearly begging.

"I want you Steven and that is my price. What is your life and the lives of your friends worth to you?" she said raising an eyebrow.

Steven swallowed; he had never been faced with such a choice. He wanted to run, wanted to go quickly back to Mama Rose's place and hide.

Hide - the thought gave him a chill. He wouldn't hide from anything ever again.

He nodded to her.

"I don't want to do this in the bedroom. I want to do this here, right here," she said drawing close to him.

"I need to use your bathroom," he stuttered.

Delicia pointed in the direction he needed to go. Steven quickly pushed passed her and went into the bathroom closing the door behind him. Leaning heavily against it he closed his eyes. Everything inside him screamed for him not to do this but he would never allow Jah-Man to harm the others, and he would go through the others to get to him, it was only a matter of time.

Turning the water on he splashed it liberally over his face; he then stared at himself in his mirror. There were dark circles under his eyes and he looked as if he had aged overnight.

"God forgive me, Sharon forgive me," he breathed softly then opened the door.

The lights were turned down low; the room was bathed in a dim glow the light bulbs emitting a tiny ball of light. At first he waited for his eyes to adjust to the low light, then he looked around. Moving into the room he looked for Delicia, he thought that maybe she had decided to go into the bedroom.

Then he noticed the candles. In front of the couch the coffee table was pushed out of the way and a thick comforter had been placed down on the floor. All around it, candles burned brightly, in the middle, lying naked on the comforter was Delicia.

For a moment he stood and stared at her, she was a beautiful woman with a body many men would kill for. But she was also evil and he felt like he had made a pact with the devil for his soul.

Slowly he began to remove his clothes tossing them on the couch. Delicia eyed him with intense lust, by the time he stood before her naked, her mouth was open and her eyes glinted back with passion. Reaching out her hand she motioned him to come to her. Steven stepped over the candles and crawled onto the comforter next to her. Her hands worked over his body and her lips hungrily began to kiss him all over. She became a live blanket as she slid her naked body over his making sure to touch his most sensitive areas.

"Keep your end of the deal," she breathed laboriously to him.

"I am, I'm here," he said staring at the ceiling.

For a moment Delicia stared at him, he didn't look back at her. She then slid her leg over him and rested herself down on him. The feeling was intense, consuming, it was like nothing she had ever felt before. Steven closed his eyes as she worked herself on him. She was aroused as never before.

"Take me Steven, take me please. Take me or I won't keep my end of the deal," she threatened him.

Steven stared up at her, slowly, he raised his hands and lightly touched her pum pum. Delicia closed her eyes at his touch. There was no other way, he would have to do this, it was his only choice.

Pushing her off him, he crawled on top of her and again slipped inside of her. Delicia was smiling, her passion consuming her.

Eve squinted and rolled over; dreams of her mama had woken her. It had been years since she dreamt of her mama. Now for some reason the dreams had returned. Pulling the covers back she wobbled to her feet, she was still groggy but she had to go to the bathroom. Walking quietly she didn't want to wake Delicia who more than likely was sleeping on the couch.

Delicia felt herself release, her legs were wrapped tightly around Steven's waist. He was an expert lover, she felt so full, so complete and that was something she had never felt in her life.

"Oh…oh my God!"

Steven and Delicia both looked up to see Eve standing looking at them with her hand held close to her mouth. Her eyes were like saucers and she quickly dashed back into the bedroom slamming the door. Getting up, Steven quickly grabbed his clothes and dashed from the room, his world had just come apart again.

Delicia lay there staring at the ceiling, savoring the warm sensation in her pelvis. She then got up and stepped over the candles. Walking over she opened the louvered doors to her entertainment center, reaching in she turned off the video camera. Her fingers shook as she ran her hand over the cold plastic casing. It was all there, there for her to watch…over and over again.

William walked the path to where he knew Junior stayed. While he walked he had a nagging feeling that he shouldn't tell Junior anything. He also loved his brother very much and wanted no harm to come to him. He also began to think about what Junior had said, about there being someone on the inside close to Jah-Man. At first he thought about everyone that was close to him, there were many but most were just there to protect him, serve him. Very few were close, Delicia was the closest and he had his own suspicions about her. Was she feeding information about Jah-Man? He didn't like her and assuredly didn't trust her.

Then he began to think about whom it might be trying to overthrow JahMan. It was true that he was changing his clients that the Columbians were no longer getting the drugs they needed. They had refused to pay the price set by JahMan. They had wanted the price lowered instead. Were they now trying to take over his organization and dominate the whole island? If they were there was only one person that was capable of such a feat - The Frenchman.

He was Columbia's equivalent to Jah-Man; he had many resources behind him and was just as ruthless, though an operation this far from home was not like him.

He rarely came to these waters and just as rarely dealt directly with JahMan. There were smaller organizations, some even from Cuba, but none had the power or brains to even attempt to bring down Jah-Man.

There were also the Americans, they had tried to bring Jah-Man down years ago but it failed and many, many people were slaughtered as a result, including Raffie's family. It was the year of blood, the year everything changed in Jamaica. It was a year that he tried hard to forget.

Junior's small bungalow sat amiss a row of palms. There was junk scattered all around, garbage strewn about along with liquor bottles. It would be a beautiful place but very <u>chaka chaka</u>. If only he had kept it neat it would be nice. Instead he lived like an animal. With all the money he had received over the years he thought Junior would be living differently. On the outside he appeared better than everyone else, but when you looked at how he actually lived, it was appalling. Reaching up, he knocked hard on the thin wooden door. At first there was no response, so he knocked again. This time Junior answered the door. In his left hand was a bottle of whiskey.

"Yeah, what do you want William?" Junior said opening the door further.

"To talk," he said stepping inside.

The inside of the bungalow was just as horrid as the outside. Dirty clothing was strewn about in piles along with food packages. There was a mattress on the floor at the other end of the room, the covers were tossed and a naked woman lay beneath. William eyed her and she just laid back down covering her body with the sheet.

"Can we talk outside?" he asked Junior.

Junior just nodded and staggered out the door, William following. Taking the lead he let Junior follow him down to the beach.

"There is a pre-shipment that will be sent sometime next week. I don't know the exact day yet since it hasn't yet been determined," William sighed staring out at the open ocean.

"When's the big one?" Junior asked sounding more sober.

"I don't know yet, that will depend on how the pre-shipment goes. Jah-Man's new buyer likes things a certain way."

"You going to know when the pre-shipment happens?" Junior asked taking a swill off the bottle.

"I assume so. What I need from you is simple. I need you to find out who is behind this," William said turning to him.

"What about the person inside?" Junior asked.

"Leave that to me, you need to just find out <u>who</u> it is that is trying to overthrow Jah-Man - is that understood?"

"Yes, but you need to keep me informed. The more I know the easier it will be to spot them," Junior explained.

"Keep your ears open also for any mention of <u>The Frenchman</u>," William asked.

"The Frenchman?" Junior looked at him in surprise.

"Have you heard that name before?" William took notice of Junior's surprise.

"No, no I have not, it just sounds so odd," Junior said looking away.

"Who is this Frenchman anyway?"

"He is a powerful Columbian drug lord who tried once to overthrow JahMan and take control of the island. That was before you began working for JahMan so you wouldn't remember," William said.

"What does this man look like?" Junior asked.

"If you ever meet the man you will know quickly who he is and you will never forget," William said shaking a finger at him.

Junior stared at him, he understood exactly what he meant, and the Frenchman was someone you never forgot. In his case though both the Frenchman and Jah-Man were people he was going to double cross. Things couldn't be going smoother, soon, possibly during the big drug exchange, the two men would slaughter each other and he would be left to pick up the pieces and assume control of the island. Soon the sweet taste of power and success would be his.

Chapter 11

Darrius yawned and rolled over, during the night he hadn't slept as peacefully as he had hoped he would. Nagging worry kept him awake, worry about the others and Yashi. He felt like he was caught between a rock and a hard place with nowhere to run and no place to hide. His imagination ran wild, images of Jah-Man butchering the others his laugh echoing from all corners of his mind. He hated the man, hated him to the point where he wanted to kill him. Kill him...

The thought of committing murder made him shudder. In the past he had thought about it but in a youthful way, now he was contemplating it for real.

"Are you alright?" a soft voice spoke.

Yashi slipped a hand under the cover and pulled the thin sheet off his chest. Her right hand ran up his arm while the fingers on her left hand gently touched the side of his cheek.

"Darrius, is there something wrong?" she breathed drawing her naked body closer to his.

"No. I was just having a nightmare. It is gone now," he whispered back.

"Care to share?" she asked with bonafide concern.

"It is of no matter, it is nothing for you to concern yourself with," he said.

Slipping the sheet further back she pulled her leg over his body and slid herself on top of him. Her hair dangled down in his face and in the early morning light that streamed through the shades he could make out the supple outline of her breasts. Reaching up he gently felt her nipple tighten against his palm. Moments later he drew her down to him.

"Let me chase away the demons - at least for now," she breathed kissing him hard.

By mid day they were leaving the motel room, the heat was not as oppressive as it was in Jamaica. He still had the nagging feeling that something was wrong, that they were all in mortal danger. It was a feeling he couldn't shake. Outside a shiny white limousine waited, its engine gently purring. Darrius opened the door and Yashi slipped into the air-conditioned vehicle with Darrius quickly following. Inside was a middle aged man, his hair speckled with more gray than one would expect. He wore a finely tailored suit and sported a black cane, which he propped between his legs. His features were stern, like they had been carved from granite. A long scar ran the length of his face just below his right eye. His brilliant blue eyes focused on them, keeping particular watch on Darrius.

"Sir, I have been requested to inform you that Jah-Man wants more per Kilo than we have offered. He also promises that he can deliver whatever we wish for volume," Yashi explained.

For a long moment there was silence, then the man pulled his eyes from Darrius and directed them to Yashi.

"Who is he?" the man spoke in a deep husky but definitely European accent.

"This is Darrius Lawson, he was sent by Jah-Man to oversee our meeting," Yashi explained.

"Why? Does this Jah-Man not trust us? We should send this young ones head back in a box to show Jah-Man what the meaning of trust is," the man said softly.

Darrius felt a chill wash over him; this man was now deciding his fate. His mention of sending his head in box made him remember Raffie's parents. Had it been this man who killed them?

"That would not be conducive to better business sir," she quickly said.

"Possibly, but I do not like dealing with someone who *thinks* they have an upper hand over me."

"He is just cautious, nothing more and Darrius was sent more of a token of *trust* than anything else," she said.

"I would rather send his head back in a box," the man said looking at Darrius.

"Now wait a minute," Darrius spoke out.

"I have no dealings with Jah-Man."

"But he has sent you to oversee this meeting. Therefore, he must have some trust in you to do that, it is a big request," the man said.

"True, he has sent me but I do not, have not ever dealt with him before a few weeks ago. I do not know nor do I care about his business," Darrius explained.

"What do you care about Mr. Lawson?" the man asked.

"My friends - Yashi," Darrius quickly said.

"I only want all of us to be away from Jamaica. Away from the drugs and death," Darrius explained.

"It is curious that Jah-Man has sent you. He obviously trusts you, why?" the man frowned.

"I do not know, it is something that I have been trying to figure out for some time now," Darrius said looking out the side window.

"How do I know you're not lying to me? How do I know that this isn't a trick and that Jah-Man has some underhanded ploy waiting for us?" the man spoke as he twisted the cane around in his hands.

"You don't and I don't. I do not know what I can tell you to change that. Jah-Man expects me to report back to him. That much I can be sure of. As long as my friends and Yashi do not get hurt, I personally don't care what you do to the man!" Darrius pointed out.

"So, you would betray Jah-Man?"

"I have no loyalties to a butcher - none," Darrius snapped.

The man turned his gaze to Yashi and just nodded. For a long moment they sat there in silence, then the man gave out a loud sigh.

"You can tell Jah-Man that we will want a pre-shipment on Saturday, say, oh, 300 kilos?" the man said to Yashi.

"Yes sir. I will inform him when we get back," Yashi nodded.

"Mr. Lawson, I do not understand what your role in all this is but I will find out.

She will stick close to you until I determine what it exactly is," he said to Darrius.

Darrius said nothing and just nodded. He then opened the door and slipped out into the ever-increasing morning heat. Yashi followed. The limousine quickly pulled away leaving them standing there.

"I think he likes you," she whispered to him.

"Likes? Yashi, he deals in drugs! I am getting sucked into something I have no desire to get sucked into!"

"You must see this out to the end Darrius. It is what you have to do," she said drawing closer to him.

"And what about you? Where do you fit into this mess?" he looked at her.

"I am the liaison and nothing more, after the next two shipments my job here will be done," she said looking away.

"And what about us?" he continued to look at her.

"Let's not talk about that now. We'll have time in the future to worry about such things, but not now," she said not meeting his eyes.

"So my heart is part of the deal? When your boss gets his new supplier, I get tossed when you leave?" he snapped.

"I asked you to leave this alone right now; we can deal with this later," she breathed softly.

"No Yashi, we deal with it now before our hearts, my heart is torn to shreds," he said softly.

For a long moment she stared out at the open ocean, then looked up into his eyes the tears welling in the corners.

"I care for you Darrius. I care very much, but when this is over I must move on to other things," she said softly the tears beginning to run down her cheeks.

"We can not be together."

"Why? Why must it be this way?" he said rubbing his hands on her shoulders.

"Because it must be that way. I can not tell you now. Later when this is over you will understand," she said wiping her cheeks.

"Understand what?" he asked.

"I can not tell you Darrius - not yet. You will have to wait, it's the only way," she said pulling herself away from him.

Darrius stood there perplexed, he didn't know what to say and didn't understand what was going on. That feeling he had earlier about being caught between a rock and a hard place was now getting worse, as though life were being squeezed out of him.

It was early morning when Raffie pulled the Rover into the Orion's parking lot. For a moment he sat there staring out the windshield, he had dropped the others off a little ways away from the resort. He had to take the blame himself and not involve the others. Slipping out of the vehicle he stopped and stared at it, the vehicle was a mess. Dings and dents were everywhere and the morning sunlight spiraled through the cracked web of the windshield. He suddenly felt depressed.

Taking the keys he walked into the main lobby heading for the supervisors office. When he reached the door he hesitated then reached out and gently knocked. There came no reply. He knocked again, and then tried the door. The handle turned and he slowly opened it stepping inside.

The office was plush with nothing out of order, nothing out of place. It looked like an office on some Hollywood movie set with every object there for effect.

Earl Nash was a big man, tall with a big frame. He towered over Raffie to the point where he had to look up at the man. Nash never took care of himself though, allowing his indulgences to get the better of him. He was overweight with a protruding gut and a double chin and a true lazy body. The man had everything going for him, a good body, if he took care of it, a good job that paid extremely well, use of everything within the resort whenever he wished, yet the man abused everything including himself.

Today, Nash sat back in his chair his eyes closed, kneeling between his legs was a longhaired waitress he knew from the dining room. For a moment he stood there and watched, the couple oblivious to him. He turned to head out of the room when he stopped himself. Turning he walked closer to Nash's desk then tossed the keys down on the hard wooden top. The noise startled them both, they split apart, the woman going for her clothes, Nash quickly pulling up his pants. He then noticed Raffie standing there.

"What in the blood fire do you want?" Nash snarled, as he watched the waitress dash from the room.

"Just returning the vehicle," Raffie said.

"So? You couldn't just wait until later? You had to burst in here and interrupt me?" Nash growled.

"What? Your early morning exercise?" Raffie frowned.

"What I do is none of your business, none do you understand that?" Nash barked.

"What about her? What did you promise her?" Raffie pushed.

"That is none of your business either. Don't you have something to do?" Nash spat.

"Actually yes but you must know that there was a problem with the vehicle last night," he sighed.

"What problem?" Nash grew quiet.

"Hail" Raffie lied.

"Hail? Hail? What are you talking about?" Nash roared.

"Hail. There was a storm last night, sudden downpour; hail the size of golf balls," Raffie continued to lie.

"There was no storm last night, the sky was clear, moon filled. Hail? We have never had hail down here. Were you drinking last night? Possibly trying to cover up for a mistake?" Nash grinned showing his missing front tooth.

"No, there was hail. It was big enough to crack the windshield and I also got a flat tire," he said frankly.

"There is no such thing as hail down here!" Nash slammed his fist down hard on the desk. The man stood up, towering over Raffie.

"If you want to continue working here…"

"I do, I just wanted to tell you want happened," Raffie said heading slowly towards the door.

"Not so fast!" Nash retorted.

Raffie stood with his hand on the doorknob as if at any moment the big man would lunge at him to tear him limb from limb. Nash walked from behind the desk tucking in his shirt as he went.

"Let me see the vehicle," he snapped.

Raffie knew what was coming, knew that his future was inevitable, unless their plan worked they would all be stuck on the island. He opened the door for him and followed him out, before long they stood in front of the Rover. Nash walked around it, then gently reached out and touched the many dents and scratches that covered the body. His eyes were then directed to the hideous crack in the windshield. Raffie stood a little distance away watching the man, he could see how quiet he was, how he was allowing his anger to seethe and build until there was nowhere else for it to go except at him.

"There is much, much damage," Nash said softly. "Much cost will have to

go into getting this fixed." "I will clean out my locker," Raffie replied.

"Oh you will do more than that!" Nash gave him an evil grin.

"You're going to work off what it costs to fix this and continue to work until it's paid for!"

"Yes, I understand, I will return to my job," Raffie said sadly.

"Oh no! You will not be returning to that job. I have another form of work that is more suited for a person like you," Nash grinned.

"What?" Raffie said almost afraid to ask.

"You will be working for Jah-Man. He needs runners, people to carry out his orders despite the danger," Nash said gleefully.

"I will not work for Jah-Man directly. It is bad enough that I have to work here for him but I will not do his illegal bidding," Raffie said putting his foot down.

"We will see about that, we will see," Nash chuckled.

"Go, clean out your locker and we will be in touch with you when you

least expect it."

Raffie turned and quickly hurried back to the resort, he needed to get some space between Nash and himself. It was a small island and now, like Steven, he was on the run too.

Steven sat on the beach staring out at the open water. After the incident last night at Delicia's he had run and run as far away as he could. He ended up here, on a desolate beach on a fairly uninhabited part of the island. He was angry, angry that he could have been so foolish; so stupid. Delicia was not going to help him; not going to get Jah-Man off his back. She just manipulated him and what was Eve doing there? Thoughts ran through his mind and he tried to put reason to them.

Eve had seen him making love Delicia. That was serious enough, Delicia had acted like she wanted Eve to catch them, wanted to destroy something in Eve. He knew that Eve would tell Sharon; knew that as soon as she found out any chance they had of being together was gone. In an instant he had destroyed his world; had taken away any chance he had of a good life. There was nothing left.

The water looked so inviting, so alluring. All he had to do was walk, walk out into the water and keep walking. They would never find him, less of course; his body washed up on the beach someplace. It was the easy way out - the chicken way out. He couldn't do it. He wasn't a quitter; he was a planner someone who needed to succeed in life, someone that succeeded at all cost, against all odds. He wouldn't give up. He would never give up.

Eve rolled over in bed, the night had been restless, and she couldn't put the images out of her mind. The images flashed back and forth, images of Steven. Steven naked on top of Delicia, their bodies wrapped tightly together. She was jealous for many years she knew that Steven had wanted her, that Steven had liked her; and now this?

The thought made her open her eyes. The large ceiling fan rotated above her making a soft swishing noise. The world rushed in on her.

Getting up she dashed to the bathroom. Opening the door she half expected to find Delicia and Steven working it. Instead an empty room greeted her. After rushing into the bathroom she looked around the large room, Delicia was nowhere in sight. The thought made her relax some and she walked more slowly to her bedroom to get dressed. She had to be at work in less than an hour.

When she was done she headed out of the room and into the elevator. When the doors opened crowds of people were milling about, most were the older guests who preferred not to sleep late in the morning. Heading down the hallway she stopped by Sharon's shop. From outside she could see her working on a woman's hair. Swallowing hard she headed for the door, then stopped herself before going inside. She wanted to tell Sharon. She knew she should tell her but found that her courage had fled her. Turning she quickly walked away heading for her job which she would now be doing alone until they could find a replacement for Tisha.

It was later in the afternoon that Jah-Man sat in one of the resorts many gardens reading paperwork, he loved the resorts gardens they were so peaceful, so beautiful.

The paperwork he was shuffling through he would rather delegate to someone else, but he didn't. The paperwork kept him focused on the tasks again, keeping his mind off all his troubles. Revenge on Steven Winter, Darrius, his son's attachment to Yashi, and the traitor that lurked close to him - somewhere. His life felt like it was falling apart around him, he was losing his grip, his control on everything. He felt weak. The thought made him angry and his hand clenched tightly on the pen he was using. Moments later, it snapped in his hand. He didn't notice it as he stared down at his paperwork.

"What is troubling you brother?" William said coming into the garden.

For an instant, Jah-Man looked up at him, his stare distant. The look was enough to root William in his tracks. His brothers' stare was that of a hideously insane person - a madman. The look quickly faded as Jah-Man's face slowly broadened into a smile.

"Hello brother, it is good to see you," Jah-Man said softly.

"You seem bothered brother, what is troubling you?" William said sitting down next to him.

"There is much that bothers me brother, many feel that they can defy and challenge me!" he said his fist clenched to the sky.

"But they are wrong."

"Would you like some advice?" William said feeling uncomfortable.

"Of course brother, your advice is the only advice I would listen to," JahMan smiled warmly.

"First off, forget Winter. Reducing yourself to these petty levels is beyond you. It is beyond Jah-Man. Secondly, we need to flush out the traitor that is close to you. That should become your first priority," William said surprised Jah-Man hadn't blown up at him.

"And finally, I have reason to believe that the Frenchman is on the island."

At the mention of the Frenchman, Jah-Man's stare shot to his brother. The insane look was back again.

"Are you sure of this brother? Are you sure the Columbian butcher is here again?" Jah-Man snarled.

"I am and I have reason to believe that he's looking to claim the island again. This time though, he will be more cautious," William pointed out.

"Then there is another war brewing, another year of death," Jah-Man stared at the slate pathway that snaked through the garden.

"The Frenchman and the traitor should be our first priority brother, forget that Winter boy and Delicia," William said softly.

"She is my woman brother, she is mine!" he snapped.

"She is yours brother, but you can have any woman you please, do not waste precious energy on her when the real danger is much closer."

For an instant Jah-Man wanted to lash out at William, but something stopped him. His words were right, they were full of wisdom and as much as he didn't want to hear them he knew William was right.

"Okay brother, let us straighten out this mess, get back on track," Jah-Man said patting William on the back.

"We should start by finding this traitor."

"We should concentrate on the Frenchman since he is the most dangerous," William said.

"He will attempt to strike your shipments from your new supplier."

"We do not know if we have a new supplier, Darrius and their agent Yashi have not returned yet," Jah-Man said a hint of worry in his voice.

"When do you expect them?" William asked.

"I would have thought they would have returned by now. There must be trouble," he said.

"Brother, why did you send Darrius with her? He does not know the operation. He has no loyalty to you. He doesn't even know who you really are," William asked.

"I wanted to show him what trust is. Maybe if I trusted him he would find that I am not what he thinks," Jah-Man said softly.

William wanted to tell him the truth in that Darrius *hated him*. Hated him beyond belief, but he kept his mouth shut.

"Brother, I also do not feel that Delicia has Eve's best interest in mind. I do not trust her brother," William changed the subject.

"She knows better than to defy me. I have already spoken to her about Eve. She will not go against my wishes," Jah-Man said.

Suddenly from the other end of the garden Yashi appeared followed by Darrius. William was the first to see them and he smiled at Darrius warmly. JahMan looked up but didn't show any expression except for the normal stern look he gave when conducting business.

"It is good that you have returned, I was beginning to think that my choice of buyers was incorrect," Jah-Man stated.

"It took longer than we anticipated," Yashi said.

"We have though, considered your offer and we accept your terms."

"Good, very good," Jah-Man finally broke out in a smile.

"But…"she said looking at William.

"Can we conduct business with him here?"

"He is my brother, anything you say to me you can say to him," Jah-Man reassured her.

"All right," she nodded. "We want a pre-shipment, 350 kilos."

"The exchange will occur day after tomorrow at Portland Point," she stated.

"There on the beach at midnight."

Jah-man raised an eyebrow at her, he never made exchanges so far from the resort, it made for trouble. Her stare never faltered as he locked eyes with her. He then looked away and nodded.

"Portland Point is acceptable to me also," he smiled.

"If this goes well, if there are no problems we will immediately go for, within a week, the big shipment. That exchange will occur here," she pointed at the ground.

"Here at the resort."

"The resort?" William gasped, as did Darrius.

"Yes here where there is less of a chance for trouble," she stated.

"I usually don't conduct exchanges at the resort, this is a place for guests, not a business exchange," he motioned with his palms outspread.

"Doesn't matter, my superiors want it done here."

For an instant, Jah-Man's face grew taut. Nobody told him what to do - nobody.

"And if I refuse?" he asked calmly.

"Then we take our business elsewhere," she said flatly.

"Okay, I will accept your terms under one condition," he began to say.
"You add an additional 5% to the total for conducting business here," he smiled.

Yashi's eyebrows drew down in a frown at his demand. She then burst out in a laugh that surprised Darrius. Moments later she extended her hand to JahMan.

"Done" she smiled.

Jah-Man shook her hand but did not return the smile. Something bothered him about her, something about the way she conducted business or perhaps something else. Either way he couldn't put his finger on it. He felt it when he first met her, something inside him began to yell, no it was more of an outright scream that danger was close to her.

"Then we will meet at Portland Point day after tomorrow?" she asked.

"We will travel there together," Jah-Man added.

"Darrius how is your sister?" William asked changing the subject.

"I do not know, I rarely saw her this summer. She spends all her time hanging around Delicia and Diamond," Darrius said to him.

"Diamond!" Jah-Man said with surprise.

"Yes, Diamond. Why does that come as such of a surprise to you?" Darrius frowned at Jah-Man.

"No reason, I have had some dealings with the man in the past. I do not like his character," Jah-Man said softly.

"So there is one thing we agree on," Darrius said to him.

"I will look into the matter," Jah-Man quickly replied.

"Why? Why does my sister and I concern you so?" Darrius blurted out.

"Because, because William has told me much about your father and he would have wanted it," Jah-Man lied.

"Uncle William knew my father? All these years and you never mentioned it?" Darrius looked at him surprised.

"It was not something your mother wanted me to discuss with you," he lied.

"I thought we could trust you Uncle William? I thought you cared." Darrius said his face showing the hurt he felt.

"I wanted to Darrius but I promised. I had promised your mother," he continued to lie.

"Look, our business is concluded, I will meet you here day after tomorrow," Yashi said quickly changing the subject again.

"I have a room prepared for you, anything you wish here is at your disposal. I can provide escorts if you wish also," Jah-Man smiled.

"Darrius has provided that service well enough, he will do," she said.

"Darrius has a job to perform here and he must get back to it," Jah-Man said.

"I will provide another for your services."

"May I request that I remain with her?" Darrius cut in.

"I said that you need to return to your job, is that understood?" Jah-Man said frowning at him.

"Clearly" Darrius said with defeat.

Sharon worked diligently all day, she was worried about Raffie, she was worried about Darrius and his closeness to Jah-Man and she was most worried about Steven. The day wore on until the shop closed at 5:00 p.m. She was the last person out of the shop and she locked the doors, turning she nearly bumped into Ohpton.

"Oh, you startled me!" she said catching her breath.

"Want someone to walk home with?" he asked.

"Sure, have you…" she began to say.

"Talked with Raffie? They didn't fire him but they might as well have. He has to work and turn his paycheck over to them until the damage has been paid."

"That will take years!" she said grabbing his arm.

"I know. He knows too, but he's going to do it and bite his tongue. He needs access to other things here to get the information we need off those disks," Ohpton added.

"Steven?"

"Don't know, I saw Eve earlier, she said nothing to me but I've known her long enough to tell when something wasn't right with her. It might have nothing to do with Steven but my gut tells me different," he said softly as they walked out the front doors.

"Darrius?"

"Back on the desk, talked with him this afternoon, he's bugged that JahMan didn't keep him with that oriental woman," he sighed.

"Guess he's got the love bug bad." Ohpton shook his head.

"What is happening?" Sharon said sadly.

"It's all falling apart; our lives are splitting in different directions. Fate is pulling us apart and if it goes on for much longer we're going to be in trouble."

"Our plans are flying out the window," Sharon said taking Ohpton's arm in hers.

"Let's not think about it tonight okay?" he whispered softly to her.

Jah-Man had gone back to his office at the resort. His desk was made of imported Oak and polished to fine sheen. All around the room were small statues of nude women in various poses. They sat on pedestals, some were mimics of European art and others looked as though they were custom-made. A few plants sat in corners for effect, he could care less if they survived, and whoever took care of cleaning the room took care of them. A majority of his business transactions took place within the confines of the office, which was the reason for it being there. He rarely spent time within its walls unless business was going on, today however he felt he needed to be here. Suddenly there came a gentle knock on the door.

"Come in," he barked.

The door slowly opened and Delicia came in. She wore a scandalous outfit that was so sheer she freely displayed her shapely breasts. Her dark nipples could clearly be seen beneath the fabric. Around her neck was a mass of gold chains of the highest quality, her arms were draped in them also and on every finger was rings, she even had multiple ankle chains. He had never really noticed it but he wondered how she moved with so much metal hanging off her. Still though, his eyes drifted back to her breasts and the way they swayed as she walked into the room.

"Jah-Man, may I speak with you?" she said drawing closer to the desk.

"Of course my dear," he said rising from the desk his excitement for her clearly visible.

"Are you still angry with me?" she said batting her long eyelashes.

"No, I was never angry with you - you were innocent in that matter," he said drawing close to her.

"Yes, I was," she whispered to him.

"I was thinking, wondering, could you please forgive him for me?"

For a moment Jah-Man hesitated, he then reached out and touched her bare shoulders caressing the length of her arms.

"Why do you ask me this? Were you not as innocent as you first told me?" he whispered into her ear.

"I want you to forgive him because he is so young and foolish. He was just overcome with my beauty. I am sure by now he is so terrified of you that he will not even come close to me," she said.

"Would this make you happy?" he said kissing her ear, then moving down to her neck.

"Yes Jah-Man, that would make me very happy. I do not want one who is so young to be harmed because of me," she replied her voice barely audible.

His hands came around and gently ran over the sheer fabric covering her breasts. Then he followed the curve of her cleavage up to her neck and unhooked the strap around her neck. He then slid his hands back down over her bare breasts gently kneading them in his hands.

Seconds later he grabbed her dress and violently pulled it down; she hungrily groped at his clothing. Within moments they were naked together, JahMan swept his arm across the desk tossing everything to the floor. Grabbing her he forced her face down on the desk, then he cocked it up. At first, she was tense and it hurt, but with his steady motion, she began to relax. She let her mind wander; let her mind envision, that it was Steven taking her, Steven the man she truly wanted. She felt herself let go.

Darrius sat fuming behind the desk. He couldn't for the life of him understand why Jah-Man had pulled him away from Yashi. Then again, he couldn't understand why he had placed him with her to begin with. He was alone behind the desk until 11:00 p.m. when his relief help would come in. The person working with him had called in sick and there was nobody else to call. It wasn't a difficult job; checking in guests late in the afternoon, calling for drivers, wake up calls for the next morning, mostly simple things. It was hard though for him to concentrate on the job. His mind kept drifting to Yashi; he wanted to be with her, both in and out of bed. He was smitten with her, which was something he couldn't understood about himself. He didn't care either; something about her attracted him. Their discussion back in Florida bothered him. Why wouldn't she want to talk about the future? What was she hiding? Was he just someone to be with while she was here? The more he allowed the thoughts to run around in his mind the more he felt like he would go mad.

"Wha'ppen," a voice said snapping him back to reality.

Standing in front of the desk was Raffie, dressed in a finely tailored suit, a broad grin forming on his face.

"Hi" he said softly.

"Where have you been? The last I saw you was the other night with that woman of Jah-Man's," Raffie said.

"She's not Jah-Man's woman." Darrius snapped.

"Whoa, sorry there buddy, I didn't mean to touch you off," Raffie said holding his hands up.

"Sorry, I didn't mean to snap. I've just got a lot on my mind that's all," he said with defeat.

"What's going on?" Raffie asked.

"You tell me first then I've got some news for you too," he added.

Darrius explained everything that happened when they were in Florida and when they came back. Raffie listened intently taking in every word. When he was done, Darrius suddenly felt better, not relieved, but at least he had gotten a load off his chest.

"Wow, I never realized you cared so much about this woman," Raffie said.

"That complicates things."

"How so?"

Raffie then proceeded to tell him the events from the previous night with Sharon and Ohpton. When he was done Darrius looked more washed out and worried. He flopped back down in his chair like a ton of bricks had just been tossed on his shoulders.

"Not that bad buddy," Raffie said.

"What I will need is access to the back office so I can use the computer; we need to access the files."

"No problem," Darrius said not looking up.

"With you knowing when and where the *big drop* will occur that will save us a lot of digging. You might just be our ace in the hole buddy," Raffie smiled.

"What about Yashi?" he said looking up.

"I don't know Darrius, but one thing is for sure. Once we swipe Jah-Man's money I wouldn't want to stay on this island very long," Raffie said raising an eyebrow.

"She could get killed," Darrius looked sadly at him.

"It's possible I suppose, but then again we're playing a dangerous game. Any one of us could get killed," Raffie pointed out.

"Maybe we shouldn't," Darrius said.

"With Steven out of a job and my own problems, chances are we won't get off this island unless we do. Maybe not for the next 2-5 years, is that something you're willing to live with?"

"No, no of course not," Darrius shook his head.

"It's just…" he began to say.

The elevator dinged to the right of the desk. The doors slowly opened, Darrius's expression instantly flew into muted shock. Out of the elevator emerged Yashi, she wore a tight shimmering gown with a plunging neckline that went to the middle of her stomach.

The gentle yet alluring cut of her cleavage could clearly be seen. She was stunning. Walking arm in arm next to her was Diamond, he was dressed in a black tuxedo and he made sure he made eye contact with him as they walked by the desk. Raffie looked first at them and then at Darrius. Trouble was close.

"Yashi!" Darrius called out to her.

Turning she looked at him and smiled warmly, then led Diamond to the desk next to Raffie.

"Good evening Darrius," she said softly.

"What are you doing with him?" he blurted out.

"He is the escort Jah-Man provided to me," she said glancing up at Diamond.

"But…but…" Darrius stuttered.

"I am her escort for tonight and I was informed that I should cater to her *every* whim, nuh?" Diamond threw Darrius a grin.

"That is insane, totally insane!" Darrius nearly yelled.

"It is what Jah-Man wants Darrius, right now neither of us has much of a choice," she pointed out.

"But that doesn't mean he has to…"

"*Anything she wants Darrius, anything,*" Diamond smiled.

Darrius was about to launch himself over the desk when Raffie grabbed him by the arm stopping him.

"What does Eve say about all this Diamond?" Raffie asked.

"I am sure she will understand that I am just doing Jah-Man's bidding," he quickly smiled at him.

"Yashi you can't, you can't do this. What about - us," Darrius blurted out.

"What about us Darrius? I told you that we couldn't think about anything until this is over and then…" she snapped.

Her tone was enough to floor Darrius to Diamonds satisfaction. Yashi tugged on Diamonds arm and they headed for the dining room. Raffie turned his attention to Darrius who watched them leave his teeth grinding together with intense force.

"I am going to put a stop to this now!" he snarled.

Raffie was quick and again grabbed him stopping him. Darrius scowled at him and tried to tear himself free but Raffie held on.

"Let go of me! You know what that bastard is going to do!" Darrius snapped.

"She can take care of herself, this isn't the time or place and you know it!" Raffie said with force.

A few moments later Darrius relaxed and Raffie eased his grip on him. He then fell back into his chair running his hands over his face.

"You're right," he sighed.

"Of course I am. If she cares about you Darrius she won't let Diamond do anything," Raffie added.

"We both know how persuasive Diamond is," Darrius said looking up at him between his fingers.

"She's not stupid Darrius. She's dealing with Jah-Man remember?"

Darrius nodded in agreement then stood up and straightened his suit. Raffie watched him for a moment then glanced at his watch.

"Look it's going on 6:30 p.m. I have to get back to work myself. Are you going to be okay?" he asked.

"Fine, I'm fine," Darrius forced a grin.

"Look, you've always been the father figure of our little group. You've always given the best advice next to Sharon of course. Keep focused Darrius. We're getting into the thick of it here and none of us can afford to make a mistake; it could cost us our lives."

"Yeah, okay I get your message," Darrius said his eyes glued to the dining room entrance.

"Focus okay?" Raffie said pointing with two fingers to his eyes.

"Yeah focus – focus. I get the picture, now get back to work before you get in more trouble," Darrius said finally looking at him.

For a moment, Raffie stood there staring at his friend, and then he tore himself away and headed for the dining room. Something about Darrius worried him; he had known him for too long not to see that he was still bothered by Diamond. Love was a silly thing sometimes, it could bring you intense joy and happiness or it could destroy you and tear your heart to shreds.

Relationships rarely started out with the pendulum hanging somewhere in the middle of the two extremes; usually they were at one end of the scale or the other. Tonight, Darrius was at an extreme - the dangerous one.

The small hallway leading to the dining room was crowded with guests waiting to enter the dining hall, which opened at 6:30 p.m. sharp. As host, he personally seated each of them, including Yashi and Diamond. He was always surprised at how the guests he saw around the resort during the day could transform in the evening. There were many older women he wouldn't give a second glance to during the day, but dressed in an evening gown with make up and jewelry they were transformed like Cinderella was by the Fairy God Mother.

Quickly he seated each of the guests until he came to Yashi and Diamond. For an instant, he glanced at Yashi who refused to meet his eyes. Diamond on the other hand looked down on him with contempt.

"Please follow me," Raffie said softly.

"A decent table please?" Diamond scowled.

Raffie led them to the outer edge of the dining room and sat them at a table for two along the back wall next to massive windows, which overlooked the shimmering ocean. The table was set with fine silverware and china with cloth linens, in the middle of the table sat a small burning candle.

The dining room was bathed in a soft dull light that provided the waiters and waitresses enough light to work but added a seductive and romantic atmosphere for the guests. In the far corner of the dining room sat a grand piano, one of the staff sat playing a soft melody that was stimulating yet calming.

"Is this adequate?" Raffie asked Yashi and totally ignored Diamond.

"Yes this will do nicely," she smiled at him.

"Good, your waiter will be here shortly to take your cocktail order," he smiled as they sat down. He then handed each of them menus and headed back to the entrance.

Yashi occasionally glanced at Diamond as she scanned the dinner menu. She had wanted to remain with Darrius but under the circumstances, she had to go with the man's wishes. Things were too close now to blow them over nonsense.

"At least he thought enough to give me someone attractive," she thought to herself.

"What are you going to have?" Diamond asked over the top of his menu.

"Food" she shot back.

"Look, Jah-Man wanted me to stay with you so you might as well get used to me," he pointed out.

"What about Darrius's sister Eve? What is she going to say if she sees you with me?"

"She's young and foolish, she doesn't understand that this is a job for me, that this is my work," he said callously.

"And she likes you?" Yashi asked.

"Like I said she is foolish. She gives her heart too easily, swayed by the pleasures between the sheets," he bluntly said.

"She is a fool, a fool for loving a man such as you," Yashi snapped.

"And Darrius is a fool for falling for you. You are not what you seem are you?" he looked at her over the top of the menu.

For a moment, Yashi was taken back at his statement. What did this man know of her? Could he have connections outside of the island? Was that why JahMan placed him with her, to spy on her?

"Whom I give myself to is my business and not yours." "Of course," he smiled at

her.

"We are much alike you and I are cut from the same cloth," he said drawing his attention back to the menu.

"We are nothing alike - nothing. I don't pretend at what I do," she said coldly.

"Oh really, you mean you don't whore yourself out for the job? Why then are you bedding Darrius? No, you are very much like me Yashi. You'll do anything if the price is right," he grinned at her.

"Bastard" she breathed.

"Slut" he countered.

"Would either of you like a cocktail before dinner?" the waiter said drawing their attention away from each other.

Darrius was alone in the lobby; most of the dinner guests had come and gone into the dining room. He would only see them when they filtered back out and headed for the elevator or an after dinner walk through the gardens or on the beach. None would approach the desk and no stragglers would arrive for rooms this late at night. It would be sit back and wait for his relief at 11:00 p.m. The more he sat and stared at the hallway leading to the dining hall the more he grew angry. His heart was winning over his mind and with each passing minute, it was growing worse. He couldn't take it anymore.

Setting the "be back in a few minutes" sign on the counter, he quickly left the desk and headed for the dining room. With much caution he peered around the corner, Raffie wasn't at his podium at the entrance. Quickly he moved to the small podium and glanced at his seating chart looking for the tables that were set up for two. He then quickly walked into the dining room weaving his way between tables heading for the far wall where huge glass windows looked out over the ocean. He knew that was where Raffie would have put them.

Within moments, he spied Yashi and Diamond sitting opposite each other. They were sipping drinks neither of them was smiling. Then again, neither was he.

Diamond looked up as Darrius quickly approached, his distraction was enough for Yashi to turn her head and look at him.

"Shit" she said softly under her breath.

"Can I talk with you in private?" Darrius said to Yashi.

"Why don't you crawl back to your desk. Can't you see you're not wanted here?" Diamond said his tone denoting anger.

"Can I talk with you in private?" Darrius again asked Yashi.

"Can this wait till after dinner? I do not want to make a scene here, not now," she said her gaze turning to see if other guests were watching.

"No, it can't wait," Darrius, said the force clear in his voice.

Sighing, Yashi nodded and put her linen on the table. She then slid her chair back to get up.

"The lady said bug off," Diamond said grabbing hold of Darrius's arm.

"Shut up," Yashi said to Diamond.

"Sit back down slut, I'll get rid of this trash!" Diamond said as he started to get up.

Raffie turned his eyes gazing over the dining guests. He then spotted Darrius standing next to Yashi's table; Diamond was rising out of his chair.

The confrontation was inevitable.

Darrius's palm shot out striking Diamond square in the face. He tumbled back, his chair overturning as he crashed into the empty table behind him.

"Darrius, please not here!" Yashi blurted out.

Diamond was quick to regain his footing and lunged with a swiftness that surprised Yashi and Darrius. His fist connected with Darrius's jaw, the blow hurling the man back onto a table behind him, its occupants startled tremendously. Darrius, his anger flaring shook his head and again went after Diamond. Screams erupted within the dining room as the two men connected blow after blow to each other. Some of the guests dashed for the door appalled at the violence that threatened to envelop them.

Raffie moved as swiftly as possible into the fray, he had to stop it before it became any worse. Though the two men were much taller than he was, he dove between them and was knocked onto his back.

"I've wanted to do this for a long time now!" Darrius snarled throwing a blow and connecting with Diamonds jaw.

"Please, stop this! Stop this now!" Yashi yelled.

Again, Raffie got between the two men trying to force them apart. Diamond lashed out with his elbow hitting him square in the chest. Raffie teetered back gasping for breath the bow knocking the wind from him.

"I'm tired of you and your sister," Diamond snapped his fist driving into Darrius's stomach.

Darrius fell back against Yashi and they both toppled back onto another table the force breaking the legs. Dishes, glasses and food flew in all directions as the table collapsed.

"Aw heck!" Raffie said, and then slammed his fist hard into Diamonds stomach.

"That's for hitting my friend!"

Moments later other waiters dashed out grabbing their arms restraining them from fighting further.

"What is going on here?" a booming voice erupted from the other side of the room.

Earl Nash walked briskly in, he was wearing sweat clothes and his face was contorted in anger. He eyed the shattered tables and the carnage that was scattered about the room. Guests stood to the side watching. Darrius helped Yashi to her feet. She immediately grabbed her purse shaking the food off it and rushed from the room. Darrius stood there covered in food, Raffie sighed loudly trying to avoid eye contact with Nash.

"Would someone mind telling me what is going here?" Nash's voice boomed.

Diamond rubbed his jaw saying nothing; he looked at Raffie, then Darrius. Nash's anger was growing as the silence continued.

"Okay, have it your way. George, Lawson, your both out of here!" he snarled thumbing over his shoulder.

"You" he pointed at Diamond.

"You I don't want to see on these grounds!"

Raffie and Darrius sullenly walked to the door, their lives had just gotten worse.

Chapter 12

Sharon and Ohpton walked quietly along the dirt road. The night was peaceful and serene and they both enjoyed the silence. They both though, occasionally glanced behind them half expecting the Duppy Children to appear, or feel the bludgeoning of rocks raining down on them. But, nothing happened, nothing appeared out of the darkness to threaten them. When they reached the trailhead, they hesitated without saying a word and headed into town to check on Steven.

Mama Rose poured herself a cup of tea; she loved her tea morning or night it didn't matter. She hummed softly to herself. Over the years she found that humming was a way for her to keep positive when everything around her had gone bad. It had helped when Jaco died and it had helped when she and Junior argued. It was during nighttime that she felt the loss of her sons - both of them. Sitting down at the table she reflected on her life, the choices she had made weather they were right or wrong and what life would have dealt her if she had taken the left road instead of the right. It was depressing.

Thoughts of all the schoolers coming into her store cheered her, children laughing and giggling as they spied the rows of candy with youthful innocent eyes. They were the reason she kept going, why she never gave up. Without them she was nothing, just another old woman without purpose. There came a gentle knock on her door.

Glancing at the small clock on the kitchen wall she got up and headed for the door. It was late; no children would be knocking on her door at this late an hour. When she reached the door, the gentle knock came again. At first she was hesitant to open it, at night death could be waiting just on the other side. Her hand shook as she turned the knob, if it was her time for God to take her, then so be it.

"Mama Rose?" Sharon said softly.

"Sharon! Ohpton! What a pleasant surprise," she smiled her fears quickly fleeing.

"May we come in?" she asked.

"We came to see how Steven is doing," she said as Mama Rose back away from the door allowing them to enter.

"He's not here. In fact, I have not seen him all day," she said.

"All day? When did he leave?" Ohpton asked.

"Last night, I heard him slip out well after dark," she explained.

"You both look like you could use a nice cup of tea! I have some already made in the kitchen, please, both of you come in and sit with me a bit."

Sharon wanted to decline, but Mama Rose was so sweet that it was impossible for anyone to say no to her. They followed her into the kitchen watching her slow and obvious painful movements as she walked. Sharon felt a twinge of pain herself. Mama Rose was getting old, the years had not been easy on her and it was clear to them that she tired easily. When they reached the kitchen she eased herself down into one of the kitchen chairs emitting a sigh of relief.

"Please sit," she said grabbing two more cups that sat on the table.

"Do you have any idea where he went?" Sharon asked.

"He didn't say exactly of course, but I'll bet that he went to see Delicia," she said pouring the tea.

"Delicia? Why in heaven's name would he go see her?" Ohpton asked.

"To try and get Jah-Man off his back and yours," Mama Rose said.

"Ours?" Ohpton looked at her with surprise.

"Jah-Man is relentless, you know that already. He would stop at nothing to get to Steven. He knows too that Steven is friends with all of you including Darrius and Eve," Mama Rose said as she added a little sugar to her tea.

"Then he went to Delicia to try and keep Jah-Man away from us?" Sharon asked.

"That is my guess," Mama Rose said.

"Then we're all in danger?" Ohpton shook his head.

"<u>Oonu</u> except for Darrius and Eve," Mama Rose said then quickly put her hand to her mouth as if she had said something she shouldn't have.

"Darrius and Eve? Why are they immune from Jah-Man's wrath?" Ohpton asked.

"Yes why? Jah-Man has suddenly taken a keen interest in Darrius," Sharon added.

Mama Rose said nothing, her face felt flushed and she concentrated on stirring her tea. She didn't want to look up at the others.

"Mama Rose?" Sharon said softly.

"There are things you do not need to know; things I should not have said. You must forget I mentioned anything," she breathed softly.

"What is this hideous secret? If it means the safety of Darrius and Eve." Sharon pushed.

"You do not understand the consequences if they knew the truth; it would be devastating, very devastating," Mama Rose shook her head.

"We won't tell them," Ohpton blurted out.

"If it's that important, they should know!" Sharon shook her head in disagreement.

"They do not need to know, not yet, not till you are off the island and will never come back," Mama Rose shook her head.

"Please Mama Rose. Do not play games with us," Sharon pleaded.

For a long moment she continued to stir her tea, then she slowly looked up at them meeting their eyes searching for trust.

"You both must promise me - <u>promise me that you will NEVER tell</u> <u>Darrius or Eve until you are off the island!</u>" Mama Rose said her voice growing stern.

Sharon sat back in her chair, she had never heard Mama Rose raise her voice or be so stern and serious. The sudden change in the woman they all knew and grew up with was alarming. They both nodded their heads.

"I mean what I say, you must never tell them! Never!" she shook a finger at them both.

"I am an old woman; an old woman who has been around for many, many years. I have seen much in my time. I remember Jah-Man when he was a little boy, he was a different child, a loner," she sighed heavily.

"And we're all orphans," Ohpton quickly added.

"That doesn't give us a right to harm someone else."

"I didn't say it did, but we all make choices Ohpton. Jah-Man was different though, you could see it in his eyes, it was like he was seeing something in you that wasn't there," Mama Rose explained.

"And what does this have to do with Eve and Darrius?" Sharon asked trying to understand where Mama Rose was going.

"When Jah-Man was a young man, he met a woman, a very beautiful woman.

They instantly fell in love but they never married. During the course of their relationship she watched him slip slowly at first; then with every increasing speed into the dark side of life. Drugs, alcohol, prostitution, all the evils that tempt us every day."

"Why didn't she just leave?" Ohpton asked.

"Because a few years earlier two children were born out of wedlock," Mama Rose said softly.

Sharon's eyes began to grow wide, her mouth hung open and her voice failed her at first. Blinking rapidly she looked at Ohpton who frowned at her like he didn't understand her actions.

"You, you can't be serious?" Sharon blurted out at Mama Rose.

"I am very serious honey. She left Jah-Man and lived on her own, raising her two children as best she could. Jah-Man would send money, at first she wouldn't use it but as things grew tighter."

"Okay, what am I missing here? You're talking about some woman that had kids with Jah-Man - so what?" Ohpton shrugged.

"That woman's name Ohpton was Evelyn Lawson," Mama Rose said.

"You're kidding right? You're telling me that Jah-Man is Eve and Darrius's father?" Ohpton stared at her shocked.

"Yes, I am," Mama Rose nodded.

"Why don't Eve and Darrius know this?" Sharon asked.

"Because their mama didn't want it and because of the circumstances surrounding her death."

"I can understand, can you imagine what Darrius would do if he found out that Jah-Man was his father?" Ohpton shook his head.

"They have a right to know Mama Rose," Sharon pointed out.

"Yes, they do, but not now. You promised me Sharon, promised me that you wouldn't tell them until you were all off the island."

"Yes I did and I will keep my promise," Sharon nodded.

"So will I, but I have to tell you it won't be easy, Eve and Darrius are my friends." Ohpton said softly.

"It is the right thing to do," Mama Rose added.

"Okay, one shocker for the night is over, what about Steven?" Sharon asked changing the subject.

"It is possible that Jah-Man has him," Ohpton added.

"We would have heard at the resort," Sharon shook her head.

"He could be back at the shack already," Mama Rose said.

"Yes, we should be going. Tomorrow is Saturday and we finally have a day off," Sharon said getting up and placing her cup in the small sink.

"Thank you for the tea Mama Rose," Ohpton said putting his cup in the sink also.

"Please come and see me again, bring Darrius and Eve too. And please, please keep your promise to me," she said almost pleading.

"We will you can count on us," Sharon said giving her a hug.

"Here, take some sweets back with you, give some to Steven and the others when you see them," Mama Rose said walking out of the kitchen to the little candy shop she had.

She filled a bag with an assortment of sweets, some homemade others imported, and all looked tasty. She handed the bag to Sharon and opened the door for them.

Raffie took a long swill off the whiskey bottle, and then passed it to Darrius. They sat outside by the swimming pool their backs resting against a handmade stonewall. Raffie had bought a bottle from the bar and he and Darrius found a quiet spot to sit and drink themselves under the table. Neither of them drank much, but right now it seemed like the right thing to do.

The pool was lit with a dull blue light that made the water look even more inviting than it was. Huge flowerbeds surrounded the stonewall, providing ample camouflage for them.

"Well I sure blew that one," Darrius said taking a drink from the bottle.

"Yes, you sure did," Raffie said softly.

"I'm sorry," he said to him.

"Look, what's done is done, we can't go back and change it we can only move on from here," Raffie said.

"Yeah, we're out of a job, Steven is out of a job and we're never going to get off this island," Darrius shook his head in disgust.

"We still have our plan remember?" Raffie said shaking Darrius.

"All we have to do is plan well and make sure we get off this island when we're done."

"This is dread Raffie, really dangerous chances," Darrius said leaning his head back.

"No loss - no gain," Raffie said reaching for the bottle of whiskey.

"Well we sure have the loss now; three of us out of jobs. That means no money coming in," Darrius said handing him the bottle.

"Like I said, we only need to pull off this plan of ours, get off the island, and we're home free!" Raffie said trying to sound enthusiastic.

"I got a bad feeling Raffie, a bad feeling," Darrius shook his head.

Suddenly they heard giggling and then the closure of a sliding glass door. Darrius ribbed Raffie in the side then pointed. From where they sat they could see a fair portion of the pool with the hot tub sitting right next to it. A man and a woman emerged, the man was considerably shorter than the woman and Darrius recognized them immediately. It was Choo Tsai and Renee Thompson, two guests that had checked in a few days earlier.

"Who are they?" Raffie whispered to Darrius.

"His last name is Tsai and hers is Thompson, checked in a few days ago." "My God she's a knock

out!" he said his voice raising slightly.

"Quiet, they don't know we're here," Darrius frowned at him.

Renee Thompson was indeed a beautiful woman, long blond hair, and a body that pleaded wanton lust. She wore a flowing flowered dress her high heels clicking on the stone that surrounded the pool. Tsai wore dress pants and a shirt with no tie. He whispered something to her that neither of them could hear; she giggled again then grabbed his arm pulling him close. It was almost comical to watch them; her taller size made him look tiny, weak and the way she pulled and tugged on him only magnified the image. They walked over to the edge of the hot tub, she bent down and swished her hand in the water and smiled warmly at Tsai.

Then to their amazement, they began taking their clothes off. Raffie took a swig off the bottle and handed it back to Darrius who instantly took another chug. Her body was more incredible naked than they could imagine, her breasts were full with large protruding nipples. Her pelvis was shaved clean and left little to the imagination. Her oriental boyfriend was obviously excited by her as much as they were as his buddy showed. He slipped into the hot water then helped her down into the tub.

"Do you think?" Raffie whispered to Darrius.

"Oh yeah, here they go!" he said sipping more from the bottle.

The couple began to kiss, softly at first then with increasing passion. His hands groped and fondled her large breasts as his lips moved down to her neck. He twitched as he kissed her and they could only imagine what she was doing to him below the water.

"I really don't need to watch this," Raffie said unable to take his eyes off the couple.

"Hey, what the heck? This is about the only thing good that's happened today," Darrius added.

Suddenly the woman pulled her body out of the tub. She lay next to it with the oriental man following. His face slide between her legs to her pum pum and though they were a little ways from the pool, they could see clearly see the effects his actions had on her. Her body jerked and twitched as his hands working over her breasts.

"I don't need this." Raffie said sadly.

"He's going to do it. I bet you he'll do it!" Darrius said pointing at them.

No sooner had the words come out of his mouth than the little man pulled himself the rest of the way from the pool, pulled her legs up and abruptly started jooking her. The woman moaned loudly and cocked her head back. That was when she saw them.

At first Darrius locked eyes with her, then she blinked and opened her mouth seductively her eyes never leaving his. She obviously didn't care if they watched. They were jammin.

"My God, she knows we're watching her," Darrius breathed softly.

"I hope you don't expect me to get up and run right now," Raffie frowned.

The woman suddenly reached her hand out as if beckoning them to come and join, the man finally looked up and noticed them also and never stopped his rhythm. For nearly a half an hour they watched the couple make love in assorted positions. They were aware that they were being watched but they didn't seem to care. When they were done, they both smiled at them, grabbed their clothes and disappeared into the resort.

"I really didn't need that, I really didn't," Raffie said shaking his head. "She was so beautiful!"

"I think they knew we were here from the start," Darrius speculated.

"Took our minds off our troubles though didn't it?" Raffie grinned.

"Made me hornier than <u>blood fire</u>," Darrius said.

"Yeah, least you have…" Raffie cut his sentence short.

"Sorry"

"That's okay, I guess it wasn't meant to be, nothing I can do about it," Darrius shrugged.

"Hey are you drunk yet?" Raffie asked.

"No, I don't feel much pain though," Darrius smiled.

"I think I can operate a computer, why don't we see about getting behind the counter and using the computer in the back office?" Raffie suggested.

"Yeah, why not? What's the worse that they can do, fire us?" Darrius smiled.

"Well, they could send some of Jah-Man's goons to kick us out," Raffie beamed.

"A few more drinks and we won't care!"

"Come on," Raffie said getting up. Extending his hand he helped Darrius up to his feet.

A pretty woman stood behind the counter. She had short reddish hair, high cheekbones, long eyelashes and very full lips. She watched the two men approach the counter; she raised an eyebrow when she saw the bottle in Raffie's hand.

"Are you two still getting into trouble?" she smiled warmly.

"Oh for sure!" Raffie smiled.

"You should try it sometime Helen."

"Maybe sometime, but right now I like my paycheck too much," she shook her head.

"I heard what happened."

"I'm sure everyone has by now," Darrius said looking away embarrassed.

"Look, both of you were kicked out. Nash is on the warpath with you two. In fact, I'm sure Jah-Man has heard about this by now," she said softly.

"I really don't care if Jah-Man has heard about it!" Darrius said raising his voice.

"Quiet please before you get me in trouble too!" Helen said trying to calm him down.

"Helen, I need to ask you a favor. Can I use the computer in the back room for a while?" This is crucial. Raffie asked as nicely as possible.

"The computer? What in heaven's name would you want to use the computer for? You two have been fired," she looked at him with surprise.

"I need to connect to the net and scope out potential jobs for us, it would be a real big help," Raffie lied.

"If I let you and someone catches us then my job is history! No way - no way," she shook her head.

"Please, just for a short time, we'll be quiet," Raffie asked.

"It would mean so much to us."

Helen's eyes went first from Raffie to Darrius. Raffie could tell she was searching for sincerity, he also knew she was afraid.

"We can do it this way, you go to the bathroom and we'll sneak into the back room and close the door then you come back. If anyone catches us, you would have never known we were back there," Raffie explained.

"Well if you do it that way," she said softly.

"Thanks Helen. Thank you very much," Raffie smiled warmly at her.

She quickly walked from behind the counter and headed for the bathroom, as soon as she was gone, Raffie and Darrius slipped into the back room closing the door behind them. The office was small, containing only a desk, two chairs, and of course, the computer. Raffie went over and sat before the keyboard, then reached into his jacket pocket and produced two 3.5" computer disks. His gaze then turned to Darrius.

"Let's hope that all those years sitting haven't corrupted the data on the disks," he said slipping the first one into the machine.

Darrius said nothing and just pulled a chair up close to the desk. He knew a little bit about computers but nothing like Raffie who began clicking away with earnest. Minutes wore on and he watched Raffie with growing impatience.

"Well?" he finally said not able to contain himself.

"I think this disk is shot, corrupted," he said softly.

"I've tried everything I could think of to get inside," he said with a sigh.

"Then we're dead in the water, no hope," Darrius said sadly.

"On this disk yes. But remember there is another one," Raffie said popping the disk from the machine.

"Yeah, but if one is bad there is a good chance the other one is too."

"Don't write it off yet Darrius, simma," he said slipping the second disk into the computer.

Darrius felt his heart thump hard in his chest, everything; their whole plan has come down to this one small piece of plastic. Without information on JahMan's operation there would be no way to sneak in, at least no way that was somewhat safe. Raffie's eyes stared at the computer monitor while his hand worked rapidly with the small mouse. Darrius licked his lips, he had never been so anxious in his life. Raffie tore his eyes from the screen and looked at him.

"Well, well, let's quash this. Is it working or not?" Darrius said overexcited.

Then, slowly Raffie's face turned into a very broad grin.

"We got it!"

Darrius jumped up thrusting his clenched fist skyward. He said nothing as he walked around the room then just a quickly came back and sat back down. His demeanor was much more relaxed.

"Okay, can you print everything out?" he asked Raffie.

"Of course, but this printer is going to make noise."

"No choice, we need that information to show the others," he added.

"I know, I know, I just hope we don't get Helen in trouble," Raffie said as he hit the print key.

The printer began to work, groaning and humming as it printed out each and every page of information. Raffie had to send multiple files and he diligently kept up with the computer, the printer never remained idle. Darrius went over and cracked the door peeking out at Helen behind the desk. She nervously looked from side to side, obviously the printer made enough noise for her to hear and whomever else was standing close by out there.

"Come on, come on!" Darrius whispered to Raffie.

"Going as fast as I can. This thing only prints out so many pages a minute you know," Raffie said not taking his eyes off the screen.

The paper began to pile up; he had to add more paper so the printer wouldn't run out. His parents had extensive files on Jah-Man - extensive.

Helen sat nervously at the desk, a few guests walked by and she smiled at them. Fiddling with her pen she occasionally glanced over her shoulder at the closed door. This was getting out of hand and she could at any moment lose her job. Glancing down at the pen she flipped it over and over within her fingers.

"Bored?" said a deep voice.

"Oh...I...no," she said startled.

Earl Nash stood on the other side of the desk staring down at her. She suddenly felt her blood run cold, the worse had happened.

"Is everything all right?" he asked her his face showing a frown.

"Oh fine, everything is fine, all the guests are happy," she quickly said.

"What's that noise?" he asked looking over her shoulder.

"What noise?" she said almost sounding stupid.

"It sounds like it's coming from the back office," he said staring at the door.

"Oh that!" she smiled at him.

"I'm printing out tomorrows guest rosters, who's staying, who's checking out, that sort of thing," she said continuing to smile at him.

"Really?" he turned his gaze back to her.

"Figured it might improve efficiency, keep everyone on their toes so-tospeak," she said.

For a moment Nash stood there and thought about what she said, then, he slowly began to nod his head a smile forming across his face.

"Good idea - very good idea. I am impressed Helen, I never thought you would have come up with such an idea," he chat bout approvingly.

Darrius watched Nash from the back room; beads of sweat ran down his back. The whole game could easily be up in a matter of moments. Over the sound of the printer, he couldn't hear what Helen was saying to Nash. The man obviously wasn't rushing back to bust down the door so Helen hadn't ratted on them.

"Come on, hurry, Nash is standing out there talking to Helen," Darrius whispered as softly as he could.

"Nash?" Raffie looked up at him with surprise.

"What is he doing here this late at night?"

"I don't know, just hurry!"

Darrius continued to watch through the cracked doorway. With each passing minute the lump in his throat grew bigger. He didn't want to see Helen fired because of them and to add insult to injury there was no other way out than through the door and front desk. The back room was centrally located and didn't provide windows that would have allowed a simple escape.

"Are you done yet?" Darrius asked nervously.

"All most. Just a couple more minutes," Raffie replied.

Nash suddenly walked away from the desk; Helen slumped back in her chair then rubbed her hand over her face. The printer finally stopped.

"Done!" Raffie said grabbing the stack of printed-paper.

"Come on let's get out of here before we get caught for sure!" Darrius said opening the door.

Helen swiveled the chair around and watched the two men emerge. In Raffie's arm was huge bundle of paper; in his, other hand was a smaller stack.

"Do you know, do you know who just showed up?" she asked her voice frantic.

"Yes we do, I was watching him from the corner of the doorway," Darrius said.

"Thank you Helen for not turning us in."

"Just get out of here before he decides to come back," she pointed to the front doors.

"I've got to spend the rest of the night trying to print up guest rosters to turn my lie to Nash into the truth."

Raffie walked around the counter, then turned and handed Helen the smaller pile of paper in his hand.

"Here"

"What's this?" she asked.

"Guest rosters, the whole nine yards," he said.

"Figured I'd produce the stuff just in case someone wanted to know why the printer was running so much."

Helen took the paper a smile forming on her face. She then looked up at Raffie.

"Thank you - but go," she said softly.

Raffie and Darrius quickly headed out the front doors into the humid night air. They didn't say anything to each other until they were outside the main gates of the resort and halfway back to the shack.

"That was pretty quick thinking back there," Darrius said.

"Just had that feeling something was going to go wrong," he added.

"Let's just hope that whatever information we got will be enough to give us an edge against Jah-Man."

"I didn't have time to skim the paper but there was a lot on his operation, we'll need to sit down with the others to go through this all," he said.

Suddenly Raffie's arm shot out grabbing hold of Darrius, the two men, stopping short in the middle of the road.

"What?" Darrius asked.

"We're in trouble - big trouble!" Raffie breathed.

"Trouble, for what?" Darrius asked concerned.

"The disks! I left the disks back in the office, left the one right in the computer!" Raffie said his voice frantic.

"You what!" Darrius nearly yelled.

"Do you realize what will happen?"

"We have to go back and get them. I should go back and get them," he said.

"Take the paperwork and keep going, I'll go back."

Darrius took the paper from him and watched as he took off with a run disappearing quickly along the dark road.

Helen read the rosters making any changes to the paperwork that Raffie gave her. She liked him, liked him a lot and that was the only reason she had allowed them access to the computer. Darrius on the other hand she didn't care for. He was pleasant enough but there was just something about him that she disliked. A click, clack noise of someone's shoes along the marble floor drew her attention from the paperwork. For a moment she didn't see anyone then from around the corner Jah-Man appeared. He stared at her for a moment his face stern and foreboding.

"Yes Sir, can I help you?" she timidly asked.

"Have you been the only person at this desk tonight?" he asked sharply.

"Huh…yes, I did leave for a short while to go to the restroom?" she squinted.

"No one was using the computer in the back room earlier?" he asked.

"I was earlier. I was producing guest rosters," she said showing him the paper, her fear beginning to grow exponentially.

"Someone was using this computer earlier and not accessing guest information," he pointed to the back room.

"Like I said Sir unless someone went back there while I was in the bathroom?"

"I will need to use that computer," he said coldly to her.

From outside, Raffie watched through the large glass entrance. He couldn't hear what they were saying but knew well enough something had happened. He watched as Jah-Man walked around and went directly into the back room.

"My God," he breathed softly to himself.

Somehow their use of the computer was being monitored or tracked. He knew that the resort's computers were on a network, but individual use of the machines weren't normally monitored - until now.

When Jah-Man disappeared behind the door Raffie knew well enough that his mistake had become a monumental one. All their lives were now in danger, especially if he put two and two together or if Helen spilled her guts. Then again, if she stuck to her story Jah-Man might just leave her alone.

The room looked ordinary, a desk with nothing more than a blotter and a computer, chairs and not much else. Jah-Man quickly went over to the desk and sat down, he turned the power on and waited. Helen stood in the doorway, trying to keep a worried look off her face. When the computer had finished booting, he began to check the system to see what was accessed.

He found nothing, whoever had used the computer had cleaned their trail well.

Getting up he was going to leave the room when something caught his eye. Sitting within the floppy disk drive on the computer was a disk; another sat on the table in front of the machine. Pushing the disk in he sat back down and accessed the information. As it came up on the screen in front of him, his eyes grew wide and a look of horror formed on his face.

Seconds later, the look of horror was replaced with sheer, insane anger.

With one quick sweep of his arms, he upturned the entire computer table, the machine smashing onto the floor. Helen had taken the earlier look on his face as a warning, she withdrew from the room and over to the corner behind the counter. With any luck, Jah-Man would burst out and forget she was even there. The door swung violently open and Jah-Man emerged. She wasn't so lucky.

At first he stood there looking around the lobby, then his insane gaze cast upon her huddled in the corner. She watched, her body numb with terror as he slammed the door and lumbered towards her. Though he was a short man, at that moment he looked like a giant.

"Who was back there? Tell me who was back there!" he ranted his voice grating and firm.

"I...I...don't know who was back there. I went to the bath..." she began to say.

With a swift motion, his hand came up boxing her across the face. The blow was enough to make her loose her balance and she hung onto the counter for support.

"Tell me." he snarled.

"Sir, Sir I am telling you. I went to the bathroom. I didn't see anyone."

Again, there was another sharp slap. Tears began to streak down her cheeks in a steady stream. Jah-Man's rage was not quelled; he wanted nothing more at this moment than to beat the pulp out of her.

"Tell me." he again snapped at her.

Helen held her hand to her face, her cheek sore. Her tear filled eyes stared into his, a new fear rumbling through her body. His eyes that were so seductive, so inviting earlier were now deep, bottomless and for a moment, she thought she could see Hell itself within them. Her instincts instantly screamed that her life was in mortal danger.

"Raffie," she said her voice barely audible.

"Raffie?" he asked.

"Winston George." she said quickly clarifying what she said.

"George!" Jah-Man's eyes grew wide with surprise.

"Who else?" he asked, moving closer causing her body to press harder into the counter.

"Darrius." she said her voice even softer.

At the mention of Darrius's name, Jah-Man's rage surged. He grabbed her by the shoulders and slammed her down to the floor with all his might. Helen let out a groan and lay there curled up in the fetal position. She waited for the inevitable blows that were assuredly going to come as he stood over her.

"Why did they come here?" he asked her.

"I don't know. They we're both fired," she sobbed.

"Fired? Fired by whom, why?" he spat.

"Nash, Earl Nash fired them, Darrius got into a fight in the dining room tonight with Diamond, Raffie tried to stop them so Nash fired them both," she continued to weep.

"Darrius? It was Darrius who got into that fight?" Jah-Man snarled.

"Yes, please, please don't hurt me," she pleaded.

"Why we're they using the computer in the back office?" he asked.

"They told me they wanted to scout for jobs."

"Get up, get up and go back to work, you mention any of this to anyone *and you won't wake up in the morning,"* he said sternly.

Helen only nodded and remained on the floor as Jah-Man lumbered off. Outside, Raffie watched the whole ordeal, he had to contain himself; contain himself from rushing in and fighting with Jah-Man. It was a fight he would only lose, Jah-Man wasn't much taller than he was, but he was considerably stronger. He also had people he could call to help; if he had gone in, he would be rushing in to his death. Watching as he struck Helen, Raffie felt the blows right along with her, not across his face but in his heart that now, cried out in pain for her.

When Jah-Man rushed from behind the counter and disappeared from the lobby, Raffie rushed in and to Helen's side. She continued to lay on the floor quaking in fear.

"Helen, Helen," he said softly scooping her into his arms.

At first, she jerked away, until she realized it wasn't Jah-Man, and then her sobbing became uncontrollable. Raffie held her tight his own rage surging through his veins.

"I tried, I tried not to tell him anything, I tried," she sobbed.

"It's okay Helen, he's gone - gone," Raffie tried to console her.

"I'm sorry I had no choice. He would have killed me," she said softly.

"It's all right. I'm sorry Helen for not telling you what we were doing," he breathed.

"I don't want to know, don't tell me anything," she cried.

"You have to leave here, get as far away as you can. He knows Raffie - he knows it was you and Darrius," she cried out.

"What about you?" he asked.

"I'll be all right, he won't do anything more to me as long as you and Darrius stay away from me," she said wiping her hand across her eyes.

Raffie helped her down into the nearest chair, then turned to leave. JahMan may have alerted his men, may have told them to hunt him and Darrius down. Turning he went around the counter, hesitating.

"Helen, I won't forget this, I'll never forget this," he said to her.

She said nothing as she watched him rush from the lobby out into the night air.

Jah-Man took the elevator down to the basement level. On one side of the resort were small three room apartments for the managers. Some lived off the resort, but many others stayed right there. Earl Nash was one of them. He had been with the Orion for well over seven years. Jah-Man had hired him because he was cocky and cheap. He was a <u>driver</u>, one that didn't cut any punches with his employees; he also scrimped and saved much money for the resort over the years. It was the primary reason he kept him on.

Reaching Nash's door he paused then turned sharply and headed back into the elevator. Within moments, he was in his office the telephone in his hand.

Earl Nash heard a crash; it was loud enough, with enough force to jar the walls. Earl Nash was asleep, least until he heard the crash. By the time his brain registered that the door had been broken in two <u>burly</u> men had grabbed him. With little effort they yanked him from the bed, seconds later he felt the first blow to his stomach knocking the wind from him. Then the second came to his jaw, then a third. Blow after blow rained down upon him until he lay in a bloody heap on the floor writhing in pain. The men said nothing and just hovered over him watching his agony. Then, as abruptly as they had come they left.

Nash didn't know how long he had remained on the floor; it could have been minutes or even hours. His body was in so much pain that time had no meaning. A searing hot pain stabbed through his abdomen, his jaw was broken and a few teeth were missing, he knew that much. His left eye was swollen shut and it felt like his right wrist was broken. He didn't understand who attacked him or even why. As far as he knew, he had done nothing wrong to anyone. The only thing of significance he had done in the past 24 hours was to fire Darrius and Raffie, nothing more. Pulling his body from the floor his hand slapped into a puddle of blood that had formed from his face. He ignored it and stumbled to his feet, carrying himself into the bathroom he turned on the water staring at the liquid that steamed out of the faucet. He didn't want to look in the mirror, didn't want to see how bad his face actually was. By the way he felt, he knew it was hideous.

Carefully splashing water onto his face with his left hand, he accidentally bumped his right into the edge of the sink causing him to scream out in pain. Yes, his wrist was defiantly broke.

He accidentally looked into the mirror and was surprised. He actually looked much better than he thought. His two front teeth were broken; his lower lip was split wide open and blood still streaked from his broken nose. His eye looked the worse of the lot and was already swollen closed a thin streak of blood trickling down from his temple.

Some of the blood was dried which gave him an idea of how long he had laid on the floor. Cleaning himself up as best as he could he made his way back into the living room and pushed the front door closed as best he could. He then went to the bedroom, glancing down at the pool of blood on the floor, it was already beginning to coagulate on the edges. He knew he should clean it up, but his body only wanted to lie down and rest. He would have to go to a doctor in the morning and have his wrist set and put in a cast.

Right now though, there was nothing he could do but try and sleep. With considerable effort and pain he pulled himself back into bed, this time though, he faced the door. Sleep wouldn't come easy as his imagination and the many shadows that prevail at night played tricks on him. Eventually though, he slowly drifted off to sleep.

A dull squeaking noise reached his ears, at first, he just passed it off, and then slowly, his subconscious fears began to take hold forcing him out of his sleepy state.

His eyes opened and darkness greeted him. The door to the bedroom was cracked slightly, the light from the hallway, which had been left on was now off.

His eyes could make out images, but nothing definite. His heart pounded in his chest, to the point where he thought he could hear it. Straining he tried to make out every object in the room, especially those close to the door. Had the power gone out? Had the bulb in the lamp blown?

Glancing over to the nightstand, his alarm clock displayed the proper time, which told him that the power hadn't gone out.

"It must be just a bulb," he said to himself.

He knew he had to get up and change it, but right now his fear kept him stuck under the covers on the bed. He usually wasn't a timid man; he was *more of an aggressor*. However, what had happened earlier in the evening had suddenly and dramatically changed him. Never before in his entire life had he been caught so unaware. Now he felt so vulnerable. Still he knew he had to get up and change the bulb. Trying to think of another reason to force himself out of bed, he concluded that he should at least; turn the overhead light in the bedroom on. That required for him to get up and flip the switch on the wall up - nothing more. That was something his reasoning could handle.

With a shaking hand, he pulled back the covers. Trying to move, he grimaced. His body so battered and bruised that every movement was a struggle. Still though, he made it to his feet and slowly moved to the light switch. Never had just a few feet seemed so far to him. Reaching out his fingers, he fumbled at the little tab protruding from the wall, then clicked it upwards. The lights didn't come on.

Uncontrollable fear swept through him as he tried to determine a reason any person was behind all this and more importantly, why. It was true he'd made many enemies to get where he was, stepped on many toes, and padded many pockets. However, to the people that mattered he had been loyal and faithful. This didn't make sense. Again, he tried the light switch turning it on and off repeatedly as if, by some miracle, it would amazingly come on. He stood in the darkness.

Then came the creaking sound, like an un-oiled cabinet or car door. It was soft, yet to him it was magnified many times over. His mouth was pasty dry and his skin cold and clammy. Suddenly his face grew hot and butterflies rolled around in his stomach.

He knew what the sound was. The front door was being pushed open - slowly. Someone was coming back into his apartment. Someone was coming back for him.

Quietly listening, he strained to hear any sound or movement the intruder might make. There was only silence. His first thought was to call out to whomever waited in his small living room, but he quickly dismissed the idea. It would alert whoever was there to his presence. Instead, he forced his body to move again and peaked through the cracked doorway into the outer hall. The apartment was entirely dark, yet he could just make out the walls of the hallway and the coffee table and couch that sat in his living room.

Suddenly, something streaked across the living room with such speed it startled him. He gasped, for whatever it was glowed dimly. Then came a childish giggle.

"Dear God!" he breathed his heart thumping wildly in his chest.

It was true; it wasn't a lie like he had originally thought when he overheard employees talking about it. The Duppy of Osirus existed. They were real and now they were coming for him.

Again, another giggle but this time much closer than the last.

"We're coming for you Nash - we're coming for you to take you back to the grave with us!" a tiny, yet haunting child's voice called out to him.

Panic surged through Nash's body. Panic like he had never felt in his life. Gasping he again rapidly tried the light switch but to no avail. Glancing around the room he tried to make out any object that he could use as a weapon - anything. A thump and then another echo just outside the door in the hallway. They were getting closer and would at any moment glide through the door or walls. He could picture them, tiny apparitions with their arms outstretched, their faces contorted in hideous snarls as they rushed through the air at him.

The vision he created was too much for him. Pain like he had never felt before surged through is chest, like an iron hand had grasped his heart and was squeezing tightly. A ringing sound echoed in his ears and he was almost thankful for it. The ghostly voices would be kept away from his mind. From the slightly cracked doorway a dull, yet a clear phosphorus glow caught his attention. The pain in his chest grew worse.

He collapsed to his knees yet his eyes didn't budge from the glowing object just on the other side of the door. Tears streamed down his cheeks but he was unaware that they were even there. His chest was on fire, his hand clutching his shirt as if it would make the pain go away.

The glow grew brighter, and although he couldn't hear the door creak, it moved ever so slowly emitting more of the horror that was coming for him. A dull glowing green hand clasped the edge of the door just above where the doorknob was. The fingers were tiny and looked solid enough, even though he knew duppies couldn't be. Then a body came through, it was a little girl. She wore a lacy dress that appeared to glow, the same color as the rest of her. The pain in his chest grew worse and he collapsed to the floor his eyes still locked on the unbelievable horror that was coming towards him. Her features were mute, he didn't care, the only thing that froze him where he lay was the fact she had brilliantly glowing red eyes.

As she moved closer to him, he noticed another duppy child coming from the door behind the first, this one was a boy wearing outdated clothing as he finally realized the girls dress was also. He too had glowing red eyes and moved alongside the little girl. He could do nothing, his chest was on fire, his body was numb and he began to gasp for breath. All he could do was stare at them as they drew closer.

When they were close enough for him to see their features they both stopped and stood there for a moment staring down at his broken body. Then, they both slowly raised their arms forcing their hands into claw shapes. The last thing Earl Nash saw was their bared teeth - then they descended upon him.

Chapter 13

Raffie arrived to find Sharon, Ohpton, and Darrius sitting on the living room floor. Scattered around them were the piles of information he had printed out on Jah-Man. As soon as he closed the door, he leaned heavily against it and closed his eyes. He was tired and downright exhausted.

"How did it go, did you get the disks?" Darrius asked glancing up at him.

Raffie remained quiet as if Darrius had said nothing. His silence was enough to cause the others to take notice.

"What's wrong?" Sharon asked sensing trouble.

Finally, Raffie opened his eyes and looked at the group, he then took his shoes off and walked over sitting beside Ohpton. The others all stared at him wondering what had happened.

"We're in trouble, big trouble," he said his voice faint.

"What happened back there?" Darrius prodded him on.

"When I got back I peered through the entrance. Jah-Man was there talking to Helen," he breathed out a sigh then explained the rest of what happened.

"Oh brother!" Ohpton shook his head. "We are in big trouble now!"

"Are you sure Helen is all right?"

Sharon asked angered that Jah-Man had struck her.

"As far as I can tell, she was more worried about anyone seeing me with her and that it would get back to Jah-Man." "I get the picture," Sharon nodded.

"So, what do we do now?" Ohpton asked.

"Nothing, we go ahead with our plan as if this didn't happen," Darrius explained.

"What! Are you crazy?" Sharon said to him amazed.

"Look, Jah-Man is going to be after Raffie and me and of course Steven, but you and Ohpton still are safe," he tried to explain.

"What good does that do? We won't have the money to get us off the island if most of us are unemployed," Ohpton pointed out.

"You are going to be the eyes and ears for us, you both need to listen to what happens around there. Especially you Ohpton, you seem to always get the scoop on what's happening long before the rest of us do," Darrius explained.

"This is getting too dangerous, way too dangerous," Sharon cut in.

"We knew it would in the beginning before we took this path," Raffie countered.

"We could get killed Raffie. I really mean it, one of us could die!" she said with a bite in her voice.

"Yes, one of us might. But then again, maybe none of us will," he smiled at her.

Sharon said nothing, her gaze turned to Darrius and she had an uncontrollable urge to tell him what Mama Rose had said. As she stared at him, she almost couldn't believe it herself. Yet, Mama Rose was seldom wrong.

"Why are you staring at me?" Darrius asked finally breaking her trance.

"No reason, I'm just worried," she said staring at the paper on the floor.

Ohpton looked over at her, he knew what was running through her mind. He too wanted to forewarn Darrius, he was his friend, his brother. Could he do no less?

The thought quickly left his mind; they had both promised Mama Rose. There was something about her, the love they felt for her that wouldn't allow them to break their promise.

"Where's Eve?" Raffie asked.

"Still at the Orion," Ohpton said.

"When I saw her earlier she was upset about something. She wouldn't even stop to talk to me," he added.

"Diamond" Raffie shook his head.

"I should have hit him harder," Darrius said looking away.

"Hit him harder?" Sharon asked.

Darrius explained with much embarrassment the ordeal that happened earlier in the dining room of the Orion. Part of her wanted to hug Darrius for what he did and another part wanted to slap him for being so stupid. Instead, she sat there saying nothing.

"Look, I'm sorry especially to you Raffie. If it wasn't for me you'd still have your job," Darrius said sadly.

"Yeah, a job where I would be working to pay off a dented Land Rover," he smiled.

"You actually did me a favor."

"Don't think you'll be off the hook for the vehicle. Nash will find a way to make you pay for it!" Ohpton smiled.

"Lucky for us nobody really knows about this place," Raffie grinned.

"Has anyone seen Steven?"

At the mention of Steven's name, Sharon turned away. She was obviously worried about him. It was also obvious to the others that there was more than just concern.

"We went to see Steven at Mama Rose's, she told us that last night he went to see Delicia to try and get Jah-Man off his back and ours. She hasn't seen him since," Ohpton explained.

"Well, we should find him and give him the update on what's happening."

"So what did you guys find in all this mess?" Raffie motioned to all the paper surrounding them.

"Not too much, most is ancient history, but we did find something about a man named The Frenchman, supposedly he is a big drug lord in Columbia or something like that," Sharon said.

"Frenchman - Frenchman, I've heard that name before. In fact, Yashi mentioned it or Jah-Man did, I don't remember," Darrius said rubbing his forehead.

"Well anyway, this guy supposedly wants to rule the drug business in this little corner of the world. In the files there is a picture of the guy," she said passing the badly taken photograph around.

"Looks mean," Ohpton said.

"Looks like a butcher," Raffie added.

"More trouble," Darrius shook his head.

"This guy is on the island."

"You mean he's here, now?" Ohpton frowned.

"Yeah, Yashi mentioned it," Darrius said glancing at the photograph then handing it back to Sharon.

"Anything else in this mess?" Raffie asked.

"No, nothing we could use against Jah-Man, but very detailed information a law enforcement agency could use," Sharon said.

"That must have been where your parents were heading with this stuff," Ohpton said to Raffie.

"Yeah, must have been I wonder." he said softly.

"What?" Darrius asked.

"I wonder if it was Jah-Man who ordered my families death or another one of the older yardies," he said his voice but a whisper.

"That's something we may never know and at this point, we probably shouldn't sidetrack ourselves with it," Darrius added.

"Yes, you are right on one hand but if he is responsible." Raffie said looking up at Darrius.

"I <u>will</u> want my revenge."

"Not a good idea Raffie, ever hear that expression <u>when you go out for</u> <u>revenge you must first dig</u> <u>two graves?</u>" Sharon said.

"Whatever it takes," Raffie said.

"So what's next?" Ohpton said changing the subject.

"Well, Jah-Man has a small drug delivery with his new buyers the day after tomorrow. It's going to happen on Portland Point. Then, if all goes well, the big shipment and exchange will occur shortly after. I don't know when yet," Darrius explained what he had heard Jah-Man talking about.

"It's time to dig our money up," Sharon blurted out.

"Why now?" Darrius asked.

"We need to get our escape route in order. If this is going down in a few days, we need to be ready."

"Good idea," Raffie smiled.

Sharon began piling up the loose paper that was scattered about, Ohpton quickly began to help her.

"Don't tell Eve any of this, least not yet," Raffie said breaking the sudden silence.

"Why not, she's part of our group," Sharon said irritated at Raffie's suggestion.

"Because she's close to Delicia and Delicia keeps Jah-Man's bed," Raffie explained.

"We can let her know just before everything happens," Darrius nodded.

"Who's going to go to Kingston to make plans to get off this island?" Ohpton asked.

"Well, Darrius and I are kind of useless around here," Raffie pointed out. "We could go tomorrow."

"How are you two going to get to Kingston, <u>walk</u>?" Sharon frowned at them.

"Get serious, you don't have an automobile and we don't have access to one at the Orion any more."

"Who else do we know who owns wheels?" Darrius blurted out.

"Forget Mama Rose," Ohpton said.

"William?" Darrius suggested.

"That's Jah-Man's brother, forget him. He would turn you two over to Jah-Man in a heartbeat," Ohpton pointed out.

"I doubt he would, he's not like Jah-Man you know," Darrius said defending him.

"They're blood Darrius and blood is thicker than water," Ohpton said pointing at the others.

Suddenly there came a loud knock on the front door. It startled them all because only Eve and Steven were missing from the group. Besides, nobody else ever came to the shack. Ohpton got up and headed for the door.

"Be careful," Sharon breathed.

"For what?" Ohpton whispered back.

"Duppy Children," Raffie cut in.

"Duppy knock on doors to come in?" Ohpton frowned.

"They throw rocks, remember?" Sharon said pointing to her head.

Ohpton reached up and felt the healing cut on his head; it was reminder enough for him to be careful. Again, there came a gentle knock on the door.
Reaching for the door handle, he stepped to the side just before he opened it. Standing on the doorstep was Yashi.

"Yashi!" Darrius said bounding to his feet.

"I'm, I'm sorry to intrude but may I come in?" she said meekly.

"Yes, please come in and join us," Darrius motioned to her.

Sharon frowned hard at Raffie who did the same to Ohpton. Their home was theirs to be private; a sanctuary for just them.

"Darrius, may I speak with you a minute?" Sharon asked getting up off the floor.

"Sure" he smiled to her obviously overjoyed.

"In private?" Sharon motioned with her hand to the hallway.

His smile quickly faded when she stared at him with a stern expression. He followed her down the hallway to the last bedroom, which was Steven's. As soon as they entered, she quickly closed the door then turned to him.

"What are you doing bringing her here?" Sharon asked with a bite in her voice.

"I didn't," he shrugged.

"Darrius, it's common knowledge around the resort that you've been hanging around with this, this criminal," she motioned with her hand.

"And now you go and bring her here!"

"I didn't bring here. Remember I was here at least a couple hours before she got here?" Darrius pointed out.

"Then what is she doing here and how did she know here even exists?" Sharon said frowning.

"I don't know. I didn't tell her where this place was - I swear!" he said holding up his hands.

"Then someone else knows and if she knows then others may too, like Jah-Man!" Sharon said the worry clear in her voice.

"Look, instead of badgering me, why don't we go and ask her?" Darrius said.

"Fine, I'll ask her," Sharon said swinging open the door and storming down the hallway, Darrius in hot pursuit.

Raffie watched Sharon moving quickly down the hallway towards them, anger written all over her face.

"Uh oh, here comes trouble!" Raffie said not smiling.

Sharon went directly up to Yashi, for a moment she was taken aback by Sharon's aggressive posture, but quickly recovered.

"How did you know that Darrius was here?" she bluntly asked.

"I have my sources," she countered.

"Mind telling me what those sources are?"

"Actually, no," Yashi said without smiling.

"Try to understand. None of us know you. You deal with Jah-Man and right now that puts all of us in a dangerous position," Sharon explained.

"Don't you think I know that?" Yashi quickly added.

"Then please tell us, why?" Raffie chimed in.

"I had to. I had to come and talk with Darrius," she said softly not meeting Sharon's intense gaze.

"But how, how did you know where to find him?" Ohpton asked.

There was a long hesitation and it became obvious that Yashi was extremely uncomfortable talking about it. Still though, the others stared at her waiting for an answer.

"I would like to know too," Darrius said softly.

"I put a bug on you," she said softly.

"A bug?" Raffie all but laughed.

"A transmitter," Yashi added.

"On me? But why?" Darrius asked aghast.

"Not on you, but in your bag that you took on the trip. I needed to keep track of you, needed to see your sincerity," she said looking away from him.

"You couldn't trust me?"

"Like I told you back in Florida…"

"Florida! You were in Florida?" Sharon looked at Darrius with surprise.

Darrius just nodded. There wasn't much he could say to them since the others would feel the same way he had on the plane. He was still feeling guilty that he was the first one to reach America.

"As I was saying, I told you back in Florida that there was more going on here than you knew - much more," Yashi explained the best she could.

"Still, if you cared, you should have trusted me," he said the hurt in his voice clear.

"I wanted to, but the big picture didn't let me. That you have to believe Darrius, you were the last person I wanted to get hurt." "Didn't work," he breathed.

"But what you did was stupid. Diamond was only an escort and nothing more," Yashi shook her head.

"You didn't have to attack him."

"He had it coming," Darrius said softly.

"Maybe, but you now put yourself and your friend in grave danger," she said.

"And why do you care what happens to them," Darrius motioned to Raffie.

"Because of what you told me of them - because of your close friendships," she said.

"Well right now you even being here has put us all in danger," Sharon piped up.

Yashi turned from them and walked over to the window. For a long moment, she stared out into the dark night beyond, then turned and walked back.

"Two of you are in danger, this man here," she said pointing to Raffie. "The other smaddy I don't see here."

"Steven" Ohpton breathed.

"Yes, that was his name. My sources tell me that Jah-Man is out for blood," Yashi said.

"What about Darrius?" Raffie asked.

"He was with me too."

Sharon shot Ohpton a serious look then they both looked at Yashi who stared surprisingly back at them.

"I don't know, Darrius seems to be in Jah-Man's favor," Yashi said lying.

"I don't understand why. I'm no different than anyone else, why me?" Darrius said with disgust.

"Don't knock it maybe we can use it later," Yashi pointed out.

"What is this, we?" Sharon frowned.

"Like I said earlier, there is more going on than meets the eye, more than any one knows and more than I can talk about. I am here to help you though," Yashi said.

"Help us? You are kidding right?" Ohpton laughed.

"You work for a drug lord. You're no better than Jah-Man."

Yashi stared at Ohpton, his words had been brutal and a hurt look quickly formed on her face. Moments later it was gone as she pressed ahead with her thoughts.

"I am here to help you all, Darrius said you all wanted to come to America, right?" she asked.

Everyone turned and looked at Darrius who held up his hands, he suddenly felt like he was under a spotlight.

"Yeah, we all do," Sharon looked back at Yashi.

"Then I might be able to help you all," Yashi smiled.

"Why?" Raffie frowned.

"And what do you want in return?" Sharon added.

"Because of what Darrius has told me about you all, because I can. I want only your cooperation if the need may arise in the future in regards to Jah-Man." "I want nothing to do with Jah-Man," Darrius blurted out.

"None of us do," Raffie added.

"I believe you all, but right now you're all in heap of trouble," Yashi pointed out.

"No, we're in deep." Raffie began to say.

"Don't go there Raffie, please don't remind us," Sharon stopped him.

"Look, if you want to get off this island then you need me," Yashi pointed out.

Silence quickly grew within the room, everyone wanted to believe her, and everyone though, was having a tough time trusting her.

Eve had stayed over an extra hour at the boutique. The day had been miserable as the image from the night before had replayed repeatedly in her mind. Why did Steven make love to Delicia? There was no sensible reason she could come up with. She wanted to tell Sharon; she needed to tell Sharon but she just couldn't find the right words. She knew it was partly jealously on her part, but she also loved Steven and didn't want to be placed in a position where she had to choose between them.

When she closed the store she went back up to Delicia's room where she hoped she would find her, instead the apartment was empty. It had remained the same, as it was the night before, Delicia hadn't come by during the day.

Taking a quick shower, she wrapped the towel around herself and flopped down on the fine leather couch in the living room. Moments later she was flipping through the television stations. This was luxury compared to the shack. A luxury that she didn't want to part with any time soon. She loved and missed the others and the shack. There were fond memories that she would never lose, but to have anything she ever wanted? There was no comparison. Delicia lived the high life and Delicia loved life.

She heard the key turn in the door and it startled her, it quickly opened and Delicia walked in. At first, she was surprised to see her, but then quickly a warm smile formed on her face.

"Glad you're here," Delicia smiled.

"Glad you're here too, now I don't have to be alone tonight," Eve pointed out.

"No Diamond?" Delicia frowned.

"Don't know, I haven't heard from him today, have you?" she asked.

"No, I've been with Jah-Man most of the day. He had some business to take care of this evening and left early. So, I figured I'd spend the night here," Delicia explained.

"Let's get some ice cream or better yet popcorn and pig out!" Eve grinned. "Got a better idea,"

Delicia smiled her one eyebrow turning up.

Kicking off her shoes she walked over to the small end table next to the couch then began fishing through her purse. Moments later she produced a round plastic container.

"Let's get high," Delicia smiled shaking the container.

"I don't know Delicia. I've never done that," she shook her head timidly.

"Oh come off it, everyone does it, maybe if you try it you'll like it!" she grinned.

"I don't know. I've seen what Jah-Man has done to the community and it isn't pretty," Eve shook her head.

"That's them and this is here and now," Delicia smiled.

"That doesn't make it right though," Eve countered.

"Look, we can have a few drinks and then do a few lines. I'll even invite Diamond over to join us, sound good?" Delicia again shook the bottle.

Eve said nothing, she wanted to be with Diamond and she trusted Delicia and her judgment. She just nodded.

"Good, I'll call him up and get him over here, then you and I can get things ready," Delicia said grabbing her cellular telephone.

Eve watched Delicia walk into the kitchen, she couldn't hear a word she said but she quickly came back with a smile on her face.

"There all set, Diamond will be over shortly. He said he'd bring a couple bottles of wine too."

"Well I better get dressed," Eve said getting up off the couch.

"I got a better idea," Delicia motioned with her finger for Eve to follow.

Delicia went into her bedroom and over to a large mirrored dresser. She opened a few of the drawers and began to rifle through the clothing within. Moments later she pulled out a set of extremely sheer panties.

"Here, try these," she handed them to Eve.

"What for?" Eve said reluctantly taking them.

"To wear silly, we're going to make you up so when Diamond gets here his head will spin when he sees you," Delicia said moving over to her hanging closet.

"Now we have to find you a negligee."

"But you're going to be here..."

"So what honey, you've never done it until you've had someone watching,"

Delicia smiled warmly.

"I don't know Delicia. Making love, well making love is private," Eve frowned.

"Come on, it's all about pleasure. It's all about trying new things," Delicia countered.

"I understand, but I feel so uncomfortable," Eve said squinting.

"That's good because that's the way you're suppose to feel. Now here, try this,"

Diamond knocked hard on the door, he hated using the doorbell. Delicia had some odd bell put in that sounded like a chorus from a stupid song he had never even heard before. She was odd that way, along with the mass of chains she wore both around her neck and around her wrists and ankles.

She wore so much metal on her body that he wondered, if he used a very powerful magnet could he possibly rip her arms, legs and head off? The thought amused him.

The door opened and Delicia stood there wearing a very sheer flowing gown. At first, he was surprised by her appearance. He had never seen her naked or even remotely so. She had an incredible body and her appearance instantly put him on edge. Smiling, he entered the apartment. Delicia took the bottles of wine from him and headed for the kitchen. He watched her bare bottom as she disappeared from sight. Maybe tonight he'd give her that freebie.

"Hello Diamond," a voice echoed from behind him.

Turning his eyes cast upon Eve, she stood in the doorway to the bedroom. His eyes opened wide with surprise. She wore high heels and an extremely short light blue teddy that left little to the imagination, as did the panties beneath.

"Do you like?" she said walking seductively up him.

"Huh...you look very nice, very nice indeed," he grinned.

"Good enough to eat?" Eve asked softly.

"Oh yeah," Diamond smiled.

Eve turned away from him just out of his reach, Delicia wanted her to tease him, tease him until he couldn't take it any more. This she explained would drive Diamond crazy for her. By the look on his face, she was right.

"Everyone grab a glass," Delicia said emerging from the kitchen with a tray.

"Are you two trying to drive me nuts?" Diamond smiled.

"Where did those bruises come from?" Eve said reaching out to touch one.

Diamond pulled away his smile quickly fading. Even a reminder of the early evening angered him.

"What happened?" Delicia asked.

"Got into a fight," he said trying not to become specific.

"A fight? With whom?" Delicia asked.

"Darrius" he said softly.

"My brother? Why?" Eve said her face filling with concern.

"He came into the dining room and attacked me." "But for heaven's sake why?"

Eve asked.

"I don't know, maybe he doesn't like me being with you," he lied.

"I can't believe my brother would do such a thing!" "Believe it because he did,"

Diamond added.

Delicia frowned, she knew Diamond well enough to tell he was lying to Eve. There was some other reason for the incident.

"Well come on you two, there's enough here for the whole night," Delicia said spilling a quarter of the bottle of cocaine on the glass tabletop. With a straight razor, she divided the drug into many lines, then handed both Eve and Diamond a glass tube.

Eve watched as Delicia put the tube to her nose along with plugging her other nostril, and then snorted one of the lines of cocaine. When she was done, she blinked her eyes rapidly then smiled.

Diamond was next and to Eve's amazement, he bent right down and snorted another one of the lines. It became painfully obvious to her that he had done it before.

"Your turn Eve, don't put the tube too far into your nose," Delicia said.

"I don't know, this doesn't feel right," Eve frowned.

"You're just scared, everyone is scared for the first time," Delicia grinned then wiped her nose.

Suddenly, Diamond put his hand softly onto her back rubbing the whole length right down to her buttocks.

"Come on, try it you might actually like it. Also, it makes sex more intense," he whispered into her ear.

Eve felt embarrassed, partly for his openness regarding sex and partly for sitting there in front of them both wearing hardly anything.

"Come on honey, just try one line," Delicia coaxed her.

Eve looked at her, and then at Diamond and then Delicia at her right. She was scared to death. Slowly she took the glass tube and bent down. Doing exactly what they did, she drew up another of the many lines on the glass table. Instantly she gasped, her sinuses burning and she blinked her eyes coughing.

"Wow!" she coughed again a suddenly feeling of <u>irie</u> sweeping over her.

"Good huh?" Diamond laughed, and then drew another line off the table.

"Get it all? It increases blood pressure you know and helps with erections,"

Delicia winked at Diamond. Eve smiled and giggled like a little schoolgirl, she never felt so elated or alert. Her heart pounded wildly in her chest. She didn't even flinch at Delicia's crudeness regarding Diamond. She then felt Delicia's hand on her arm motioning her to do another of the lines. She nodded and bent down sucking in more of the white powder.

"Oh!" she moaned closing her eyes.

"Better isn't it?" Delicia asked.

Eve just nodded, it was a feeling she had never before experienced and it was highly stimulating. Diamond looked over at Delicia who just nodded to him. He then reached over and lightly ran his hand through Eve's thin curly blond hair. His touch was magnified to her and it made her sigh, when his other hand lightly caressed her breast. She felt tingles all over her body. She wanted him.

Delicia grinned, then got up and sat in the nearest chair as she watched Diamond make love to Eve. She had to admit it was stimulating even to her to watch them; then again, the cocaine could very well be the cause of her feeling. Eve lay back and was like a rag doll in Diamond's hands, she was absorbing every minute, every second of him. The stimulation was incredible and beyond her wildest dreams.

Delicia watched Diamond; he was definitely an experienced lover. He was a true <u>Teg-A-Reg</u>. He turned and pulled Eve in a variety of positions and by the expression on her face; he was having the desired effect. After nearly an hour, she watched Diamond's face tense as his own passion built to a crescendo, he then released and collapsed on top of an exhausted Eve. The moment was at hand.

Rising from the chair, she went over and laid beside Eve her hand lightly stroking her damp hair.

"Honey, can I ask you a question?" Delicia asked.

Diamond frowned at her withdrawing, then leaned back against the couch. He watched Delicia and was erotically turned on by her body. He was still under the effects of the cocaine.

"Yeah sure," Eve muttered, her eyes closed.

"Do you remember much about your mama?"

"Of course I do," Eve frowned but didn't open her eyes.

"Do you remember her saying anything about your father?" Delicia asked.

"No. Well I do remember her saying that maybe someday we might meet him."

Delicia pushed.

"No. I had asked her if his last name was Lawson but she only shook her head," Eve explained.

"Can I ask you another question?" Delicia prodded.

"Sure"

Delicia looked over at Diamond then motioned to Eve. Diamond pursed his lips and scowled at her. He then moved back on top of Eve, sliding himself deep within her <u>pum pum</u>. Eve's expression was utter ecstasy.

"Are you sure?" Delicia asked again.

"Oh yeah, yeah," Eve grinned her legs wrapping around Diamonds waist.

"What do you know about Jah-Man?" she asked.

"He's a bad man," Eve said her expression remained the same.

"No. .that's not what I want to know, do you know anything <u>about him</u>?"

"Not much, only from what Uncle William would say about him." "What did Uncle William say about him?" she pushed harder.

Diamond half-listened as he made love to Eve. He was shocked at Delicia. She was digging information up on Jah-Man - for what reason he could only guess. Blackmail most likely. Here Delicia was trying to pull a skank.

"Uncle William never had anything bad to say about him, Jah-Man is his brother you know," Eve grinned.

"Yes, I know, but is Uncle William your real uncle?" Delicia asked.

"No silly, we just call him Uncle William. He was always around as we grew up, he used to give money to my Mama," Eve said her smile fading as she remembered her mama.

"Money? For what?" Delicia became interested.

"I don't know, I only saw him give her an envelope a few times. I did hear Uncle William say it was from Jah-Man though," she frowned opening her eyes.

"Why would Jah-Man give your mama money?" Delicia asked.

"My Mama worked here you know," Eve stated.

"Yes, but what did you mama do? Was she a lady of the evening?" Delicia said trying to sound as mellow as possible.

"Mama? No way, she was a front-end manager," Eve scowled at her.

"I'm sorry Eve, I didn't mean anything by that," Delicia apologized.

"That's okay, that was the first thing I thought of too. I asked Mama about it, and she told me that Jah-Man gave us money because out of all the people we were special to him," Eve said.

"I never told Darrius that though, he hates Jah-Man," she giggled again.

"Is there anything else you remember?" Delicia asked.

"Not much, Jah-Man never came to the house, only Uncle William."

Delicia backed away from her and sat down into the chair again, while Diamond again made love to Eve. There was some connection that Jah-Man had with Eve and Darrius. All the pieces of the puzzle were there, she just had to put them in the right order. Then a thought came into her mind, it was a thought that suddenly astounded her. She got up and walked over to the curio cabinet, sitting on top was a picture of Jah-Man. Grabbing it she walked over and stood above them, they were oblivious to her consumed by their own passions.

She glanced at the picture studying it, then looked down at Eve. It then hit her like a ton of bricks. Jah-Man was Eve's father.

Steven wandered about; he had stayed on the beach most of the day then decided to wander back to town. He was trying to think of a way to get himself out of his problems. He also needed to find a way to explain what had happened and why he had done what he did to Sharon. What he felt for her was something he didn't want to lose.

By the time he reached their small town, it was near midnight. He hadn't eaten anything and was ravished. As soon as he got home, he knew there would be something to eat. The shack wasn't far from town.

Something rustled in the bushes alongside the road. It was enough to startle him. He stopped and strained his eyes to see into the dark foliage that lined the roadside. He remained motionless for a few minutes then continued on down the road. He was about to make the turn that led onto the path to the shack when the noise again occurred. The first time he thought it had been him, that he inadvertently mistook some other sound, but now? There again came a rustle in the bushes right next to him.

Suddenly, without warning something rushed out at him. At first terror took control, his mind couldn't comprehend what he was seeing. One of the duppy children was lunging at him, a huge butcher's knife poised high above his head. The duppy silence, save for the swishing sound as the knife plummeted towards him.

Steven yelled, his instincts forcing him to react and move. However, it was too late, the knife sliced down skimming his left arm and slicing deeply into him. He howled in pain clutching his arm, his blood leaking between his fingers. He let his first thought take over. He ran towards town. As he ran, the jostling motion caused the pain in his arm to be magnified. He felt suddenly nauseous, but his fear drove him on. Glancing over his shoulder, he watched as the glowing duppy child followed, the knife poised again over his head. This time though, his blood was covering it.

The town was not far off and he ran as fast as his legs would carry him, every so often he would glance over his shoulder to see how close his pursuer was coming.

The duppy was gone.

A new fear swept into him and he stopped dead in the road, his ears straining to pick up any unusual sounds. He tried desperately to control his labored breathing; the noise he created made it difficult to hear anything else.

"Why, why me?" he thought.

"Jah-Man wants me dead not some duppy children from the turn of the last century."

Wheeling around he had a sudden feeling of dread. He half expected the apparition to be standing there a hideous screw face as the knife sliced into him again. Only the darkness greeted him.

"Okay" he thought to himself.

"These buggers glow, which means they can't hide very well at night. All I have to do is keep sharp and make sure nothing sneaks up on me."

Slowly he began to walk into town. Blood dripped down his arm and hand; tiny droplets fell from his fingertips onto the dry dirt. He was light headed, hungry, tired and more importantly, scared. He knew well enough that heading up the shack would endanger the others, but where could he go?

"Mama Rose" he muttered under his breath.

She lived on the other side of town, not too far normally, but every step he took was becoming laborious. He tried to grip the slice in his arm as tightly as possible; it might stop the bleeding if it wasn't too deep. If it was deep, he knew it would require stitches that would have to be done at a hospital.

A sharp rap of metal against metal forced him to a stop. The sound originated to his left and behind. Whirling around he held his breath his eyes ready and expecting to see the duppy coming for him but nothing. He waited longer than he should have before continuing. His arm now throbbed and was growing hotter by the second. Every step became intolerable and he wanted nothing more than to lay down on the filthy ground and go to sleep. He pushed himself on.

"Steven, Steven, we know it's you Steven. We're coming to get you Steven," a tiny childlike and very giddy voice called out to him. He again stopped dead in his tracks listening. The sound had originated to his right now, opposite to where the last noise came from. There was more than one child aboard the Osirus. The legend stated a whole boat full of children. Glancing up he cocked his head about scanning everything he possibly could. If was dealing with a whole boatload of duppies, he would have no chance, but just one?

There came no apparent sound, just his heavy breathing. Again, he continued into town the small run down houses providing better cover for his attacker. It would also provide him with a little cover. All he had to do was get to Mama Rose's place, there he could lock the door, hide until he could figure out what to do or how to get rid of the duppies. Were they after him because of his childhood? He was found abandoned in a church, whoever his mama had been had just delivered him. His umbilical cord and placenta were still attached, according to the nuns, the only reason they knew he was there was that he cried out. Maybe these duppy children were after him because of that, because maybe he was left in a church. It was the only rational explanation he could think of.

"Steven, stop running. Steven, your time is near Steven. Come to us, come to us Steven," a ghostly voice cried out to his left.

He was terrified; a duppy was hunting him. How could he defend himself from something that was dead already? Crosses, wooden stakes, silver bullets, there had to be something he could use that would work. Hollywood, in America would love the terror he was experiencing, it would make for a good horror movie.

"Please Steven. Your time has come. We will get you Steven, we will, we promise." the ghostly childlike voice cried out.

"Then come and get me duppy!" he cried out in defiance.

Wheeling around, back and forth, he continually looked around; only darkness surrounded him, enveloping him. With much effort, he gritted his teeth and continued. He was almost at Mama Rose's place – his sanctuary.

Something darted across the street in front of him and it glowed. It was one of the duppy children. He didn't get a good look before it disappeared behind one of the houses. Now it was in front of him, laying in wait for the precise moment to strike.

"Come on out! Are you scared, are you chicken?" he yelled trying to taunt it.

He figured his yelling would awaken someone in one of the many houses within the town. Nevertheless, all remained quiet, almost tranquil.

"Come on out - I dare you!" he yelled again at the night.

Suddenly something darted to his right. The duppy child was edging his way closer, foot-by-foot, until it reached the opportune time to strike the one fatal blow. Steven spun around his teeth clenched and his anger rising sharply. He let go of his wounded arm and balled his hand into a fist.

"Come on out of hiding. Come on out and see if you can take me!" he ranted his voice yelling.

There came no response, not a sound came from the direction that he had last seen the duppy. Paranoia quickly set in and he spun himself about in all directions wondering when the attacker would make their move.

He had no weapon and no flashlight to search for one either. If he could only find a suitable stick, an iron pipe or better yet an axe, he would feel much better about his threats. He continued towards Mama Rose's.

Mama Rose slept soundly, at least as soundly as could be expected for a mama since one of their children died. Since her son's death, her nights started out sound, but quickly turned into terror as nightmares claimed her subconscious. They were always similar but not exact. She was running, trying to make it to the beach in time, and though the reason for going was different, the end product was the same. Jaco was laying on her kitchen floor, his blood spilling out, and the wood floor soaking it in leaving a dark oval. This night though, the dream was different. When she entered the kitchen Jaco's body wasn't on the floor in a pool of blood, he sat upright in one of the many chairs that surrounded him. His eyes were lifeless, yet they still looked up staring at her.

"Mama" his voice creaked like it hadn't been oiled in a thousand years.

She wanted to run to him, hold him close, but her fear kept her at a distance. His lifeless eyes were haunting and they looked about the room as if not settling on her totally yet.

"Mama, please help me, help me please Mama," Jaco croaked.

"I can't honey - I can't!" she yelled out frantically.

"Come to me Mama, please - hurry!"

Mama Rose shook her head as tears fell down her cheeks. Her heart ached at seeing her beloved son but her stomach had butterflies over what he had become.

Suddenly, from behind Jaco, Jah-Man emerged a broad grin on his face. He walked over and placed his hand on Jaco's shoulder like a father would with his son.

"No!" she croaked.

Sitting quickly upright in bed, she clutched her chest for fear that a heart attack would claim her. It didn't. Sweat poured off her, she pushed covers away and forced herself to get up. Maybe a cup of hot tea would help. The room was dark and only faint images could be seen. She ordinarily loved the dark, but tonight the comfort she usually felt was replaced with dread. Was it because her dream had been different than all the others? Was something wrong with Junior? Despite her attitude towards him, he was still her son and she loved him very much.

There was something else, something was definitely <u>wrong</u>. Then she heard someone yelling, at first she thought one of the towns' people had gotten drunk again. However, there was something distinctly different with this voice. It had fear in it.

Grabbing a cane she kept by her bed, she used it to help her to her feet. Ordinarily she would leave it there but this time it was needed. With as much speed she could muster, she moved to a window and pulled the bamboo blind to the side. She saw nothing; the back of the house was quiet, undisturbed.

Another yell, this time it was closer and coming from the front. Navigating her house, she stumbled and nearly fell on the lip of a door. Stress was claiming her now making her forgetful. When she reached the front door she was about to pull the blind to the side like before, but instead unbolted the door and swung it open. What she saw made her gasp and make the sign of the cross down her chest.

Steven stood about 30 meters away from her yelling and shaking his fist at the dark alleyway across the street. What he didn't see was the small child that was running up from behind him crouched. The child seemed to glow - like a duppy.

"Steven! Turn around!" she yelled with all her might.

Steven turned just in time; the duppy child came sharply up behind him wielding the butcher knife. With a swift kick, he slammed his foot into the duppy's stomach. It let out an exasperated wheeze and collapsed to the ground, the knife falling from its hand.

The effort it took to swing himself around had cost him; he collapsed to the ground also. Spots swam before his eyes and he tried not to pass out. It was inevitable though, and the last thing he witnessed was Mama Rose hurrying out from her house trying to reach him.

Mama Rose panted and wheezed as she rushed from the house her own ailments forgotten. As she drew nearer to Steven, the duppy child quickly got up and turned towards her. For a moment it stood there staring at her, then dashed off across the street disappearing behind one of the many houses.

"Steven, Steven can you hear me?" she said reaching him.

There came no reply, she noticed the gash on his left arm. It was a serious cut, but one she knew she could mend. Then something caught her eye a short distance away from him. A glowing object lay on the dirt. Hobbling over, she bent down and picked it up. It was a glowing butcher knife.

Chapter 14

The world spun in circles and he felt his stomach do flip-flops. It was exhilarating to say the least. He had never been on an amusement ride, but for some strange reason, he knew it would feel this way. For all the pictures he had seen and all the articles he had read described it this way.

America was a beautiful place, he was glad he was here.

The amusement ride changed suddenly enough where he felt a twinge of apprehension. However, the feeling quickly faded as a sandy beach took its place. The setting was warm, quiet with the only sounds coming from the lapping of tiny waves against the shoreline and the soft breeze coming in off the ocean. The sun was beginning to set; red, yellow, pink, and orange colors captivated his attention. In the distance he noticed a lone figure standing on the edge of the water. He couldn't make out who it was, but for some strange reason he already knew.

As he drew near, he noticed she wore a long flowered sarong that blew in the steady breeze. The way the waning sun was shining he could nearly see through it.

Sharon stood watching the horizon. Her hair was down and it blew along with her sarong. She was stunningly beautiful and for a moment he stood and stared taking in every curve. The setting sun made her skin a glowing metallic. Taking a deep breath, he approached her. As he drew near he noticed the sarong was just tied around her waist.

The gentle yet large curve of her breasts were stimulating, he wanted nothing more than to draw up behind her wrapping his arms underneath them and holding her close. Instead, he chose to break the silence.

"Hi" he said softly.

She didn't turn to him, never uttered a word. She abruptly turned and began walking along the edge of the water. Steven followed, his heart beginning to pound in his chest.

"Sharon, please stop, please forgive me," he pleaded.

She said nothing. The sun had gone and night was coming quickly to take its place. He tried repeatedly to get her to notice him, but to no avail. Then something else caught his attention, behind him in the distance was something tiny, something glowing. He stopped to stare at it and when he turned again, Sharon was gone. His attention was now focused on the glow as it quickly, almost inhumanly, rushed towards him.

As it drew closer he realized it wasn't just one glow, but a mass of tiny lights bobbing up and down. It was the duppy children. Fear quickly rushed into him and he turned to run but found his legs were stuck in the sand, the water rushing around his ankles. The duppies were close enough for him to make out the first one, it was a little girl her lips pulled back and hideously sharp teeth gnashed together. Her eyes were glowing red as if the fires of Hell itself were lighting them. Upraised in her right hand was a gleaming and overly shiny knife.

There was nothing he could do; he couldn't move. All he could do was scream as the knife slashed down against his arm, the pain unbearable.

Steven's eyes burst open and he let out an anguished cry. Mama Rose sat on a small chair next to his bed and carefully stitched the outer skin together. The wound hadn't been that serious and it didn't require any internal stitches, but the outer cut needed something to hold the skin together.

"Glad to see you're back with me," she smiled warmly to him.

"What happened?" he croaked his mouth dry and parched.

"Well, you have a nasty cut on your arm, but I think you'll pull through just fine."

"What about…"

"That duppy child?" she asked, knowing exactly what he was going to ask. "Yeah, that duppy kid," his voice belaying the fear he felt.

"Well, he ran off when I came out so maybe he's scared of me!" she laughed knowing full well that the whole experience was terrifying.

"I know I hit something hard," he added.

"You sure did, you dropped him quick, he was out like a light until I nearly got to you," she explained.

"He followed me from the outskirts of town, I couldn't lead him to the shack, to the others," he swallowed.

"You did the right thing coming here Steven, that was the right thing to do," she nodded to him.

"I have to warn the others," he said closing his eyes.

"They'll be fine, you need to rest. We'll talk more about it in the morning," she said lightly kissing him on the forehead.

She was about to get up when she heard something behind her. Swiftly she swiveled in her chair and looked where the noise had come.

"You shouldn't have him here," Junior said a grimace on his face.

"He needs help, he is injured," she scowled.

"Jah-Man wants him dead," Junior stepped further into the room.

"Jah-Man is a fool. Jah-Man will get his in the end," Mama Rose spat.

"Perhaps quicker than even he expects," Junior said the corner of his mouth turning up in a smile.

"What are you doing here this late?" she asked changing the subject.

"No reason, can I not come home whenever I please?" he looked at her.

"You never do anything without a reason unless of course, it benefits you," she snapped.

"Why mama, aren't you proud of your son? He has more money than anyone in this village. I can do whatever I please, is that not something to be proud of?" he smiled.

"You have material things but you lost your soul Junior, lost it many years ago and you took your brothers along with you!"

"I was not to blame. I did not force him to go with me!" Junior snarled, the mention of Jaco's death instantly throwing him into a rage.

"It was your fault, your brother would be alive today if you had done the right thing!" she said with anger.

"It was just as much your fault as it was mine! You are to blame mama! If you had been there for him and for me instead you spent all your time with other children!" he yelled.

"I worked doing whatever I could to put food in your mouths, clothes on your back, it wasn't easy! How could you be so, so horrible to me?" she said a tear streaking down her cheek.

"I wanted more out of life mama, more than you could ever possibly provide!" he shrieked.

"I tried so hard, so hard to put you on the right path - an honest path. Yet you chose to follow the darkness just like Jah-Man," she cried. "And your bother paid the price for you." "Stop it! Stop it!" he screamed.

"I hate you mama, hate you!" he said then turned and headed for the door. When he reached it he stopped and turned back to her.

"I would not keep him here or any of the others," he said then left the room.

Mama Rose wiped her cheeks and stared down at Steven. She then took the cool washcloth and placed it back on his forehead.

"Why couldn't you have been my son?" she thought to herself as she stared at Steven.

Day broke sharp and crisp. Sharon and Ohpton went into work while Darrius, Raffie and Yashi took off in another of the Orion's Land Rovers. It was nearly noontime when they reached Kingston. Yashi parked the Rover along side of a curb and slipped the transmission into park.

"So what now?" she asked.

"We have to figure out where to begin looking," Darrius said.

"Maybe asking along the street?" Raffie suggested.

"What, anybody that happens to come along?" Yashi frowned.

"Excuse me, do you know where to get fake passports?" she mimicked.

"Got any better ideas?" Raffie shook his head.

"Actually, I do," Darrius said softly.

"We need to find a sleazy joint. That's where we'll find what we need." "Sleazy huh?" Yashi said pursing her lips.

"Look, you can stay here while we go in and ask," Darrius shot back.

"Yeah, like you two will be able to accomplish anything with these people. This kind of stuff is my specialty remember?" she said.

For a moment, both Raffie and Darrius stared at each other, and then without saying a word, they nodded. Yashi grinned; they knew when she was right.

It didn't take them long before they found themselves in a very depressed area of the city. There were a few Neon lights, but mostly posters and signs denoted what each establishment was specialized in. Darrius looked up at a large sign that sported the word <u>Toppers</u>, it was an older sign, back in the days when they used light bulbs. Some of the bulbs were blown leaving gaps in the red and yellow blinking mass. The "T" was missing, as was the right side of the "O". For a moment he stood laughing, it was ironic that the name now spelled <u>Coppers</u> as if it was a police hang out.

"Are you sure this is a good idea?" Raffie frowned.

"There has to be someone inside that has connections, they hang around these places don't they?" Darrius shrugged.

Yashi shook her head and chuckled to herself, she knew better. There wasn't going to be anyone here that could set up illegal passports for them. She could easily have taken control of the situation and solved their problems, but there was something to be learned here and she wanted to see how bad they wanted those passports.

A cylindrical booth sat in the entrance, peeling yellow paint surrounded it. All windows were covered to keep prying eyes from watching without paying. Behind the cracked glass of the booth sat a fat woman. At first Darrius was surprised at woman was selling tickets to a men's establishment, then when she looked at him he knew. She looked mean, terribly mean.

"Twelve…" the mean woman spat.

Darrius reached into his pocket and produced the coil for them; it was more expensive than he thought. Handing the money to the woman he thought she was going to snarl and foam at the mouth. The woman then eyed Yashi and for a moment the woman's demeanor changed.

"She looking for a job?" the woman asked.

Yashi's eyes opened in amazement and she nearly burst out laughing. That is until Darrius spoke.

"Maybe, is there someone we can talk to?" he asked.

"The boss is in the back, all of you go in and get a drink and he'll come out and see you," she said not looking at him.

Darrius nodded and they headed inside. Yashi was angry now; she grabbed Darrius by the arm halting his advance into the building.

"What are you doing? Do you realize what your messing with here?" she snapped.

"Easy there, we're just going to talk to the man go right to the top so to speak," he said.

"Yeah, but with my body as a bargaining chip?"

"No, I only said that to get us close to the guy," Darrius explained.

"You don't get it do you? These people <u>are criminals.</u> They are just as bad, most likely worse than Jah-Man. You don't go pulling their strings, you don't screw around with them!"

"She's right Darrius, we could be in a lot of trouble," Raffie agreed.

"So what do we do now, walk away? Go back into the hole we dug for ourselves? Allow Jah-Man to win?" Darrius blurted out his frustration.

"Look, if this goes South in a hurry just don't get in front of me okay?" Yashi frowned.

The inside was dark and it took a few minutes for their eyes to adjust. When they did they noticed three stages, they were short and jutted out from the far wall.

Standing on them were dancing women wearing little clothing. Chairs and tables sat around them and in the back of the room was a long wooden bar with stools. Dim lights lit the whole room, the main lighting focused on the women. The place also reeked of stale cigar and <u>spliff</u> smoke. Men sat staring at the women, transfixed by their supple bodies and jutting breasts. Darrius motioned to the others and they headed for the bar. Two other men sat drinking, oblivious to them as they sat on the stools. The <u>bar tender</u> was big, <u>burly</u> with eyes that made him look like he was half asleep. He was cleaning the bar with a dirty rag when he noticed them.

"What is your drink?" he asked.

"Red Stripe" Raffie said.

"Wine" Yashi added.

"Wine is fine for me also," Darrius said not looking at the man.

He scanned the room for anyone that may look like the owner, the fat woman in the booth had said he would seek them out. He was nervous, he had never been in a place like this, it didn't seem right to him and he felt filthy even being here.

"So, you guys come here often?" Yashi said breaking the ice.

"Yeah, in our spare time," Raffie scoffed.

"I wish this guy would show so we can get the <u>blood fire</u> out of here," Darrius breathed taking a sip of his wine.

"You're not going to find what you need here," she added.

"Why not?" Raffie asked.

"No, I want to know how you know so much about this kind of stuff," Darrius added.

"You forget? I work for a drug lord?" she reminded him.

"There is much you don't know about me Darrius, much," she said.

"I think who we're looking for is on their way over here," Raffie said watching three men walk towards them.

The man was dressed in a finely tailored white suit, his hair was slicked back and his features were strong, and cut sharply. The two men beside him were obviously his muscle, their large forms strained at their finely tailored clothing. The man came up to them and instantly drew his attention to Yashi. Reaching out he touched the very tip of her hair.

"Nice, very nice, she would do nicely here," he smiled.

"Shove it," she barked pulling away from him.

"Fire in this one. That is something I have not had the chance to extinguish in quite some time now," he continued to grin.

"Mr..." Darrius began to say.

"Mahoe, you can call me Mahoe, and yes, that is after the tree," he smiled.

"Mahoe, we did not come here to bring you another dancer," Darrius said.

"Then why have you decided to waste my time?"

"We're looking to acquire passports to go to the United States," Darrius said.

"Why have you come looking here?" the man frowned.

"Because this seemed like the logical place to start," Darrius explained. "Can you help us?"

"Possibly but the price tag will be high," he said looking at Yashi.

"We need passports for 6 people," Darrius said.

"The number is unimportant. Are you willing to pay the price?" Mahoe asked not taking his eyes off Yashi.

"And the price?" Raffie butted in.

"An evening with this beautiful radiant flower," he said reaching out to take Yashi's hand.

"Your price is too high," Darrius said.

"I could just take what I want. You and your friend will be powerless to stop me," he said softly.

"You're forgetting that I have a say in what happens to me," Yashi began to say.

"I am going nowhere with a filthy slob like you!"

"You my dear do not have any say in anything," Mahoe barked.

"I do not think it would be wise to anger Jah-Man," Darrius blurted out.

"Jah-Man!" Mahoe said in amazement.

"What do you know of Jah-Man?"

"We, we work for him, she is one of his contacts," Darrius pointed out.

"Our business is done here. If you are with Jah-Man than death soon follows!" Mahoe said sliding off the barstool.

"Wait a minute, what do you mean death soon follows?" Darrius asked.

"There is conflict brewing, much death is near. Anyone close to Jah-Man is in danger," he explained.

"The Frenchman has returned."

"The Frenchman, but what does that have to do with our passports?" Raffie asked.

"Nothing, except that you will not get anything from me. Just being near you is dangerous!" Mahoe said.

"Remove them from here," he said to the two huge bodyguards.

Darrius jumped off the barstool and was about to take a swing at one of the huge men when Yashi intervened.

"We can walk out of here under our own power," she smiled at Mahoe.

"Please do not come back ever," he said watching them leave.

Once they were out on the street again Darrius turned to Yashi who quickly put her arm through his.

"What does this Frenchman think he is going to do, take over Jah-Man's empire?"

"That is exactly what he's trying to do. Gain control over Jah-Man's empire and he controls the island," she explained.

"I personally don't give a hoot if this French guy wipes out Jah-Man, actually I hope he does succeed. What I do care about is getting these passports, we don't have much money and we still have to rent a plane," Raffie said.

"I might be able to help you with the passports," Yashi breathed softly.

"How? Why?" Darrius asked.

"No, why didn't you say so before we went into that joint?" Raffie asked.

"Because I put myself out on a limb - way out," she sighed.

"I can get your passports and papers but you need to get your way off the island," she explained.

"How much?" Raffie asked.

"We can worry about the bill later. Right now you two can help me with something in return," she began to say.

"I knew there was a catch!" Raffie grinned.

"Mahoe in there was right, there is a war brewing - a big war. This Frenchman and Jah-Man are going to get dirty soon," she said.

"How do you know this?" Darrius asked.

"I have my sources," she said softly.

"But you are negotiating for Jah-Man to supply you with drugs. I do not understand," Darrius shook his head.

"I can't explain but not yet. You'll have to trust me Darrius, you and the others," she said.

"Easy for you to say," Raffie scoffed.

"Why should I? How do I know you're not going to use us?" Darrius explained.

"That question doesn't even deserve an answer," she frowned.

"What do you want us to do?" Raffie asked.

"Simple, I want you to go ahead with your plan. I will try to smooth things out with Jah-Man and get you both back into the Orion," she said.

"Just inform me when you hear anything that could have the potential to harm me or my associates."

"And if Jah-Man finds out we're passing information to you?" Raffie asked.

"You're dead." Yashi calmly replied.

Raffie rubbed the back of his neck and walked away then turned and quickly returned. Darrius could tell there was something on his mind.

"What about the computer disks I know he has? How are you going to smooth his feathers and get me back in?"

"I might not be able to pull that one off. You, Raffie, might be the one who has to remain low, and I mean low to the ground till this is over."

"You expect me to sit and let the others endanger themselves for me?" Raffie yelled.

"You'll endanger them more by trying to help," she said.

"This is becoming a mess," Darrius shook his head.

"Look, let's go and find a way for you all to get off the island. Let me worry about the passports and papers okay?" she said taking Darrius by the arm.

As they headed back to the Land Rover Darrius felt uneasy, there was something about Yashi that bothered him. There was much she wasn't telling him also.

Sharon was working with a customer's hair when she looked in the mirror and realized that she looked like hell. Worry was taking its claim, worry about the others, and worry about not getting off the island. All their dreams seemed to be dissolving before their eyes, all their hopes and desires were locked on committing a crime. Staring into the mirror she realized she had bags under her eyes.

"Oh, oh yes sir," she heard one of the other workers say.

Moments later, as she continued to work on the customer she glanced up in the mirror again. Jah-Man stood next to her his face drawn and serious. At first her body went numb and she tried to act like it was no big surprise.

"Can we talk?" he said to her.

"I have to finish with my work first," she explained.

Jah-Man snapped his fingers and motioned to another one of the workers, who promptly came over and took over for Sharon. Something was wrong. Taking her jacket off she grabbed her purse and followed Jah-Man out of the salon. Guards waited for him and she felt strangely uncomfortable as she walked next to him. All she could think of was that standing next to her was Eve and Darrius's father. It was odd after so many years of knowing them and him that she learned this secret.

He led her out of he Orion and into a waiting limousine. Jah-Man was the only one who sat in the back with her, the other guards sat up front. The limousine pulled out and drove quickly out the gates of the Orion and headed along the coast.

"It is a beautiful day is it not?" Jah-Man said staring out at the ocean.

"Yes it is," she said.

"Do you know why you are here?" he asked not looking at her.

"No" she lied.

"I need information from you, information about the others in your little group."

"Why?" she played dumb.

"Don't insult my intelligence, you know why I need the information," he said finally looking at her.

His eyes were hollow. Dead and the sight of them sent a chill up her spine.

"Why would I give you information about my friends?" she asked.

"Because it would save their lives, it will save your life," he said again looking out the window.

"What do you want to know?"

"Winston George III. Why does he have information regarding my business affairs?" Jah-Man looked sternly at her.

"I didn't know he did. His parents, his whole family were Babylon," she said.

"Yes, I already knew that, they were police," he grinned.

The smile he radiated was one of a cold-blooded killer. There was no doubt now that he was the man behind the death of Raffie's family.

"Maybe he found the information and didn't know what it was?" she lied.

"You must think me stupid. The information he has was not some simple records, he has access to information that belongs to me, me!" he snapped.

"But what good is it if it's old?" she asked not wanting to pry.

"That is my business and not yours, I only want to know where Winston George III is, nothing more. I can get what I want from him when I find him."

"And that's all? You want me to just turn over to you one of my friends so you can torture and eventually kill him?" she snapped.

Jah-Man scowled at her his anger was quickly growing. He had no time to waste with these children, there was more on the horizon that needed his attention.

Still though, the information Raffie wielded was dangerous to him.

"So, are you going to tell me where he is?" Jah-Man looked sternly at her.

"What about the others?" she asked.

"The others are of no concern to me, all except Steven Winter," Jah-Man said.

"Can't turn the other cheek huh?" she pushed.

"I have told Delicia that I would forget about the incident, but I can not. He has done me great harm and must be punished for it."

"What if it was Delicia that was at fault. What if she was deceiving you?" Sharon pointed out.

"It is possible but highly doubtful, she is not a fool, she knows her place," he said.

"Your friend took liberties with her, liberties that were against her will," he said angrily.

"Well then, I guess you are out of luck Jah-Man. I will not turn my friends over to you. I will not betray them."

"Your loyalty is admirable but very, very foolish."

"So what are you going to do with me? Are they going to find my body floating in the surf like they did Tisha?" Sharon spat.

"I had nothing to do with that - nothing. It was unfortunate though, very unfortunate. I have other plans for you my dear. The others will show themselves when they find that you are missing," he smiled.

The limousine pulled back up to the entrance of the Orion. A valet came out and opened the door. Sharon stared out then back at Jah-Man wondering if he was going to allow her to leave. Sliding from the seat she was going to head back into the hotel when Jah-Man called out to her.

"Your time will come my dear. You have no way off the island, I will find you again," he smiled.

The valet shut the door and the limousine pulled away leaving her standing there stunned. He was right, she had nowhere to go, and nowhere on the island was she beyond his reach. He would be watching and sooner or later he would find Raffie and Steven and when he did they would be killed.

Delicia sat on the veranda overlooking the resorts beach and ocean. In her hand was glass of vodka. She needed it after learning the truth about Darrius and Eve. It was perplexing and she wondered how she could use it to her advantage. For Delicia, it was always I & I.

"She is asleep, I have given her a sedative," Diamond said sitting down in one of the wicker chairs.

"She is of no further use to us," Delicia said taking a swill from her glass.

"What do you mean us?" Diamond looked at her wondering why she was such a dogheart.

"I mean you are in this up to your ears with me, there is no getting out easy now," Delicia said taking another swallow.

"My part of our bargain is finished, I want nothing more to do with her. She is Jah-Man's daughter. She is dangerous..."

"Especially if Jah-Man finds out how you were using her," Delicia said giving him an evil grin.

"I will take you down right along side me," Diamond said his voice belaying his fear.

"I am not worried. I share Jah-Man's bed," she smiled.

"You do not have that advantage."

"Maybe not, but I am sure that he would get rid of you just as quickly. You are no more safe from him than I am." "So?" she asked.

"So you and I should forget we ever started this; ever heard what we did. We should go back to you being his whore and me doing my job."

Delicia shot him a hard cold look, resting the glass down she sat upright in the chair and resumed looking at the ocean.

"Is that all you think of me, his whore?" she said softly.

"Earlier you wanted to take me to bed for free remember?"

"I do not want to get close enough to you to touch you with a 10 foot pole," he breathed.

"You are playing a dangerous game with Jah-Man, you already have him riled up over Steven Winter," Diamond pointed out.

"That my dear Diamond has been taken care of, it is over, Jah-Man has told me so," she sighed remembering the night she and Steven had made love.

"You think so? That is not what I heard Delicia. Jah-Man may have told you he was forgetting the whole situation but he still has his muscle out looking for him with the intent to kill him on the spot!"

"Your information is bogus Diamond, I know what Jah-Man is doing not you!" she said the irritation in her voice clear.

"You believe what you want but either way it doesn't concern me," he shook his head.

"Our business is over."

"Our business is over when I say it is and not before."

Diamond felt rage rush through him, tossing the glass it shattered against the corner of the wall. Lunging over Delicia he grabbed the arms of her chair bringing his face close to hers. Delicia stared into his eyes not flinching.

"You do not control me Delicia - nobody controls me! Our business is done, do you understand? Done! I want nothing more to do with you, Jah-Man, or Eve. I find you too <u>fassy</u> for me so I'm walking away from all this now!" he snarled, then headed for the door.

Delicia never flinched and she acted like his words were meaningless. Just as he opened the large sliding glass door to her room she called out to him.

"I'm sure Jah-Man would love to hear what you've been doing to his daughter, how you used her sexually," Delicia sighed looking at her nails.

Diamond stood there for a moment his rage unchecked; he then headed into the room slamming the glass door behind him. Delicia heard it slam and grinned, Diamond wouldn't step out of line she was quite sure of that.

Outside of Kingston sat The Palms, another small resort. It wasn't as grand or lavish as the Orion was but it was clean and catered to the middleclass tourists. It had all the amenities that most resorts sported with the addition of one of the best beaches in Jamaica.

In Kingston, Yashi, Darrius and Raffie had asked around for anyone who chartered a airplane. More than one person directed them to the Palms and a man named Jack Griff. Arriving at the Palms a Valet parked the Rover; they headed in and inquired at the desk. Moments later they walked out into the sunshine and the huge cabana bar that sat on the beach next to the two huge outdoor pools.

Women milled about in bikinis, Raffie grinned, and some of the women didn't wear their tops.

"I like this resort - maybe they're hiring?" he laughed.

"You Mr. Big Bad Wolf?"

Yashi shook her head. "Men"

The bar was crowded as were the many tables that sat scattered around it. Darrius went to the bar and asked where he could find Jack Griff. The bartender pointed, sitting at one of the far tables was a man reading a newspaper. He was older with tasseled gray hair and a very wrinkled face. He was unshaven and appeared to keep his clothes <u>wrinkled</u>. In one hand he held a newspaper, in the other a large Cuban cigar.

"Mr. Griff? Darrius said approaching him.

The man said nothing and continued to read his newspaper, moments later he turned the page.

"Mr. Griff?" Darrius asked only this time louder.

"Who wants to know?" the man said in an Australian accent.

"Do you have a plane we could charter?" Darrius asked.

Griff lowered the newspaper and flicked the ash from the end of his cigar. He stared at them for a moment paying particular attention to Yashi. He then motioned for them to be seated.

"Yeah, I got a plane to charter. First off, where you want to go?" he asked. "United States, anywhere in Florida," Darrius said.

"Florida huh? You got papers and the whole nine yards?" Griff said rubbing his chin.

"Yes, we have papers and passports," Darrius said looking at Yashi.

"Well we'll sure as hell need them, customs in the States is pretty strict regarding incoming private flights from third world countries."

"We're aware of that. Like I said we have the correct papers," Darrius again pointed out.

"Yeah you may have the papers but do you have the money to rent the plane?" Griff said taking a swill off his beer.

"Depends on how much you want," Raffie cut in.

"Depends on a lot of things, how many, where to exactly, possible trouble," Griff explained.

"For an idea of what we're talking, let's say Miami for a destination. There are six of us going and no trouble following," Darrius said.

Griff rolled his cigar around between his lips then took a long hard draw from it. Seconds later he blew the smoke out into their faces.

"Twelve grand, two grand a head. You pay the fuel both to get there and for me to get back. All money is American too," he pointed out.

"None of this Jamaican currency."

"Is that all?" Raffie said with irritation.

"No, I want half up front, the rest when I get you there," Griff grinned showing a missing front tooth.

"Half up front, you pay the fuel," Yashi blurted out.

"Look missy, I'm talking to the men folk here not you," he said his grin falling.

"Come on Darrius, let's get out of here. This guy is going to rip us off," Raffie said tapping Darrius on the shoulder.

"Yes, maybe you're right," Darrius said softly.

They turned to leave, Griff watching them closely. They made it to the Land Rover when he called out to them.

"Okay, okay. You folks drive a hard bargain, half up front and I'll take care of the fuel to get there but you buy the fuel for me to get back. Is that a deal or what?" he smiled again displaying his missing tooth.

Darrius looked at Raffie then to Yashi who nodded slowly. He then walked over and shook Griff's hand.

"What kind of plane do you own Mr. Griff?" Darrius asked.

"Well, glad you folks asked. Why don't we use your vehicle and I can go show you the old girl," he said continuing to grin.

As they walked to the Land Rover, Griff put his hands on Raffie and Darrius's shoulders. At first Darrius wanted to knock it off, but he didn't want to upset the man since he was their ticket off the island.

As Griff sat in back with Raffie, Yashi drove with Darrius next to her. Griff gave them directions, which led them out of Kingston heading east. The surroundings grew desolate and homes faded until there were only palm trees and brush. Yashi glanced over at Darrius, he instantly understood her look, and she was wondering if Griff was setting them up for something.

Finally, he directed them to a small clearing. As they entered, Yashi, Darrius and Raffie gasped. Sitting at the other end of the clearing was an aged twin engine DC3 airplane.

The DC3 was a reliable plane and was in circulation since the Second World War, which Griff's plane looked like it had been through. It was a dependable design that never seemed to quit. Griff's plane was rusty; the aluminum had separated on various points leaving gaps along the fuselage. There was faded paint on the tail section and newer peeling paint along the sides beneath the small windows. The peeling paint said "Griff's Charter" but looked more like "iff's Chater" which meant nothing to anyone.

"Isn't she a beauty?" he said with obvious excitement.

"Does it fly?" Raffie breathed.

"Does it fly? Why my boy this plane has seen, has seen," he stuttered.

"Vietnam?" Yashi frowned.

"Actually, Korea," Griff said thinking. "Maybe it was the end of the

Second World War?" "But does it fly?" Raffie asked again.

"Of course it does! It may not look like much on the ground but when it's in the air?" he grinned.

They parked the wheels next to the rear of the plane. They all got out, Griff being the first one. He went up and lowered the stairs so they could climb aboard. Yashi and Darrius climbed up the stairs behind him while Raffie walked towards the front of the plane.

"Oh brother," he muttered staring down beneath the engine.

On the ground was a huge saturated puddle of oil.

He looked at the props, there were chips and gouges taken out of them and a huge dark streak ran the rest of the engine and down the wing. Walking reluctantly back, he too climbed the stairs into the plane.

Inside Yashi and Darrius stood staring at the main cabin. Troop seats filled each side, they were worn, and some even ripped showing shredded foam beneath. There were no seatbelts.

Griff went into the cockpit and sat down in the pilot's seat. Moments later the three of them heard a dull whine, then a chugging sound. Seconds later, a huge cloud of black smoke poured into the cabin.

"Don't mind that none, it'll clear up quick enough. Always does that when I first start em'," he yelled grinning from the cockpit.

The noise was horrendous also and they all held their hands to their ears. Darrius then went over to Raffie and yelled at him.

"We've got to be kidding," he yelled.

"This thing is leaking oil bad!" Raffie yelled back.

"Look you two, this guy is your only ticket. I don't think we have much choice!" Yashi yelled at them.

Suddenly the engine cut and silence returned, though they all had a ringing in their ears.

"Well what'd ya think? Sweet huh?" Griff grinned.

"Mr. Griff..." Darrius began to say.

Yashi was quick; she nudged him in the side reminding him that they didn't have many choices.

"Mr. Griff, the plane is fine," Darrius lied.

"Great, great, now let's talk mass," he said coming from the cockpit.

"Six of ya, at two grand each makes 12 grand, half up front like we talked," he said extending his hand.

"We're not carrying the money on us Mr. Griff; we'd have to be fools to do that!" Raffie pointed out.

"So, when do you plan on getting me the dough?" Griff asked.

"Soon, by next weekend," Darrius said.

"Not soon enough mates! This here baby requires maintenance, no parts, no fly," he shook his head.

"You'll just have to wait until next weekend Mr. Griff, we can not get the money to you sooner than that," Darrius shook his head.

"When we're you planning on flying out of here?" Griff asked.

Darrius turned to Yashi, if anyone knew the schedule of events she did. For a moment she stood there speechless, then sighed heavily and spoke in a soft voice.

"Next Sunday," she breathed.

"Sunday!" Raffie exclaimed.

"Wow isn't that a little soon for Jah-Man?" Darrius blurted out.

"Jah-Man, Jah-Man, what does this have to do with Jah-Man?" Griff asked nervously.

"None of your business," Yashi pointed out.

"Now hold on a minute here. If you people are somehow wrapped up with Jah-Man..."

"It's none of your business," Yashi again spat.

"Sorry honey, as long as you people are talking Jah-Man, either the price goes up or you find yourselves another pilot!" Griff exclaimed.

"You are the only pilot," Raffie shot back.

"Precisely my point. Look lads, I've been on this bloomin island long enough not to mess with the likes of Jah-Man. People turn up missing you know!" "We already know that," Raffie pointed out.

"So what do you three have to do with him?" Griff asked not really wanting to know.

"He's after him and I," Darrius pointed to Raffie.

"She does business with him," he pointed to Yashi.

"Yikes! I think maybe you three should get back in your wheels there and head back to wherever you came from!" Griff said heading for the door.

"Look Mr. Griff, you're our only way off the island, our only hope of getting to America!" Darrius blurted out following him.

"Not my problem mate, not my problem!" Griff said checking the wheel chocks.

"My friend and I are dead men if we don't get off this island!" Raffie added.

"You should have thought about that before you crossed Jah-Man!" Griff said continuing to circle the plane.

Things were heading south in a hurry. They were losing their only way off the island. Darrius glanced over at Yashi then rushed after Griff.

"How much?" he yelled to him.

"Sorry mate," Griff yelled back.

"We'll double the amount!" Darrius yelled.

"Forget it, money isn't going to do me much good if I'm not alive to spend it!" Griff said continuing to circle the plane.

Yashi quickly circled around the other side. As Griff rounded the nose of the plane, he came face to face with her stopping him in his tracks.

"How much Mr. Griff?" she said her voice stern.

For a long moment, they stood in muted silence staring at each other. Then finally, Griff broke his stare and turned away.

"How much Mr. Griff?" she asked again.

"Ten times the amount." he said softy leaning against the plane.

"120 thousand!" Raffie yelled choking.

"Take it or leave it, the choice is yours. You're asking me to put my life on the line by messing with Jah-Man who is dangerous. That's stupid!"

"You're asking us to put our lives on the line by even going up in this thing!" Raffie said gesturing to the plane.

"Yeah maybe but this plane isn't going to hunt you down, cut you up into small pieces and feed you to the sharks," Griff said. "Take it or leave it."

They watched him disappear up the boarding ladder and into the plane. Grouping together, they walked to the edge of the wing.

"That is a lot, a lot of money!" Darrius shook his head.

"We'll have it if we pull off our plan!" Raffie pointed out.

"How are we going to come up with half up front?" Darrius added. "We're lucky if we have a tenth of 60 thousand back home."

"Negotiate, that's what you have to do, negotiate," Yashi grinned.

"Leave this to me," she smiled.

Swiftly she walked back around the plane and up the boarding ladder. Darrius and Raffie were afraid to follow; they didn't want to hear what she was saying. They could see no way for her to negotiate Griff into allowing them to pay after.

"We're going to be out of luck my friend," Raffie sighed.

"Maybe we better go back into Kingston and try to find another pilot."

"Remember, this man was the only one. Even if we did find another, it would be no different. As soon as they found out Jah-Man was involved we'd be dealing with the same problems," Darrius replied.

"Maybe and maybe not, I don't think we're going to get anywhere with Griff though," Raffie said slowly walking back to the Rover.

Darrius followed, every so often, he would glance over at the plane wondering what Yashi and Griff were talking about.

Suddenly, she emerged rapidly hopping down the stairs. Both Darrius and Raffie froze as they watched her approach.

"Well?" Darrius was the first to say something.

"You're all set, he'll take what you have up front with the assurance that you will pay him when you arrive in the Florida," she explained.

"I don't believe it! How did you manage to get him to agree?" Raffie leaned against the Rover, a bewildered look spreading over his face.

"Trade secret," she smiled.

"No seriously, how did you pull this one off?" Darrius asked amazed.

"Trade secret. I'm not kidding. Like I said earlier, you have to negotiate and that's what I do, negotiate," she smiled.

"Come on we have a long drive back."

Both Darrius and Raffie stared at each other for a moment then slid into the Rover. Moments later they were back on the road leading back to Montego Bay. The ride back was silent and extremely unnerving. Yashi could feel the tension; feel them occasionally stare at her as they tried to figure out how she convinced Griff.

When they arrived back at the shack, Ohpton was the only one there. He came out and stood on the porch as they got out of the Rover.

"So?" he called to them.

"Where's Sharon?" Raffie asked.

"And Eve?" Darrius chimed in.

"Don't have a clue where Eve is, probably still with Delicia. I saw Sharon before I came home early, not much for me to do there on Saturday," he explained.

"She said that she would be going to see her mama and little brother tonight. She would be back tomorrow night for sure."

"Great! She picks the worse times to do this, we have to make some decisions," Darrius shook his head.

"Did you find us passports and a plane or boat?" Ohpton asked as they came up onto the porch.

"The passports weren't a problem, Yashi is going to do that for us. The plane, well the plane…" Darrius explained shaking his head.

"We found a plane," was all he said.

"That's good, right?" Ohpton winced.

"That's very good!" Yashi added.

"Then what's the problem?" Ohpton asked.

"Oh not much, we only owe the guy 120 thousand," Raffie added.

"120, 120 thousand!" Ohpton blurted out nearly gagging.

"Yeah and we cleaned out our life savings," Darrius grinned.

Yashi stared at them; she understood how much of a fine line they were all walking. She also knew that eventually they would discover the truth about her.

Chapter 15

The Frenchman stood on the upper bridge of his yacht. The sun was shining and the temperatures were stifling hot even under the huge canopy. Standing with him was the Captain who wore a white Naval uniform though no medals or insignia were present. Below on the foredeck and on the transom beautiful women lay on towels and chairs, their bodies completely naked. Crewmembers went about their work oblivious to the women around them. The Frenchman eyed their tan, supple bodies one by one. He loved having them around him, flaunting their flesh, submitting to his every whim. He felt like he was a sheepherder and they were his flock.

Licking his lips he tried to choose, which one, he would take next. Maybe the dirty blond, her breasts were enormous, or maybe the Asian with her firm tight body. There was always the islander, her dark supple body, and her large firm buttocks. Yes, he liked her the most; he had a weak spot for islanders. He was becoming excited just thinking about it.

A small boat sped towards the yacht, two men sat in the small launch, moments later they tied themselves up to the Yacht. One of the men quickly walked across the deck, stopping briefly to admire the nude women around him, then came quickly up the ladder to the bridge. The Frenchman kept his eye on the island girl even as the man approached.

"What have you learned?" he said not turning.

"Sir, Jah-Man is having a small pre-shipment sent tonight," Junior said.

"Tonight? Why is it that I am learning about this now? I should have been informed days ago," the Frenchman said still not taking his eyes off the island girl.

"I just learned about it myself sir," Junior said nervously.

"Where?"

"Portland Point," Junior added.

"Is this new supplier going to be there?" he asked.

"She is suppose to oversee the operation to make sure Jah-Man does what he says he will," Junior explained.

"She is an ordinary ting, when will someone that matters arrive?" the Frenchman asked.

"I do not know Sir. It is very difficult to get close to Jah-Man right now. He suspects someone close to him is betraying him," Junior said.

"Well now, he's right isn't he?" the Frenchman grinned.

"He also knows you're here sir," Junior said softly.

"I am sure he does, he wouldn't be very much of an adversary if he didn't," the Frenchman continued to grin.

"What do you want to do?" Junior asked.

"Nothing, this shipment is meaningless to us," the Frenchman mused.

"Yes sir," Junior said turning to leave.

"However…" the Frenchman said holding up his hand.

"…we could take the goods away from his buyer after they make the switch. We could make it look like Jah-Man was seizing his own goods back; double crossing his new buyer," the Frenchman beamed.

"How are we going to do that?" Junior asked blinking.

"We're going to slaughter his buyers when they come to pick up the goods!"

"But sir, won't that send a message to Jah-Man, a message for all out war?" Junior said his voice nearly breaking.

"Perhaps, but without his main buyer what good is he?" the Frenchman beamed.

"Slaughter the girl too - no wait! Bring the girl to me. I could find a use for her first," the Frenchman said drawing his attention back to the island girl.

Sharon grabbed a palm frond and sat it down on the white sand; she then sat down and stared out at the open ocean beyond. A large white yacht sat at anchor, people milled about on its decks but it was too far away for her to see any detail. Her attention was drawn though to the ocean. Letting her imagination run she could envision Florida in the United States, it was so close now, so very close. All their dreams were emerging, finally coming together. She tried to see the lives they would have, the fun they would share together, the joy of being free to become whatever they wished. Then reality set in.

She shivered, as a chill rushed through her body as she thought of what Jah-Man told her. Her life was in danger; he had told her as much, he would use her to get to Raffie and Steven. There was nothing she could do about it either, unless of course, she got off the island. She had other problems too; she had to go home. The thought of seeing Elmo made her suddenly feel sick. She wanted to see her mother and brother but the confrontation that may happen between her and Elmo made her want to stay away, forever.

Realization set in though, she never shrugged her responsibility, never walked away from family. She would keep her chin up, her hands clenched into fists in case she had to punch Elmo and go home to see her family.

The Frenchman spied someone sitting on the beach, walking over he grabbed his binoculars and held them up. In them, he spied a woman, a very beautiful woman; an island girl. He licked his lips hungrily. She was more beautiful than his own, more exotic and sensual looking. Pulling the glasses down he grabbed the arm of one of his men.

"See that girl sitting on the beach?" he said handing the glasses to the man who held them up and looked.

"Yes sir," the man said.

"Find who she is and bring her to me. Offer her money, jewelry, whatever she wants!" he said chuckling.

"Yes sir," the man said handing the binoculars back.

"Sir" the Captain said walking up to him after the man left.

"What is it Carl?" the Frenchman said not taking his eyes off the girl.

"We have a situation brewing sir," the Captain said softly.

"So handle it, that is why I pay you is it not?"

"Huh? Yes sir, I will haul anchor immediately," the Captain said.

"Haul anchor? What are you talking about?" the Frenchman said looking away from the girl.

"The weather service from the United States has posted a Hurricane. They're calling it Millie, it's still off Africa, but close enough that it looks like it's heading this way," the Captain explained.

"Africa? What do we care about the weather in Africa?" the Frenchman scowled.

"Sir, Hurricanes are produced between the land masses of Africa and South America, they brew then head west towards either South America, the Caribbean isles, or the United States."
"So what do you propose?" the Frenchman said raising an eyebrow.

"We should raise anchor immediately, and either make for home or the States," the Captain suggested.

"The States are out of the question and leaving Jamaica is out of the question," he shook his head.

"But sir, they're saying this one has the potential of being a big one," the Captain explained.

"No, I don't care what you have to do or what it costs, but we're staying here! Is that understood? I don't care what you do here but do it here," the Frenchman said tapping his finger on the railing.

For a moment, the Captain stared at him with a serious concerned look bleeding over him. He then turned saying nothing and went back into the wheelhouse. The Frenchman again hauled them up and stared at the girl, his eyes working over every inch of her body. Sharon again glanced up at the yacht and wondered what it would be like to have so much mass.

Jah-Man paced the room in his townhouse. He was unusually nervous; it wasn't like him to feel the way he did. He never had in the past, he had made important decisions before without problems, why then were these bothering him so? He already knew the answer; his son was involved; his son had betrayed him. His daughter didn't know about him either, it was time that they both had.

There was also the problem of the Frenchman; he was here on the island and more than likely planning something sinister. His new supplier bothered him also; they were up front and agreed to his terms, but there was something about them that raised a warning flag. Tonight was the first shipment he was to bring to them, Portland Point was their meeting place. The meeting place was quiet, out of the way, and also an ideal place for the exchange.

However, using the Orion for the big shipment, that bothered him, never in his life had he used the Orion for <u>any</u> exchange. It was too open, to vulnerable, to easy for the Frenchman to make a strike at him.

Suddenly he became rooted to the floor, was it possible? Was it possible that Yashi and her buyers were working <u>for</u> the Frenchman? It would explain why the Orion was being used for the big shipment. It would also explain the inside man whom he hadn't found yet. Wheeling around he grabbed the telephone and quickly pressed one of the many speed dial numbers. Almost instantly, a man with a gruff voice picked up.

"Yush?" the man said.

"This is Jah-Man, is everything ready for tonight?" he asked.

"Yes sir, everything is on schedule and we're ready in case <u>anything else</u> <u>happens</u>," the man said.

"Good, very good, I and my buyer will meet you there," he said.

"Yes sir, we'll be waiting," the man said.

He grinned hanging up the telephone, then walked briskly around the desk and sat down. Contentment washed over him, he now had the upper hand, and he now was in control. At that moment, a gentle knock resounded off the door.

"Come in." he blared.

The door opened and in walked Kingston's <u>Babylon chief Sam Fisher</u>. His uniform was spotless and finely pressed each crease perfect. He was a balding man with strong cut features; his eyes though, were soft and made him look weaker than he actually was. He had a large puffy moustache that nearly blocked his upper lip. His frame was well taken care of too, his arms muscular. Despite his soft casual appearance, he was not a man to turn your back on. He wasn't an islander; instead, he came from <u>Chile</u> where he was a police chief. Things in his country had gotten bitter and dangerous and when his family was in danger he packed his things and left. He knew when to turn and look the other way; he knew where the money was.

"What can I do for you today Chief Fisher?" Jah-Man said not smiling.

"We have some problems," Fisher began to say.

"There have been a few deaths now that seem to point in your direction." "Me? That is absurd!"

Jah-Man scoffed.

"We have been doing business for some time now right?" Fisher asked.

"I am not a fool Jah-Man. I am not a fool not to see what is coming here. That large yacht out in the bay; we are heading for another blood bath!"

"Times change my friend, people change. Yes the Frenchman is here again, yes there is something up his sleeve and no, I will not let him roll over the island!" Jah-Man spat his anger flaring.

"How can you be so sure this time?" Fisher frowned.

"Do you doubt me <u>mon</u>?" Jah-Man said rising to his feet.

"This is not like many years ago Jah-Man. An incident like we had many years ago will assuredly bring news reporters and cameras from other countries. It will be like a huge spotlight aimed right at us!" Fisher bellowed.

"Do you doubt me?" Jah-Man asked again.

"I do not know. Before I would have never thought, but now?" Fisher said staring at the floor.

"Maybe someone else has offered you more money?" Jah-Man said raising an eyebrow.

"No, nobody has offered me anything Jah-Man. I came to you out of concern and worry that this whole thing is starting to get out of hand," Fisher said.

"It sounds like you don't trust me anymore," Jah-Man said walking around the side of the desk.

"We all have much to lose," Fisher said softly.

"Maybe you should think about that Chief Fisher; maybe you should think very hard," Jah-Man said his voice but a whisper.

Fisher felt the hair on the back of his neck rise. His instincts were telling him that it wasn't a very good idea to come here. Jah-Man walked over to the bookshelf along the wall. Fisher tried to follow him with his eyes but the man had gone behind him.

Suddenly he felt a sharp searing pain in his side. Jah-Man stood directly behind him with a large knife that he had embedded into Fisher's side. With his other hand, he grabbed hold of the man's throat keeping him from turning. Then, with satisfaction, he twisted the knife sideways.

Fisher crumpled to the floor dead. Jah-Man let go of the knife and stared down at the body. He had the man's blood on his hand and it dripped off the tips of his fingers onto his finely tailored carpet. Then other thoughts began to seep into his brain. Thoughts of his son and how he betrayed him. Maybe if Darrius knew the truth, maybe his son would see the reality of life and stand at his father's side. He loved Darrius, loved him since the day he was born. He cared for Eve also, but every time he looked at her all he saw was Evelyn, and that fateful night so long ago that changed him - robbed him of his soul.

The thought chilled him as he stared down at his bloody hand. Bounding over Fisher's body, he dashed into the bathroom and began scrubbing his hands, repeatedly.

"Cleanliness is next to Godliness - cleanliness is next to Godliness," he repeated aloud over and over again. He became a man obsessed.

For nearly fifteen minutes, he stood there scrubbing and washing and rewashing his hands removing every speck, every trace of blood. Suddenly he glanced up into the big mirror above the sink. For an instant, he felt hollow and very alone. His eyes were blank, lifeless, he felt abandoned.

His fist slammed hard into the mirror shattering it into fragments and cutting his knuckles. Staring down at the glass protruding from his hand, he ignored the pain and began removing the shards of embedded glass. The pain made him focus; the pain gave him purpose; the pain kept him alive.

Darrius, Raffie, Ohpton walked out of the shack and into the forest, Yashi followed saying nothing. Darrius thought about all that had happened in Kingston, they needed to remove their money from where they buried it. He wished Sharon, Eve and Steven were here but it couldn't wait. This was the moment they were all waiting for, this was the moment that would determine the outcome of the rest of their lives. He hoped they were right. They knew exactly where to go since they had done it so often in the past; the spot was second nature to them. Ohpton used the old shovel and began digging. Moments later the tip of the shovel clinked onto the large metal box. Darrius knelt down reaching into the hole he pulled the box out shaking the dirt from it. Yashi watched saying nothing.

"I wish the others were here," Raffie said softy.

"Me too," Ohpton said.

"It doesn't feel right pulling the box without the others."

"We all have the same goal, we all have the same dream," Darrius breathed. "It must be done now."

Setting the box down he used a small key and unlocked the tiny padlock. Opening the top slowly he had to push the many loose stacks of bills back in. For years, they'd been saving for this very moment. He was about the close the lid again when Raffie spoke up.

"Count it here, now," he said.

"Are you sure? We could just bring it back to the shack and do it there," Darrius said.

"No, Raffie's right we should do it here," Ohpton nodded.

"We've always done it here, don't break tradition."

Darrius just nodded and again opened the lid. Grabbing a handful of money, he began to count. The others watched closely as he shifted the bills through his hands.

Yashi was impressed as she watched Darrius count the money. They were all so diligent, so loyal to each other. They were truly family to one another and in a way that she would never be with her own, she was envious of them.

It took nearly an hour for Darrius to count the money twice. When he was done, he again closed the lid on the box then looked up at the others.

"$13,542, that's it," he breathed.

"Lot less than it looks," Raffie sighed.

"Better than nothing," Ohpton said optimistically.

"Yeah and only $106,458 to go," Raffie laughed.

"We better hope that we can pull off our plan."

"We're only going to get one shot at it too," Darrius added.

"Anyone have any idea <u>how</u> we're going to pull it off?" Ohpton asked.

"Don't know, we need to know how Jah-Man is going to set things up for the big shipment," Darrius said.

"That's where I come in," Yashi said finally speaking.

"You, I don't understand. You're going to help us?" Raffie looked at her with surprise.

"I already am by getting your papers and passports," she said.

"I can get the information you need."

"But you're going to be going against your own employers," Raffie said.

"Yes, maybe, but it's the only way," she said.

"As long as my employers get what they pay for, we don't care what happens to the money."

"I want to know why you're helping us; why risk your own neck?" Ohpton asked.

Yashi turned to Darrius, "Because I love you," she said.

At that moment Darrius felt proud, devoted to this woman. She was everything he ever wanted and more.

"Why risk your life for us though?" Raffie asked.

"Because I have my reasons," she said.

"We're trusting you…" Darrius said softly.

"I know," she breathed.

"I realize that all of you have to," she said looking at the others.

"A lot is riding on this - this gamble," Raffie shook his head.

"Well, things have to move if we're going to get off this island; if we're going to have a future," Darrius stated.

"We're all messing with death too you know," Ohpton pointed out.

"One wrong move, one slip up and one of us could get killed." "That's why you're not going to have a slip up," Yashi said.

"Plan, that's what you have to do now; plan and research. Then trust that I'll do the rest," she said.

"I have to go now."

"But I thought you were staying with us tonight?" Darrius asked.

"Got my meeting with Jah-Man?" she said to him.

"I'll be back though."

"Is there anything we can do to help you?" Ohpton asked.

"Stay away" she said.

"The best thing you can do to help me right now is to stay out from <u>underfoot</u>. Remember, this Frenchman is here too and things could get messy," she said.

Darrius felt a sudden lump stick in his throat. Until this very moment, he hadn't considered the possibility that Yashi could be hurt or killed.

He wanted to be with her, wanted to protect her but after the altercation with Jah-Man, he would be endangering her by being there. They walked back to the shack; Yashi kissed Darrius and slipped behind the wheel of the Rover. Moments later she disappeared down the rough path leading to the edge of town.

Darrius watched until he could no longer see her brake lights, then, he reluctantly went into the shack with the others.

"Darrius, we have to talk," Raffie said as he entered the shack.

"Okay" he said.

"Yashi, I'm sorry to say this but my gut tells me she's not what she seems," she shook his head.

"What do you mean? You heard her earlier, she's going to help us!" Darrius said his voice raising.

"Yes she may but remember I come from a family of cops. They dealt with crooks, criminals and thugs; I've seen the type," Raffie began to say.

"Yeah, so?" Darrius blurted out defensively.

"She doesn't fit the profile," he sighed.

"Profile? What are you talking about Raffie?" Ohpton cut in.

"Criminals have profiles, quirks that they all share. Some can be as subtle as where they get their coffee in the morning, or who does their books. Others can be as obvious as how they commit their crimes. She doesn't fit anything I've ever known," he explained.

"And your point?" Darrius said his anger flaring.

"My point is this, she is not and does not match the criminal mentality. There is something else also - she is hiding something," he said.

"What?" Ohpton asked.

"Don't know, but I do know this, we're putting all our futures in her hands - totally," Raffie said bluntly.

"No, not only our futures but also our lives," Ohpton agreed.

Darrius suddenly felt sick to his stomach. His emotions were in turmoil, his heart wanted to trust and love her unconditionally but his brain screamed out warnings. He understood their apprehension to trust her and he didn't blame them. He also realized that with the money they had getting off the island together wasn't an option.

Sharon watched the yacht for a while, the sun was setting and a gentle breeze began to blow in off the ocean. The yacht was beautiful; it had sleek lines and was three decks high. It was solid white with a large green strip running down the side. She couldn't see the name from where she was at, but guessed that it had to be named after a woman. Anyone with enough money to buy something so grand would be eccentric. She watched the yacht for a while then got up brushing any loose sand from her skirt and headed off to do the inevitable.

It was early evening when she arrived at her mother's house. There were a few lights burning inside. A wave of apprehension rushed through her she wanted to turn and leave. The thought of seeing Elmo again made her sick. Still though, she pushed open the squeaky gate and walked up to the front door. Taking a deep breath, she reached out for the doorknob and then hesitated.

For some strange reason she felt a wave of fear rush through her. It was something she had never experience before, something that shook her from head to toe. Her palms suddenly became cold, clammy and the doorknob felt cold and alien. She turned the knob.

The inside smelled of cigar smoke and she waved her hand in front of her face in an attempt to whisk it away from her. The living room was empty with only one small lamp shining in the corner. Peering down the hallway the bathroom light was on, in the opposite direction she glanced towards the kitchen, all the lights blazed on there also. She was surprised that Ronald, her little brother hadn't been playing in the living room when she came in. It was early yet and not passed his bedtime, but late enough to be after dinner.

Walking towards the kitchen, she half expected to see her mother baking something by the stove, her brother sitting by the table taste testing or licking out the mixing bowel. Instead, she found Elmo.

He was standing next to the sink cutting something on the cutting board. An ashtray sat next to it with a pungent cigar burning. Sitting half empty on the table was a whiskey bottle, another empty one sitting next to it.

She understood now why her senses had screamed so. She turned to walk out, when Elmo finally realized she was there.

"Oh so miss high and mighty finally comes home!" he said slurring his words.

"Mama around?" she asked not wanting to stop and talk.

"Working late. She's got to make that extra money now that Old Elmo got fired!" he said his voice full of sarcasm.

"Ronald?" she asked.

"Staying over at a friends house, it is Saturday you know. But Miss high and mighty probably forgot what day it was," he said shaking the large butcher knife at her.

"Tell my mama I will be by to see her tomorrow," Sharon said as she headed for the door.

She made it into the hallway when she felt Elmo's firm grasp on her arm. She tried to shake him loose but he held on tightly.

"So what's the rush? Why don't you come back into the kitchen and have a small drink with me?" he stuttered.

"Because I have things to do and I don't want to have a drink with a pervert like you," she snapped.

"Pervert? You think I'm a pervert?" he gasped.

"How can you call me a pervert Miss high and mighty when you walk around here sometimes in those really short tops and shorts?" he spat.

"Let go of me or so help me I'll gouge out your eyes!" she snarled.

Elmo let out a large belly laugh and made a screw face. At the same moment Sharon struck. Her hand came up clawing across his face leaving deep gouges. Elmo yelled but didn't let go of her arm, instead he clamped down on it tighter, then with one swift move brought his other free hand up slamming it hard against Sharon's face.

She registered the blow and it hurt fiercely but she attacked again this time bringing her face down and biting hard into his arm drawing blood. Elmo yelled in pain his grip on her arm releasing. Sharon didn't waste a second; she dashed for her room down the hallway. Elmo though, was just as quick and he grabbed hold of her legs tripping her.

"Get off me! Get off me or I swear I'll kill you!" she screamed.

"Oh like to play rough now do we?" he grinned.

Before he could advance further, she managed to reach up and snatch the small lamp off the nearest table. With a crash, it smashed down on top of Elmo's head shattering into pieces. He groaned for a moment and fell off her.

Sharon bounded to her feet and continued for her room, once there she shut the door hooking the hasp and shoving another chair under the doorknob. Her heart pounded in her chest, the beat sounding like horse's hooves. The window; she dashed for the window, pulling the curtain back she gasped. Beyond the glass, Elmo had barricaded the window taking away her only chance for escape. It chilled her to think that he had planned from their last encounter - he was ready.

"Sharon, oh Sharon, why won't you come out to play? I know you want me. I know you want me to take you; take you anyway I want!" he called to her from the other side of the door.

"Leave me alone!" she shrieked.

"Just leave me alone!"

"I'm going to find a way in there and when I do you better be ready for me!" he yelled.

She was terrified, things had spun out of her control, and she was now the prey being stalked. There was nowhere for her to run, no place to go and hide, she was trapped.

Sitting down on the edge of the bed, tears rolled down her cheeks. First Jah-Man and now Elmo, there was nothing she could do.

Suddenly there came a loud crack, and then another. For a moment, she thought that Elmo was trying to come in through the window, and then realized that he was coming through the door.

Two more cracks and she could see the blade of the axe as it drove through the wood of the door. He was coming for her.

"Leave me alone! Go away and leave me alone!" she screamed at the top of her lungs.

"Oh but you and I are going to have so much fun tonight! I will make you scream in pleasure!" he yelled back as he continued to hack through the door.

Sharon's terror was numbing, her body at first wouldn't respond then, slowly, she glanced around the room looking for anything she could use to defend herself. Getting up off the end of the bed, she grasped the small nightstand next to her bed. Raising it up off the floor she slammed it down repeatedly until the wood splintered and shattered. Grabbing one of the wooden legs that had broken off she swished it back and forth, in front of her testing the way it felt in her hand.

The door had shattered enough for Elmo to get his arm through, with one swift effort he pushed the chair way from the door. Then launching his body against it, the door hasp crashed and broke from the molding. He now stood before her, axe in hand.

"I've waited too long for this; too long to have you," he said his voice but a whisper.

"Stay away from me; stay away or I'll use this!" she said shaking the broken jagged leg of wood at him.

"I can't stay away. I want you Sharon, I want you!" he said moving slowly closer.

When he was within reach of her, she swung the wooden leg the jagged edge connecting with his arm drawing first blood. He yelled in pain then tossed the axe to the side, seconds later he launched himself at her. Sharon swung the stick again hitting him hard across the chest but it wasn't enough to stop his momentum.

His body collided with hers knocking her clean off her feet, the stick bouncing out of her hand. She yelled and clawed as he groped her body. Twisting she tried to free herself from his grasp but his body weight was too much and it pinned her down.

"Are you ready to have some fun?" he said his whiskey-laden breath causing her to gag.

She continued to wiggle and twist trying desperately to free herself. Then something moved out of the corner of her eye. Elmo's hand came down sharply. Boxing her, the blow sent her into darkness.

Eve stirred and rolled over. Blinking she sat up in bed and looked around. She was in Delicia's bed and she tried to remember how she had gotten there. She also had one massive headache. Pulling the covers down she realized that she was naked, that was something else she didn't remember. Grabbing the nearest bathrobe, she slipped it on and walked sluggishly out into the living room.

"Delicia?" she called out.

There came no answer. Walking around the apartment she checked each room, it was empty. Delicia had gone out leaving her alone. Walking back into the living room, she suddenly cried out in pain as she stepped on a small stone with her bare feet. Her left hand instantly reached out to balance herself and knocked some of the videotapes off the shelves.

Reaching down she started to scoop them up when she noticed one that stood out.

It had Diamond's name on it. Curiosity got the best of her; she walked over and slipped the tape into the machine then sat down turning on the television. Her finger hovered over the play button, something inside of her didn't want her to push the button, but she did.

What appeared on the television before her made her gasp. Diamond lay naked with another woman, another woman that she had seen around the resort. They were grining. Tears streamed down her cheeks. She had been betrayed, Diamond had cheated on her and had made love to another woman.

Delicia came into the apartment and froze when she saw the television screen with Eve sitting in front of it. Eve finally saw her and turned her cheeks wet with tears.

"How, how could he?" she cried.

Delicia said nothing; she just stood there staring at her.

"How could you?" Eve yelled.

"What are you doing with this tape anyway? How did you get it?"

"Eve honey, you are so naïve. You think the world revolves around you. You think everyone should drop what they're doing for you!" Delicia yelled back. "Well maybe it's time to grow up!"

"How could you? I thought you were my friend," she cried.

"Little fool," Delicia muttered.

"Stupid little fool," she said walking further into the room.

"How did you get that tape?" Eve said wiping her cheeks.

"That tape? What do you mean that tape?" Delicia said walking over to where Eve had found the tape.

"See this wall?" she pointed to the dozens of videotapes.

"This wall is full of videos of Diamond; Diamond with customers; Diamond with clients."

"What?" she gasped.

"Are you that stupid honey? Are you such a fool that you couldn't see that your true love, the man of your dreams is a male prostitute?" Delicia said bluntly.

Eve sat there staring at her the tears welling up in her eyes. Her world, her love had just been destroyed. The others had been right about Diamond; she was just too stubborn to listen. She had given herself to him totally, done things she knew were wrong, and now it was being thrown back in her face.

Delicia felt a twinge of pity for Eve, for an instant it was like she was looking at herself not too long ago. Once she was as blind as Eve was, then, like Eve someone had woken her up and shown her the real world.

The moment quickly passed, the girl sitting broken on her couch was no longer her friend; she was really nothing to her anymore except for a way to get to Jah-Man. She knew that Eve didn't know, didn't realize that Jah-Man was her father. That was a crucial piece of information she could possibly use later.

"Get over it honey," Delicia said kicking off her sandals.

"But I gave myself to him. I thought he loved me," she began to weep uncontrollably.

Probably half the customers he services feel the same way. Look at the bright side honey, least you didn't have to pay for it!" Delicia said letting out a loud abrasive laugh.

Eve's emotions surged through her and she bounded off the couch racing into the bedroom. She ran back and forth frantically looking for her clothes. When she found them, she quickly dressed.

"Grow up Eve, this is the way life is," Delicia said coldly.

"Shut up! Shut up!" Eve sobbed.

"Why don't you look at this as a learning opportunity?" Delicia said callously.

"Why don't you shut up?" Eve blared.

"Just shut up!"

Delicia frowned at her, nobody told her what to do - nobody that is except for Jah-Man. She didn't have to listen to Eve, didn't have to put up with her mouth.

"Get out! Get out and never come back here!" Delicia snarled.

Eve slipped her shoes on and dashed for the door. Delicia was saying something but she didn't listen, didn't want to listen. Her life was a ruined mess now, anything more that Delicia would have to say would just add to her misery. She didn't want that.

As soon as she was in the elevator, her world closed in quickly around her. What could she do? Where could she go? She knew that she needed someone to talk to, someone who would listen. There was really only one person who would, one person she could depend on. Sharon.

Sharon felt a tug, and then another, then she heard a ripping sound. Her body tensed then her eyes slowly opened. Nearly nose-to-nose with her was Elmo's grinning face. She started to scream but as soon as she opened her mouth, a rag was stuffed in it and tied tightly around her head.

She noticed her hands were tied tightly together and bound to the headboard of her bed. Her legs were splayed open and each ankle was tied to the footboard. Her heart beat like a jackhammer and perspiration dripped down the side of her temples. Her eyes looked around the room finally settling on Elmo. He sat on a chair staring at her.

"Finally, finally the time has come. You can not believe how long I've waited for this," he said softly.

"All those years watching you, stripping your clothes off with my eyes was almost more than I could take!"

Sharon muttered something but the gag prevented any legible sounds from making sense.

Elmo smiled and got up; reaching inside his pants pocket, he produced a small folding pocketknife. Sharon's eyes went from his to the knife then back again. Was he going to kill her? Possibly, cause her much suffering before finally plunging the knife into her heart? Her mind raced with possibilities.

"You and I are going to have such fun, such fun," he smiled warmly at her his unshaven face making him look more threatening.

Leaning over he grabbed hold of her skirt and drove the knife through the fabric then slowly pulled it from the bottom to the top where he grabbed hold of the waist and sliced clean through it.

Sharon struggled as best as she could but the bonds that held her were taut, preventing any movement. With care, he pulled the rest of the skirt away leaving only her panties and shirt. Setting the pocketknife on the small dresser, he grabbed hold of the bottom of her shirt. With both hands, he savagely tore the fabric ripping the shirt from her body and exposing her bare breasts beneath.

Tears streamed from her eyes and she struggled to free herself the bonds beginning to cut into her skin drawing blood. Elmo stood back and stared at her nearly naked body. His eyes were penetrating, boring. She could see the hideous lust in his eyes and he licked his chapped lips slowly with his tongue.

"You have me so excited," he breathed heavily.

"To take you, to have you submit to me wholly is beyond my wildest dreams!"

Sharon stopped squirming, her wrists and ankles were chaffed raw and the pain making her nauseous. Elmo then slowly began to remove his clothing his eyes locked on her rising and falling breasts. As he removed his clothing, he tossed them across the room. It was obvious by looking at his buddy that he was excited and when he removed his shorts, she began squirming again despite the pain. Walking over he gently touched her ankle and slowly began to slide his fingers up her leg, to her knee and then her thigh.

Sharon wept tugging with such force on the bonds that held her that her extremities were turning purple from lack of blood flow. His fingers lightly touched over her panties feeling her through the fabric. Then with one swift swipe, he grabbed the top of them and ripped them off her body leaving her totally exposed to him.

Then she felt his touch against her bare skin, she froze her body going ridged. She whimpered and cried as he explored her pum pum.

"You are much better than I could have dreamed. I can not wait any longer. I just can not wait," he muttered to her.

Climbing up onto the bed, he reached over and grabbed the pocketknife off the dresser then with a quick swipe he cut first one bond, then the other that bound her feet. Before she could draw her legs up and kick, he tossed the knife and grabbed each of her ankles. Sharon fought as much as she could her body coming off the bed.

"Ah yes, fight me - fight me hard!" he yelled to her.

Drawing himself close to her, he leaned forward forcing her legs up. Sharon then felt him rubbing his manhood against her before he forced himself inside. The room was suddenly distant to her, hollow, she couldn't bear to look at him and closed her eyes tightly with the hope that maybe he would disappear and she would be safe. Her other senses unfortunately took over and the only sound that reached her ears was the sound of Elmo's breathing. The only smell she could sense was the rancid odor of whiskey. The only thing she could feel was the brutality of his manhood against her entrance. She was about to be raped!

Suddenly something warm splashed onto her chest, then she felt little splatters on her face. She then heard soft yet firm grunts in repetition. The noises were enough to force her eyes open again.

The look on Elmo's face was muted surprise, which quickly changed to horror. Standing next to them was Sharon's mother Leeann, in her hand was Elmo's pocketknife, which she now plunged repeatedly into his back. The force of the knife plunging into his flesh was enough to cause his blood to splatter down upon her.

His eyes were now beginning to roll white and the muscles in his face were beginning to sag. Her mother continued to plunge the knife down in rapid secession her rage consuming her. Teeth bared as she tore at him with insane fury. Sharon stared at her as she felt Elmo's body slump down upon her the trickling of his blood running from his back onto her naked body.

Her mother continued to stab him, both hands held together around the knife.

"Mama, stop," she muttered though she wasn't even sure she had said anything.

Leeann didn't hear, didn't care, insane rage had consumed her and she wanted revenge, revenge for her ignorance, revenge for her own faults.

"Mama, stop. Stop, he's dead," Sharon said softly.

Slowly, Leeann began to stop, her breathing labored the front of her dress was covered in blood, as were her hands and the knife.

"Cut me loose," Sharon said trying to force Elmo's body off her.

"Oh my God!" Leeann muttered as she used the knife to cut the bonds holding her hands.

As soon as her hands were free, Sharon forced Elmo's lifeless body off her. It collapsed to the floor beside the bed and with a thud, his blood continuing to leak from the mass of multiple wounds. Sharon glanced down at her body; his blood covered her breasts, stomach, and pelvis, even parts of her legs. She felt so soiled, so filthy, she suddenly leaned over and vomited.

"Sharon, oh my Sharon. I am so sorry - so sorry!" Leeann said grabbing her.

For a long moment they sat there embraced, rocking back and forth as Sharon wept uncontrollably.

"I didn't listen and I should have listened," Leeann breathed.

"You tried to tell me; you tried to tell me. My God why didn't I listen?" she said continuing to rock her back and forth.

"I love you mama," Sharon whispered holding onto her tight.

"I love you too honey. I love you so much," Leeann cried softly.

Sharon didn't know how long they sat there together; it could have been minutes or possibly hours. Nevertheless, Leeann finally pulled her away from her and looked into her eyes.

"Come with me, let's get you cleaned up," Leeann said softly.

Sharon nodded and followed her into the bathroom. Glancing into the small mirror she stared at herself, she looked hollow and old; so old.

"Can you forgive me? Can you ever forgive me?" Leeann said wiping the blood off her.

"I forgive you mama and I love you," Sharon muttered not able to take her eyes off her image in the mirror.

"He won't ever touch you again, ever," she said continuing to wipe the blood away.

Suddenly a dull whine reached their ears. Leeann stopped what she was doing and looked up at Sharon.

"Babylon coming," Leeann said.

"Finish cleaning up I will tell them what happened."

Sharon nodded and sluggishly began to clean herself. Leeann left the bathroom closing the door behind her. Police were already knocking on the front door and she slowly walked up and opened it.

The shocked look on their faces told her that she wasn't a pretty sight. She didn't care though and backed up allowing them to enter.

"What has happened here? Why are you covered in blood?" one of the officers forcibly asked.

"I killed my boyfriend. He was trying to rape my daughter," Leeann said.

One of the officers quickly went down the hallway to the bathroom where he opened the door slowly his gun drawn. Sharon stood on the other side she had slipped clothing on but was still covered in Elmo's blood.

"Please step out of the bathroom," he ordered her, his gun pointed at her.

Sharon said nothing and stepped from the bathroom walking down the hallway to the living room where her mother was.

"Where is your boyfriend?" one of the officers asked them.

"End bedroom." Leeann breathed softly.

Two of the officers quickly went to the bedroom where they looked in on the grisly sight of Elmo's naked body. His entire back was torn to shreds; lying on the floor next to his body was the murder weapon.

Eve ran as fast as her legs would carry her. She knew that Sharon would either be at her mother's or at the shack. She hoped that she was staying at her mother's; she couldn't face the others right now. She felt so ashamed. As she rounded the corner she stopped dead in her tracks, three police cars sat outside Sharon's house, a tiny blue light revolved on each of the vehicles. Something was terribly wrong. She dashed towards the house. When she reached it the front door opened and Leeann, Sharon's mama emerged her hands handcuffed behind her back, the front of her dress, her face and arms were covered in blood. A chill raced through her.

"Leeann, Leeann what happened?" she called to her.

Leeann stopped and looked up at her. Eve got goose bumps, she was looking right through her. She said nothing though and the police continued to escort her to one of the cars. As she watched, two more police officers emerged causing Eve to gasp. They were escorting Sharon out of the house and she too was in handcuffs.

Chapter 16

Yashi arrived at the Orion a little after 9 p.m. The place was still alive and guests milled about either going to the nightclubs, the game rooms, or the pool and hot tub areas. Parking the Rover she followed the route she had taken earlier to Jah-Man's room. Gently she knocked on the door. There came no reply. She was about to knock again, when the door opened. Jah-Man stood there wiping his hands vigorously with a bath towel.

"You are punctual. I like that," he said backing up into the room.

Yashi entered closing the door behind her. Then something struck her, there was a strong odor, and it was something she had smelled before it was the odor of death. Her eyes quickly locked onto a huge dark stain that had soaked into the carpet. Someone was killed here; someone very recently. Jah-Man noticed her staring at the stain. He walked around his desk tossing the towel down on the green blotter, and then sat down.

"Someone disagreed with me," he said casually.

"So you rubbed him out?" she looked up at him.

"I cut my loose ends, my problems, away quickly. I find that if they are left to linger, they usually come back to haunt you," he said.

"Understandable" she nodded.

"I understand that you are fond of Darrius," he began to say.

"My fondness of anyone is my business, not yours," she quickly replied.

"Perhaps, unfortunately Darrius has gotten himself and his friends in trouble."

"There are more serious things to worry about. My superiors want tonight to go off without a hitch," she explained.

"It will," he said getting up.

Walking around the desk he stood directly in front of Yashi. His eyes looked her up and down, and then bluntly, he reached out and put his hand against her left breast. Yashi didn't back away she just frowned at him.

"Do you always fondle your clients?" she said sarcastically.

"Only when they are as beautiful as you are," he grinned.

"I can see what Darrius sees in you," he continued to smile.

"And what is that?" she asked.

"A cheap lay," he said pulling his hand away.

Yashi wanted to box him for that comment. This man had no understanding of women or of Darrius.

"We must leave," he said.

She watched as he opened one of his desk drawers and then withdrew a Smith & Wesson 45 caliber semi-auto pistol. He chambered the first round then tucked it in the waist of his pants under his beaded shirt. Yashi swallowed, JahMan was insane that was easy enough to see and hard enough to deal with without having a gun in an insane man's hand.

He opened the door for her and motioned her to go first. Below outside the Orion's main building another Land Rover waited. The driver was skinny and he looked nervously at them as they slid into the rear of the vehicle.

"Junior, let's get going," Jah-Man barked.

Junior pulled the vehicle out and headed out the main gate, he repeatedly looked in the rearview mirror at them. Yashi was quick to catch him, each time she did he would quickly divert his eyes forward.

The road to Portland Point was not smooth, it was a dirt road that was so rough Junior had to slow the Rover down to a crawl to negotiate some of the huge rocks and pot holes. Still though the Rover was the ideal vehicle for the conditions, no ordinary vehicle would have made it this far. Yashi occasionally stared at Jah-Man; she was surprised that he didn't have a stream of cars following with dozens of his men for protection. She also hoped that her own people would be there waiting. Glancing at her watch she noticed they were nearly 15 minutes late. Her people would already be there - waiting.

"You seem preoccupied with something," Jah-Man noticed her agitation.

"We're late," she breathed.

"Nothing to worry about, you and your people will not walk away tonight empty handed," he said not smiling.

"What about the Frenchman?" she asked.

Jah-Man's expression turned from calm to sheer anger at the mention of the Frenchman's name.

It was obvious that the man was someone Jah-Man feared; that was good to know.

"What do you know of him?" he asked his voice belaying his anxiety.

"I know, we know that he tried to muscle his way into your territory years ago. There was a slaughter and he went back to Columbia. I also know that he's been spotted here again and my sources say he's been asking questions," Yashi explained, then again glanced into the mirror.

Junior's eyes locked with hers and she could see or sense panic in them.

The trickle of sweat gave him away also.

"You know much about him, do you also know that I defeated him once and I will do it again?" he stated.

"It's been years Jah-Man, how can you know what has changed in the man since then? For all you know he may have more backing, more muscle, and more firepower," she pointed out.

"Perhaps, but I do know that he came to his island in a yacht and that can only hold so many people and equipment. So I doubt that he came here with much and probably left more behind him," Jah-Man smiled.

"Never underestimate your opponent," she said softly.

"A very wise and true statement my dear, and which are you?"

Yashi cut him a sharp look. His stare said what was on her mind, the tiny amount of trust that was there before was gone, replaced with caution and doubt. Fear ran through her body, intense fear, enough to make her shudder.

The Rover's headlights cut through the dense foliage onto the open and clearly uninhabited beach of Portland Point. The point stuck out like a finger into the ocean, the beach they were on made up the base. It was at the edge of the sand that Junior stopped the vehicle. What they saw drew silence from each of them.

On the beach there were two inflatable rafts, scattered around them were bodies, many bodies. Yashi pushed open the door and dashed out towards them. Reaching inside her purse, she drew out her own maggy. When she reached them she stood and looked around, they were all dead. Bodies twisted and racked with bullet holes. They were her people and she was late.

"Are they your people?" a voice called from behind her.

"Yes" she said sadly.

"Seems the Frenchman was here already," Jah-Man said looking about.

"Or your men were here already," she said coldly.

"My men do as I say. Why would I want to kill the people who are buying my product? That does not make sense my dear," he nearly laughed.

"Why would the Frenchman cut down my people when they could potentially buy from him?" she countered.

"Mistaken identity?" he shrugged.

"This changes things - changes things drastically," she said staring at one of the bodies.

"This changes nothing," he stated.

"We had a deal and I expect you to keep your end of it." "I would have until this,"

she said softly.

"No my dear, <u>you will</u>," he replied.

Suddenly from the dense underbrush came hoards of Jah-Man's men, in their hands were various weapons, mostly, <u>matics</u>. One of the men walked directly up to Jah-Man and whispered something. The two men walked off beyond the range that Yashi could hear. Moments later the two men split up, JahMan walking briskly over to her.

"It seems my men watched the whole thing," he said.

"It was definitely the Frenchman."

"What happened?" she asked coldly.

"It seems that your people came in the rafts, the Frenchmen's men were already here and were waiting for both of us," Jah-Man pointed out.

"Because we were late, they couldn't wait and cut your people down." "That doesn't make sense,"

she shook her head.

"It could be that the Frenchman hates me so much, he wants to destroy anything and anybody that deals with me. Think how powerful of a message he just sent to your people," Jah-Man grinned.

"If that's the case, he is asking for trouble," Yashi shook her head.

"You must talk with your people and get them to help me, get them to help me eliminate the Frenchman once and for all! With both of us working together he will not be able to stop us!" Jah-Man said excitedly.

"You ask us to get involved in your problems," she said coldly.

"Yes, I do. It will only benefit both of us in the long run," he said.

"I must talk with my people," she said again staring at the bodies at her feet.

"Good, very good," he smiled.

"As a show of good faith I will reduce the price per kilo," he stated.

"We must fight together."

Yashi stared at him, he was smiling - the fool was smiling like the death around him meant nothing. His fist was clenched in an act of defiance; he was so sure of himself, so confident that she would get her people to side with him. The whole operation was coming apart, soon there would be nothing left. Then she noticed something.

"It's gone," she said looking around.

"What is gone my dear?" Jah-Man asked.

"The money, the money is gone," she said.

"It was in a gold briefcase."

"I will have my people search, maybe it is still here somewhere though I doubt it.

The Frenchman has it by now," Jah-Man stated.

"What I want to know is how the Frenchman knew about our meeting or the place of our meeting."

"There is a rotten tomato in your organization," she said.

"All of my men are loyal to me - me!" he stated obviously irritated by her comment.

"Yes, they may be loyal to you now but flash a few hundred grand in their face and I wonder how loyal they will actually be," she said sarcastically.

"Do not push me my dear. Choose your words carefully or you might end up right here along with the rest of your people."

The coldness of his voice chilled her, he was making no idle threats, and he meant what he said. She had to get back to tell her people and Darrius.

Steven sat upright and for a moment he felt disoriented but the feeling quickly passed and he remembered he was at Mama Rose's. Standing he flexed and stretched, then nearly doubled over in pain. His arm was still tender, the lighting flash of pain told him so. Yawning, he rubbed his other hand through his hair and walked from the small bedroom into the kitchen. Mama Rose stood by the stove stirring something that smelled delicious, everything she made was and he loved to eat what she cooked.

"Good morning," he said softly coming into the kitchen.

"Good morning Steven, are you feeling better?" she asked her spoon still rotating inside the pot.

"Better, my arm hurts though but I guess I'll live," he said remembering the pain he felt.

"You were lucky, that knife could have gone much deeper," she said.

"If I knocked one of those duppy children out, then please explain to me how a duppy can get knocked unconscious?" he asked.

"They obviously can't, take a look at what's on the counter over there," she motioned to him.

Steven walked over to the counter. Upon it lay the duppy child's knife. For a moment, Steven stared at it then reached out and touched its cold blade. Then something struck him like a wall of water. On his finger was a dull green hue that had rubbed off the blade; it was phosphorous.

"They're using phosphorous!" he exclaimed turning to Mama Rose.

"What's that?" she asked not looking away from the pot she was stirring.

"It's a chemical that absorbs light and gives the appearance of glowing in the dark," he explained.

"That may explain why they look like duppies. But who are they and why are they doing this?" she asked.

"Children, someone must be using children for their crimes," Steven said still surprised.

"Who in heaven's name would use children for such horrible acts?" Mama Rose said stopping what she was doing.

"Someone with a lot of pull and a lot of power. Enough power to corrupt young children," Steven frowned.

"But to make children killers? That doesn't seem possible, children are so, so innocent!" she blurted out.

"Maybe not all children," he sighed.

"If only I got a good look at one, we might be able to identify whose child it is."

"The orphanage," Mama Rose said sadly.

"If you wanted to use children, you would get them from the orphanage."

"We need to go there and check, maybe, just maybe I can identify one of them or spook them."

"Not punning are you?" she smiled.

"Come over here and eat some breakfast."

Steven sat down at the table smiling warmly as Mama Rose filled his plate. He loved her, all of them did. He was also scared for her, she allowed children into her home on a regular basis selling them candy and treats. What if one or more of those children where one of the duppy children?

"Mama Rose?" he said softly.

"Yes Steven, is there something wrong with your food?" she asked sitting down at the table with him.

"Can I ask you a very big favor?" he said putting down his fork.

"Of course you can, you know that," she said.

"For the next few days would you lock your door and not allow any <u>schoolers</u> in?" he asked.

What he said made her stop eating; she looked up at him as if he had just driven a dagger through her heart.

"I have given and sold treats to children all of my life Steven - <u>all of my life</u>. I have seen much death, senseless death and it has not stopped me then and this will not stop me now!"

"But Mama Rose, there is great danger with these children. Look what happened last night," he stated.

"I chased them off!" she said shaking a finger at him.

"But for how long? Now that they know you're associated with me they might come here looking for me and hurt you instead. Or worse yet, as an example."

"No" was all she said.

"Please Mama Rose, please, just until I can figure out who these children are," he pleaded.

"I will not be frightened away. I will not let the other children who count on me suffer," she said.

"I will not close my door."

Steven stared at her, when she was determined - she was determined. There would be no convincing her. His only hope was that he could find who these children were before they decide to pay her a visit.

"Do you have a hat? Anything that I can use to hide what I look like?" he asked her.

"I am sure that Junior has a few things still here. He'll never use them and I think he might have a hat or two," she said.

"You really shouldn't go out, if anyone else sees you..."

"I don't have a choice. I have to go around the orphanage and try to locate these duppy children," he said.

"I also need to see the others; I need to see Sharon."

"You are fond of her?" Mama Rose grinned reducing the tension in the room.

"Very, I never knew it until a short while ago; all these years," he said shaking his head.

"Sometimes it is best that way. At least you found each other, that is more than many in this world can say," she smiled.

"Now eat, after we will find you at hat."

Ophton rolled over then fell out of bed hitting the hard floor with a thud. Muttering something under his breath, he staggered to his feet tossing the blanket back onto the bed.

All of the sudden there was a crash from the living room. The noise was enough to startle him causing him to jump backwards a few feet. Then, thinking more of the others than himself he bounded for the door ripping it open.

In the living room, he watched Eve pace back and forth and back and forth. She acted like a wild animal that was caged and wanted nothing more than to be free. He also had never seen her act this way either.

"Eve?" he called out to her.

At that moment, Darrius opened his door along with Raffie who stretched his arms high into the air.

"Eve?" he called again this time walking further out into the hallway. "What's wrong?"

"Everything is wrong, everything!" she snapped.

Darrius burst past him and rushed up to his sister. For a moment he stood staring at her, she looked frazzled, tired and <u>more worrisome</u>, strung out.

"What happened?" Darrius asked.

"Sharon..." she began to say then burst into tears.

"What happened to Sharon?" Raffie asked.

"Something happened at her house. The <u>Babylon</u>, they had her in handcuffs. They were taking her to jail Darrius, to jail!" she wailed.

"I'm on my way!" Raffie said dashing back to his room to dress.

"I'll go with him," Ohpton followed.

"She was covered in blood Darrius, covered in blood!" Eve wept.

"It's okay, Raffie and Ohpton will find out what happened, they'll find out," he said taking her into his arms and hugging her.

"He, he used me, used me," she said softly between sobs.

At first, Darrius wasn't sure what she meant, and then he realized that she was talking about something else. She was talking about Diamond.

"He used me. I gave myself to him and he used me!" she shrieked.

"I'm sorry Sis, so very sorry," he said running his hand through her hair and hugging her tightly.

"I trusted him and trusted her too! But they both used me. They both had their fun," she sobbed.

At that moment Raffie and Ohpton appeared. For an instant, they stared at Eve and Darrius, and then Raffie nodded to him.

"We'll let you know what's going on," he said, and then both of them headed for the door.

"It's okay Sis, trust me it will be okay," he said.

"You need to get some rest, let us find out what's going on alright?" he asked leading her to her bedroom.

She said nothing; she just nodded and continued to cry. Darrius's rage was building; Delicia and Diamond had done something to hurt Eve something horrible. Now Sharon was in deep trouble. Fate was throwing them curves; fate was trying to keep them from escaping.

Sharon sat huddled in a jail cell, she was brought in with handcuffs, strip searched for no apparent reason, and then thrown into a filthy jail cell.

She had no idea what happened to her mama, they apparently had her also. In a fit of pity she began crying, her life was a shambles and the two people she loved most where in trouble. Her mother was in jail for Elmo's murder and her brother was alone without his family. She had failed them both.

A clinking sound snapped her out of her self-pity and she wiped her eyes. Footsteps resounded down the hallway and they were drawing closer. A police officer appeared and for a minute he stood staring at her, then reached along his side and produced a key, which he used to unlock the cell door.

"Come on, you're getting out of here," he said to her.

"Really?" she said again wiping her eyes.

"What about my mama?"

"I don't know, I was just instructed to come and get you," the officer said as he waited for her to leave the cell.

Sharon walked cautiously out past the officer as she closed the door behind her. He then walked around and motioned her to follow. She felt a bit of apprehension, it was much to early for the police to make a determination about the murder, even if her mama did confess and Darrius or any of the others wouldn't have known so quickly. Her answer to the question came quickly as she followed the officer out into the lobby. Jah-Man stood there staring intently at her an evil yet provocative grin forming on his face. Sharon stopped short her breath caught in her throat at the sight of him. She then reached out at the nearest officer halting him.

"Officer, officer take me back to my jail cell," she said not taking her eyes off Jah-Man.

"Miss, this man has paid your bail, you are free to go. You would prefer to be locked back in a jail cell over freedom?" the officer frowned.

"I do not wish to go with this man," she breathed softly.

"What you do is your choice, you are free," the officer said shaking her grip on his arm off.

Sharon was left standing with Jah-Man still intently staring at her. There was no place to go, nowhere to run. She glanced to each side; maybe if she attacked one of the officers they would throw her back in jail. She knew the truth though, she could do virtually anything she wished and Jah-Man had enough pull to get her out. Finally, he casually walked up to her. Sharon remained rooted to the floor.

"Why are you so afraid of me?" he grinned.

"You know why," she said.

"I have purchased your freedom, you are obligated to come with me. I told you before that I would be seeing you again, I'm giving you a great bligh," he smiled.

"So you will use me as a hostage to get to the others?" she snapped.

"That is one possibility," he chuckled.

"I have something else in mind though."

His words chilled her to the bone. He had something tucked up his sleeve, something sinister. He wanted Raffie and Steven quite badly that was apparent, he would go to any lengths to get to them.

"I won't help you," she breathed.

"You my dear, don't have a choice," he continued to smile.

"Shall we?" he motioned to the door with his hand.

At that very moment, Raffie and Ohpton came through the front door. JahMan turned his gaze casting upon them both. His expression turned into a vengeful frown, he didn't know who Ohpton was, but he knew Raffie and he was one of the two he wanted.

Raffie's gaze first shot to Sharon, and then to Jah-Man, he instantly knew that he had made a monumental blunder. He had thrown himself into the lion's den without looking if the lion was waiting inside. Jah-Man's expression told him so.

"You!" Jah-Man barked.

"Sharon are you all right?" Raffie called out to her.

"I'm fine but Jah-Man came here to take me with him," she quickly said.

"Come on, run!" Raffie yelled.

Instantly, Sharon bolted towards them and freedom. Jah-Man was quick though; he reached out snatching her long dark hair yanking her back with extreme force. Sharon was taken clean off her feet.

Raffie bolted forward but was quickly stopped in his tracks by Ohpton who grabbed hold of his shoulders.

"What are you doing? Let me go, we have to help Sharon!" Raffie yelled.

Ohpton never let him go, two of Jah-Man's guards stood poised with a few of the police officers to cut them down. The situation was growing critical by the minute.

"Come on, we have to leave - now," Ohpton said softly.

"You are going no where!" Jah-Man pointed to Raffie.

"You have something of mine. It took me a while to figure it out but I finally remembered who you really are!"

Raffie's expression grew into intense anger and he struggled even more against Ohpton's grasp. He realized fully now, that it was Jah-Man who had his family slaughtered. He was responsible.

"It was you. All these years I suspected but not until this moment did I know for certain, you killed my family!" Raffie snarled.

"They were too close - much too close. They weren't bothered by the threats. They kept digging and digging getting closer every day. I could not allow this, it was intolerable!" Jah-Man snapped.

"And you keep the law in your back pocket too I see!" Raffie said looking at the officers who just looked away.

"Money buys everything and anything. If you have enough anybody can be bought, even you," Jah-Man grinned.

"You're family got what they deserved."

Raffie strained against Ohpton's grip, his anger was out of control; his hate for this man was consuming him. Ohpton's grip tightened on Raffie.

"Come on, time to leave," Ohpton breathed.

"What about Sharon?" Raffie snapped at him.

"Live today, fight tomorrow," Ohpton said.

"Come on before someone gets trigger happy."

"We'll be back for you Sharon, we'll be back," Raffie yelled to her.

"I'm sure you will. In fact, I'm counting on it," Jah-Man smiled.

Sharon watched them disappear out the door. Her heart sank at the prospect of being Jah-Man's hostage. He was going to use her to get to the others.

"What about my mama?" she snapped at him.

"Your mama is in jail for murder," Jah-Man pointed out.

Sharon said nothing; there was no way for her to help her mama. Worry began to grow deep within her, worry about her little brother who was innocent to the world.

"You do have options though," Jah-Man grinned.

"We can talk about those later."

Sharon was roughly pushed towards the door by one of Jah-Man's thugs. She wondered what was coming next and what she could do to stop him.

The front door burst open, Yashi quickly looked around the shack. Finding it empty, she dashed out leaving the door open. She then remembered that they sometimes went swimming near a waterfall not far from the shack. A rough foot trail led into the dense underbrush. She followed. Within minutes, she heard the rushing sound of water. It was a pleasing sound and for a moment she let it sooth her rough shattered nerves. Continuing on, she found Darrius and Eve sitting next to a massive pool of water. Behind them, a huge waterfall cascaded down. Darrius noticed her and motioned with a smile for her come closer.

"Eve - this is Yashi," he introduced her.

"Hi" Eve said her voice barely audible over the rushing water.

"Darrius, we have to talk…it's important," Yashi said ignoring Eve.

"Sharon was arrested," he said.

"What? What was she arrested for?" Yashi blinked at him with surprise.

"Don't know yet, Eve saw her being escorted out of her house in handcuffs. Raffie and Ohpton went to find out what's going on."

"It wasn't wise for Raffie to go. He's still wanted by Jah-Man," she said.

"He's got experience dealing with the law. His whole family was into law enforcement."

"It still wasn't smart since Jah-Man is out for blood," she said.

"Listen Darrius, we have to talk," she said again.

"Okay, so talk, what's going on?" he asked.

For a moment Yashi stared at Eve, she didn't know if she could trust her. There was too much riding on her and one wrong move would send the whole stack of cards tumbling down on their heads.

"This is my sister Yashi, my blood. You can talk freely," Darrius said.

"Darrius, what I'm going to tell you could get me killed - it's that serious," she began to say.

"I understand," he said.

"Darrius, I work for the DEA," she breathed her voice barely audible.

Darrius's face instantly turned into a shocked expression then he frowned sharply when the impact of her words sunk in.

"It was a lie, all of it was a lie," he said sadly.

"No Darrius you must believe me not all of it was a lie," she said.

"You tricked me," he said looking away.

"I trusted you and you tricked me."

"Darrius, try to understand. My government has known about Jah-Man for sometime now and plans were in the works months ago for a sting operation to shut him down."

"What about my government? Do they know about this?" he asked.

"No, your government has too many ties to Jah-Man. It would have compromised our operation," she explained.

"And why should I believe you now?" he sharply asked.

"Because last night we were suppose to receive a pre-shipment from JahMan. When I got there with Jah-Man for the meeting, all our people were slaughtered - killed where they stood," she said over the sound of the rushing water.

"These were my co-workers; many of them my friends." "I'm sorry Yashi," Darrius

said.

"They were killed by the Frenchman of that I am positive," she nodded.
"He doesn't want Jah-Man shipping out to anyone including us. He most likely thinks that we will drop

Jah-Man and deal with him."

"Sounds like you and your people are caught between a rock and a hard place," Eve cut in.

"Yes, I suppose we are and that's putting it mildly," she nodded.

"We do though, have a unique opportunity. We can shut not only Jah-Man down but the Frenchman too."

"You and your people have the muscle and firepower to do this?" Darrius asked.

"Of course, but to limit the bloodshed we need help," she said.

"Help from you and your friends."

"What can we do? I mean half of us have been fired from the Orion and the rest of us are in some form of trouble or are hiding out from Jah-Man. What can we possibly do to help you?" Darrius asked with a baffled look.

"There is plenty you can do. For starters I want you to continue with your plans to get off this island. I will still get your passports and papers though they will be illegal."

"Will customs in the States notice that?" Darrius asked.

"They shouldn't. They're going to be the best forgeries that my department can make."

"What else?" Darrius asked.

"I want to use some of you, mainly Raffie and Steven for bait," she breathed.

"Jah-Man wants them both dead and that will give me an edge when the time comes."

"And what's going to keep them from getting killed in the crossfire?" Darrius asked.

"Nothing. I didn't say that this wasn't going to be dangerous. But, if you all follow my directions, nobody should get hurt." "Should?" Eve said raising an eyebrow.

"Like I said, I can't say wants going to happen when the time comes. We can only hope that things go the way we plan them," she sighed.

"And if they don't?" Eve asked.

"Then we have to limit how much damage we create," Yashi said, her voice turning cold.

"Can I count on all of you?"

For a long moment Darrius wouldn't meet her eyes, then, slowly he looked up at her and slowly nodded his approval.

"And what lies did you tell me, about us?" he asked softly.

"None. I meant every word," she smiled warmly to him.

"You and my brother?" Eve looked at her then Darrius.

"Time will tell," Darrius said, embarrassed.

Yashi just smiled at them, the future could bring many things and to plan and hope or even discuss it was a bad omen. Suddenly, there was a ringing sound, Yashi snatched her cellular phone from her hip and opened the protective cover. She then held it up to her ear, turning she quickly walked out of earshot. Darrius watched her, for a moment he wondered why if she wanted their help she couldn't discuss or talk with them around. It raised a warning flag.

Moments later, she closed the cover back on the phone and hooked it back onto her hip clasp. She then walked over her expression drawn and serious, she wouldn't meet their eyes either.

"What's wrong?" Darrius quickly noticed her mannerism.

"That was my superiors," she said.

"They want, they want to end the mission. They've called for me to withdraw immediately."

"What!" Eve blurted out.

"Those are my orders," she said.

"So what does that mean for us? You won't be getting out passports and papers will you?" Darrius asked his heart beginning to ache.

Yashi said nothing, she couldn't meet his eyes and she looked away ashamed.

"And Steven and Raffie are fed to the wolves?" Darrius shot out.

"Look I don't like this any more than you do but I do have my orders," she said.

"Blast your orders! What about doing the right thing? What about saving people?" Darrius snapped at her.

"Darrius, try to understand. My people just got word that a whole team of agents were killed. Do you realize the impact that will have back in the States when the media gets wind of it?" she frowned.

"So you're going to let him get away with it?" Eve cut in irritated also.

"This is a media and information age. Almost all those people had families, children and believe me they're going to want to know what happened here! Once that leaks to the media inquires will be made, Congressional panels formed to investigate, and blame will be laid on someone."

"So you're worried about your own skin?" Darrius nearly laughed.

"I wasn't the one in charge of this operation; that man lying dead on Portland Point beach was," she snapped.

"I don't think you understand," she shook her head.

"I understand fully. You want to use people to accomplish your goals but when it gets rough, your people fold and run away," he shook his head.

"That's unfair," she said her own anger flaring.

"Nuh true??" he looked sharply at her.

"What's unfair is most likely when you pull out of here, half of my friends are going to be killed."

"I'm sorry," she said turning away.

"I'm sure you are," he said curtly.

Darrius quickly got to his feet and headed back down the trail towards the shack. Yashi watched him, she wanted to reach out to stop him and hold him but his anger was great and at this moment in time there would be no reasoning with him. The sad part was that she knew he was right.

"How could you do this to him?" Eve asked drawing Yashi's attention.

"I didn't do anything, my supervisors made this decision." "So you're a dog?" Eve asked.

"A dog? I don't understand," Yashi frowned.

"Dogs we tell to come, go, and sit. They never usually ask for much, which is how they live their lives. Are you like a dog?"

"I do what I'm told. If all Federal agents ran off and did what they wanted to, then our country wouldn't be what it is," she stated.

"If everyone in your country doesn't give a damn about the next person, then I'm not sure I want to live in your country," Eve said sadly.

"Look what do you expect me to do?" Yashi said her anger flaring.

"Nothing, just the right thing- the honest thing," Eve said getting up and following Darrius down the trial.

Yashi was perplexed, deep down she wanted to help them, defend them. She wanted to crush Jah-Man and the Frenchman but doing so meant going against her oath as a Federal agent. She was also troubled by her feelings for Darrius; she cared for him that she was certain, but in the long run... Turning, she began to follow the trail down to the shack.

Darrius had just opened the door when Raffie and Ohpton came up the path leading to town. Even from a distance, he could see that they were both visibly shaken. Eve was close behind him and she stopped to stare at them also.

"What's wrong?" he asked as they drew closer.

"Sharon's in a world of hurt," Raffie said wiping the sweat from his brow. "Jah-Man has her and he's going to keep her to get to Raffie and Steven," Ohpton said sitting down on one of the porch stairs.

"Has she been harmed?" Eve asked.

"No, but Jah-Man yanked her off her feet when she tried to come with us," Raffie quickly said his anger again rising.

"The Babylon?" Eve asked.

"Sewn up in Jah-Man's hip pocket, they would have shot us down just as quickly as Jah-Man's men." Ohpton shook his head.

"So what can we do?" Eve said concern washing over her face.

"You need to go along with your plans just as if this didn't happen," Yashi said coming up behind them.

"You can say that after you were going to feed us to the wolves?" Darrius said turning to her.

"Look, in my book, problems are just situations that need to be figured out. Nothing, I mean nothing is insurmountable," she said.

"We just need to figure out a solution that covers all the bases." "Is that a yes I'm going to help you?" Eve asked.

"Yeah, I'm going to help, but we could all end up in at ditch someplace. I just want you to know that up front," she stated.

"What difference is it going to make? If we do nothing we're going to end up in a ditch anyway," Darrius shrugged.

"So what do you suggest?" Ohpton asked.

"Let me find out what the police were holding her for and why Jah-Man is holding her. It may not be to get at Raffie and Steven," she said.

"Why else?" Darrius asked.

Ohpton stared at Darrius, he already knew the reason why. Jah-Man was his father and right now, he was upset with his son, but he had promised Mama Rose that he would never tell him.

"There may be other reasons," Yashi said not elaborating.

"So what can we do?" Eve asked.

"Like I said, continue to plan your trip out of here. The way you can help me is to assist by taking both Jah-Man and the Frenchman down." "Gee, you sure ask a lot lady," Ohpton shook his head.

"Two massive drug lords and a bunch of teenagers are going to bring them down?"

"Either we do or they make us disappear," Darrius said cutting in.

"What about Steven?" Raffie asked.

"Has anyone seen him?"

"I don't know…" Darrius shook his head.

"So when does the big shipment of Jah-Man's drugs go out and your money come in?" Raffie asked Yashi.

"Don't know yet, after what happened last night it might not be for a while, or if I can convince my superiors to continue, it might happen quickly," Yashi speculated.

"What happened?" Raffie asked looking around.

"Yashi lost many of her agents," Darrius said.

"Agents?" Ohpton frowned.

"Oh, we forgot to tell you that Yashi is an agent for the DEA in the United States," Eve said.

"DEA? What are you doing here? Isn't this out of your jurisdiction?" Raffie asked.

Not as long as the drugs being shipped come into the Unites States. As long as that happens I have jurisdiction anywhere," she said.

"So you're here to take down Jah-Man?" Ohpton asked.

"And the Frenchman," she said.

"That is if I can get your help."

"And what can we do to help you?" Ohpton asked.

"Bait" Raffie said already guessing.

"You're kidding me. Doesn't that mean someone usually gets killed?" Raffie asked.

"No, it doesn't have to go down that way. If we plan this right nobody will get hurt," she explained.

"That is a big chance you're asking us to take," Ohpton sighed.

"Nothing comes without risk. You people want off the island, then this is the only way," she stated.

Silence grew amongst them and it told her what she wanted to know. None of them wanted to stay on the island, they wanted the freedom that the United States would offer. They would stick their necks out for a chance, which was something she already knew.

"We'll do it," Darrius said softly.

"But we need to know if and when you plan on the big shipment."

"Agreed, now I must go. I have to talk with my own people then try to repair the damage done by the Frenchman."

Before any of them could say anything, Yashi turned and walked briskly down the trail leading to town. She didn't want them have the chance to back out. They all watched her walk down the trail quickly disappearing from sight. Raffie was the first to turn to Darrius.

"You've spent time with her, is she on the level?" he asked.

"As near as I can tell she is, but then again, before today I had no idea she was a DEA agent either," Darrius shook his head.

"What about our passports? Raffie asked.

"She says she will still get those for us," Darrius said.

"Maybe she's just using us like Delicia and Diamond used me," Eve blurted out.

"What? You mean you finally figured that one out?" Ohpton looked at her.

"It was a learning experience," she said.

"Actually more of an embarrassment. I want to tell you all how sorry I am for not listening," she said sadly.

"It's not really us you need to tell that to - its Sharon," Raffie said.

"You loved him didn't you?" Ophton asked.

"Yes, very much," she said wiping a tear from her cheek.

"I'm sorry," Ohpton added.

"We're going to America; that is where my future is," she said with confidence.

Yashi sat in her wheels talking to her superiors trying desperately to convince them to continue with the operation. At one point, her voice raised and then became deathly silent as she held the telephone away from her ear. It took much convincing; both holding truths and lies but she managed to get a 48-hour window. She was told that if she could solidify the operation within that period then it would be a go and they would support her. If not, her badge was to be turned in. Everything was riding on this operation.

By the time she reached the Orion it was mid morning. She now had to convince Jah-Man that her superiors still wanted to deal with him; she knew would take some convincing. Slipping her <u>maggy</u> into her purse along with her cellular phone, she was about to get out of the Rover when she felt a rag cover her face, seconds later someone turned her lights out.

Sharon was escorted into a very plush and very spacious townhouse apartment. Two female servants then led her through two massive doors into a bedroom that was about as big as the shack. They said nothing to her and quickly left closing the doors behind her. Turning she watched them leave, she was surprised that Jah-Man hadn't posted any of his muscle in the room with her. The room had thick tan carpeting with rosewood dressers and hutches lining the walls.

A humongous oval bed sat against the far wall with a silk comforter and pillows covering it. Swivel lights were mounted just above a velvet headboard. It was lavish and she had never been in a room so grand. There were even mirrors mounted above the bed. Obviously, Jah-Man had particular tastes. Walking over she peeked into the bathroom. There was a separate shower, a large oblong whirlpool bath, a double vanity and obviously a john. Then she noticed something that chilled her.

Hanging on the towel racks where monogrammed towels. Each had JahMan's initials sewn into the lower left corner. This was his bedroom.

Turning she walked back into the middle of the room, then noticed laying on the bed were neatly folded clothes, he obviously wanted her to change. That was something she wanted to do also, the shirt she wore was covered in Elmo's dried blood. Picking up the clothing she held it up, there was no doubt that whoever brought them knew her sizes. The thing that made her dizzy and weakkneed was the clothing itself. It was a sexy black lace negligee. Then she remembered when she and Darrius were invited by Jah-Man to the dinner party and how Jah-Man had danced with her, erotic and slow. He obviously had something else in mind for her.

Chapter 17

Steven walked along the busy side streets. Every so often, he would tuck the brim of his hat low. He knew the dangers if anyone caught him; he would be fed to Jah-Man for lunch. Still though, he had to find the answer to the duppy children. They were obviously not duppies but just children, schoolers. However, what disturbed him was that fact a child could commit such crimes they were so horrendous. As he walked along the street, he passed many people, each time he would try to keep his face out of direct view. Before long, he had reached St.Vincents orphanage. He was familiar all to well with it. The schoolers played about in the yard on their rickety swings and teeter-totters. Some had rubber balls they kicked about. For a moment he stood staring at them looking at each of their faces when the opportunity became available.

He recognized no one. He also didn't want to seem too obvious; some people would notice the fact that he stood there staring. Moving further down the street, he walked through an old wooden gate that led into the orphanage. Taking his time, he scanned the children with care. It was possible that the duppy children weren't here, that maybe they had parents and a home. He doubted it though.

The stairs squeaked as he climbed them and entered the rundown building that was the home to so many lost children. Upon entering he took a deep breath, it had been many, many years since he stood inside these walls. A flood of memories rushed in on him and he staggered backwards a few steps.

"Are you okay mister?" a soft and very innocent voice said to him.

Steven looked down, standing next to him was a little girl her dark curly hair dangling down in locks across her brow. He hadn't heard her approach and that bothered him.

"Huh, yes I'm fine. Tell me is Mother Francis here?" he asked her regaining his composure.

"Sure, she's in the kitchen," the little girl pointed.

"You want me to get her for you?"

"No, I know where the kitchen is. You should run along and play," he smiled warmly to her.

"Okay, nice to meet you," she said then dashed out the front door.

Steven moved through the large hallway. St. Vincent's was primarily run by Nuns, most of them were of French origin but there were some from all corners of the globe. Most were white, quiet spoken, and fun to be with. However, there were a few that he could remember who loved to take a switch to you at the drop of the hat. Mother Francis was in charge of the orphanage and not much got passed her. When he was growing up here, she was a young woman with very blond hair, now, she was much older and her hair had gone silver gray. He also loved her dearly.

When he entered the kitchen, she was busily at work mixing something in a huge pot. She didn't have her habit on and a lock of her short hair was dangling down. She wore a flowered apron that had splotches of flour dusted over it.

"Hello Mother," Steven said softly.

Mother Francis stopped what she was doing and turned. For a brief moment, they locked eyes and said nothing, and then a broad smile formed on her face.

"Steven!" she said rushing over to him.

For a long moment, they stood hugging, and then she stood back holding him at arm's length looking him up and down.

"It has been many, many years. You have grown into a handsome young man! It is so good to see you! You know not many children that leave St. Vincent's come back to visit," she rambled.

"I came for a purpose," Steven said not wanting to detract from the woman's expectations.

"Oh, I see, what could possibly bring you back here?" she said her smile fading.

"To see you and the others," he said trying not to totally burst her bubble. "I also need some information."

"Well, I have a few minutes before I prepare lunch for the children. Come, let us grab some milk and cookies and sit down," she ushered him over to one of the tables.

Steven followed her. He didn't really want milk and cookies since he wasn't five years old anymore. Still though, he humored her and sat down accepting the food.

"So, what information are you looking for?" she asked placing a small plate of butter cookies in front of him.

"Information on some of the children. I need to know if you found any phosphorus on or around any of the children," he asked.

"Phosphorus? Isn't that strange - Sister Mary just asked me about that last week. When doing some laundry, she found some of the clothes had a <u>dull yellow</u> <u>tint</u> to them," Mother Francis said not meeting his eyes.

"Very strange indeed."

"Can you tell me which of the children the clothing came from?" Steven said excitedly.

"Oh that was simple, it was the twins," she smiled warmly.

"The twins?" Steven frowned.

"Delvin and Devilia Hellton."

"Twins…" Steven said looking away his mind racing with thoughts.

"Steven, why do you ask me about them and what does the phosphorus have to do with them? They are such sweet children, very respectful and helpful. I'm actually surprised that they weren't adopted quickly," she explained.

"Where are they now?" Steven asked.

"Well, they could be in the yard playing or they could be up at the Orion," she said.

"The Orion?" Steven asked with a baffled look.

"Yes, the Orion. It's very unfair to the rest of the children, but the Orion takes certain children up there to spend the day; sometimes even a night or two."

"You let strangers take the children away from here?" Steven blurted out.

"My, there is nothing to worry about. They've been doing this for some time.

You know there are many children's activities up there, games, swimming pools, horseback riding.

Why shouldn't some of them have the option to go? They're children they want to play and the Orion is a public place that <u>has childcare already</u>," she pointed out.

For a moment, Steven said nothing, and then just nodded his head in agreement. If what Mother Francis said were true, it would be a pleasant thing for some of the children. Nevertheless, he already understood the truth, Jah-Man was the owner of the Orion and he was using children to do his dirty work.

"You haven't explained to me why you're so interested in the Hellton twins," she asked.

"Because" he began to say then stopped, catching himself. He couldn't let Mother Francis know the truth, not yet.

"I work up at the Orion as a lifeguard, swimming instructor and all those sort of water activities. I noticed some children and I wondered if they came from here," he said feeling guilty for lying to her.

"Oh I see," she smiled again.

"What does that phosphorus have to do with this though?"

"Well, we were painting one day and some of the children got too close to the mixers and sprayers and I wondered if they got coated with some," he said feeling more guilty.

"Oh it wasn't too bad, came right out of the clothes."

"Well Mother it has been nice to chat with you. I must be going," he said getting up.

"Must you go so soon?" she smiled standing also.

"Yes, I must get back to work," he said giving her a kiss on the cheek.

"Please come back and see us again, Sister Margaret would love to see you again. She speaks of you often!" she smiled and escorted him to the kitchen door.

Steven just nodded and slipped out, moments later he was on the street again. It was time to head back to the shack and tell the others.

Mother Francis resumed stirring her pot humming softly to herself. She was pleased that Steven had come to see her. She was pleased when any children came back for a visit. Unknown to her, the kitchen door squeaked as it slowly opened. The noise was enough though, to cause her to stop humming. For some reason she felt a twinge of fear, but she quickly scoffed at herself for it. What was there to fear in an orphanage?

Grabbing the pot, she lifted it off the counter and swiveled around to put it on the stove. She abruptly stopped. There wasn't much pain, only a burning sensation. For an instant, she stood there, and then stared down at her feet. Protruding from her abdomen was a large butcher knife. Hanging onto the handle of the knife was a child's hand. For an instant, her eyes looked up into the child's. It was Delvin Hellton. Seconds later, he twisted the knife and yanked down. The pot slipped from her hands and her life slipped from her body.

Sharon sat on the end of the bed, there was no way she was going to put on a scant negligee, she would rather stay covered in Elmo's blood. She needed to escape and right now, that was priority one on her list. Glancing around the room she looked for any objects that she could use as a weapon. There were none.

Jah-Man had been meticulous in adjusting the room. He expected her and knew that she would be staying here.

He had removed anything that could be used defensively. She also let a thought briefly pass through her mind; if she couldn't get out she could always use one of the bed sheets out the window. That is, if satin would hold her.

The door clicked and opened. Jah-Man walked through and slowly closed it behind him, then turned to face her. His expression was mild, placid and she could detect nothing from it.

"Why haven't you changed?" he said softly.

"Give me some real clothes and I will," she barked back.

"That clothing is _more_ than adequate for you," he said stepping further into the room.

"It might be if I was a cheap whore," Sharon quickly replied.

Jah-Man held his arms behind him and slowly walked around the room, stopping briefly by the large window that overlooked the ocean. He stared at the majestic water beyond for a long moment then turned to her his look sterner.

"I have watched you over the years with keen interest. As you already know your association with my son has kept me watching your whole group."

Sharon gasped at the mention of Darrius being Jah-Man's son. Mama Rose had only told her and Ohpton. Somehow, Jah-Man knew that she had.

"Don't look so shocked, I know that Mama Rose told you. Mama Rose has a labba mout and that is something I will quickly correct," he sighed.

"She told me nothing..." Sharon quickly said trying to protect her.

"You do not lie well. It isn't in your blood; you're too honest, caring. You extend you help to others freely. You're little group is a reflection of that," he said casually.

"We just have a lot in common," she said softly.

"Yes you do, but it's more than that. You have become family to each other," he said with a hint of jealously in his voice.

"Some of us wouldn't have if you hadn't slaughtered Raffie's family," she snapped.

"That was unfortunate, but like I said earlier, they couldn't take the hint," he smiled remembering.

"My, the look on his face when he opened those boxes!" "You're sick," she said.

"No, just a <u>craven playboy</u> and powerful!" he said with glee.

"Yes you might be but you lack the one thing you can never have - family," she quickly shot back.

Jah-Man's expression quickly changed and he stared at her with intense anger. She had struck a raw cord with him - a very raw cord.

"I have a son and a daughter," he barked.

"Eve and Darrius have never been your children, never! You abandoned them when they were young, when they needed you most after their mama died!" she snapped.

"Her death, her death…" he stuttered.

Sharon suddenly felt the oxygen get sucked out of the room. Her lungs ached as she stared at him in muted shock.

Jah-Man had killed Evelyn Lawson. He murdered his own children's mama.

The silence in the room was enough to alert Jah-Man to the fact that now she knew the truth. He stared at her with glaring, murderous eyes. Sharon couldn't take her own off him, she was afraid that if she did he would strike her down in one swift blow.

"She, she was - I loved her so," he said his voice cracking.

"Then why did you murder her?" Sharon said softly.

"She knew too much. Our children, she would have turned me in, betrayed me!" he shrieked.

"So that was reason to murder your children's mother?" she pushed.

"She made me, she made me do it!" he ranted.

Sharon realized that if she continued pushing the man he would kill her on the spot. He was clearly insane and going over the edge further by the moment.

"That was a long time ago," she said trying to diffuse the situation.

Jah-Man continued to stare at her with insane hatred. His hands were clenched tightly into fists as they shook.

"Who else other than Ohpton Manley knows that I am Eve and Darrius's father?" he snarled.

"No one," she said hoping that he would believe her.

"You lie."

"No, none of the others know. I am telling you the truth," she said again.

"They will all die. I will kill each and every one of them! I will start with Steven and Raffie, then Ohpton," he smiled with satisfaction.

"That will bring you closer to your son and daughter or are you going to kill them too?" she again pushed.

"If they disobey me, they will be punished - severely!" he snarled.

"So what happens to me?" she asked.

"You, you I have always had a <u>taste</u> for," he grinned.

"I have use for you. Now do not make things difficult for yourself, please, change out of those filthy clothes."

Sharon knew she had no choice; she was most likely dealing with a predator that was ten times worse than Elmo was. Reaching down she grabbed the lacy clothing, then turned and looked at him.

"What? Are you going to stand there and watch?" she scowled at him.

"Of course," he said his voice but a whisper.

The tone of his voice chilled her and for a moment, she stood there staring at him. Then, reluctantly, she unbuttoned her blouse letting it fall to the floor. She then slipped out of her shorts; all the while, her eyes were glued to his. When she removed her bra, she watched his eyes widen the lust clear in them. Grabbing her panties, she slipped them off then, breaking eye contact with him reached over and grabbed the negligee.

The brief moment was all he needed. Jah-Man moved quickly behind her drawing his hands up and cupping her breasts. Sharon panicked.

She tried to pull away from him but his arms were strong and held onto her tightly. Instinctively, without thinking, she snatched her shirt off the floor. Taking it, she rubbed the dried blood into his face. He instantly withdrew.

"You, you hellion!" he spat, and then swung his hand the back of it connecting with Sharon's jaw.

The blow knocked her clean off her feet and she collapsed to the floor in a heap. Jah-Man became frantic as he stared at the filthy shirt on the floor by his feet. His eyes locked on the large dark patch of dried blood. Blood!

With a strength he never knew he had, he began tearing at his own clothing, slinging it in all directions. Seconds later he stood there naked his taunt chest rising and falling, his breathing labored.

Sharon rolled over the room still spinning for a moment before clearing. Her jaw ached and she held it with one of her hands. She stared at him as he stood there naked before her, and then abruptly, he began rubbing his hands over his body as if he was trying to rub something out of his skin. His movements showed panic, his eyes were wide as if they were seeing a horror no one else could. Abruptly he turned and dashed to the bathroom, seconds later she heard the shower come on. He was muttering something but it was so soft that she couldn't tell what it was. He was also very oblivious to her.

Getting up she grabbed the first piece of clothing she could find - the negligee and dashed for the door. Reaching out she grabbed the handle flinging the door open. Standing on the other side was Delicia.

For an instant the two women stared at each other, then Delicia, her mouth agape looked down at Sharon's naked body.

"What in the…" Delicia snarled.

"Move!" Sharon demanded as she tried to get past Delicia.

"Wait just one minute here! What are you doing in my - Jah-Man's bedroom naked?" she blurted out.

"Trying to get out of here!" Sharon said drawing back.

At that moment, out of the bathroom came Jah-Man, still naked. Delicia looked up at him and then at Sharon, she was speechless. Seconds later, Jah-Man grabbed Sharon by he hair and tossed her to the side.

"Get dressed," he snarled.

"What happened here?" Delicia demanded.

"Nothing that concerns you," Jah-Man spat.

"What do you mean nothing that concerns me?" Delicia yelled.

"Nothing that concerns you," he said again.

"Am I not your woman?" she blurted out.

"You are what I decide you will be," he said walking casually over to a large dresser.

"I demand to know what this tramp, this whore is doing here!" she screamed.

Slipping on his pants, he buttoned them, then abruptly turned and grabbed Delicia by the throat. She instantly shut up making only a gurgling sound as her hands tried frantically to remove his hand.

"When I say that nothing happened, nothing happened. Do I make myself clear?" he said his teeth grating together.

Delicia slowly nodded her face showing the strain from the lack of oxygen.

"And if I choose to bed another woman, I will bed another woman. I don't care if you like it or not. Do I make myself clear?" he snarled.

Again, Delicia nodded the gurgling noises becoming more pronounced.

"Let her go Jah-Man. Let her go before you kill another woman!" Sharon snapped.

Jah-Man shot a harsh gaze to her, and then back to Delicia whose eyes were now beginning to roll white. He then let her go, her body crumpling to the floor. Delicia gasped drawing a large deep breath, seconds later she wretched.

"You and the others will pay, do you hear me? You will pay!" he snarled shaking a finger at her. He then finished dressing.

Sharon slipped the clothing over her head and adjusted it around her breasts.

She then sat on the edge of the bed her arms folded covering her nearly bare breasts. Jah-Man walked over and stood before her glaring down at her with evil intent.

"I have a deal to make with you."

"I don't make deals with yardies," she spat looking away.

Again, Jah-Man's hand came up boxing her on the other cheek, the blow strong enough to knock her flat onto her back on the bed. He was quick crawling his way on top of her pinning her wrists back.

"You would be wise to listen," he said with a bite in his voice.

"I have a simple offer to make you. Help me get two of your friends, Raffie and Steven and I will spare the others," he began to say.

"Go to hell!" she snarled as she struggled against him.

"Put simply, you want to help your mama?" he looked at her smiling.

Sharon stopped struggling and stared up at him her eyes wide.

"I can make it so she gets out of jail tonight. So look at my offer this way, you help me and I not only save the rest of your friends, but your mama gets out of jail and, your little brother stays alive."
"Bastard!" she cursed at him.

"The choice is yours and I'll give you till tonight to make it," he said slowly pulling his body off hers.

Sharon quickly pulled herself away from him and huddled towards the head of the bed her arms and legs, drawn up close. Jah-Man walked over and scooped Delicia up off the floor, she was quiet and her hand rubbed slowly across her throat. He then brought her over to the bed and laid her down. He then began removing her clothing, she murmured and tried to stop him but he just pushed her hands out of the way. Within moments, Delicia lay naked before him. Rolling over onto her side she curled up into the fetal position and mumbled to herself. Jah-Man stared intently at Sharon as he undid his trousers and shorts. He was clearly aroused; the violence of the moments had done this to him. Grabbing Delicia he pulled her onto her back and forcibly spread her legs. Moments later he started grining her taking her as he pleased, all the while keeping his eyes locked on Sharon.

Sharon tried to look away, tried to take her eyes away from his and his muscular body but she found she couldn't. She had no idea how long they stared at each other, it could have been seconds or minutes but abruptly Jah-Man's motions became quick and forceful as he released. Pulling himself away, he watched as Delicia again rolled over into the fetal position. Grabbing his trousers he slipped them on and headed for the door, opening it, he glanced back at Sharon.

"Let that be a lesson to you - I take what I want," he said then left.

Sharon glanced nervously down at Delicia who began to sob. Her own tears began to glide down her cheeks and she reached out running her hand through Delicia's messed hair.

Shortly she would have to make a choice. Save her mama and little brother by condemning Raffie and Steven to certain death or killing her mama and little brother by keeping her mouth shut. The tears began to fall harder.

Junior closed the door to his little shack down at the beach. He leaned up against it, and then rushed forward to an old wooden cabinet against the wall. With shaking hands, he opened it and pulled out a large leather bag. For a moment, he held it close to his chest, then went over to the bed and unzipped the bag. Inverting it, the contents fell out; thousands of nannies fell out onto the bed until there was a small pile in the middle. Tossing the bag, Junior reached his hands into the pile and brought it skyward to his face, smelling deeply into the green currency. He was happy, happier than he could ever remember. He was rich; rich to do and go wherever he wanted to. No more would he be Jah-Man or the Frenchman's flunky. He could choose and go wherever he pleased.

Laughing uncontrollably, he crinkled the money between his palms and brought it up letting the bills fall back to the top of the bed.

"Oh my! That is a lot of money!" a voice called from behind him.

His neck snapped around to see one of the whores he slept with standing in the doorway, her eyes glued on the mass of money lying upon the bed.

"What are you doing here?" he snapped.

"I came by. Thought you'd like me to spend the night again," she smiled warmly.

"Care to share some of your new-found wealth?"

"No, go away," he said his voice clear and concise.

"You mean you don't want someone to spend those lonely nights with; someone who'll look out for you and give in to your every whim?" she said drawing close to him.

She was now close enough to the money to touch it. Junior let go of the bills in his hand and grabbed her by the shoulders.

"No, no you can't have it - none of it!" he snarled.

Moments later he slammed her body into one of the center posts holding the roof up. The force was enough to crack and split the beam. The girl let out a yelp then collapsed to the floor.

"Nobody is going to get my money! Nobody!" he ranted, and then began bludgeoning her with his feet.

Minutes later the girl lay dead upon his floor her lifeless eyes staring intently up at him. He stood there staring at her his anger continuing to swell, then, just as quickly it subsided and he staggered back collapsing onto the edge of the bed. He continued to stare at the girl and he suddenly felt sad, she was great in bed. His hand drifted to the pile of money sitting next to him. Picking it up again, the feel of the bills between his fingers gave him strength. He again looked at the girl, she didn't matter, his mama didn't matter, and all that mattered was money. Money was the only joy in his life. He had outfoxed Jah-Man and the Frenchman and taken money from the Americans.

"The fools. They're going to fight each other till they're both dead!" he laughed aloud.

Again he stared at the girl's body. He had killed before for what he wanted, this was no different. Scooping his money up he began to put it back in the bag and plan his next move.

"That double crossing bastard!" the Frenchman screamed at the top of his lungs.

Moments later he grabbed a statue of Venus that stood in the corner and began beating the nearest object, a solid rosewood cabinet. The wood splintered as he continued to hammer away, finally the statue fractured and fell apart. The man stood there gasping for breath his anger boiling over.

Yashi awoke to yelling. She was face down on a plush bed her arms were tied behind her back, her legs were tied together, and she was naked. Her mouth was dry and she licked her lips repeatedly to try to moisten them.

"Ah you are awake!" a voice behind her called back.

She then felt fingertips lightly touch her calf and slowly run up the back of her leg and over her buttocks to the small of her back. The touch chilled her and she rolled quickly onto her side to avoid it.

"Oriental women hold a special place in my bed," the Frenchman smiled.

"I'm sure they've all gone there willingly too," she said staring at the man. "Most have," he grinned.

"I must apologize for the ropes, but until I know I can talk with you civilly it will have to be that way."

"Oh a woman scares you?" she frowned.

"Oh yes, some women do scare me!" he grinned.

"Can you stand?"

"Yeah, and you want me to hop like a rabbit or something?" she snarled.

Reaching into his short's pocket, he produced a small pocketknife. Leaning over he slipped the cool blade between her ankles and sliced the two ropes with one quick jerk.

"Any chance of getting some clothes?" she frowned as she stood up.

"I prefer my women natural," he smiled.

"Come"

She followed him out of the main cabin onto the back deck where a large table and chairs sat. All around them were loungers filled with beautiful women - all naked.

Yashi stared at them; there were all races, Black, White, Oriental, Arab, and Mexican. It also made her feel greatly inadequate; all the women were buxom with hourglass shapes and long shapely legs. She couldn't understand what the Frenchman saw in her, with her average breasts, wider hips, to strip her naked. Turning she held her hands out for him to cut the ropes binding them.

"Can I trust you not to create trouble?" he asked.

"Give me some clothes and I might agree," she said wiggling her hands behind her back.

"I was tempted you know, I just wanted you to know that," he said cutting the rope.

"Tempted?" she said realizing at the last moment that she didn't want to know.

"Like I said, I have a weakness for the Oriental type of women. I was tempted to taste what you would be like," he said licking his lips.

"Thank you for refraining," she said sitting down.

"Can I have some clothes?"

"In a while, I enjoy staring at your naked body," he smiled.

"Do you know why you are here?"

"Because you find me attractive?" she countered.

"Hardly, compared to my other women you're just average," he said raising an eyebrow.

"Why then?"

"You were going to buy from Jah-Man, am I right?" he asked.

"Maybe"

"Well that wouldn't be a wise idea, I know that you know who I am and what I can provide if you give me the opportunity."

"Why should I?" she asked rubbing her wrists.

"It is good for your health and it's good for business?" he gave her a frightful grin.

"Your people wiped out mine last night. Why should I deal with you at all?" she scowled.

"It wasn't my people," he shook his head.

"Then who was it?" she said leaning forward.

"The person you're planning to buy off of," he explained.

"Jah-Man? Why would he shoot the people who are going to buy his product?"

The Frenchman got up and walked casually over to one of the wet bars. He grabbed a glass and dumped two ice cubes in then filled it with whiskey. "What would you like?" he asked.

"Vodka straight up," she said.

The Frenchman poured her drink then brought them both over to the table. Moments later he sat down and took a sip from the tumbler.

"Jah-Man doesn't realize that there was a person very close to him, that was feeding me information. He wanted me to send a hit team to take out your people. However, I was quick to retract the order, there was no use in me fighting with people that will eventually give me money for my product - not good business I tell you," he said taking another sip.

"So what happened to my people?" she looked at him with great interest.

"I wanted information on Jah-Man so I hired one of his own to feed it to me. What eventually happened was that the little punk double crossed me and took the money."

"Ripped off by your own people?" she all but laughed.

"Actually it was not very funny, that money was yours remember?" he looked at her coldly.

"Oh yes we know, we would also like to find who it was too," she said her laugh subsiding.

"I know whom it is remember, he did work for me," the Frenchman said taking a sip of his drink.

Next to the yacht a piece of driftwood floated, it bumped gently into the bow, then methodically moved along the waterline to the stern of the yacht.

Two small snorkels came up along with two small heads. Devilla Hellton was the first out of the water. Around her neck was a large clear sealed bag containing a silenced maggy and extra clips and a small electronic listening device with a tape recorder. Looking back at the water, she watched her brother Delvin slip away from the stern. Moving with extreme stealth, she slithered onto the transom and onto the stern deck. Nobody saw her, walking on the balls of her feet to limit the amount of noise she quickly moved over to the first of four lifeboats. Pulling the cover back, she slipped beneath it into the lifeboats belly. From the plastic bag, she withdrew the listening device and tape recorder, moments later she protruded the microphone and started the tape.

"So are you going to share that information with me?" Yashi asked.

"Depends, depends on if you plan on carrying through dealing with JahMan," the Frenchman asked.

"Why can't we deal with both of you?" she asked taking a different tack.

"Rivalry" he said quickly.

"Even if we could buy everything you make?" she looked at him.

"Everything?" he asked raising an eyebrow.

"Everything" she quickly said.

"And we'll keep the prices the same for both of you to ensure that neither of you feels ripped off," she said.

"You do realize that you are talking about tons?"

"Obviously, we have distribution points throughout the country and connections in the DEA to ensure that none of your shipments get stopped," she said.

"Now do you mind getting me some clothes?"

The Frenchman raised his hand snapping his fingers. Instantly two naked women came up carrying the clothing she was wearing, it was neatly washed and pressed. Yashi took them and got dressed under the Frenchman's glaring eyes. When she was done, she sat back down and took a long swill of vodka draining the glass. She then held it up to him and he again snapped his fingers. Another naked woman came and refilled the glass for her.

"Now, does that sound like a viable deal?" she asked.

"No" he countered.

Yashi instantly frowned, something else was going through the Frenchman's mind. He wanted something more of her.

"What then?" she asked, not really sure she wanted to know the answer.

"Jah-Man has to be out of the picture," he said.

"But I already told you that I can handle both of your products," she quickly countered.

"This goes beyond that. I wish to rule Jah-Man's territories. For many years he has been my most hated enemy and now I have the chance to crush him, once and for all," the Frenchman said clenching his fist.

"You don't make good business sense," she shook her head.

"You can have your cake and eat it too, yet you insist on a nonproductive vendetta."

"Call it what you will but Jah-Man will fall. I promise you that, he will fall and I will kill him," the Frenchman snarled.

"Whom do you have working on the inside?" she asked.

"That really doesn't concern you does it?" he shot back.

"The man is untrustworthy and will be dealt with accordingly."

"So why not tell me who it is, so I can find him and eliminate him. He is obviously the one who wiped out my people."

"I already told you who did that - it was Jah-Man," the Frenchman said with irritation in his voice.

"Jah-Man would not jeopardize such a lucrative deal. I highly disagree with you on this," she shook her head.

"Believe what you will, either way it is you who are the loser," he smiled.

"This is the way things are going to work. Deal with me or deal with no one," he said coldly.

Yashi stared at the man; he was obviously serious about his intentions. There was no way she was going to get both of these men in one corner to take them out together. Jah-Man was her main objective; the Frenchman came second on the list.

"I will need to inform my superiors," she said softly.

The Frenchman slid a cellular phone across the table at her. She stopped it but didn't pick it up.

"Call here, now," he ordered.

"I will call when I deem it is appropriate," she shot back.

"I said, call now!"

Yashi stared at the man, he was growing angrier by the moment. There was no way she could give the man an answer here and now. If she used the phone he could speed dial the number back and eventually find out that she was not what she seemed. She slid the phone back across the table at him.

"I will call when I decide to call and not before. I am not one of your whores to order around. If you want to deal with us, you better get your priorities straight."

The Frenchman sat there for a moment, then grabbed the cellular phone and slung it out over the side of the yacht. It plunked down in the water nearly hitting Delvin Hellton who skirted around the hull.

"That was not the correct answer," he said rising from the chair.

Yashi watched him her blood beginning to run cold. Before she could jump from the chair two powerful hands grabbed her shoulders holding her down. The Frenchman walked around the table his hands in his pockets. He never took his eyes from her either.

"I think I need to send your superiors a message - a powerful message," he said softly.

Nodding to the two men next to her the forcibly hauled her to her feet, moments later she felt the hard snapping blow of a hand across her cheek. The box was enough to daze her; the ones that followed quickly sent her into darkness.

By the time they were done, she was a limp rag in their hands. The Frenchman walked over to her and grabbed her bloodied face. Holding it by the chin, he raised her head.

"You could have just agreed you could have done the smart thing. Now, well now you will join your other friends," he said.

"Throw her over the side."

One of the two men hefted her into his arms and carried her along the edge of the deck. Passing one of the lifeboats, he noticed that the edge of the canvas top was pulled out.

"Check that out," he said to his partner.

The man grabbed the canvas and hauled it back exposing an empty lifeboat. He then shook his head to his partner who took Yashi and tossed her over the railing. Her body hit the water hard, then, rose to the surface, face down. The men watched her for a second then went back to their duties.

The Frenchman paced the deck; he was angry, angry that people didn't do what he wished. When the men returned he paced back and forth a few times then stopped before them.

"Go, find that little punk. Find Junior and bring me back his head!" he snarled.

The men both nodded and quickly headed for the stern of the boat where a launch was tied. The Frenchman heard the motor start when the Captain came up on deck holding a piece of paper.

"Sir, this just came in from the American weather service. We defiantly have a big, big hurricane coming. The other one missed us, they're calling this one Alma," he said.

"How long?" the Frenchman asked.

"Maybe 48 hours; most likely less," the Captain said.

"I want to hold off for another 24 hours, is that understood?"

"But sir, that won't give us much time to evade this one! According to the United States weather service, Alma is a category 5 - maybe even bigger. We need to get to the States as soon as possible."

"The United States?" he nearly laughed. "That is totally out of the question. You know as well as I do that I set foot on U.S. soil and I will immediately be in their drug enforcement hands."

"But sir, this is big enough to kill us all!" the Captain shook the paper at him.

"24 hours and then you can do what you want," the Frenchman said.

"But sir..."

"Enough! If you feel incapable of carrying out my orders then I will find someone who will," the Frenchman snarled.

The Captain nodded and quickly headed back to the bridge. The Frenchman cursed and walked over to the railing. Staring at the water, he noticed something moving. It was a piece of driftwood and quite a ways away from the yacht. What he found odd was that Yashi's body was floating face up; next to it he noticed the snorkels.

"Sound the alarm! Kill them, kill them!" he screamed to his guards, his finger pointed to the floating body.

The red digital timer ticked down from five, four, three, two, and one. The blast engulfed the entire yacht. Fragments of fiberglass, chrome, body parts and wood flew high into the air along with a huge black mushroom cloud. Fire burned in splotches across the top of the water. Where once there was a magnificent large motor yacht, there now remained only debris.

Two small heads emerged from the water; they both looked back at the destruction smiling at each other, and then continued on dragging Yashi towards shore.

Steven burst through the door of the shack. Everyone was inside except for Sharon whom was the one person he wanted to see. His excitement was clear as he closed the door and quickly sat down.

"Where have you been?" Raffie asked.

"Mama Rose's," he said.

"Look, I've done some digging and I figured out who the duppy children are!"

"We have a lot to tell you too," Darrius said softly.

Steven could see the seriousness in their faces. Darrius began to recite what had happened to them all since they last saw him. He could see Steven's face fall when he told him about Sharon.

"Me, he wants me," Steven said staring at the floor.

"No, not only you, me too," Raffie added.

"We have to go and get her," Steven said shaking his head.

"That would mean both of us would get killed," Raffie said.

"It doesn't matter, only Sharon does. She has done much for every one of us over the years. We owe her and owe her big!" Steven pointed out.

"Didn't you hear me? We will be killed Steven, killed!" Raffie shook his head.

"Doesn't matter - only Sharon does," he said heading for the door.

Ohpton jumped up grabbing him and holding him back. Steven struggled with him but Ohpton had him pinned so he couldn't move.

"Let me go! I have to go get her - I have to!" he yelled.

"Relax, relax, we'll get her out, we'll all get her out!" Raffie said.

"What did you have to tell us?" Darrius said changing the subject.

Steven stared at him as if he was <u>daft</u>, then resigned to the fact he wasn't going after Sharon alone. He then remembered why he was so excited.

"Oh, I figured out who the duppy children are. They're not duppies I can tell you that!" he said explaining what he had found.

"That sure would explain much," Ohpton said.

"Yeah it sure does, but why would Jah-Man use kids?" Darrius said his tone belaying his irritation.

"They're efficient and nobody would give a couple of kids a second look. They can come and go in most places without detection," he explained.

"So Jah-Man is using kids as hit men, what are we going to do about it?" Eve asked.

"Yeah, she does have a point, we stick our necks out now and Jah-Man will probably lop it off," Ohpton said.

"Kids are fairly silent too," Darrius said.

Raffie stared out the window at the dense jungle beyond. A chill swept through him and he turned to the others his face showing shock.

"There's no telling when or where they could come. For all we know they could be out there already," he said looking out the window again.

"We have to continue with our plan - it's our only way out," Darrius breathed.

"This is our moment."

"What is our plan?" Steven asked.

"Okay, Yashi is going to let us know when the big shipment is, she's going to keep us on the inside track even though we're out of the loop," Darrius said.

"What about our jobs?" Eve asked.

"Well, as it stands, you, Sharon and Ohpton are the only ones that have them," Raffie said.

"I'd say keep working."

"Good idea," Darrius said.

"Anyway, Jah-Man will have to receive payment for his goods and that's where we'll make the hit," he said.

"The hit?" Eve looked at her brother oddly.

"Okay, that's where we'll take the money, does that sound better?" he looked at her.

"This sounds shaky, you know that Jah-Man has muscle all around him," Steven said.

"But he doesn't when he conducts business," Darrius grinned.

"Yeah, but how are we going to know?" Eve asked.

"Yashi"

Ophton let Steven go and resumed his place in one of the chairs. Steven got up brushing his shirt then looked out of the window.

"We have another problem too," Steven said.

"What else can go wrong?" Eve shook her head.

"Mama Rose" Steven breathed.

"Mama Rose? What's wrong with her?" Ohpton asked.

"She's in danger," Steven said explaining how he found out Jah-Man was using children to do his dirty work.

"Then we need to protect her," Darrius said.

"And how are we going to do that?" Eve frowned.

"One or two of us need to go and stay with her until this is all over," Darrius said.

"One or two of us? Who?" Eve blurted out.

"You and Ohpton," Darrius said.

"Why me?" Eve asked.

"Because you've been through a lot lately and right now I think you'd be the best thing for Mama Rose," Darrius said.

Ohpton said nothing, he wanted to tell Darrius the truth, wanted to tell him that he should be the one staying with Mama Rose because he was actually JahMan's son. Instead, though, he kept his mouth shut and just nodded.

"So what happens after we get the money?" Eve asked.

"We meet Jack Griff at a predetermined spot, get on this plane and we're off to the United States!" Darrius smiled.

"That simple?" Steven asked.

"Hopefully, yes," Darrius nodded.

"What happens when Jah-Man's men start lobbing bullets?" Ohpton asked.

"Pray, really pray." Darrius breathed.

Chapter 18

Jah-Man slid a few sunflower seeds through the tiny bars of the birdcage. The bird stared at him trying to judge if the food was a trap. Jah-Man smiled at the bird, he loved them. When the bird didn't jump down for the seed Jah-Man's smile turned to a frown.

"Hello Darwin," William said coming out onto the large veranda of JahMan's townhouse.

"Brother!" Jah-Man smiled warmly.

"It is good to see you," William said hugging him.

"Much has happened, much, we must talk," Jah-Man said pulling a chair out for him.

William sat down as did Jah-Man. Silence grew between them, and JahMan turned his attention back to the bird that now fed on the seeds.

"Stupid bird, you would think they would try to please me. They would get much more from me if they did," Jah-Man said.

"I do not think they actually care," William said.

"Perhaps, but I think they know more than they let on," he said winking at him.

"How did your initial meeting go the other night?" William asked.

"Bad, we didn't unload any merchandise and our clients people were cut down by the Frenchman," Jah-Man explained.

"Cut down?" William said with surprise.

"Yes, cut down," Jah-Man added.

"Brother, I am here because something is troubling me," William said.

"Tell me your worries my brother, tell me so I can make them go away for you."

"I have learned that you still have a price on Steven Winter and Winston George?" he asked.

"You concern yourself with things that have no matter," Jah-Man scoffed.

"Yes, maybe, but I watched those children grow. They may have made mistakes, but I do not think that is a reason to put a price out on their heads," William said.

"Brother, I do love you dearly, I really do. But you are weak brother, terribly weak," Jah-Man shook his head in disgust.

"You do not know how things work."

"Darwin, killing children, young adults is not the way to do things. Haven't you done enough to Winston George? His family was wiped out!" William said defiantly.

"That family got what it deserved, I gave them many, many <u>blys</u> to withdraw from the investigation. Nevertheless, they decided to press on, keep digging. That was something I couldn't allow, the information that young adult has could cause many problems," Jah-Man explained.

"And Steven Winter?" he asked.

"Winter is a thorn in my side. He has taken liberties that cannot be forgotten. With George it is business and with Winter, it has become personal," Jah-Man said.

"But enough of these two, there are other things we must discuss." "But Darwin..." William

began to protest.

"No brother, they are no longer your concern; they never have been your concern. I will deal with them now," he said with a bite in his voice.

"Brother, I can not and will not let you harm them," William said surprised at his own outburst.

Jah-Man stared at him with savage intensity. Never before had William defied him, never had he been bold enough to speak his mind. Maybe William was not as weak as he had always thought.

"I admire your new found strength brother, but my decision is made. What do you intend to do about it?" Jah-Man pushed him.

"Brother, I have always done as you asked, all through the years. Please, this once, forget them; forget them all and let us move on with life," William said trying to reach his soft side.

"You obviously have not listened to me. My decision is made. What do you intend to do about it?" he asked again

"Whatever I have to," William said his voice faint.

"Ha! You have always humored me so!" Jah-Man said laughing.

William watched him laugh; it was the laughter of a madman. Darwin Stone no longer existed; his brother was gone, replaced by some hideous savage beast that just looked like him. He realized then, he had said too much.

"Brother I have other news to tell you," Jah-Man said changing the subject.

"Remember when I mentioned that last night our suppliers were wiped out by the Frenchman?"

"Yes," William said softly.

"Well, I have something to show you," Jah-Man said rising from his chair. "Follow me."

William followed him into the townhouse and up the long winding spiral staircase to the second floor. William knew the layout of the townhouse well; his brother was leading him to the guest bedroom. Upon opening the door, he instantly noticed a figure lying in the bed the sheet drawn up over them. It was a woman; the subtle outline of her breasts could plainly seen through the sheet. Walking closer, he gasped. Lying there was Yashi, her face bruised and battered. Her left eye was swollen nearly shut, her lip was split and dark bruises splotched her face.

"What have you done?" William turned to Jah-Man his voice revealing his anger.

"Me? I have done nothing to her brother, actually, I saved her," he smiled.

"It would seem that the Frenchman wanted her to forget dealing with me and just work with him. Her loyalty to me was clear, she would have no part of it," he smiled.

"How did you find this out?" William asked.

"My operatives," he grinned.

"I sent them on a job, a big job," he continued to smile.

"I don't understand," William said.

"I sent them to eliminate the Frenchman," he laughed.

"They did such a good job - they remembered their training so well. There is nothing left of him to speak of!" Jah-Man said with glee.

"You sent the children to blow up his yacht?" William said with surprise.

"Of course, why not?" Jah-Man asked.

"Brother I never liked your idea to use these children as assassins," William shook his head.

"They are only children - children brother!"

"They are tools, very good tools also, nothing more," Jah-Man, said his expression falling his mood quickly changing.

"What has happened to you brother, what?" William shook his head.

"Come with me, I have one more thing to show you," Jah-Man motioned.

William followed his heart pounding wildly in his chest as he tried to figure out what Jah-Man's next surprise was. He led him down the hallway to his own bedroom. Hesitating he grabbed the handle then turned to him.

"This is my ace in the hole," he smiled, then opened the door.

Sharon was still huddled at the head of the bed the comforter drawn up tightly around her.

"What?" William gasped upon seeing her.

"Uncle William!" she said equally surprised.

"What is she doing here?" William turned to Jah-Man.

"Insurance, insurance brother," Jah-Man grinned.

"This has gone too far - this must stop now!" William snarled.

Sharon yelled but she was too late, Jah-Man was quick, he grabbed hold of William and slammed him hard against the wall knocking the wind out of him.

"You are beginning to have a big mouth brother, a labba mout!" Jah-Man snarled.

"Like I told you once before I can shut that mouth of yours forever!"

Sharon launched herself off the bed colliding with Jah-Man. He lashed out at her striking her against the side of her arm. The blow wasn't deadly but it was enough to push her aside.

"Sharon no!" William yelled.

Jah-Man swung, his fist connecting with her jaw. The blow instantly turned out her lights and she crumpled to the floor in a heap. He then turned and swung at William who dodged the blow. Jah-Man's fist smashed through the sheetrock leaving a huge gaping hole.

William wasted no time; he dashed from the room taking two stairs at a time. He didn't look back to see if Darwin was chasing him, it was pointless. What he did anticipate though, was the hot piercing blow as a bullet tore through his back. Neither one happened.

William kept running as fast as his legs would carry him. Soon he was out of the Orion heading for town. He couldn't go home, Jah-Man would have men waiting for him or worse, the children would be sent on another mission. He needed a place to go and he knew exactly where.

It was going on 9 p.m. when Yashi woke up. Her body ached and every movement was painful. Still though, she got up and staggered to the bathroom. She had no idea where she was. The last thing she remembered was the Frenchman's thugs kicking her, as she lay curled up on the floor. As she went to the bathroom she nearly doubled over, her abdomen was so sore and she was peeing blood. When she looked in the mirror, she gasped. The person looking back she didn't recognize, the face was grotesque, puffed and swollen her cheeks misshapen. Still though, she should be thankful for even being alive.

Looking around she found her clothing draped over the end of the bed. With much effort, she dressed then limped out of the room. Wherever she was, it was quiet. She stood listening, her ears straining to pick up any sounds that would tell her where someone was. She heard a faint groan from the other end of the hallway.

She had no weapon and not even her hand-to-hand training would be effective given her current condition. Tip-toeing to the end door she put her ear against it and listened, there was definitely sounds coming from the other side. Glancing down at the lock, a key protruded from the knob. Turning it, she slowly opened the door.

Sharon lay on side her hand held to her cheek, her sobbing was continuous and she didn't bother to look up as she heard the door open. Yashi knew exactly who it was.

"Sharon!" she said moving as swiftly as possible to her bedside.

"What, what are you doing here?" Sharon asked wiping her cheeks.

"Me, the others are worried sick about you," she said trying to force a smile.

"I'm worried about them. Soon Jah-Man is going to want an answer," she sniffed.

"An answer? An answer to what?" Yashi frowned.

"He wants me to betray Steven and Raffie in order to save my mama and little brother," she said.

"He's an animal," Yashi breathed.

"Why are you here, your face…" Sharon said reaching up and gently touching one of her swollen cheeks.

"Sharon, I'm here to bring down Jah-Man. I work for the DEA," she whispered into her ear.

"Then why don't you just bring in the Marines?" Sharon breathed softly back.

"It doesn't work that way, we're not in the United States," she said.

"Can't we just slip out of here while Jah-Man isn't around?" she asked.

"No, I have to set up the final deal with him for tomorrow night," she shook her head.

"Look I will inform the others that you are here. Stay put I'll figure out a way to get you out."

Sharon nodded as Yashi headed back to the door. Moments later she was alone again. Worry began to seep in, worry for her mama and little brother. What would happen to them if she was gone? She then began to think of Steven, it was too long since she last saw him, and too long they were apart. She wanted to tell him what she felt, how her heart ached.

Looking around the room she noticed that Delicia had left her purse, it was laying in the corner where she had dropped it earlier. Not long after Jah-Man had left, she got up took a shower, dressed and left the room saying nothing.

For a moment earlier, she had felt for the woman and what she had experienced. However, Delicia said nothing to her and just left. The feeling passed quickly.

Getting up, Sharon walked over and grabbed Delicia's purse from the floor. Something fell out crashing to the carpet. A videocassette lay at her feet. Grabbing it, she looked the tape over; there were no markings to indicate what was on it. Taking it, she walked over and slipped the cartridge into the tape player. Seconds later what came on the screen made her stagger back and fall. Delicia lay naked upon the floor her legs wrapped tightly around Steven's bare buttocks. He was thrusting himself deeply within her.

Tears began to fall in a steady stream. She couldn't believe her eyes, the man she loved had jooked with the woman she despised. In a fit of rage, she yanked the tape from the machine and repeatedly smashed it against the television and bookshelves. The plastic quickly gave way, spewing yards of thin glossy ribbon. She then collapsed to her knees, losing all hope.

Mama Rose sat by her kitchen table drinking a hot cup of tea. The house was empty, lonely and the four walls around her suddenly seemed to shrink in. Today was a slow day, not many schoolers came in to see her. It was unusual; almost every day hoards of children would come through her door their beaming smiles brightening her spirits. Why today had been different, she could only guess. Fear.

A hush was forming around the community; something was brewing, something dark and sinister. Rumors had abounded around the community about a huge yacht exploding.

There had been many deaths. Rumors also were circulating that Jah-Man was behind it. This she believed without a doubt. Through all the years watching him grow, she could see that he was following the darkness. Even as a child he was cruel, playing pranks on other children that sometimes got them hurt.

She then began to think about the duppy children. If Jah-Man was using orphaned children to do his dirty work, how could he accomplish this without drawing attention? She then began to think about her own children. Junior was her only living child, she loved him as she always would, but he was following a darkness also one that she was sure would eventually claim his life. Her other child Jaco, was dead, he died because he loved his brother and his brother never looked out for him.

The thought of her children made her weep, it was a burden she alone had to bear and most of the time she bore it in silence. There came a gentle knock on the front door.

A chill washed through her. Who could it be at this time of night? Without any regard to her own safety, she got up and hobbled into the storefront to the door. Again a gentle knock came.

"Hold on, I'm coming," she called out.

Opening the door she came face to face with Eve and Ophton. Seeing them both brought a light into her face and she smiled warmly at them.

"My, what brings you here this time of night?" she asked standing back out of the doorway.

"We came to be with you," Eve said stepping into the house.

"Be with me? I don't understand," she said frowning.

"We have reason to believe that Jah-Man may send someone to kill you thinking Steven or Raffie is here," Ohpton explained.

"Why would he want to do that?" she looked at them wide eyed.

"Because you helped them and because you mean so much to them," Ohpton added sitting down.

"I help everyone, even Jah-Man knows this," Mama Rose scoffed.

"Yes he may, but you were hiding Steven and he knows that," Eve said.

"You should come with us, leave this place, make it harder for him to find you," Ohpton said looking around the shop.

"I will not leave my home, this house. This candy store has been my life. It is all I have," she said softly.

"I will not leave."

"Then you have two house guests for the duration," Ohpton smiled.

"Well then, come with me to the kitchen. I have some tea brewed already if you would like a cup," she motioned then turned and slowly walked back towards the kitchen.

Eve looked at Ohpton and shook her head; getting Mama Rose away would be the best option, now they were in danger too.

When Yashi reached the foyer she looked around, the house was quiet. She gazed around the room looking for anything she could use for a weapon. Being defenseless was not something she liked to be. The far wall of the living room was decorated with weapons, knives, spears, and axes, odd items that were used in times past. Jah-Man obviously liked that type of décor. Walking into the living room, she eyed the items on the wall and decidedly chose a small knife. Reaching up she was about to take it from the wall when the hair on the back of her neck rose.

"Looking for something?" Jah-Man called out from behind her.

Yashi quickly withdrew her hand and turned around to look at him. She tried to smile to give the illusion that she was happy to see him but it was too painful.

"You have a very nice collection," she said.

"It is attractive is it not?" he smiled walking up next to her.

"Very, I particularly like this one," she said, pointing to the small knife she was going to grab.

"That one was came from the Middle Ages, a dagger used in torture chambers," he said pulling it from the wall.

"Feel the craftsmanship, the balance of the weapon," he said handing it to her.

Yashi took the weapon and hefted it in her hand. Surprisingly it was well crafted. Reluctantly she handed it back to him, he then placed it back onto the wall.

"Are you feeling well?" he asked.

"I have been better," she said.

"The Frenchman would have killed you," he said adjusting the blade.

"Why didn't he?" she asked the obvious question.

"Because I didn't let him," he said.

"You saved me?" she looked at him dumbfounded.

"Yes is that so strange? You have proven to me where your loyalties lie. I could do no less," he said.

"And what of the Frenchman? Isn't he going to be angered by your intervention into my death?" she asked.

"Ha! Not if he can reach out from the sea," Jah-Man laughed.

"Right now many, many fish are feeding on his remains," he said with joy.

"You killed him?" Yashi looked at him with surprise.

"Obviously"

"Well, that eliminates one problem," Yashi said forcing a smile.

"One problem," Jah-Man said.

"You have seen my guest?" he asked.

Yashi was taken back by his question; he obviously knew she had been in Sharon's room. There would be no hiding that, she only prayed that the room hadn't been bugged.

"Yes, I heard something when I got up," she said.

"You know her?" he asked.

"Yes, through Darrius," she said.

"Ah, yes, Darrius, I forgot your association with him," Jah-Man nodded.

"Why is she here?" Yashi asked.

"She is here to ensure I achieve my goals," he said.

"What are you're intentions regarding Darrius?"

"I do not understand," she said again taken off guard.

"The question is simple. What are your intentions regarding Darrius?" he asked again.

"You have taken to his bed more than once, what else have you done?"

Yashi tried to think quickly; it was plainly obvious that his man knew more than she even suspected he would. He had informants everywhere; she had to assume that he already knew of her involvement with Darrius.

"He is special," she said.

"Special? Have you taken to him?" Jah-Man bluntly asked.

"Well I did share his bed, that should answer your question," Yashi countered.

"Whores share beds also but they don't let their emotions get tangled up with their bodies."

"I am not a whore," Yashi snapped.

"I did not imply that, my apologies for my misunderstanding. I just want to know what your intentions are with my - with Darrius," he asked.

"I do not know, our paths are very different. When we have finalized our deal and the first shipment has been made then I must move on to other areas. My job here will be done."

"Then you do not intend to see him after that?" Jah-Man asked.

"I do not think our lives will permit that, but you never know what life throws at you," she shrugged.

"Yes, that was put very well," he nodded.

"Now let's discuss business out on the veranda, I have ordered some food for you. You can eat while we talk," he motioned her to follow him.

Yashi followed trying to determine if the man knew she was not what she professed to be. She also wondered why he was so interested in her relationship with Darrius; this hadn't been the first time he asked her about him.

The veranda was round, a large black wrought iron table and chairs sat in the middle. Flower boxes were positioned all around with blossoming colors spewing from their thin stalks. On the table were a variety of foods and one plate. A chilled bottle of champagne sat next to the table the top already drawn.

"Please help yourself," he motioned to her.

Yashi sat down and pulled some of the food upon her plate. Her jaw was so sore that she wondered if she could even chew. Still though, she tried. As she nibbled on her food Jah-Man stared at her intently as if every little facial muscle was a lie detector.

"When can you get the <u>mass</u> for the shipment?" he asked

"The money is there already, we have yet to find the briefcase from the other night. We lost much cash and would like to retrieve it," she said.

"Fortunately the product was not lost also," he said.

"We still have yet to receive any product from you," she added.

"Then you would have no objections to moving ahead with the large shipment?" he asked.

"Not if you can deliver the goods," she said.

"Excellent! I would like to conclude our business day after tomorrow," he said.

"I will have the product brought here in trucks. From there you can have it moved to wherever you wish," he said.

"You want to do business here?" she looked at him with surprise.

"Yes, this is where I want to make our exchange," he nodded.

"Wouldn't you like someplace more remote?" she asked.

"No, I own this resort so I can and will do as I please with it," he stated.

"What about your guests? What if they observe or see the exchange?" she asked.

"I have areas here that are private, the people here are loyal to me. They want to keep their jobs," he smiled.

"So you will have the shipment brought here, then I can have it picked up?"

"Of course, I assume you will also bring the money, all 16 million of it?" he asked looking at her.

"16 million? We agreed on..." she began to say.

"Yes, that was before I had to eliminate the competition," he smiled.

"The price has gone up."

"I will have to check with my superiors, you have asked for much," she shook her head.

"In return I will add a bonus shipment to the order, more than enough to compensate you for the increase," he smiled.

Yashi stared at the man then slowly nodded her approval. Her superiors were not going to like coming up with 16 million in cash even if it was left over drug money.

"I must go," she said.

"There is much I have to arrange."

As she headed for the door, he called out to her stopping her in her tracks.

"I will see you here day after tomorrow?" he called to her.

"Of course," she said.

"Be careful of whom you associate with, there is much danger out there," he said coldly.

His words were enough to chill her and root her to the floor. It took much effort but she nodded and slipped out into the foyer. Moments later she was outside breathing in the cool night air.

Jah-Man watched her leave. No sooner had she disappeared than a side door to the room opened. Devilia Hellton walked in her little legs moving swiftly. She went up and sat down in one of the high back chairs. Jah-Man sat down opposite her and for a brief moment they stared willfully at one another.

"What have you come to tell me?" he asked his voice soft and sweet.

The little girl said nothing; she just reached inside the big pocket on her dress and withdrew a tape recorder. Reaching her little arm out, she handed it to Jah-Man, and then bounded off the chair. Skipping across the polished floor she disappeared behind the door, she had come through. When she was gone Jah-Man pressed play on the machine, the voice he heard was that of the Frenchman as he talked to Yashi. Seconds later he heard a name, a name of a traitor. He heard Junior's name.

Uncle William leaned heavily up against a palm tree, his breath was ragged and he sweated profusely. He was not used to vigorous climbs, his limbs were not as agile as they once were. He glanced up at the night sky, usually he would have expected stars to twinkle back but tonight the sky was dark and ominous. The air was heavy and the smell of ozone thick. A storm was brewing, a big one. He had listened to the news earlier in the day; a hurricane was bearing down on the island. Alma had turned into a category 5 hurricane that made it one of the worse to hit the island in many years. There would be undoubtedly many deaths and many homes lost. Still though, he had a task.

When he reached the shack, he saw the warm glow of candlelight within. He was thankful that some of them were home. Knocking on the door he waited, there was no answer. He was about to knock again, when the door cracked.

"Uncle William?" Darrius's voice said softly.

"Yes, I am sorry for coming here, I must talk with you all. May I come in?" he asked.

Darrius opened the door allowing him entry. He had never been in the shack, he had only heard about it from the others. The insides were modest, plain actually. However, there was a warmth, a feeling of home. For an instant he stood there letting the feeling wash through him, it had been many, many years since he had felt the same.

"This way," Darrius motioned.

When he reached the living room, he found Steven and Raffie. They both looked at him with surprise.

"What are you doing here?" Steven asked.

"How did you know where to find it?"

"I am an old man Steven, I hear many, many things. Over the years, I derived a conclusion and figured out where this place was. Do not be concerned, I have not told and will not tell anyone," Uncle William reassured them.

"Why are you here?" Darrius asked.

"Sharon…"

"What about her?" Steven bounded to his feet.

"Jah-Man has her and is holding her captive," Uncle William explained.

"We already know that, we were at the police station when he pulled her from Jail," Raffie explained.

"What you don't know is my brother is using her to get to you two," he pointed to Steven and Raffie.

"What do you mean?" Raffie asked.

"Jah-Man is going to use her to get to you two. He is holding her mama and little brother over her head," Uncle William explained.

"He's what? He has taken them too?" Darrius frowned.

"No, Leeann Cunnings is in jail for the murder of Elmo Lester," Uncle William explained.

"In jail for murder?" Steven frowned.

"I found out that she killed him when she found him trying to rape Sharon," William breathed a sigh.

"Did he, did he…" Steven mumbled.

"No, she killed him before he had the chance," William said seeing his concern.

"So Jah-Man is using her as bait?" Raffie scowled.

"Yes"

"We have to get her out," Steven said his voice growing frantic.

"We will, trust me we will," Darrius said.

"We can't forget what we have to do either."

"He also has another woman there - Yashi," William said.

"Why is she there?" Darrius took notice.

"It would seem that she was abducted by the Frenchman and beaten when she refused to forget dealing with Jah-Man. Fortunately though, Jah-Man had the Frenchman assassinated," William breathed.

"They managed to get Yashi away before she was hurt." "So why did you come

here?" Darrius asked.

"My brother is insane," William said.

"I pleaded with him and demanded that he forget his revenge against you and Raffie," he said to Steven. "But he threatened me also." "He would kill you too?" Darrius asked.

"Yes. I think he would in a heartbeat. He is not the person whom I grew up with, he as turned foul and is evil," William sighed.

"Why tell us?" Raffie asked.

"Because here is the only place where I know I can be safe, I can not go home as his little assassins will be waiting for me," William said.

"Duppy children!" Raffie blurted out.

"Yes, they are your duppy children. Jah-Man has been training orphaned children to become assassins."

"That would explain everything I found out today," Steven said.

"They even killed Mother Francis," William said.

"Killed her, killed her?" Steven gasped feeling his body go numb.

"Yes, they found her body in the kitchen today," William said.

"May I sit down?"

Darrius motioned him to come in; Uncle William sat down in the first chair. His face showed the relief of standing for so long.

"Where are the others?" he asked.

"Eve and Ohpton are at Mama Rose's, we think the duppy children may try to harm her," Darrius explained.

"Why?" Uncle William asked.

"Because she was hiding me," Steven said.

"I do not know where this is going. I do know that we are all in danger," he explained.

"We must find a way off the island."

"We have that already," Darrius said.

"Off the island?" Uncle William looked at him with surprise.

"Yes, you've known for some time that we wanted to go to America. Well now we have the opportunity," Darrius said making sure he left out their plans to steal Jah-Man's money.

"Do you have room for one more?" he bluntly asked.

"I am sure we can fit you," Darrius smiled softy.

There came another knock on the door. The suddenness of it made them all jump. Darrius bounded from his chair and cautiously walked to the door. When he noticed whom it was he swung it quickly open.

Yashi stood on the doorstep her eyes tired. He stared at her bruised and battered face, then leaned forward and gently kissed her swollen cheek.

"Are you okay?" he asked softly.

"I've been better," she breathed stepping inside the house.

"We have to talk."

"I heard what happened, I…" Darrius began to say.

"We have to talk now." she said walking into the living room.

Her gaze quickly shot to Uncle William then snapped back to Darrius.

"What is he doing here?" she looked at him with surprise.

"What are you doing here?" Uncle William countered.

"You do realize that he is Jah-Man's brother?" she said to Darrius.

"We know that, he is also on the run. Jah-Man has threatened him also," Steven said.

"This is getting out of hand - it's becoming too dangerous!" she shook her head.

"You can trust him," Darrius said.

"I trust no one," she snapped.

"You wanted my help but every time I turn around you're coming up with something new."

"He wants to come with us when we go to America," Darrius explained.

"What are you doing here?" Uncle William asked changing the subject.

"She works for the DEA," Darrius said.

"Darrius!" Yashi yelled at him.

"The DEA! You're setting Jah-Man up? This is all a ruse!" William blurted out.

Yashi looked to each of them as the silence filled the room. Darrius had let the cat out of the bag to the one person whom she knew would run back to JahMan. The operation was destroyed, blown apart before it began.

"It's over Darrius," she said turning.

"Wait! Where are you going?" he said grabbing her shoulder.

"Keep your hands off me! I trusted you, and now you endanger my life by telling Jah-Man's brother who I am," she snapped.

"I already told you, you can trust him. He has always looked out for us growing up. He has always helped whenever he could. I trust him Yashi," Darrius quickly explained.

"Do you know why? Do you have any idea why?" she snapped at him.

"What do you mean, what are you talking about?" Darrius withdrew his hand.

"Please this is not the time." Uncle William cut in.

Darrius looked back at him his face showing bewilderment. There was obviously something more going on than he knew about.

"What are you talking about?" he asked softly.

"Maybe you should ask him," she motioned to William.

Darrius turned to him, Uncle William stared at the floor, and he could not meet his eyes.

"Uncle William?" Darrius asked.

"Darrius, would you believe me when I tell you that you really don't want to know?" he asked.

"No, what's going on?" Darrius said his voice becoming even more faint.

Uncle William took a deep breath. Silence grew within the shack, a silence that was thick and penetrating.

"You do not know the truth," he began to say.

"Truth? Truth about what?" Darrius asked frowning.

"For one, the truth about your mama," Uncle William said.

Darrius felt his skin grow cold at the mention of his mama. Everything else seemed to disappear and he hung on his every word.

"You're mama was a special woman, a beautiful woman and you can see much of her beauty in Eve," he said.

"The night she didn't come home she was at the Orion and had just finished work."

"And?" Raffie chimed in.

"She was going home when she happened to witness something," Uncle William said.

"Witness, witness what?" Darrius said his anger growing.

"She witnessed Jah-Man making a drug exchange with a magistrate," Uncle William explained.

"And he caught her? Raffie asked.

"No, he never knew she was there," Uncle William said.

"It was my fault."

"What was?" Darrius snapped.

"I saw your mama hiding in the shadows and I mentioned it to Jah-Man.

He was very unhappy; he went after her and eventually found her walking along the road. He said he tried to reason with her; tried to make her understand," Uncle William said his voice breaking.

"And, and?" Darrius screamed.

"He killed her Darrius, he accidentally killed her that night," Uncle William said his voice but a whisper.

"Jah-Man murdered my mama?" Darrius blurted out his anger out of control.

"Yes, and I have known this for all these years - it was my fault. I should have said nothing. I should have told Jah-Man nothing," Uncle William shook his head.

Darrius rushed forward grabbing Uncle William by the shirt. He hauled him to his feet with an ease that surprised the others.

"How could you? How could you betray her? How could you lie to us for all these years?" he shrieked.

Yashi watched Darrius's anger; she could also see the concern in William's face. It was plain to see that he loved them, loved them all. Maybe Darrius had been right about him, maybe they could trust him. Right now though, it looked as if Darrius was going to kill the man.

"Darrius, stop," she said to him.

"I trusted you. I believed everything you said - how could you?" he snarled.

"Stop it Darrius, it won't change what happened," she said.

"But it's his fault that's she's dead. It's because of him!" he yelled.

"It's Jah-Man's fault Darrius - Jah-Man. He's the one who killed her - he is!" Steven added.

Darrius shook William, and then let him go. William fell back into the chair like a limp doll. Darrius pushed past Yashi and stormed out of the shack. Raffie jumped to his feet to follow but Yashi stopped him.

"He needs to be alone for a while," she said.

"You don't understand. Jah-Man not only killed his mama but he wiped out my family too! I owe him just as much!" Raffie snarled.

"I know about your family. They were supplying information to us for quite some time," she said.

"I'm sorry Raffie. I'm sorry for both you and Darrius and Eve." "He has to pay. Jah-Man

has to pay!" Raffie snarled.

"He will, but not by an act of revenge!" she said.

"Let me deal with him. I'll take care of Jah-Man!" Raffie yelled.

"No, he has to go down our way not yours," she flatly stated.

"Let me deal with Darrius, let me go to him," she asked.

Turning she quickly headed out of the shack, glancing behind she wanted to make sure that none of them followed. She followed the well-worn path away from the shack that led to the waterfall and hot springs. When she got there, she found him sitting on the edge of the hot spring staring down at the water.

She slowed her advance, when she reached him she reached out and gently touched his arm.

"Darrius" she breathed softly.

"No, I don't want you to try and convince me of anything," he whispered his voice barely audible over the waterfall.

"Darrius, you can't change the past, you can't bring your mama back," she said lightly stroking his arm.

"I may not be able to change it but I can get revenge for what he did. I can make my mama rest in peace," he said looking into her eyes.

"You have to keep to the plan, stay focused. Things are moving quickly now. You have to make plans if you and the others want to get out of here and back to the states. I have your passports coming - they should be here tomorrow," she said.

"Doesn't matter anymore, things have changed," he shook his head.

"No they haven't, nothing has changed," she said.

"Haven't they? I know now that's what's changed - I know the truth!"

"What about the others? Do they have to pay the price for your revenge?" she asked.

"They can continue on with the plan. They can get his money and go to America," he said.

"And what about Sharon? Does she become a casualty in all this, her mama and brother too?"

Darrius stared into her eyes her words sinking in deep. He loved the others and would put his life on the line for any of them. He also was fighting his anger, his wanton desire for revenge.

He wasn't surprised either, he had suspected all along that Jah-Man was responsible for her death. Eve would be devastated.

"We have to get Sharon out," he said.

"We will but you have to stick to the plan. This is crucial" "We don't have a plan," he

breathed.

"You do now, everything is going down day after tomorrow. I'm doing the exchange at the Orion. I'm not sure where yet, but it will be there," she said.

"We have to know where," he said.

"Do you want to know something else?" she said forcing a painful smile.

"More good news?" he squinted.

"You're going to be heisting 16 million dollars," she said smiling.

Darrius looked at her his eyes widening. Slowly his jaw dropped until she though she would have to push it closed.

"You can't be serious?" he asked.

"16 million, and yes I am serious," she laughed.

"I can't believe it - I just can't believe it!" he shook his head.

"Well you better start believing it, day after tomorrow it's going to be here," she nodded.

"This isn't going to get you in trouble? Losing all that money?" he asked.

"My government won't like it, but the money is drug money. The stuff was just sitting in storage nothing more," she shrugged.

"I'll probably take some flak for losing it but as long as we shut Jah-Man down I should come out of it okay," she smiled.

"How much security is there going to be? I mean you're not going to be hauling around a briefcase with 16 million all by yourself are you?" he asked. "No, so whatever you plan on better be pretty crafty," she said. "Can you tell me what type of case you're going to be bringing it in?" "I can find out," she smiled.

"I still want Jah-Man to pay for my mama's death. I want him to pay with his own blood," he said solemnly.

"He'll pay Darrius, pay by doing hard time in prison," she said.

"That's not enough, he has to be made to understand what he did, made to bleed," Darrius snarled.

"Violence isn't the only way. Think of it this way, you and the others pull off getting that briefcase from him and you'll all be rich! What do you think your mama would think?" she asked.

"I don't know. I would like to think she would be happy but I just don't know," he shook his head.

"I think she would. I think she would be proud that you chose a different path instead of reducing yourself to your enemy," Yashi smiled.

"Is that suppose to make me feel better?" he grinned.

"Maybe, but I can think of something else that would," she said.

Grabbing his shirt, she tugged and pulled until it slipped over his head. She then went for his shorts. Moments later he was naked before her.

"Get into the water," she said giving him a slight push.

Darrius slipped into the hot refreshing water. Watching, Yashi slipped her own clothes off and stepped into the water next to him. Reaching up she touched his face; he could feel the smoothness of her body against his, her taut nipples, the curvature of her pelvis as it touched against his thigh. She stimulated him tremendously; taking her into his arms, he watched her wince.

"Sorry, I'm sore," she whispered to him.

"Then slide down into the water with me," he said pulling her down.

She closed her eyes as the water enveloped her body; she then felt his lips as he began to kiss along her neck and shoulder. Rising up out of the water she felt his tongue dance down between her breasts then hungrily circle around her left nipple. He was excited also; she could feel it as her hand stroked his <u>buddy</u> beneath the water.

"Love me," she breathed into his ear.

His actions became more bold his hand reaching between her legs, touching her <u>pum pum</u>. His touch was electric and it made every fiber of her being spring to life.

"I want you Darrius - I want you," she whispered.

She felt him enter his strong body supporting her as his lips hungrily caressed her upper torso. The pleasure was so intense, so fulfilling that for a brief moment all the pain in her body and all the problems in the world went away. Wrapping her arms around his neck, she felt his hands grab hold of her waist slowly moving down to her buttocks.

"I love you Yashi," he breathed to her as he tensed then released.

Moments later their arms tightened around each other, as they remained motionless. Yashi felt so complete, so full, she only hoped that the future wouldn't tear them apart.

Chapter 19

Eighty miles off the <u>Jamdung coast</u>, the freighter Joule rode up and down each massive wave. Captain Preston Jackson hung onto the center support post as the next wave battered his vessel. The Joule was a 650-foot cargo freighter. Leaving the <u>Azores</u> three days before, he had tried desperately to outrun the monster that was now beginning to slam them about. Their port of destination was Miami Florida; they were carrying everything from sugar to engine parts. The huge crates that swamped the deck were lashed down with massive cables and the howling wind made them vibrate; the sound resonating within the bridge of the ship.

Hurricane <u>Alma</u> had started like all hurricanes start, the warm waters between Africa and South America were breeding grounds. Alma had started small and nobody really showed much concern. Her track would lead her further north and away from the Americas. However, in a sudden shift, the tropical depression had grown rapidly and had turned into a level 1 hurricane. Still nobody thought there was much to worry about – until Alma rapidly grew to a level 5.

Captain Jack, as his crew liked to call him, had made the decision to cross when Alma had only been a tropical depression. Once she turned to a level 1 hurricane, he had contemplated heading north to outrun it. He had made the wrong call.

Now Alma was clipping them from behind with waves and swells that towered to 50 feet or more. Many of his men were seasick; the motion of the ship causing even the simplest of acts to be more like a circus show.

"Captain do you think it would be wise to head to South America, maybe skirt this monster to the side?" the first mate asked.

"We turn in this and we risk broaching, this ship would be rolled. Our only choice is to stay on course and pray," he said looking out the forward window.

"Most of the crew is sick…" the first mate began to say.

"Stay on course," Captain Jack said softly.

The first mate nodded and resumed his position on the other side of the bridge. Joule's bow plowed deep into the oncoming wave. Thousands of tons of water slithered across the deck as the bow came up from beneath the water. Captain Jack watched the motion of his ship, and then made his way over to the first mate.

"Take on more water, settle us down in the water more," he said to him.

"But, but sir…" the first mate said softly.

" We've taken on all the ballast we can."

Captain Jack said nothing as he continued to stare out the forward windows as the water pelted them. There was nothing more they could do - nothing but pray.

Delicia turned the key of the door lock and entered the room. The inside was brightly lit.

Sharon sat in one of the chairs against the large glass window. Her gaze then turned to the strewn mass of ribbon scattered across the floor. Sharon stared at her with contempt.

"I see you found it," Delicia said not smiling.

"What didn't you expect me to?" Sharon snapped.

"Of course I wanted you to find it, that's why I left it," she said walking over and sitting in the chair opposite her.

"So, what do you want?" Sharon asked.

"I've gotten what I want," she smiled.

"So?"

"I've come here to talk with you," Delicia said crossing her legs.

Sharon stared at her; Delicia wore a tight halter-top that freely displayed the shape of her breasts. She wore a short skirt that most women would constantly be pulling down. She on the other hand, let it ride up. She also wore an array of jewelry, a <u>mass</u> of gold chains around her neck and silver amulets around her wrists and ankles.

"You dress like a <u>skettel</u>," Sharon said not holding back.

"Thank you, at least I have what I want," Delicia countered.

"All you are to anyone is a sex object," Sharon spat.

"Of course, why do you think we were designed the way we are?" she laughed.

"I'm sure Steven thought the Prestone way."

Sharon frowned at the mention of Steven's name. Images of Steven naked, thrusting himself inside of her was enough to almost bring her to tears. She fought them back.

"You've never had him, you've never <u>worked</u> him have you?" Delicia said a smile forming on her face. Sharon said nothing.

"I was the reason why Jah-Man put a price on his head. I tried to make an advance on him. I threw my body at him and he turned me down!" she said.

"But he came to me to try and persuade Jah-Man to leave him alone and all the rest of you. I managed to persuade him and bargained with him…"

"That you would help him if he made love to you?" Sharon snarled.

"Yes, oh yes. You cannot imagine the way he made me feel! The sensation of him deep inside within my <u>pum pum</u>." she began to brag.

"Shut up!" Sharon said turning away.

"Does that bother you? Does it turn your stomach to think that he gave himself to me and not you?" Delicia said tauntingly.

"Shut up"

"I came here for another reason," Delicia began to say.

"I found out a bit of information, something that was, well, shocking." "What that you're a slut?" Sharon snapped.

"No, that Eve and Darrius are actually Jah-Man's children," she said.

Sharon turned looking sharply at Delicia. How she found this information out she would never know. It was possible that Jah-Man had told her, but she highly doubted it.

"So what?" Sharon acted stupid.

"So, do you realize that neither of them know this?"

"What does it matter?" Sharon asked playing stupid.

"Jah-Man doesn't want them to know. For some reason he doesn't want them to know that he is there father," she said.

"He would probably pay handsomely to keep that secret intact."

"You're talking about blackmailing Jah-Man?" Sharon turned to her laughing.

"Not me directly," Delicia said.

"Who then?" Sharon asked.

"Diamond?" Delicia said.

"Why tell me this?" Sharon changed the subject.

"Because, because you could get in on this, maybe get enough money to get off to the United States," she said.

"I don't understand you Delicia, you let me find a video tape of you and Steven having sex, and then you tell me you'd like to help me get off the island? You're making no sense," Sharon shook her head.

"I'm tired of Jah-Man, tired of being at his beck and call. I don't like you or the others I never have. But I do admire you all for what you want and how you're going about getting it," she said.

"So you want to blackmail Jah-Man? You're out of your mind. In case you haven't noticed, the man is insane," Sharon pointed out.

"Jah-Man is not the point, his <u>mass</u> is," Delicia said.

"You do this and they'll find you in a ditch someplace," Sharon said.

"I want no part of it," she shook her head.

"I know him and I know how to get around him," she smiled.

"Good, then you don't need my help. If you haven't noticed, I'm being held prisoner."

"I can get you out," Delicia said.

Sharon stared at her wondering if she was being sincere. Her gut told her Delicia was not to be trusted, but any chance to get away made her mind race with possibilities.

"And what if Diamond blackmails you?" Sharon asked.

"I have an ace in the hole," Delicia smiled.

Suddenly the door opened. To the surprise of the women Diamond walked in closing the door behind him. Delicia looked at him, the surprise clearly written on her face.

"What are you doing here?" she demanded.

"I was asked to come here," he said.

"By whom?" Delicia frowned.

"You - I got a message at the front desk that you wanted me to come here," Diamond's words trailed.

Delicia bounded from the bed, she dashed into the bookshelf and yanked out a bundle of books. Moments later she yanked out another bundle the books falling to the floor in heaps.

"My God it's gone!" she shrieked.

"It's gone!"

"What's gone?" Sharon asked.

"The tape, the tape is gone," Delicia turned to them.

"He has it - he has the tape!"

"What tape?" Diamond asked.

"This tape you fool," Jah-Man said surprising them all.

Walking into the room, he shook the tape in his hand. Everyone drew silent as he walked along the room and over to the television set.

"Did you think I was that much of a fool?" he said to Delicia.

"I don't know, I don't know what you're talking about honey," she said in a soothing voice.

"Really?" he said pushing the tape into the video cassette player then pushed the play button.

The television came on and the lines of static were quickly replaced with images. The images were of Diamond and Eve. Diamond giving Eve drugs and then having sex with her.

"You evil witch," Diamond breathed softy.

"I have watched this video over and over and each time I watch it I see my little girl, my daughter being manipulated and used," Jah-Man said sighing.

"This is my little girl," he said turning to Diamond.

"I was paid by Delicia to do it," he said drawing back further away from him.

"I know you were and I told Delicia that I wanted her to stay away from Eve and Darrius. Still though, she pushed defying my wishes!" he said moving closer to Diamond.

Suddenly he lashed out with his fist striking Delicia across the face. Delicia staggered back hitting the bookcase, the blow stunning her. Jah-Man continued to advance towards Diamond.

"You have taken many women, many women and have made a lot of money in the process. I have even used you from time to time with clients, but your actions with my daughter, my daughter have made you cross the line."

"I didn't know. I had no idea that she was your daughter," Diamond said holding up his hands.

"Of course you didn't. But there was also no profit in it for you except from what Delicia was paying you. You knew better Diamond, you should have known," Jah-Man said softly.

"I'm sorry Jah-Man, I didn't mean to, I wouldn't have," Diamond pleaded.

"That my boy, is water under the bridge. Your words come too late. The damage you wrought can not be taken back," he said his right arm reaching behind him.

Diamond felt a chill run through him; the look in Jah-Man's eyes told him there was no chance of escape. With a burst of energy, driven by fear, he leapt towards the man. Jah-Man hadn't expected his move; the gun he was beginning to withdraw fell out of his hand hitting the floor in front of Sharon.

Jah-Man was quick though; he grabbed hold of Diamond and wheeled him around slamming him hard into the mirrored dresser. The mirror shattered into thousands of tiny fragments as Diamond bounced off and hit the floor. He recovered quickly and again moved against Jah-Man. His fist slammed hard into Jah-Man's stomach. But the man just laughed and grabbed Diamond around the throat.

"You think you can fight me boy? Do you think you have the strength to over power the mighty Jah-Man?" he snarled.

"Please..." Diamond pleaded.

"You are nothing to me, nothing, I have put up with your arrogant ways far too long now," Jah-Man snarled squeezing tightly against Diamond's neck.

Seconds later, a snapping sound was heard. Diamond's arms dropped hanging slack against his body. Jah-Man had snapped his neck. Letting the body go he watched it crumple to the floor, then turned his attention to Delicia who pressed herself against the bookcase.

"And you my dear, you are far too nosey. You have a real labba mout. It wasn't enough to have wealth and power and to be the woman at my side. You wanted it all, all for yourself," he snarled drawing closer.

"Stay away!" she shrieked.

"Oh I am going to make you pay the most," he began to laugh.

"You, you played me for a fool," he said reaching down and scooping up the broken videotape Sharon had smashed.

"I already know about this. Do you think you're the only one who can manipulate others?"

Delicia's face dropped and her head slowly shook from side to side.

"You wanted him - you always wanted him," Jah-Man snarled.

"No, you have it all wrong Jah-Man. I never wanted him - he forced me and raped me," she yelled.

"Your lies mean nothing any more Delicia, nothing," he breathed as his hand reached up to grab her.

Suddenly there was a loud rapport as a bullet tore into one of the books above Jah-Man's head. He wheeled around his eyes showing intense anger and rage. Sharon sat on the end of the bed Jah-Man's pistol held in her hands.

"Put the gun down," he growled.

"Move away from her. Move away or I put the next bullet where it counts," she said the gun shaking in her hands.

"You think you can kill someone?" Jah-Man grinned.

"The Babylon think I did, so why not?" she spat.

"Put the gun down and I will let you live," he said again.

"Delicia, move away from him, come over here," Sharon said ignoring Jah-Man.

Delicia moved quickly away, Jah-Man eyed her as she moved. When she was close to Sharon, she looked back at him.

"You never wanted to share your life with me, you never truly loved me," she said to him.

"I always loved you," he said softly.

"You never loved me. You only love that other woman, Evelyn - Evelyn Lawson," Delicia said.

At the mention of Evelyn's name, Jah-Man's face contorted in anger. Delicia had brought up a subject he obviously tried very hard to forget.

"You will die right along with her for mentioning that name," he breathed softly.

"Time for us to go," Sharon said keeping the gun trained on him.

"She can not be trusted," Jah-Man said to Sharon.

"You don't think I know that? Regardless, she doesn't deserve to die," Sharon said heading for the door.

"Run far and run fast, because when I come for you will not see the light of morning," he gave her an evil grin.

"I should just put a bullet into you now and end the problem," she said.

"You are not a killer," he said.

"Stop yapping and let's get the heck out of here!" Delicia said to Sharon.

Sharon kept the gun trained on him as she slipped through the door. When she was through, she shut it and locked it.

"We need wheels," she said to Delicia.

"Mine is down in the yard."

"What about guards?" Sharon asked.

"Unless they hear from Jah-Man, they won't bother me," Delicia said.

"Yes, maybe not you but what about me?" Sharon asked.

"Well, maybe by the way you're dressed," Delicia said.

Sharon scowled at her; she didn't need a reminder that she was wearing a nearly see-through negligee.

"Don't worry about it, you're with me," Delicia added.

They dashed down the long spiral staircase to the first floor. Once there Delicia was the first one out the front door. Three guards stood with weapons, they turned upon seeing her. When they saw Sharon, their eyes widened, Sharon slipped the pistol beneath her arm covering her breasts that could clearly be seen through the thin fabric.

"She's with me," Delicia said to them.

One of the men nodded, as they casually walked down the stairs another one of the guards yelled to them.

"Stop!" he yelled.

Delicia turned but Sharon froze where she stood. The guard came down the stairs his automatic weapon still cradled in the crook of his arm.

"Why does she not have shoes?" the man said to them. "And why is she dressed so, so…" his words trailed as he stared at her.

"I'm taking her to the doctors, she doesn't feel well," Delicia lied.

"She looks pretty fine to me," the man grinned showing his missing front teeth.

Sharon didn't move if she did one of the guards might see the gun tucked beneath her arm. The guard moved closer, then she felt his hand pat her behind. Turning she scowled that the man and moved away from him. Delicia opened the door to the Rover and Sharon slipped into the cool leather seat. Moments later they zoomed out the front gate.

"That was close, real close!" Delicia sighed.

"Filthy animal, I should have boxed him where he stood for touching me," Sharon snapped.

"Sometimes, having someone is better than having no one," Delicia said.

"So what happens now?" Sharon asked.

"I don't know Jah-Man will want both our heads on a platter!" Delicia said.

"Can I ask you something?"

"Depends"

"Why did you help me back there? Why did you risk your life?" Delicia asked.

"Especially after, after…" her words trailed.

"I risked not only my own life, but my mamas and brothers," Sharon sighed remembering Jah-Man's threat.

"I'm sorry about them," Delicia said.

"Yeah, me too, look just bring me to town and drop me off. You can go where ever you want," Sharon said.

"But I don't have anywhere to go," Delicia said.

"That's not my problem," Sharon said softly.

"You can take care of yourself well enough." "Can I come with you?" she

asked.

"No"

Delicia said nothing more; there was nothing more to say. She had burned her bridge with Sharon years ago and there would be no rebuilding it. The Rover quickly made it to town; Delicia pulled it over in front of the large covered building that sat in the middle of town. Sharon opened the door and sat there for a moment. She then slipped from the seat, keeping her breasts and the gun hidden. Turning she looked back at Delicia.

"If I were you, I'd keep driving, go to the other side of the island," Sharon said.

"And go where? It is still an island." Delicia replied.

"I'm sorry for you Delicia, sorry that you couldn't see the error of your ways years ago. Family is more important than anything else, including money," Sharon said.

"Could you do a favor for me?" Delicia asked.

"Depends"

"When you see him, could you give Steven a message?" she asked.

Sharon looked at her the air again being sucked from her lungs as she remembered that scorching video. Delicia didn't wait for an answer.

"Could you tell him, tell him that I think he's special and I'm thinking of him always?" she asked.

Sharon just stared at her saying nothing; she then slowly nodded then closed the car door. Seconds later Delicia zoomed away leaving her standing there. For a long moment, Sharon stood there watching until the vehicle disappeared. Then, she turned and headed for the outskirts of town and to sanctuary, the shack.

Mr. Griff took a long swill of bourbon then capped the bottle tucking it back into his pants pocket. Wiping his unshaven face on his sleeve, he stared up at the sky. Ominous clouds were rolling in, dense, thick and oppressive. He turned and headed back to the plane. Drawing near he turned and saw a vehicle coming churning a cloud of dust from the dry road. Spitting, he stood there and watched as the dust cloud settled.

Yashi emerged from the drivers seat along with Darrius and Raffie. He stared intently at Yashi.

"What happened to you?" he asked spitting again.

"Trouble" was all she said.

"Here is the money we promised; the rest when we arrive," Darrius said handing him a container with all their savings.

"You might as well hang onto it," he said.

"Why?" Raffie asked.

"Take a look at that sky," Griff pointed upwards.

"We have one hell of a hurricane coming."

"But can't we fly out of here before it arrives?" Darrius asked.

"You want to leave tomorrow night right?" he asked.

"Yes, tomorrow afternoon or evening," Darrius nodded.

"Well you might be in trouble, this monster that I hear is coming could be on us by then," Griff said.

"What are you saying? You won't fly us out of here?" Raffie cut in.

"No, but I'm not going to crash my plane by trying to fly through a hurricane."

"So take your money and keep your end of the deal," Darrius said handing him the money.

Griff hesitated, and then reached out taking the case. He opened the lid and looked at the money within.

"It's there," Raffie said.

"I'm sure it is," he said.

"Is there any way you people could leave any earlier?" "Not likely," Yashi said.

"Okay, where do you want me to meet you?" he asked.

"Montego Bay," Darrius said.

"Oh brother, right into snake territory," Griff shook his head.

"This is how things are going to go. If the weather permits me to fly, I'll be there. If not, then I sit right where I am now," he pointed to the ground.

"Fair enough," Yashi said.

"What about passports and all the paperwork for you people?" Griff asked. "Right here," Yashi said handing him a zippered bag.

Griff took it and opened it glancing at the small books within. He then closed the bag and looked up at them.

"I'll wait for an hour, if you people don't show, I keep the money and we're even," he said spitting again.

"Just be there," Darrius said coldly.

As they drove home, Darrius stared out the side window. Suddenly he turned to Yashi.

"You know about these people, do you think this guy is going to rip us off?" he asked her.

"No, I think he'll be there as long as this hurricane coming doesn't ground him," she said.

"Maybe we should plan something for after this hurricane, wait till it blows over?" Raffie said from the back.

"Can't, the exchange has to go down tomorrow. My superiors are sending in a few men with the money. Look, I can't be tied with losing this money. My career is on the line and I personally don't want to flip hamburgers at some burger joint," she said.

"Are you going to come with us?" Darrius said softly.

"Don't know yet. Once this goes down, I might have to stay here for the clean up. We have to ensure that once Jah-Man is out of the picture that nobody else steps into his place and starts the whole operation off again."

Yashi waited for Darrius to respond, he didn't. She understood what he was thinking, how he was feeling. Tomorrow might mean the last time they ever see each other. She didn't like it either, but she was a realist, if this was the way it was meant to be then so be it. Still though, her strength was not enough to stop her heart from aching.

Sharon stood at the end of the trail; in the distance was the shack. She stood there staring at it, never before had their hideaway looked so secure, so reassuring to her. She half expected the others to be milling about; instead, the place was quiet and serene. When she arrived at the front door, she hesitated, then reached out and turned the doorknob. The inside was quiet, empty, where had the others gone? From what she knew, their jobs were virtually gone at the Orion, so they couldn't be there. Suddenly from the back hallway, a door opened.

Steven walked out and closed the door behind him. When he looked up, he locked eyes with Sharon. For an instant, they both stood motionless their eyes locked on one another. He then rushed down the hallway to her. Sharon wanted to rush to him, wanted to hold him tightly but the memory of the video tape flashed through her mind. She held her hands up stopping him.

"How, where…" he stuttered stopping.

"I escaped with Delicia," she said softly.

"I am so relieved! I was worried sick about you!" he smiled.

"Steven…" Sharon began to say.

He could see the concern in her face, something was wrong something was bothering her.

"What's wrong Sharon?" he asked his smile fading.

Sharon turned her back to him, walked over to the window and looked out. She didn't turn around to look at him, she didn't want to.

"Delicia, I found a video tape that she had," she breathed softly.

"What where you thinking?" she said her voice but a whisper.

Steven's blood ran cold, somehow Delicia had tricked him, she had video taped the whole thing.

"I was trying to solve a problem," he breathed.

"I didn't want to."

"Didn't want to?" Sharon nearly yelled.

"You sure looked like you wanted to!"

"She said she would talk to Jah-Man and make him understand that it was a mistake. She said she could make him forget about me, all of us," he said.

"I did what I thought was right."

"You were intimate with her, you made love to her!" Sharon said beginning to cry.

"Sharon, you have to believe me I didn't want to. I begged her to help me but that was her price," he tried to explain.

"Her price, her price?" Sharon scowled.

"What if she gets pregnant?" Sharon snapped.

Steven blinked at her the words caught in his throat. He had never considered the fact that she could, that he could father a child with a woman he despised.

"I didn't think…" he muttered.

"No, you didn't think!" she yelled at him.

"You didn't think about that nor did you think about me!"

Steven shot her a hard look his face quickly showing his anger.

"That's where you're wrong. I did think about you. In fact it was thinking about you that even got me through."

It was Sharon's turn to stare at him wide eyed.

"I care about the others and I would do whatever it takes to help them, but - I love you," he said softly.

"You were all I could think about and after all these years I never realized just how much I was in love with you. I thought about Eve but in reality it was you," he said.

Sharon's mouth dropped, she never realized how he felt about her. She was always hiding her feelings, trying not to interfere with the others personal lives. Now, she stood here in front of the man she fell in love with listening to him tell how much he loved her.

She began to cry.

"Please Sharon, try to understand, try to forgive me. I never wanted to, I never intended to. It was my putting Delicia off, that started this whole mess," he explained.

"You really love me?" she breathed.

"Yes, I really love you," he smiled at her.

Sharon fell into Steven's open arms; he wrapped them tightly around her drawing her close.

"Oh Steven. I've wanted you for so, so long. I wanted to tell you so long ago but I couldn't. For many nights I've dreamed of this, being in your arms and making love to you," she said as she continued to cry.

"As I did you," he whispered to her.

She looked up at his smiling face; bringing his hand up he wiped away the wetness from her cheeks. Slowly, ever so slowly their lips gently touched. At first, their kiss was soft, supple, and then as if a light switch had been turned on, it became frenzied and intense. They kissed with uncontrolled passion. His lips moved from hers to her cheek, then her ear and neck. Sharon felt her legs grow weak at his touch. He sensed this, his strong arms holding her close.

"The others?" she whispered between gasps of passion.

"Gone" he replied his tongue lightly flicked across the lower part of her ear.

"I want to," she breathed.

"We have time," he replied.

When they reached her bedroom, she turned to him yanking and tearing at his clothing. Within moments, he stood naked before her, his excitement for her clearly showing.

Her heart raced as he reached up and lightly touched the side of her face bringing his lips to hers again. Slowly he lowered her to the bed his body becoming her live blanket. His hand squeezed and kneaded her right breast the nipple swelling to his touch. Pulling and tearing he slipped the negligee off her leaving her exposed. She laid back the wanton look of passion clearly written on her face. She then extended her arms to him.

For hours, they explored and teased each other to insane heights of passion until finally she felt him press against her. At that instant, they stared into each other's eyes, there was nothing to say, the look of love they gave each other was enough. They hungrily kissed as he slowly slid himself deep within her. Her whole body trembled to his touch; years of desire had built to his one tender moment. Her desires quickly rose and fell in crescendo with each thrust. She had never experienced such passion, never realized how an act of love could be so intense. Suddenly his rhythm became faster more chaotic then, abruptly, she felt him release.

"I love you," she breathed in his ear.

"I love you too, more than you can possibly know," he replied kissing her ear.

They lay entwined; his body pressed up behind her his hand cupping her left breast. Sharon could feel him inside, the warmth of his body against hers, his hot breath against her shoulder. Staring out the window of her room, she was surprised that the sky was dark, ominous. A storm was coming, a big one.

"Where are they others?" she whispered to him.

"Eve and Ohpton are at Mama Rose's, in case the duppy children, which are orphaned children Jah-Man has transformed into professional killers." He said pecking her shoulder.

"Darrius and Raffie?" she asked.

"Gone to meet this guy named Jack Griff, he's a pilot who's going to fly us out tomorrow after we get the money from Jah-Man," Steven said.

Sharon turned onto her back; Steven slid to the side then slowly began to kiss her breast lingering casually over her swollen nipple.

"We're going ahead with the plan?" she asked.

"Yes, this time tomorrow we should be in the air and heading for the United States," he said sliding his arm around her stomach.

"Steven, Jah-Man wants me and the rest of us dead!" she said. "How are we going to get

close enough to him to get his money?" "We have a plan," he smiled.

"Darrius's girlfriend, Yashi is helping us," he explained.

"I know but…"

"She already got our passports and papers," he said running his hand gently over her pelvis.

"But…" she began to say closing her eyes. His touch was stimulating, she tried to keep focused on the matters at hand but she found it difficult. Her heart raced with excitement, with each stroke, each kiss from him.

Again, they made passionate love.

Rain began to beat down and the wind gradually increased. Mama Rose lit the oil lamp in the kitchen. All day long, the candy shop was empty, not one child came in to see her or to get her treats. Eve and Ohpton tried to be as supportive as possible; they could see the tension, the disappointment in Mama Rose. Without her schoolers, there was nothing more for her. As night began to fall and the wind began to pick up, a new worry seeped into her.

"What about the others, Steven, Darrius, Sharon and Raffie?" she asked. "Shouldn't they be here with you?"

"They have things to work out for tomorrow," Eve explained their plans.

Mama Rose frowned upon listening to them. It was clear that she didn't approve with what they planned.

"Stealing from Jah-Man is a dangerous thing," she pointed out.

"We're not really stealing from him, just from some other yardie," Eve smiled.

"Our friend in the DEA is helping us."

"You can trust her?" Mama Rose asked.

"Darrius does and I trust Darrius," Eve said.

"We don't have any other choice," Ohpton spoke up. We all have lost our jobs at the Orion. We either make it now or we're stuck here for the rest of our lives."

"It is dangerous, one of you could be hurt or killed," she shook her head.

"We'll be fine. We already have a plane that will take us to Miami," Eve smiled.

"In this weather? You have heard that a big, big hurricane is bearing down on us?" she asked.

"We will hopefully be in the air and heading for the United States long before it hits us," Ohpton added.

"And what if something goes wrong? Have you planned for problems that may arise?" Mama Rose asked.

"Nothing will go wrong," Eve said.

"You can not say that, you can not predict the future," she said shaking her finger at them.

"No, but like I said we don't have a choice," Ohpton said.

There was a clicking sound from the storefront. They were on edge the sound making them all jump. Someone was coming through the front door. Ohpton grabbed the first thing his hand encountered, which was a large butcher knife that Mama Rose had used to cut a succulent rum pie she made.

Junior appeared in the doorway, his gaze went to his mama, then to Eve and finally, to Ohpton and the knife in his hand.

"What are they doing here?" he barked shaking off the water from his raincoat.

"They are here because they feel my life is in danger," Mama Rose said.

"Danger? Danger from what, the only thing that could cause you to be in danger is if you are still allowing Winter to stay here," he snapped.

"He has left," she said.

"I came here mama because I want you to come with me," he said.

"Go? Go where?" she frowned.

"We can leave the island. I have money," he said limiting what he wanted to say.

"I can not go, my home is here. It has always been here and it will always be here," she shook her head.

"Don't be foolish, there is nothing here but poverty. With my money we could live much, much better than this," he pointed out.

"Your money is blood money Junior," Mama Rose pointed out.

"Blood money? I have earned that money. I risked all to get it!" he yelled.

"You have lost your way, lost all that is important. Money is not the only thing in life and that is something you have never learned. That is something Jaco tried to show you," she said.

"My brother, my brother was a fool. He thought that hard work would get him riches and get him off the island, but he was wrong!" Junior spat.

"No, he was right, you have embraced the darkness Junior. I fear for you and fear for your life," Mama Rose said her voice breaking.

"You never cared about my life only Jaco's!" he yelled.

Eve and Ohpton felt like crawling into the wooden floor. They felt sad for Mama Rose. They also felt some pity for Junior who couldn't see the love his mama had for him and others.

"That is not true, I loved you both so much - so much," she shook her head.

"If you loved us so much then why didn't you try to give us a better life?" he yelled.

"Did you think we would want to run a candy shop when we got older?"

"No, I tried to give you the best that I could. I didn't want you both to end up along the road or in the gutter. I wanted you both to have hope. I tried to give you hope!" she cried.

"You gave us nothing, nothing but despair," he shook his head.

"I love you mama but I don't agree with you."

There came the loud sound of a horn blaring. Junior was the first to jump his hand reaching for the maggy under his raincoat. Ohpton took notice and nudged Eve not to get to close to the man. Peering out the side window he tried to discern who was in the Rover outside of the house. The pouring rain limited his field of view.

"Damn" he breathed sliding the pistol back into the waistband of his pants.

Darrius and Raffie ran up to the front door. They pulled their raincoats over their heads trying to keep the rain from running down their backs. Darrius was the first to knock; Junior opened the door allowing them inside. When Darrius dropped his coat and looked at him he frowned.

"Hello Junior," he said.

"Darrius!" Eve smiled at him.

"Look, there is a big storm blowing in. Can you get Mama Rose to come home with us? It would be much safer for her if she did," Darrius asked.

"I can't get her to come with me, what makes you think she's going to go with you?" Junior scoffed.

"Mama Rose, please come with us, at least for tonight," Darrius asked her ignoring Junior's comment.

"I will not run. I will not leave my home out of fear," she shook her head.

"Just for tonight Mama Rose, just tonight!" Eve pleaded.

"No"

"You all can go. I will not leave here till tomorrow anyway," Junior said.

"You're staying with me?" Mama Rose looked at him with surprise.

"Yes mama, I will stay with you tonight," he nodded.

"Did you not think I would?"

"Actually, none of us did," Raffie said.

"I will stay until tomorrow and then I will leave and go my own way. Maybe tonight we can talk, maybe tonight I can convince you to come with me," he said to her.

"Come on, we have to get going," Darrius said.

"Are you sure you will be all right?" Eve asked Mama Rose.

"I will be fine. You go along, come back in the morning and have tea with me," she smiled warmly.

They all gave her a hug and a kiss then disappeared out into the torrential rain. Mama Rose watched the Rover pull away quickly disappearing from sight. She then turned to her son.

"Come let us have a nice cup of tea," she smiled to him.

Junior was about to say something but stopped himself. Tonight he would try not to argue with her. Their relationship had been marred with arguments; tonight he would try to be different. Tonight he would show her how much he loved her.

Sharon slipped into her clothes under Steven's watchful eyes. She knew he was staring at her, absorbing her naked body. They had made love repeatedly, she knew that her love was genuine, knew that his was too. Each time it felt <u>Prestone</u>, each time the passion had been intense, unyielding. They would have continued to <u>wuk</u> all night but they knew that the others would be arriving shortly. They were both surprised that no one had showed up already.

"Steven…" she began to say.

"Was it like you expected?" she softly asked.

"Better" he smiled.

"It felt like we were meant to be together, forever," he smiled.

"I have to tell you something. I have to give you a message," she said.

"Delicia wanted me to tell you that you will always be special to her; always be close to her," Sharon said trying to remember Delicia's words.

"That's nice," he said slipping his shirt over his head.

"I really don't care what Delicia feels about me," he said.

"You on the other hand, I love you Sharon," he said softly.

"I love you too Steven. I have another problem. I have to figure a way to help my mama and little brother. I'm fearful that Jah-Man will go after them to get to me," she said softly.

"Maybe we can figure a way to get her out of jail?" he said.

Suddenly, over the sound of the pounding rain they heard a vehicle approach. Their conversation abruptly ended as they both headed for the living room. Steven glanced out the side window at the white Rover. Moments later the front door burst open and the others entered. Upon seeing Sharon, there was a joyous reunion. They all gave many hugs, many smiles, and each had a story to tell.

Junior sighed heavily, for the last two hours he had repeatedly tried to convince his mama to come with him. At first, he had tried the soft, emotional route then when that didn't work, he began to grow angry. His voice raised and he got up pacing the room with frustration. He didn't know what to do, thoughts ran through his mind, thoughts of just leaving.

"For the last time mama, please come with me," he snapped at her.

"No son, you must go on your own. This is the day I knew would come. Go and try to be happy," she said.

Junior stared at her; a knot was welling up in his stomach. Still though he turned and grabbed his coat. Slipping it on he headed for the door. Outside the rain beat down in buckets. Never since his brother's death had he felt so guilty. Grabbing the doorknob, he opened the door. For an instant, he stood there staring his eyes not believing what they were seeing. Standing in front of him was a small figure swathed in a dark green raincoat. The hood was drawn up hiding the person's facial features. In the dim light, he wouldn't have been able to make them out anyway. The figure just stood there saying nothing.

"My mama's shop is closed, go away and come back tomorrow," he said angrily.

The figure continued to stand there the rain running off its tiny form.

"Are you deaf? I said there is no candy, go home!" he snarled.

"I do not want candy," a soft meek voice said barely audible over the pounding rain.

"Then go home, there is nothing here for you," he spat.

"I came here for another reason," the tiny voice said.

"Another reason?" Junior frowned.

"I have a message," the tiny person said.

"A message, from whom?"

"A message from Jah-Man," the tiny voice spoke.

Junior's eyes grew wide with horror as he finally figured out whom the tiny person was. Reaching for the gun in the back of his pants, he tried to quickly draw it out. From beneath the child's raincoat, a small thick barrel protruded. There was a soft rapport from the end of it.

Junior felt the bullet drive into his stomach. The pain was excruciating as he toppled to the floor. The tiny figure came further into the house. Reaching up a small hand pulled back the hood. Delvin Hellton stood there staring at a bewildered Junior. In his hand was a spechie. He walked over standing to the right of him making sure the doorway to the kitchen was visible.

"Jah-Man wanted me to give you a message," the small boy said.

"You will not get the chance to spend his money."

Junior gasped his mouth hanging open in surprise. He tried to say something but his voice failed him. The last thing he saw was the dull flash from the end of the barrel, the bullet penetrated his skull and he fell back dead.

Delvin walked casually towards the kitchen, when he entered through the doorway he found Mama Rose sitting at her kitchen table.

At first, there was a look of surprise on her face but it quickly faded replaced with the warmth and love the old woman bestowed on every child.

"For heaven's sake what are you doing out on a night like this?" Mama Rose asked.

"You know why I am here," he said.

"Where is your sister? Is she out in this terrible rain?" Mama Rose said not answering him.

At first he was shaken by her mannerisms, she was not like the others she did not show fear. The feeling quickly passed though and he moved further into the room.

"Jah-Man says he is sorry for what must be done," he said.

"He says you should have stayed out of this and you should have just peddled your candy and not been a labba."

"Give Jah-Man a message. Tell him that darkness has claimed his heart and soon it will not protect him," she said finally acknowledging him.

She felt the bullets hit, felt her body fall from the chair onto the floor, and saw the tiny child walk up to her. As her life ebbed from her body she stared into his eyes, she realized that there was nothing there - the beauty of being a child was gone. All that remained was the cold heart of a killer.

Delvin watched her slump over dead her blood pooling on the wood floor beneath her. For a moment he stood staring at her open lifeless eyes, then, turned and walked back into the shop. He went behind the counter and reached into the large glass candy container. Grabbing handfuls, he dropped a few as he placed the candy in the small paper bag.

Eating a few pieces, he again slipped the hood onto his head and tucked the bag of candy beneath the raincoat. Opening the door, he stared out at the driving rain. He and his sister had one more job to do before they could go back to he orphanage and enjoy the bag of candy.

Chapter 20

The corner edge of the glass cracked, as a monstrous wave pounded the bridge. The <u>Joule's bow</u> buried deeply into the frothing mass of water, it hung there for what seemed like an eternity before pointed steel protruded back out. Captain Jack and his crew hung onto anything that they could. Hurricane Alma had overtaken them; they were in the mists of one of the biggest storms to batter the small island of Jamaica.

"Captain, I don't know how much more we can take," the first mate said the fear clear in his voice.

"Hold our course, she'll take it," he said his voice unfaltering.

As if to defy his words, the ship plunged down a massive wave with the bow slamming into the torrent sea. The ship groaned, creaked, and shuddered to an abrupt halt. It then began to rise, the bow creeping from the water and now pointing to the slate gray sky. Two of the ships cargo containers that were lashed with 2" cable were gone, the frayed end of the cables wiped about like live electrical wires.

Captain Jack felt his mouth go dry as he stared out at the angry sea. It was possible, very possible he had been wrong.

Sharon and the others had spent hours talking, planning until each of them could recite their plans word by word. Eve had broken down in tears when she learned of Diamonds death. Ohpton offered his shoulder and she readily took it.

When they finally retired the others were surprised, especially Eve when Steven followed Sharon into her room. Neither of them wanted to hide their love for each other, neither of them wanted to be apart during the night.

The next day was as dark and foreboding as the day before. Hurricane Alma was bearing down hard. The rain had continued to fall in buckets and the winds were beginning to wail with incessant regularity. Darrius sat in the living room alone; he had gotten up early after a night of restless sleep. Yashi had stayed the night with him; he was worried that it would be the last night they would spend together. He was also worried about their plans; a mistake could mean death for one or all of them.

"What's wrong?" Yashi whispered coming into the living room.

Darrius looked up at her, she was wrapped in a sheet wearing nothing else beneath. She looked so lovely, so radiant, and so original. Walking over she sat down next to him tucking the sheet tightly around her.

"Nothing" he breathed.

"Couldn't sleep."

"Relax, things will go well if you all just relax," she said.

"I'll keep my end of the deal," she said.

"I know you will," he breathed.

"Darrius, I wanted to talk with you earlier but things happened and I never got the chance," Yashi began to say.

"I don't want to talk about it," Darrius said looking away.

"We have to, we both know that sooner or later we're going to have to deal with this," she said.

"I would prefer later, much later," he said not meeting her eyes.

"We can't hide from this; we have to be adults," she breathed.

"I don't want to leave you either," she said lightly touching his bare shoulder.

"Then why do you?" he asked.

"My job, I am a DEA officer Darrius, I put myself in dangerous situations on a regular basis all over the world. You and the others are struggling to get to the United States to start your lives," she said.

"We both know that our paths go in different directions." "I know," he said.

"We'll meet again, you'll probably be married with twelve kids…" she joked.

"I would rather have them be ours," he said looking at her.

"Kids and danger don't mix, nor do relationships in the field. I broke one of my own rules Darrius, never to fall for someone while on the job. Now look what I've done, broke my own rule."

"Why does it have to be this way, why can't we still try…" he started to say.

"Because I think in the long run we would both be unhappy," she said holding her finger to his lips.

"Yashi…" he began to say.

"No, don't," she whispered.

"Today you start your new life, today you get a chance that most people in the world won't ever have. Do this for me," she asked.

Darrius said nothing, he just stared into her soft warm eyes then reluctantly he nodded his approval.

"We should wake the others," he said.

"Yes, get the massive together. I have to tell all of you how this is going to play out," she smiled.

Two hours later, they all sat somber and quiet. Yashi told them what each had to do, what dangers were involved. The reality of their situation was finally sinking in. The moment had come.

"I want to check on Mama Rose," Eve asked.

"I'll go, you stay here and finish packing," Darrius said to her.

"I'll go with you," Sharon said.

"I need to talk with her anyway to say my good-byes." "Me too," Raffie added.

"I'll stay here with Eve," Ohpton said.

"I'll stay too," Steven said.

"Packing our things," he smiled at Sharon.

Sharon stared at him, then looked to the floor. There was something on her mind and it was clear to everyone there.

"Steven, can I talk with you privately?" she asked him.

"Sure" he said his smile quickly fading.

She led him down to her bedroom, once inside she closed the door so the others wouldn't hear. Steven watched her pace the room for a moment, and then she sat down on the edge of the bed.

"Steven, I won't be going with you and the others today," she said softly.

"What!" he blurted out his voice nearly shouting.

"I can't go. My mama is still in jail, my little brother hasn't seen me since that day. I can't abandon them," she shook her head.

"But, but..." he stuttered.

"I love you Steven, I love you so much. But I can't abandon them, not now. If I can, if I can take care of them here, I'll find a plane and follow," she said her eyes welling up with tears.

"Sharon, I can't leave you. If you stay then I do too," he said.

"No, you have to go. You have to make the best of things. If I can follow, I will and I will find you. Trust me Steven, please trust me," she said the tears finally beginning to fall.

"I promise I will find you."

Steven felt the lump quickly form in his throat. It was choking and it became increasingly hard to breathe. His own emotions were starting to show, as was his love for her. Walking up to her, he reached out and gently touched her cheek. Sharon closed her eyes feeling the warm of his hand.

"You promise? You promise me that you will come as soon as you can?" he said his voice barely audible.

"Of course I will, I will I promise," she said bounding off the bed into his arms.

They stood there embraced for what seemed like an eternity. Their lips hungrily kissed, with a passion that neither had ever known. Finally, Sharon forced herself away from him, wiped her eyes and headed out of the room without saying a word. She didn't want to look back; if she did, she would never tear herself from him.

Darrius watched her emerge, his instincts told him what had happened. Her wet cheeks did also.

"Are we ready?" he said to her and Raffie.

"Yeah, let's go," she said heading for the door.

When they opened the door a gust of wind slammed into them, torrents of rain pelted down and for a moment they stood staring at the maelstrom. Finally, Darrius turned to Yashi.

"Can you give us a ride?" he asked

She just nodded and dashed out the door to the Land Rover. Moments later they cautiously drove down the hill to town. The wind was blowing so hard and the rain coming down in sheets it was increasingly hard to see.

"This could cause us some trouble," Yashi said.

"From what I heard this hurricane was suppose to be bad, the worse one in years," Sharon added.

"Jah-Man won't care, he'll still do his business as normal," Raffie added.

"Yes, but once you get the money it might be hard to get off the island," she said looking at him in the rearview mirror.

"Judging by the pilot, if we offer him enough money he'll fly through hell itself," Raffie grinned.

"I'd offer you the resources from my people, but if you get caught with that money, all of you will end up in jail," Yashi said.

"This hurricane could also be a blessing," Darrius said.

"How?" Raffie asked.

"It might provide a very good cover for the disappearance of the mass," Darrius said looking over his shoulder.

"Good point," Yashi nodded in agreement.

"Just remember what you have to do."

"We will, just don't leave us high and dry," Sharon said.

Yashi said nothing; she understood that many of them didn't trust her. They never had much time to spend with her like Darrius did. No matter what, she would keep her end of the bargain. Maybe not for the others, but for her love of Darrius.

The town looked like a ghost town as they slowly drove through it. Nobody was outside; then again, the weather was so bad everyone was staying in. Yashi pulled the wheels in front of Mama Rose's place. Sharon, Darrius and Raffie wasted no time bounding from the vehicle to the small awning in front of the candy shop. Darrius for a moment stood and stared at Yashi.

"Be careful," he said to her his voice shouting over the howling wind.

"You too," she gave him a reassuring smile.

He closed the door and dashed to the awning with the others. Sharon knocked on the door, it was still early in the morning and she wasn't sure Mama Rose was up yet.

There came no answer.

"Maybe she's still asleep," Raffie said.

"I doubt it, she was always an early riser," Sharon said shaking her head.

Reaching out she tried the doorknob it turned freely. She gazed up at the others concern quickly forming on her face. Pushing the door open she slowly entered.

The first thing they came upon was Junior's bloody body. It lay sprawled out on the floor his lifeless eyes staring at he ceiling.

"Mama Rose!" Sharon called out in panic.

There came no reply. Sharon was about to dash through the house when Raffie grabbed her holding her back.

"Let go of me!" she snapped.

"No, their attackers may still be here," Raffie, whispered to her.

Darrius knelt down and lightly touched Junior's neck. He then looked up at Raffie shaking his head.

"This happened last night sometime - his body is cold."

Raffie let go of Sharon who bolted through the house frantically calling for Mama Rose. Suddenly she screamed. He Darrius and Raffie rushed to where she was. Lying on the floor was Mama Rose; she laid on her stomach a huge puddle of blood surrounding her.

"Oh my God!" Sharon screamed falling to her knees.

"Look," Raffie said pointing.

Above Mama Rose's head was a message written in blood. She had obviously tried to tell them something. The message said. "Child - Jah-Man." "The butcher, that butcher did this!" Darrius snarled.

"He killed my mama and now Mama Rose!"

"Those children, like Steven said he's using orphaned children as assassins," Raffie said.

"This has to end now - now!" Darrius yelled.

Turning he dashed for the front door. Sharon bounded to her feet and quickly followed. Before Darrius could open the front door, she grabbed him.

"Darrius wait!" she yelled.

"Forget it, Jah-Man is going to pay for this and he's going to pay dearly!" Darrius yelled.

"Darrius you don't understand. You don't know the full truth," she yelled.

"What is there to know? He killed my mama and maybe my real father too! Now he killed an innocent old woman who cared about children? No, he will pay!"

"Darrius, Mama Rose told me and Ohpton something a few days ago," Sharon said.

Darrius stared at her his anger seething through him. Sharon searched his eyes, the hatred for Jah-Man was clear. Darrius wanted revenge – he wanted blood.

"Darrius, Mama Rose told us but made us promise not to tell you," she began to say.

"Tell me what?" he yelled.

"She didn't want you to know. She was afraid for you," Sharon said. "She told us, she told us about Jah-Man." "Yes, so what?" he snarled.

"Darrius, she told us that Jah-Man - Jah-Man is your real father."

Her words struck him like a bullet. His face screwed and twisted in abject horror and he staggered back slamming into the covered candy counter breaking it. With his eyes locked on hers and slowly shook his head from side to side.

"No, no there is no way, no way," he muttered still shaking his head.

"It's true Darrius, Jah-Man is your father," Sharon nodded.

"It makes perfect sense too," Raffie said.

"That would explain why he has taken particular notice and has paid much attention to both Eve and Darrius."

"No, that butcher can't be my father. He can't be!" Darrius snarled.

"Darrius, right now it doesn't matter." Raffie began to say.

"No!" Darrius yelled and dashed out the front door into the maelstrom beyond.

"Darrius don't!" Sharon yelled to him.

It was too late though; her words were ignored. Darrius was gone.

"Come on, there is nothing more we can do here. Mama Rose is gone and we can't bring her back," Raffie said to her.

"Raffie what are we going to do? What is Darrius going to do?" Sharon turned to him.

"We have to continue, continue to pray that Darrius will do the right thing for all of us," Raffie said.

"He'll kill him," Sharon shook her head.

"No, I am," Raffie professed.

"What?" Sharon looked at him in amazement.

"I owe him, I owe Jah-Man for many things; the death of my family, Mama Rose and now the pain he has caused Eve and Darrius. I will kill Jah-Man, I swear I will before we leave," Raffie said his face showing anger.

"No Raffie, let's just get the money and leave. Go far away from this place and start our lives," Sharon blurted out.

"What about your family Sharon? You're not going to leave with us are you?" he asked.

"How, how did you know?" she asked not meeting his eyes.

"We all know, we've all been together for so long that we know Sharon," Raffie said.

"I have to get him, get him before he does something to your family too," he said.

"What about the DEA?" she asked.

"If they get to him first, so be it, regardless, today Jah-Man will end up in prison for life or die," Raffie said his teeth clenched.

Ophton and Steven helped Eve with everyone's bags. They didn't say much; they all felt the same way. Things were spiraling nearly beyond their control; everything they had was riding on this one day. All their lives were uncertain, riches or destitution would be decided by the time night fell again.

Occasionally, Steven would stare out the window at the howling wind and driving rain. He worried about Sharon, his heart ached for her, never in his life had he felt this way. He wanted to stay, help her with her family, but he also respected her wishes.

"I'm worried," he said softly to Ohpton.

"Yeah, so am I. I have to tell you something my friend. I am very pleased, no, very happy to see that you and Sharon have gotten close," he smiled.

"It is clear to see that she loves you very much," he continued to smile.

"I love her too but I'm worried sick about her," Steven fretted.

"Things will turn out okay. I am confident they will be fine." he said trying to make him feel better.

"What time is it?" he asked.

"About an hour since the last time you asked. Don't worry Steven, trust in God, he will see us through this," Ohpton said.

"I'm worried about his weather. How will the plane be able to fly in this?" Eve asked coming into the room.

"Don't know, I don't know what it takes to fly a plane," Ohpton shooed his head.

"It won't be fun I can tell you that," Steven said glancing out the window. "When is this guy supposed to pick us up?" Eve asked.

"He's not, we have to make it to the clearing on the outskirts of town," Steven explained.

"In this <u>weather</u>?" Eve looked at him with surprise.

"Yeah, this weather," Ophton said.

"I better go get our rain coats from the shed, I can't remember the last time I had to use one," Steven said.

"Our bags are going to get soaked too," Ohpton shook his head in disgust.

"Oh well, if things go well we won't need these clothes any more," Steven said, giving them a false smile as he headed for the door.

Ohpton had to help him. He opened the door but the gusting wind forced them both backwards. Steven went outside into the storm while Ohpton struggled to shut the door. Clinging to the side of the shack, Steven slowly clawed his way along to the edge of the shack. When he reached the edge of the shack, something caught his eye. Two children were crouched low wearing dark green raincoats'; they were placing something along the side of the shack; a bomb.

Steven turned the wind battering him against he side of the shack as he dashed back to the front door. When he got there, he pounded heavily against it yelling his voice carried off on the wind.

Ohpton swung the door open causing Steven to fall inward to the floor. He then tried to close it again.

"Forget it, come on we have to go! The <u>duppy</u> children are planting a bomb!" he yelled to them.

"A bomb?" Ohpton yelled.

"Yes, a bomb! Now come on we have to get out of here," he said clawing to his feet.

Both Eve and Ohpton followed Steven out into the screaming wind. On the other side of the shack, Devilia and Delvin Hellton worked as quickly as their tiny hands could. They tried to brace themselves against the hurricane but their bodies were too small and light. More than once Devilia was blown backwards landing in the sodden earth. They continued to work and neither of them saw Steven round the corner of the shack. Delvin grinned as he placed the timer against the side of the shack. He was going to enjoy watching it blow, enjoy the brief yet agonizing screams from those within. Jah-Man would be pleased at their work and overjoyed at the elimination of his enemies. He would do anything for him, as would his sister. They <u>loved him like the parent they never had.</u> Staring down, he only needed to connect the proper wires and set the timer. Then he and his sister could hide behind some trees and wait.

His small hand shook, blown by the wind as he began connecting the wires. He had done this so many times in the past he could do it with his eyes closed. First the negative wire was connected, then neutral wire, finally all that remained was the positive, hot wire. Slowly he brought the small red wire to the connector, the savage wind that roared all around him was gone, and he heard nothing save the beating of his small heart. He didn't even acknowledge his sister's scream as another huge gust of wind blew her sideways - against him.

Devillia crashed into her brother the wind nearly carrying her off her feet. The blow came as a surprise and caused his hand to shift with the wire to the neutral, completing the circuit.

Neither of the children knew what happened, nor did they feel the blast. All they saw, the last thing they saw was a blinding flash of light.

Eve, Steven and Ohpton heard the explosion. Wheeling around they watched the shack, their beloved home, disappear into a ball of fire. Shards of wood were flung by the force of the explosion, and then propelled by the sheer force of the wind.

"Get down!" Ohpton yelled forcing both Eve and Steven to the ground.

Debris rained down on them, pelting them, causing them to yelp with pain. Within moments it was over, all that remained was the charred ground where their home once stood.

"Our home!" Eve wailed.

"Gone, it's gone," Steven shook his head.

"Come on, we can't stay out here," Ohpton nudged the others.

With much effort, they pushed on to their part of the plan, each with a heavy, saddened heart.

Yashi dashed from the Rover into the Orion. Once she was inside, she stood for a moment and watched the driving rain. Palm trees whipped about bending further than she would have thought they could. This hurricane could change things.

"It's about time," a voice called from behind her.

Yashi turned to see a tall dark skinned man with broad shoulders. Denzil Simms gave her a broad smile as he approached. Denzil Simms was one of the DEA's top agents. On more than one occasion he had worked with her, they were also good friends.

"I figured they'd send you," she smiled warmly then gave him a hug.

"Wouldn't want to miss this one, not after you stuck your neck so far out to get this guy," he whispered to her.

"What in blood fire happened to you?"

"The Frenchman is gone - out of the picture. I kind of got caught in the middle, you bring the goods?" she asked.

"Yes, and it took a lot to get this much. Do you realize how many agencies we had to tap into?" he said raising an eyebrow.

"Well, let's hope we don't lose it," she smiled.

"We lose this suitcase we better figure on getting a new line of work," he grinned.

"So when is this going down?" "A few hours from now," she said.

"Where?"

"Right here," she pointed to the ground.

"You're kidding me, here in a resort hotel?" Denzil frowned.

"That's where he wants it," she said pursing her lips.

"Are we ready?"

"All I need to do is call," he said patting his coat where his cellular phone was.

"Let's go eat, I'm starving" she smiled taking him by the arm.

Jack Griff sat in the cockpit of his old C47 airplane. The rain pelted down upon the fuselage so hard it made it hard to even hear inside the cockpit. He was fighting with himself, part of him wanted to just go sit in the back and crack open a new bottle of bourbon, the other half wanted to crank up the engines and try like blood fire to help these kids. He hated himself.

Rising from the cockpit, he went to one of the seats in the rear and sat down. Reaching inside his flight jacket, he produced a flask of bourbon. Uncapping the bottle he held it to his lips, then drew it away staring at the dark liquid within. At one time, in his life, he had been important, people had depended on him, and he made a difference. Nevertheless, something had happened, something within him changed. Now he was a pale image of what he once was, flying a derelict airplane that was barely safe to fly. He was now angry with himself.

His hand shook as he brought the open end of the bottle to his lips. Then, abruptly, he slung the bottle shattering it against the bulkhead. Rising from the seat, he went back into the cockpit and began putting power to the engines.

Captain Jack Griff had returned.

Sharon and Raffie reached the Orion, shaking their rain coats off they entered the lobby and looked around. None of Jah-Man's men were standing guard, nobody noticed them, and people were more concerned with the hurricane outside.

"Come on, it's almost time," Sharon said.

"We need to slip into the kitchen, this way," Raffie motioned to her.

Raffie led Sharon down a service hallway then through a set of doors that led to the kitchen. From the linen room he produced two white frocks and hats. Slipping them on they went into the kitchen, grabbed a large cart and began to do their part of the plan.

"What are we going to do without Darrius?" Sharon asked.

"I don't know, one of us had to make the switch," Raffie said.

"No you don't," a familiar voice said from the other end of the kitchen.

Darrius stood smiling at them, in his hand was a large blue suitcase. He weaved his way around stainless steel counters.

"We were worried," Sharon, said relieved.

"I won't let you down," Darrius said slipping the suitcase on one of the shelves of the large cart.

"Come on, we don't have much time. In about 30 minutes, crews will be coming in to prepare lunch. We have to be out of here before that," Raffie said glancing at his watch.

"Are you alright to do this?" Sharon asked Darrius.

"Like I said, I won't let you down," Darrius said.

"Are you sure this cart will hold me?" Darrius pointed to the cart.

"You'll be cramped but I don't think anyone will take notice that you're there," Raffie said looking at the shelves.

"Have either of you seen Yashi?" he asked.

"No and we won't either, not until we make the switch," Raffie said.

Sharon could see the concern in Darrius's face. He loved her that much was clear, he worried about her and that could possibly cause problems.

It took them nearly 25 minutes to finish filling the cart with various foods. It was a ruse, they only hoped that Jah-Man wouldn't notice them, especially Sharon. Darrius crawled onto the top shelf of the cart. He was cramped; the space was tiny with not much airflow. Beneath him was the blue suitcase that he would make the switch with. They entered the elevator and headed up to the first floor.

Yashi and Denzil walked along with three of Jah-Man's guards. They were led into a large enclosed arboretum; the room was round with a large frosted glass dome above them. Various flowers bloomed displaying their multitude of colors. In the center of the room, sat two padded park benches, sitting upon them waiting patiently was Jah-Man. He wore a multicolored tunic with many beads around his neck. When they approached, he turned then rose up off the bench a broad smile forming on his face.

"Jah-Man, this is my representative," Yashi said.

"It is good to finally meet you," he smiled warmly at them. "Shall we conduct our business?"

"Of course," Denzil smiled and sat down on the bench.

"I trust that you have delivered on your end?"

"Yes, the material is sitting on the docks waiting for you now, 6 tons of material mixed in with sugar cane and other staples," Jah-Man said.

"Do you mind if my people verify this?" Denzil asked.

"Of course not, I would be worried if you didn't," Jah-Man said.

Denzil reached into his jacket pocket and produced his cellular phone. Punching in a number, he held it to his ear. Jah-Man watched him as he explained to his men where to go. Moments later he ended the call and slipped it back into his pocket.

"They will call me back when it has been verified," Denzil said to him.

"Now your end?" Jah-Man asked.

Denzil was hesitant but he pushed the blue suitcase towards Jah-Man. Yashi watched them both and the suitcase. As Jah-Man reached out to grab the suitcase, she checked her watch. She hoped the others were keeping to their plan.

Jah-Man pulled the suitcase onto the bench next to him then tried to open it finding it locked. Denzil reached into his pocket then tossed him the keys.

When the lid opened, Yashi watched his eyes light up.

"I trust the amount is correct?" Jah-Man asked closing the lid.

"Yes, 16 million in large bills," Denzil said nodding.

"Good, very good, now as soon as you have verified that your goods are there we can conclude our business," Jah-Man said slipping the suitcase next to the bench.

Suddenly, two of Jah-Man's men came in walking up to them. Jah-Man frowned at them; he didn't like his men around when he did business.

"What is it?" he snapped.

"Sir, there are two servants here with a cart. They have food prepared," one of the men said.

"I didn't order any food…" Jah-Man frowned.

"Actually, we have not had lunch, it would be rather nice," Yashi said to Jah-Man.

Jah-Man at first frowned then looked up at his men who stood waiting for an answer.

"Do not let them in, tell them to wait outside. Wheel the cart in here yourselves," he ordered.

The men nodded and quickly left. Within moments they returned pushing the large cart of food. They positioned it right in front of them. Yashi was quick, getting up she moved the cart off to the side next to the suitcase, then began pulling the lids off.

"This food looks good," she said grabbing one of the small plates.

"I am happy you like it," Jah-Man said coldly.

"I trust that we can do business in the future?" Denzil asked creating small talk.

"Of course, you have proven yourselves trustworthy," Jah-Man grinned.

Yashi watched as Darrius's hand came out from beneath the white linen cover. With an ease that amazed her, he casually and quietly switched the briefcases.

At that moment, Denzil's cellular phone rang. He reached into his pocket pulling it out then holding it to his ear. Jah-Man watched as Denzil nodded then slowly a broad smile began to form on his face. Seconds later he looked up at JahMan.

"Your goods are secure, you have kept your end of the deal," Denzil added.

"Good, that means our business is concluded. If you do not mind I have other business to attend to," he said getting up.

Yashi took a bite of food then smiled at Jah-Man as he picked up the suitcase. He then headed for the door. Yashi nodded to Denzil who pushed one of the buttons on his cellular phone. All <u>blood fire broke</u> loose.

By the time Jah-Man reached the doors, he began hearing gunfire. Turning he looked at Yashi and Denzil who now had their guns drawn pointing them directly at him.

"Drop the suitcase! Jah-Man, you are under arrest," Denzil yelled to him.

The look on Jah-Man's face started as shock, and then quickly turned to rage, insane rage as he realized he had been double-crossed. Denzil squeezed off a round as Jah-Man dashed behind a <u>mass</u> of large ferns.

"Damn it don't lose him!" he yelled to Yashi who dashed around the side in order to cut him off.

When she rounded one of the many bushes she was greeted with empty space. Jah-Man had disappeared, where she could only guess. Somehow, he had made a rapid escape. He had obviously prepared for such an occasion.

"Where did he go?" Denzil yelled.

"Gone, disappeared," Yashi yelled back.

"We have to find him, remember he has the money," Denzil pointed out.

"Wait a minute," she called to him.

Yashi noticed something out of place on the floor. Moving closer, she kept the gun trained on the floor. A huge floor tile was twisted off to the side, with much caution, she reached down and pushed it the rest of the way to the side. Beneath a dark foreboding tunnel greeted her.

"He went into a rabbit hole," she called to Denzil.

"Damn it! We have to follow him!" he snapped.

"Forget it, this tunnel will be booby trapped. Any of us go down there, which he expects, will end up dead."

"So what do we do? Did we lose both him and the money?" Denzil snapped.

"No, lock down the Orion and the grounds, he had to appear someplace," Yashi ordered.

Beneath the cart, Darrius listened to the whole ordeal. He had to remain motionless; it was the only way to ensure he wouldn't be caught. They would leave shortly, and then Sharon and Raffie could come in and pull him out. He hoped it would be soon too, his legs were beginning to cramp.

Ohpton who struggled against the wind pulled Eve along, Steven was ahead and he finally stopped staring up at the slate gray sky.

"He's not coming," he yelled back to the others.

"What are we going to do?" Eve yelled back.

"This guy was our ticket out of here," Ohpton screamed back.

Suddenly over the roar of the wind, they watched the old hulk of Jack Griff's plane rise up over the treetops. The plane pitched from side to side as if out of control, then the landing gear lowered and the plane began to descend.

Pitching from side to side, they were surprised that the wings didn't connect with the ground. The plane though, managed to straighten then come a halt. The side door opened and Jack Griff's concerned face emerged.

"Come on, get aboard," he yelled above the howling wind.

"We didn't think you'd be coming," Eve yelled.

"I almost didn't," Griff said.

"This hurricane is nasty."

"Will we be able to take off again?" she asked.

"I'll take off, don't you worry about that," he reassured her. "Are the rest of you on track?" "Yes" Ohpton yelled back.

"Good, because if we don't take off soon we're all going to be stuck here," he yelled to them.

"They'll be here," Eve reassured him.

Darrius waited and waited, finally the cover of the cart was pulled up and he looked up into Sharon's worried face.

"What's wrong?" he instantly asked.

"Raffie, Raffie disappeared," she said.

"Disappeared, disappeared where?" Darrius asked.

"If I knew I wouldn't be so worried," she said.

"He said he was going to take care of Jah-Man once and for all."

"Damn him! We're so close, so very close," Darrius said stretching his legs.

"What are we going to do?" she asked.

"Nothing, we can only head back to the others," Darrius said pulling out the blue suitcase from the bottom tray of the cart.

Raffie stood in the lobby, in his hand was a public telephone. He waited patiently as the telephone rang on the other end. Finally, it was picked up and he heard Jah-Man's voice.

"Do you know who this is?" Raffie spoke his voice stern.

"I do not care, whoever you are I will have you torn limb from limb!" Jah-Man snarled.

"Don't threaten me - ever!" Raffie retorted.

"Have you checked your briefcase yet?" he asked.

There came a long pause on the other end of the telephone. Raffie could tell that Jah-Man was doing just that.

Tossing the suitcase on the bench, he used the keys he had and tried to open the locks. The keys didn't work. He then tried the suitcase directly. The latches opened and he raised the lid. Inside was mass of shredded paper and rocks.

Raffie could hear him yell on the telephone, the sound was so sweet to him. Abruptly though, Jah-Man picked up the telephone.

"Where is my money?" he snarled.

"How does it feel now Jah-Man when the shoe is on the other foot?" Raffie snapped.

"Where?" Jah-Man snarled.

"You want your mass? Meet me in the center of town at the gazebo, that is where I will give you your money," Raffie snapped then hung up.

Jah-Man gripped the telephone with such force his entire body shook. With all his strength he slung the telephone against the wall tearing a huge hole in the sheetrock and smashing the telephone. Moving swiftly behind his desk he opened the bottom drawer and drew out a 9mm semiautomatic pistol. He then headed for the door and his money.

DEA agents swarmed over the Orion like locust over a wheat field. Many of Jah-Man's men put up a fight only to be cut down in a bloody gun battle. Yashi and Denzil went down the tunnel, moving cautiously they moved as quickly as possible through the darkness their small flashlights bobbing back and forth.

Finally, they came out in an office, one that Yashi recognized. "We're in his office," she breathed.

"Where did he go now?" Denzil asked.

"I don't know, start looking for other tunnels. Maybe he has a way out of the resort," she said.

"We miss him and the chief will have our heads! The money we can write off but losing Jah-Man isn't an option," Denzil breathed as he began to look over the office.

Yashi nodded her agreement, it was true, the money was a write off and she already knew where that was, but she wanted Jah-Man just as bad as Denzil did.

Jah-Man stood in the center of the gazebo, the wind and rain pounded all around him, much of it driving in through the sides. He was soaking wet the air chilling him, yet he didn't feel it. His hatred consumed him; his world was crumbling all around him. The people he trusted most, people whom he gave much to, and people who stabbed him in the back when he needed them cheated him from success.

Raffie stepped quietly up the first step of the gazebo, Jah-Man hadn't seen him yet, his back was to him and if he were quiet, he would have the advantage. His own hatred burned deeply inside, images of the horror he witness as a child, this parents severed heads, their bloody severed heads staring intently and forever quietly at him. That image was burned into his soul and now he tapped into that hatred.

Jah-Man turned slightly, just enough to see movement out the corner of his eye. His hand grabbed the pistol and quickly drew it from his belt. Raffie lunged, his body colliding with him driving him to the floor of the gazebo the pistol falling from his hand to land in the mud. Jah-Man was considerably stronger than he was and it became apparent as he hefted Raffie clear off the floor and slammed him into one of the gazebo's posts. Raffie wheezed as the wind was knocked from him yet he struck back with his fists drawing first blood.

Jah-Man's nose was instantly broken as Raffie's fist slammed into it. He reeled backwards allowing Raffie to drop to the floor.

"You think you can defeat me? You think your puny will is stronger than mine?" Jah-Man snarled the blood running from his nose.

"You murdered my family. You butchered them and left that grotesque nightmare for me to see. You deserve to die and I will kill you, you nasty naayga!" Raffie said again launching himself at Jah-Man.

Sharon and Darrius arrived at the gazebo just as Raffie was again driven back by a shocking blow from Jah-Man.

"I have to help him…" Darrius dashed forward.

For an instant, Sharon was trying to figure out whom Darrius was referring to. But when she saw Darrius jump on Jah-Man's back, she knew her answer. Jah-Man spun wildly trying to dislodge the new attacker. When he found he couldn't, he slammed his body against the nearest roof post. Darrius felt the blow, it was shattering and enough to bring spots to his eyes. His limbs grew numb and he was beginning to lose consciousness. His body fell to the floor with a thud. Jah-Man wheeled around to strike the attacker, when he noticed whom it was he stopped. His rage was unchecked, and he snarled at Darrius who looked up at him with glassy eyes.

"Why? Why did you kill my mama?" Darrius spat.

"I…I didn't mean to; I loved your mama. She was going to turn me in, she saw something she wasn't suppose to….she knew too much!" he snarled at him.

"You have become a traitor to me also. You could have been at my side. You could have been rich with incredible power!" Jah-Man ranted.

"I would rather die than be at your side," Darrius snarled forcing his body to sit upright.

"Then I will give you your wish my son, I will give you your wish!" JahMan spat grabbing him around the throat.

"No!" Raffie yelled over the howling wind.

Jah-Man felt the blow strike him in the side of the head. His ear rang and he instantly let go of Darrius. Raffie was quick, he pushed him back and grabbed him around the throat his thumbs pushing against his windpipe with all his might. Jah-Man kicked and bucked trying to free himself; his mouth opened making a gasping noise. Raffie hung on drawing on strength he never knew he had. JahMan did also.

With a blow so forceful, Jah-Man struck Raffie in the side of the head. Raffie's grip loosened as the ringing in his ears became a roar. The moment was all he needed, Jah-Man grabbed him and forced him down onto his back the tables now turned. Raffie quickly felt his throat constrict as now Jah-Man tried to strangle him.

"You are nothing and your family was nothing. I will kill you like I had them killed!" Jah-Man yelled.

Raffie saw spots before his eyes as his world quickly began to fade. Struggling he tried to wrench free Jah-Man's hands but it was useless, the man's grip was like iron.

He suddenly knew he was going to die.

Straining, he tried to reach Jah-Man's face to gouge out his eyes to make him release his grip but he couldn't reach the man's hideously twisted grin. With desperation he groped his hands around him trying to grab anything he could use, anything that could provide a means for his freedom. His fingers touched something metal.

Sharon dashed forward, she couldn't let Jah-Man kill Raffie. Moving with considerable speed she took the steps of the gazebo two at a time. She had no weapon, so she used the only thing she had. Hurling her body against Jah-Man's, Raffie swung the metal object he had found. It was an old rusted fork.

His aim was for Jah-Man's face and he would have connected had Sharon not collided with him, instead the fork embedded itself deeply into Jah-Man's neck. Blood spurted out as he and Sharon hit the floor hard. Sharon was quick to distance herself from him, she rolled over and quickly got to her feet.

"No more, no more death, no more pain. You will never hurt anyone ever again!" Raffie croaked rubbing his throat.

Darrius staggered to his feet leaning heavily against the railing. Jah-Man glanced over at him his eyes pleading for his son to help. Darrius turned away.

Jah-Man's body went limp; Raffie stood staring at the man gasping until Darrius touched his shoulder startling him.

"Raffie, it's over," Darrius said softly.

Raffie stared down at Jah-Man's lifeless body, a sudden calm washed over him as sense of peace filling his soul. His revenge was complete, his parents, his family had been avenged. He then looked at his hands they shook uncontrollably.

"What have I done? I've killed, I've killed." Raffie yelled horrified by his actions.

"You did what you had to, you did what you had to," Darrius said softly.

"But, I killed a man. I killed your father!" Raffie looked up at him.

Darrius could say nothing, it was true he hated Jah-Man as much as Raffie did, he put out of his mind the fact that the man was his father. To him his father was living somewhere else and he was a man, not a monster. Darrius reached his hand down to Raffie to help him up.

"Come on it's time to go," Sharon said to them.

As they turned to leave, they were amazed to find many of the town's people standing staring at them. With Jah-Man's death, they too were now free. As they disappeared a lone figure watched from the crowd.

Uncle William emerged pushing his way past everyone until he reached his brother. Kneeling down he touched his fingers to his neck, then glanced from side to side keeping an eye on the crowd. With much effort he picked his brother up and carried him off the gazebo the crowds parting giving him a path.

He would care for his brother - he would always care for him.

Yashi and Denzil pushed their way through the crowd towards the gazebo. Huge crowds had formed and were now cheering their fists clenched to the sky despite the hurricane that raged all around them. When they pushed through the crowd, they tried to figure out what the crowd was ranting about, the gazebo floor was empty, Jah-Man's body was gone.

Sharon stood rain soaked as she watched Darrius and Raffie board the plane. The wind was so strong the droplets of rain were painful as they beat against her face. Nobody smiled; nobody wanted to go without her. The anguish they all felt was clearly seen on Steven's face. He looked so somber, so alone.

Suddenly Eve emerged from the door of the plane, she dashed to her and for a long moment they embraced.

"I can't leave without you, I just can't!" Eve yelled above the howling wind.

"You have to. Trust me Eve, go with the others and I come later. Go now while you all can," Sharon said keeping her own emotions back.

Eve blinked at her wiping the water from her face. Sharon tried her best to keep strong, at any moment though, Eve would see through.

The moment was long enough. Eve reluctantly turned and dashed back to the plane. Jack Griff increased power to the engines and spun the plane into the wind. Moments later it became airborne the engines straining to keep the plane in the air.

"They're gone?" a voice called to her as she watched the plane disappear into the cloudy sky.

Sharon turned to see Yashi and Denzil standing there. For an instant, she stared at them then turned her gaze away.

"He's dead," she breathed.

"We know, we saw," Denzil said.

"But someone carted off his body," Yashi added.

"So what happens to me now?" she asked them.

"Nothing, in fact we have reason to believe that your mama is in jail due to a problem with Jah-Man?" Yashi asked.

"Yes, how did you know?" Sharon looked at them baffled.

"We've watched your little group for some time now, ever since we learned that Eve and Darrius were Jah-Man's children," Yashi explained.

"You can help me?" Sharon looked at them hopeful.

"Yes, we can get your mama out of jail - right now," Yashi smiled through her wet hair.

Sharon's smile broadened and they all turned heading back to the Land Rover.

It didn't take much to convince them to stop by the shack on the way. When they reached it her breath caught in her throat.

"It...it's gone!" she said faintly.

Getting out from the Land Rover she forced herself through the shrieking wind, standing where her home for so many years had been. She began to cry.

Moments later she turned, Yashi was standing right next to her.

"I'm sorry," she breathed.

"So am I. This was my home; this was all I had," she shook her head.

Yashi didn't know what to say, instead she just squeezed Sharon's shoulder and turned to go back to the Rover.

"Please, can you hold on for a few minutes?" Sharon yelled to her.

Yashi just nodded and continued on to the wheels. Sharon moved up beyond the ruins of the shack, eventually coming to where the little tree was and also where the can was, at least she would have some money, a little. To her surprise she found a large flower there, bent over due to the driving rain but a flower none the less. Tied to it was a small piece of string. With her hands she began digging, following the string. She didn't have to dig far before she came a large pouch. Pulling it out she opened it. Inside, the pouch was filled with money, coils and a note.

"We will be waiting for you when the time is right. Our family isn't complete without you."

She couldn't hold back the tears nor did she want to.

The plane banked and turned rising and falling with violent regularity. Jack Griff struggled to keep the plane airborne.

They were over the ocean now; even though they couldn't see it, they knew that huge waves rocked the sea below. Darrius was quiet until she told Eve the truth about Jah-Man. Like him, she denied it, she couldn't believe it, but finally she broke down in tears.

Jack Griff's teeth were clenched together as the plane was buffeted by hurricane Alma. For the first time in his life, he began to pray, softly at first but with ever increasing volume.

Then, every light began to blink red, one of the engines, not able to handle the strain, coughed sputtered then finally spun to a stop. There was no way they could remain in the air.

"Buckle up people, we're going down!" he called out over the planes crackling intercom.

The group grew silent; the plane was going down, most likely over the ocean, somewhere between Jamaica and the United States. There were so many horrible ways for them to die. Nobody said a word; even when they felt the plane suddenly lurch to the right. Eve clung onto Darrius, Raffie, Ohpton and Steven sat quietly their hands gripping the steel armrests of the seats.

Jack Griff struggled with the controls; the plane that he loved so was now dropping from the sky like a rock. Hurricane Alma raged all around them and even he knew their chances of survival were slim to non-existent. Still though, he fought to keep the nose of the plane up.

When they hit, the plane struck the top of one wave and skimmed across them like a stone on a pond. The left wing snapped off in a grinding roar, the right engine collapsed shattering like a twig against the walls of water. Jack felt the water crash through the cockpit windows and he thought he heard the others scream though he couldn't be certain. All he knew, he wasn't coming out of this alive.

The Joule groaned as it rode each wave, railings were shattered and they lost the last of the cargo containers that were strapped deck side. Captain Jack kept an uneasy crew confident as the ship progressed through the monstrous nightmare around them.

"Captain look!" the first mate yelled.

Captain Jack turned to see a plane swoop down from the sky striking three waves before finally burying itself into one of the waves directly in front of them.

"My God!" he breathed.

"Heave to, prepare a rescue party!" he ordered.

The fuselage bounced a few times then rolled completely over as the waves bashed it about. Darrius and the others were tossed about like rag dolls. With much effort Darrius reached the door, opening it water flew in painfully striking his face. What surprised him the most was the face that looked down in on him.

"Ahoy! Are there any other survivors?"

Darrius grinned with a joy he had never felt before. The men from the Joule helped each of them out and into the launch, which was pitching so violently that it also threatened to capsize. Raffie was the last, he moved quickly towards the door when the fuselage groaned and rolled completely over tossing him towards the front of the plane.

Two of the Joule's crewmembers were hurled off into the raging water. Darrius went over the side for them while Steven went over the other side for Raffie. Eve sat there in horror as she watched a huge wave toss the fuselage over.

Then it sank.

"Steven, Steven!" she screamed, though her voice was carried away on the howling wind.

Darrius managed to drag one of the crewmen to the launch, the other one he couldn't find.

"Eve, Ohpton, help me," he called to her from the side of the launch.

"Steven went after Raffie, but the plane it's gone!" she shrieked.

"There's nothing we can do, nothing!" he yelled, trying to haul himself back in the launch.

Steven swam like he had never before. He reached the fuselage just as it slipped beneath the water. The suction was incredible, and he used it to his advantage. Forcing his way through the fuselage door he saw Raffie struggling, his ankle caught between two bend seats. Air was running out fast.

The launch bounced and pitched, the men stayed as long as they dared and finally turned towards the Joule. Raffie and Steven were gone their bodies lost forever beneath the boiling water.

"There!" Eve shrieked.

Everyone turned to see two heads burst from the water not far away. Steven gasped for air his arm locked tightly around Raffie's chest. He coughed and tried to draw in more air but the water was too rough. Then out of the corner of his eye he saw the launch heading for them and Ohpton's outstretched arms waiting to grab him. Their struggle was over, they were safe, and God had seen them through hell to a new life of hope, promise and love.

Epilogue

Steven stared into the full-length mirror, he adjusted his tie and stared at the cut of the new suit he wore. For an instant, he stared into his eyes. He looked tired, worn. It was not the look of a wealthy man.

The Joule had rescued them, pulling them from certain death. Jack Griff hadn't made it; the fuselage of the plane had disappeared beneath the waves before they could reach the cockpit. By the time, they made it to Miami the realization of what they had come through and what they left behind had taken hold. They were sullen, sad, yet tremendously excited. Yashi had made excellent passports and papers including birth certificates. They were now American's.

Steven forced himself away from the mirror. A month had passed since they made their exodus from Jamaica; a month that they all worried about Sharon. Darrius also had become more quiet and reserved, without Yashi something inside him had died. Ohpton and Raffie on the other hand had taken to the American way of life quickly. Raffie had resumed his pranks and Ohpton spent much time on the receiving end of them.

Each day for the entire month they all dressed in the best clothes they had, then traveled to Miami International nearest airport. There they would spend much of the day waiting and looking as the passengers, mostly tourists came off the planes from Jamaica. Each day they prayed that Sharon would be there. Each day they were disappointed.

They tried to communicate with her but since the overthrow of Jah-Man, there had been many changes within the Jamaican government. They tried the Orion, but nobody had seen nor heard of her whereabouts.

"Maybe today will be the day," Raffie said to the others.

"Maybe" Darrius breathed as he watched a huge plane land.

"We shouldn't have left her, I shouldn't have left," Steven said sullenly.

"You say that every day we come here. Give it a rest okay? You can't change the past, none of us can," Ohpton said.

"Maybe something else happened. Maybe one of Jah-Man's men…" Steven speculated.

"Cool it," Eve said giving him a sharp look.

"She's fine, I know she is."

"Sorry" Steven sighed.

The plane slowed then taxied up the gate. A huge boarding tunnel moved out and pressed itself against he side of the plane. Steven and Darrius both rose from their seats with eager expectations.

The doors opened and people began to disembark, most were tourists, laughing and chattering amongst themselves. To them Jamaica was a tourist spot and nothing more. Finally the flood of people exiting the plane stopped, for a moment they all stood waiting then realizing that today wasn't the day they all got up to leave.

"Where are you all going?" a familiar voice called out to them.

Steven wheeled around his body instantly becoming numb with excitement. Sharon moved swiftly over to them followed closely by Yashi.

Their embrace was passionate; his arms enveloped her pulling her tight. His lips pressed hard against hers, her scent overwhelmed him and he stood there feeling the moistness of her lips and the warmth of her body. Yashi flew into Darrius's arms her momentum carrying them backwards until Darrius tripped and they fell to the ground. It didn't matter though they were together again.

"Where have you been?" Eve asked hugging Sharon, the tears falling.

For a long moment they both stared at each other embraced like two lost sisters. Then Sharon found her voice.

"It took a while, but with Yashi's help I managed to get my mama out of jail. I set them up in a new house and all that stuff," she smiled.

"I thought something had happened," Steven breathed.

"No, things just took a lot longer than I would have liked," she nodded.

"Miss?" a voice called out to them.

Sharon turned to see one of the flight attendants rushing over, in her hand was a carry on bag.

"You forgot this," she smiled handing the bag to Sharon.

"Thank you," Sharon smiled back.

The woman grinned at them, then turned sharply and headed back to the gate.

"You know her?" Darrius asked.

"Her name is Monique and she's single," Sharon grinned looking at Raffie and Ohpton.

"Always looking out for us aren't you?" Raffie smiled back.

"Always" Sharon grinned.

"So it's finally over, everything turned out okay," Eve smiled.

"Yeah, it seems so," Raffie grinned.

"I've been wondering about something," Ohpton frowned.

"What ever happened to Delicia?"

Sharon nearly burst out laughing. The others stared at her for a moment wondering what had happened.

"She found me nearly two weeks ago, when she found that Jah-Man was gone and his empire wiped out, she came back," Sharon began to say. "She wanted to come with me, come here and stay with us!" "No, you're kidding?" Raffie shook his head.

"No I'm not, anyway, I told her there was no way she could come," Sharon said.

"Then as we began to go through all of Jah-Man's books and papers we found some interesting information about Delicia. Seems she was also doing some illegal things on the side," Yashi explained.

"So she's in jail?" Darrius asked.

"No, but we made a deal with her. Seems she kept many records on JahMan and many of his buyers. A lot of information we can use to shut down other organizations," Yashi smiled.

"So, what happened to her?" Ohpton asked.

"She's under the witness protection program, not as glamorous of a life as she would like, but it's not a jail cell," Yashi grinned.

For a long moment they all stood together in silence, the joy they all felt needed no words. Finally, Ohpton spoke up.

"So what happens now?" he asked.

"We have enough mass to last us all the rest of our lives, where do we go from here?"

"We take things one day at a time," Sharon said hugging Steven.

"But, what comes next?" Eve asked.

"Life" Darrius smiled.

"We all start to finally live our lives, together."

"We spend so much time Rationalizing Mediocrity, We have forgotten what greatness looks like."
~ ALMA

Love Alone